M000313438

Beyond
The
Hallow Grave

Editingle Hallween Anthology

EDITINGLE INDIE HOUSE

Mumbai, India

www.editingleindiehouse.com

www.indiebookcafe.com

BEYOND THE HALLOW GRAVE

Copyright © 2020 Editingle Indie House

All rights reserved.

This book is a work of fiction. Names, characters, places and incidents are either the product of the author's imagination or are used fictionally. Any resemblance to actual persons, living or dead, or to actual events or locals is entirely coincidental.

This book is not sold to subject to the condition that shall not, by way of trade or otherwise, be lent, resold, hired out, or otherwise circulated without the publisher's prior consent in any form of binding or cover other than that in which it is published and without a similar condition, including this condition, being imposed on the subsequent purchaser.

For more information, please contact:

Contact: - www.editingleindiehouse.com/contact

Editor: In-House

Cover Photo : Designed by Portia Ekka

ISBN : 9788194192831

First Edition : October 2020

Dear reader,

It is to our great pleasure to showcase of the following authors on our second year of Halloween Anthology: Mark Boutros, D.A. Schneider, Phil Hore, M.M. Ward, Brandon Ebinger, Danielle McNeill, and Catherine Edward.

We appreciate the authors for believing in us and submitted their stories for publication, their trust in us is our strength.

As a publication indie house, we strive to deliver best stories and bring out the potential in authors. Our company values are driven by authenticity, originality, and leaving readers with unforgettable tales.

From bottom of our hearts, we are thanking to all of our authors for believing and keeping faith. Most importantly thank you to the readers for giving our stories chance. No words will be enough to express our gratitude.

Now we will stop here and let you enjoy the amazing stories from our amazing authors.

Happy Reading!

CONTENTS

DOG

I'm finally going to share my story. I'm not even sure I want to, but I feel like I have to. I haven't told anyone what happened for over thirty-five years. I was only fourteen and nothing made sense. I'm forty-nine now, and with all the time I've had to think, it still doesn't make sense. I guess I hoped that by never talking about what happened that it might make it less real, or make the whole thing disappear.

I didn't even talk about it when it happened. Even during the conversations, I wasn't so much quiet as I was absent. People had shouted in my face but my mind was blank, numb and empty. But, as this is the last night, I'm going to be alive, I need to share my side of the story. It's not out of bravery or some desire to change. It's because I've lost, and my story is my final fuck you to whatever caused this tragedy. I don't care what happens to me after this.

Who knows what I could've made of my life. It was on the horizon, glistening under the sunrise full of options and possibilities. I loved physics and would've probably pursued something in that. Sure, forty-nine isn't exactly the end of my life, but I feel as though the sun is setting on that horizon, and on it is nothing but death and decay.

I drag a plastic chair away from the kitchen wall and place it facing the steel counter. I sit and take a breath, cracking my fingers back to loosen the rigid joints. I shuffle in the seat, but it seems to have been deliberately designed to create discomfort.

Everyone read about what happened in the newspapers, heard about it on the radio and saw the pictures on the TV, but nobody ever got my side. They didn't need it, because of what they saw when they found us. Any time I felt like talking about it my throat tightened and burned, and my heart thumped. Evil's hand grabbed my neck and squeezed until the words were crushed. It wanted me to be the only one who knew, so I could suffer alone.

I came close to telling my aunt, Jaz. All the words were in a letter, but something compelled me to tear that letter up and flush it down the toilet before I could send it. I even had a documentary maker visit, excited to be the first to get my story, but I sat there in total silence and stared at the poor kid, probably traumatizing her. Whatever force was at play teased me, letting me think I had control over what I was doing, then it reminded me that choices didn't exist.

Last I heard Aunt Jaz died of cancer. For her, the last thirty-five years were a series of ailments until her body just gave up. It's hard to tell what's true or false when it's all second or third-hand info.

I look up at Danny, a young man so relaxed from his hair to his toes that I'm amazed he's ever awake. He hangs his chef's apron on a hook behind the kitchen door and turns to me. "If you're gonna talk for long, keep the phone plugged into the charger. Battery's crap so it'll die on you in about three minutes." He runs his hand over the immaculate kitchen counter as though there's some dirt still there. "I've been meaning to get a new phone, but the fuckers cost more than rent. Fuck London."

I chuckle. "Thanks, Danny. I appreciate it." He's a good man. Deserves a lot better than being in here, cooking for and serving people who don't appreciate the importance of what he does.

He takes his jacket that's draped over a chair. "You remember how to send the video, right?" He hands me his iPhone.

I'm glad I never had one. There's too much going on in my head to have just as much going on in my hands. "Yeah. Once it's recorded, I open the message, write the number in that bit at the top, press the photo icon that opens your photos and choose the video. Then I press that arrow that sends it up."

Danny chuckles. "Yeah, you send it up."

I take the glass of water from the steel worktop and have a sip. I haven't eaten all day and the water swims through my body as though it's cleansing the rusty pipework. My hands tremble so I clasp them together.

"And what else?" Danny asks.

"Don't eat any of the food," I reply.

"Yes, that. Though I've made you a couple of sandwiches for when you're done. They're on the bottom shelf. A farewell surprise." He nods, pleased with himself. "I was thinking the more important 'anything else?'"

I raise a finger, remembering. "Don't look through your

photos. Unless I want to see things I can't unsee." I smile.

"Exactly. What people do in their spare time is their business." Danny takes the keys to the kitchen from his pocket and has one last look around the room. "And once you've sent it, delete the video. I don't want to feel compelled to watch it."

"Thanks, Danny. I remember how." I stand up and shake his hand. "You've been a good friend." He half smiles. I think I've made him uncomfortable. Perhaps being acknowledged as a friend by me is seen as a bad thing, but I mean it. Danny seems like someone who understands pain. Sometimes you can just tell by the way someone looks at you, or the tone they use with you.

He walks towards the door. "When you're done, leave the phone in the charger. Then lock the door and slide the keys under it. I'll head back after I've been for a few drinks and get everything." Danny scratches his cheek and opens the door. "Good luck, Ray. I'm sad to see you go, but I'm obviously happy for you. I hope things work out." He turns and closes the door.

Things will work out, just not how he imagines they will. I go and lock the kitchen door from the inside. I don't want anyone to interrupt me and my audience of none. The air feels heavy, suffocating. I've held onto this for too long.

I walk over to the pile of boxes Danny placed at the ideal height for me to film from and lean the iPhone against the five-liter can of olive oil, unlocking the phone with Danny's password. His year of birth, 1991. I switch the choices on the camera to video and press the icon with the arrows in a circle so it shows me. My face on the screen makes my heart heavy. Is it the effect of the screen or are my eyes that lifeless? I see a wasted life, buried beneath fear and confusion. Could I have done anything differently? The lone thick black hair on my head is the only thing of my past that hasn't packed up and run away. It's a reminder.

My finger moves towards the red record button but I hesitate. What am I hoping to achieve with this? I don't really know, perhaps peace. Perhaps acceptance. It doesn't matter. I need to share what happened. But keeping quiet has served me well these decades. Why risk it? What if it comes back? I don't care.

"No turning back," I tell the air, hoping if it's listening it knows I mean business. I press the button a bit too forcefully; knocking the phone down so put it back in place. It's recording.

I walk back to the chair and my body feels not so much lighter, just empty.

"Hey Becca, remember me? Your cousin Ray?" I shake my head. "That's a stupid question, of course you do. What I mean is, remember the me you knew as a kid before that day? Not the one from the news." My voice cracks and my mouth is already dry. I take a sip of water and lick my lips. "I hope life's been good to you and you got to become a vet like you wanted." I smile at the camera, wishing I'd looked after my crooked teeth better.

"I want to tell you my side of things, because I want to answer questions you might have. You might not even have any. Maybe you don't even give a shit. But if you do, I'll try. I might not be able to answer them all. I haven't been able to answer a lot of them myself, but I hope it helps." I slump in my seat, already exhausted. The air gets colder and I fold my arms.

"As you know it was summertime in 1986. Mum and Dad loved to have their yearly trip to Avebury, near Stone Henge, while

I dreaded it. They loved that Avebury had the largest megalithic stone circle in the world. I still don't know what megalithic means. I think it's just a more powerful word for unnecessarily big. I'm not sure and I don't really care." I shrug.

"People think the place contains psychic traces of ancient people and times. And there's no end to the ghost stories. From a lady in a white hood who haunts Avebury Manor, to a rock that crosses the road at midnight. Sounds fun but it's far from it." I gaze into the kitchen corner then back at the camera. Bringing up ghosts makes me uneasy.

"Mum and Dad would swarm like flies with other weird-minded people to sit in the center of the stone circle to meditate. They'd try to suck in this invisible energy and they'd go and touch the big stones. I never quite got it back then, being a kid. But what was so empty in their lives they had to try to fill themselves with something invisible? It was as though they hoped whatever they needed would be carried to them by the wind, or transmitted through a rock. I found it so weird. So desperate." I sit up straight.

"Looking back, I feel like they were tricking themselves, believing in something they couldn't see, hoping it'd bond them, because there was nothing else tangible apart from me. I don't think I ever even saw them kiss each other." I scoff, feeling slightly guilty, because they probably would've gone their separate ways if they didn't have me. I trapped them. I run the back of my hand over my forehead to wipe the sweat.

"I hated them for wasting my summers. I was a kid. I should've been spending the holidays playing football with friends or falling in love with girls who had no interest in me. Instead,

Mum and Dad dragged me away from any chance I had at a normal kid's life. I tried to be part of groups during term times, but Dad didn't like the kids at my school. He'd say the parents had negative energy and that it was likely transmitted onto their child. Sometimes Mum would come by the school early to take me out of it. I thought it was because she wanted to spend time with me, but it turns out it was just to get me out of school sooner. Only reason I was even in school was thanks to Grandma insisting they send me. Thank fuck she existed. Rest in peace." I kiss my fist.

"So, while kids bonded during the most important years of their lives, I stood in a field with a bunch of old folks and touched cold rocks. The biggest crime a parent can commit is to make their kids prefer being in school to being on their summer holidays." I take a breath. This is weighing me down and the resentment towards my parent's bubbles, but also a deep resentment towards myself. I'm blaming myself for their problems again. But it pisses me off. I was a fucking kid.

"We always stayed in a barn a few hundred yards outside the stone circle. I showed you photos of the barn once and you said it looked like a place old people die in. It was stuck in some forgotten era and didn't even have a TV! There were about twenty houses on the road, all backing onto fields, and yet we spoke to nobody from any of them. We got funny looks off the neighbors a few times, but that was about it.

"I'd spend the days walking around the barn looking for anything to capture my imagination. During the nights I wished I could be magically teleported back to London so I could have the life a kid should have. It would've been okay if I could play with the other kids, but my parents had an ability to make us repellent to anyone that didn't fit their criteria. With another kid I could've had a great time in those fields, but instead, I'd have to talk to flies and whatever creatures I'd find crawling around. One summer I spent three hours talking to an ant in my room." I shake my head at the ridiculousness of it. "That was the best part of the holiday!"

"I wished you and Aunt Jaz could've joined us, but you were both smarter than to waste your summers." I stop for a moment. My heart clenches. I don't know if it's glad I'm finally talking about this, or trying to eat itself.

"Some nights Mum and Dad left me alone. They'd go off into the fields and do whatever they did with the other energy hunters. I sometimes heard chanting and caught the flicker of candlelight in distant fields." My neck muscles tighten. "Hold on, Becca." I worry I'm not alone. I get up and grab a cleaver from its hook on the wall and place it by the chair, out of camera shot. Not that it'll do any good. I sit back down and feel slightly safer.

"I'd count the minutes in my room. It had nothing but an old wooden bed, an oak bedside table and a single window. The window faced out onto the endless fields. There was also a wardrobe built into the wall, but I preferred to keep my clothes in my suitcase. I don't know what it is, but something about wardrobes built into walls scares me. They're more like doors to a neglected place as far as I'm concerned. I made sure my suitcase blocked it as well.

"A lot of the time I'd stand in Mum and Dad's room and stare out of the window into other houses where families sat together. They were homes filled with smiles, togetherness. I'd end up walking around this barn getting freaked out by noises that old houses make. It was as though the barn was talking to me through its creaking. Probably telling me to stop stomping so heavily, or to wipe that bit of jam off the precious wooden floor.

"I looked everywhere I could for any sign of fun. Only thing I found were tools - a shovel, a hatchet. I took a torch and kept it with me in case the lights went out. Once, I got so bored I used a screwdriver to take a chair apart, just so I could figure out how to put it back. I did manage to find an old book under the sofa, The Magic Cottage by James Herbert, but Dad took it off me and threw it away before I could even open the cover. He'd tell me, 'You don't need someone else's imagination to entertain yourself when you have your own.'" I shuffle in my seat. "He had this weird idea that other peoples' imaginations pollute your own, diluting your clarity of thought and messing with your energy, somehow killing its purity. It's safe to say Dad was a moron." I poke my fingers into my lower back, wishing I could be bothered to stretch in the mornings. But even with so much time, it was the last thing on my list after - sit, nap and stare at the wall.

"Anyway, you get it. I was bored, my parents shouldn't have been together and they shouldn't have been parents. I'd complain, cry, beg, but they weren't going to let me go home. About three weeks into this six-week hell, I tried to walk all the way back to London. I got about a mile into it before night descended over the nothingness. It was all flat fields and the occasional tree. The silhouette of a horse or something appeared in the distance, but it was perfectly still. It was the strongest case of the chills I ever got, so I turned and ran back to my summer prison. I don't think I've ever run faster. I decided the only option to get through summer was to try to get into the energy nonsense." That same chill attacks the back of my neck so I rub it.

"I remember the day clearer than anything else in my life. It was baking hot. The kind of heat where you take a shower, dry yourself, and then instantly sweat again. The day was weird from the start. I woke up with a burning in my mind, like something was broken and I didn't know how to fix it. I cried that morning for no reason other than I couldn't not cry. All I wanted to do was go back to bed and sleep until the summer was over.

"I dragged my heavy legs down the creaky barn stairs and my dad packed the picnic basket. He was on his knees rolling his meditation blanket methodically and gently. I felt like he cared about that blanket more than he cared about me. He wiped his long hair away from his face and smiled up at me. The bright light caught his face and made him look more welcoming than he had in a while. 'Are you ready to feel the buzz?' He clenched his fist and the tiny muscles on his weedy arms became more pronounced." I mimic the gesture to the iPhone.

"Dad looked happier than I'd ever seen him. No idea why. It's nice to think that, though, isn't it? That sometimes people can be happy for no reason. Makes it feel like it's possible to be happy more often if there's no reason attached to it. He stood and straightened his t-shirt, then came and gave me a hug. I almost burst into tears again. For a moment he felt like an actual dad, rather than someone just playing the role of one when he thought he had to.

"Mum was smiling too. She'd tied her dark hair back and

wore a bright blue dress that stopped at her knees, like she used to when we'd go to my grandma's on weekends, before Grandma died. Mum always wanted Grandma to see her looking her best, so that Grandma wouldn't worry. Mum still had a hint of worry in her eyes, but that seemed permanent since the day her and Dad came back from hospital and she was no longer pregnant. I didn't realize the severity of it back then."

I take the biggest breath I have for years. I'm not sure I'm ready to confront the next part. I glance at the cleaver.

"Sorry," I tell the iPhone, as though Becca might actually watch this video and not instantly delete it. I rub my temples and steady myself. I take another sip of water.

"We went to a field together, as a family, like the families I'd seen in the houses. The grass was green in patches, and flattened and duller where people stepped on it around the rocks. Beyond the rocks a tiny hill cut out the distant view, likely just more fields. That's all this place was, fields, stones, a pub that claimed to be haunted, and shops where people sold smaller colorful stones. If you weren't in Avebury for the stones, then you were likely an alcoholic or lost.

"Even in the sweaty heat, it was pretty windy. Probably because the trees were so far apart. Maybe they knew about social distancing well before our time." I chuckle to myself, but notice my face fall on the iPhone screen. I don't have the right to joke with Becca.

"Mum and Dad got straight to stone touching. Both pressed their hands-on opposite sides of the rock and stood there with their eyes closed. So. Damn. Boring. I watched for what was about ten minutes but felt like ten years. Dad patted the stone like it was a pet. 'You ready to try?' he asked me. I falsely smiled and walked over to the giant stone. It was pretty impressive to see something so big. But that was about it, it was impressive. I had no need to spend time with it. I pressed my palms against the cold grey stone and pushed, trying to eek out whatever was supposed to be inside it."

I hold my palms out open to the iPhone. I mime pushing against a rock, my fingers tensed.

"Mum and Dad asked me if I felt the energy. I genuinely felt nothing; just annoyance that my hands were touching something hundreds of other people had touched, probably without washing their hands. I concentrated, imagined colors in my mind, begged for something, but I felt absolutely nothing. I started to wonder whether I was lacking something and if I was the one with the problem. 'Yeah, it feels kind of fuzzy,' I lied. I took my hands off the stone and opened my eyes. Mum and Dad smiled. 'It'll take time but that's a good start, Ray,' Dad said. Mum's smile was bigger than when Ms. Molloy told her I was the best pupil she'd ever taught.

"I figured I may as well carry on lying throughout the day. Touch a stone, say it's warm. Touch another stone, say it made my neck twitch and my head lighter. I hoped it'd make time speed up. Eventually we sat and ate our picnic, thankfully. Dad had made those coronation chicken baguettes you loved when you'd visit. I even remember the bread being that perfect, spongy softness that we always hoped for when we'd go to the bakery. Even though the day was dull, at least it felt like we were a family. Mum and Dad even took an interest in what I had to say, for once.

"I told them about a computer game a kid at school claimed he could get early versions of from Japan. It was called Castlevania and was due out in September in Japan, but not in the UK until 1987. It was about a vampire hunter who has to kill Dracula in his castle. Dad hated the thought of me playing computer games and he worried that games would make me lazy. Mum seemed a bit more open, though. 'Maybe for your birthday in January we can talk about you having some games.' She shrugged at Dad who shook his head."

I scratch my nose and rub my neck. Something about talking to a camera makes me tense. I like feeding off peoples' reactions, but all I can see are my own and I don't like them.

"Do you remember that Christmas we came to stay with you and we played Duck Hunt all night? That's what this conversation with Mum and Dad reminded me of. They were letting me be a young, and they seemed to like me that afternoon. It felt like we could be friends, not just family. I guess the trade off was showing them I could be what they wanted in a kid by pretending to feel the energy.

"But sadly, our bonding was ruined by some other energy hunters. 'Laura! Benik!' a nasal voice called out. I turned to the source and a guy in his early twenties who looked like he hadn't had a haircut since birth walked towards us. He wore a vest to show off his developing arms, and shorts way too wide for his stringy legs. It seemed all of his exercise went into the upper half of his body. He was flanked by two girls styled out of the same catalogue, who wore gowns that likely swept up every piece of dirt from the grass.

"Mum's eyes lit up and she bounced up to her feet faster than a released spring. She hugged the man she called Lucas, while Dad was much slower to stand and shake Lucas' hand. He greeted the two girls, Paula and Larissa, who nodded at him like he was a teacher. They shook Mum's hand from as far as their arms would extend. Chat turned to energy.

"I stared at the few clouds to busy myself. I made out an ostrich, a shark, and a creature I made up. I called it a Bagdola. The Bagdola was big as a tree, arms like a bear, and could eat stones. I imagined it eating all the stones in Avebury, and then we might not have to come here anymore. Mum and Dad talked to Lucas about things like ley lines and entities, and then Lucas showed them a little white hexagonal box. It had circular mirrors on the sides and a dial on the top with a compass. Lucas said there were magnets in it. Apparently, it helped people to balance out their energy. All they had to do was hold the box out in front of them. I imagined the Bagdola could pick Lucas up and throw him miles away, then boot the box into the nearest river.

"Mum didn't hesitate to grab the box of pointlessness, and that's where it got way too boring for me. So, I got up, dusted the baguette crumbs off my shorts, and told Dad I wanted to go and explore. Anything was better than watching people stare at someone holding a box."

The strip light on the kitchen ceiling flickers. I look up as though my eyes will do anything, but the flickering continues. I reach for the cleaver and place it on my lap, out of camera shot.

"Dad told me to stay within the rock circle. To be fair, that was a pretty massive area, and he wanted me to be back in a couple of hours, max. So off I walked, away from the boredom and into the unknown that was also likely to be boring. I walked around the outer part of the stones, thinking I'd do a lap and see what caught my eye.

"It got busier towards the Tolkien trees; apparently inspiration for the Ents in The Lord of the Rings. People tied ribbons to the wishing tree but a frog distracted me. I dropped to my knees to pick it up but it leapt away. 'Do you want me to follow you?' I asked it, and it leapt away, so I took that as a yes. It jumped away out of the stones and up the tiny hill on the outskirts of the stones."

The light stops flickering and dies. I'm sat in darkness, so I stand and take the iPhone. I unplug the charger.

"Sorry, Becca." I lean against the sink and put the cleaver down on it. I stand in the streak of moonlight streaming through the window bars. I turn the tap on and fill my glass with water then take a sip. I turn the tap off and plug the charger in and hook up the iPhone. I'm a bit silhouetted, but it doesn't matter.

"I obviously followed the frog. Who cares that it was outside the stones? It was all fields and over the hill that seemed more like a swollen speed bump were more fields. If it was a spooky wood, I would've never followed the frog, we know how that stuff tends to end! But I could still see the stones from where I was and it was all so open and sunny.

"I followed the frog for a few minutes, into longer grass up to just above my knees. The frog jumped, but this time it vanished. I looked around, confused and worried that I'd been imagining this frog, such was my boredom. But I took a step forward and my heart leapt back in my chest so hard it knocked me back onto my ass. I crawled forward and there was a pit, about a grown man and a half deep, and the same wide.

"I couldn't see the frog but a dog as dark as soot stared up at me. And I swear, Becca, this was no normal dog. It had the shape of a normal dog, like a Great Dane, but there was something missing. First thing I noticed was that it looked sad, forgotten. And it was damp, but I don't know with what. It was almost slimy." I rub my thumb and forefinger together. "I stood up and took a step back. The dog oozed the stench of an old bin bag full of rotten food, and that horrible choke-inducing smell you get when people burn sticks in their gardens. I retched and swallowed a bit of vomit, not wanting to throw up into the pit and onto the thing. It gave me that feeling you get when something gets into your chest. Know what I mean? As though if I had a soul it was trying to break out of my body to run away.

"The dog had these bony legs, like they'd been squeezed, and the muscles just hung off it. The nails on its paws were broken too. But what hit me the most was how expressionless it was. There was something off, like it wasn't real."

I choke up. I've never spoken of this dog since that day and I worry it'll somehow appear right in front of me. I place my hand over the cleaver handle and run my eyes over the corners of the kitchen.

"But it was real, Becca. It stared right at me. Its eyes weren't like the dogs we know though. You know how Turbo looked at us with curiosity and playfulness? This dog's eyes were black all over. There was a hint of orange behind them, like a dull flame in the dark, but it was all so numbing. The skin on my left forearm itched uncontrollably and I raked my nails up and down it. I wanted to rip my forearm off and throw it away." I mime scratching down my left arm and remember how deep my nails went.

"I called out to the dog, hoping to get a reaction, but it just stared. I wanted to leave it, but even though it looked out of this world I kind of felt sorry for it. I asked it, 'What's your name?' Nothing. It didn't look like it had a collar and I couldn't see a way for it to get out of the pit, thankfully. I looked around for an owner, but it was just me and this dog.

"The frog seemed okay though. I spied it by the dog's back leg. The frog jumped around, trying to get out of the pit, and that's when I saw something I could never have imagined, Becca." I bite my bottom lip and the pit of my stomach burns.

"The dog, in a flash twisted its head to near a hundred and eighty degrees. A barbed tongue stretched out of its mouth, grabbed the frog and pulled it into the dog's mouth. The dog turned back to me and stared, expressionless, frog's blood on its lips.

"My body never felt so weak. I inhaled my shock, turned to run and fell face first into the turf. Grass and dirt went in my mouth and nose. I scrambled back to my feet and bolted, pulling grass out of my teeth. I was too scared to turn around but imagined the dog leaping out of the hole and speeding towards me to take a chomp out of my calf, or worse yet, neck."

"I got to the top of the small hill and turned back, relieved to see nothing. I nearly cried and I saw that my blue shorts had a darker pool of blue where I'd pissed myself. I looked towards the stones and everything on this side of the hill was back to comforting and boring. I took my t-shirt off and tucked it into my shorts so most of it hung over the piss-stain.

"I returned to my parents and whispered to my dad that I'd found a dog in a pit and what it had done. I hoped that we would get the dog taken away by someone so I\d know it wasn't lurking. 'Are you making stuff up again?' Dad asked. But I think he could see how scared I was, so he stood up. He glanced towards my mum for acknowledgement, but she was sat leg-to-leg with Lucas, discussing that stupid box. 'Show me where,' Dad said, and we walked to the long grass.

"When we got there, we couldn't find the pit. 'Are you sure you saw anything?' Dad asked, frustrated. 'I swear I did,' I told him, and then he looked down at my shorts and must've seen a bit of the piss stain under the t-shirt. He huffed. 'Right, go home and change.' He shook his head at me like I was a disappointment! I asked him to go to the barn with me, but he said he couldn't, because he had to get back to my mum. At the time I didn't realize, but it's obvious now he was going to keep an eye on that slimy shitbag, Lucas.

"So, I walked back to that miserable barn alone, terrified that a hell hound was going to leap out at me. All I wanted was for my dad to be a dad in that moment, but he didn't care. I didn't want to be spoiled. I just wanted to be more than an inconvenience."

I clench my jaw and slump to the floor, holding the iPhone as far away from my face as the charger wire will stretch and with the cleaver by my side. I'd take my anger out on the boxes of onions if

I wouldn't have to clean it all up afterwards.

"I got back to the barn and washed some bits of grass off my teeth then showered. A nasty acidic taste hung in my throat. I was scared that every time I turned my head that I'd see that dog. Thankfully I didn't. I closed the curtains in my bedroom and went to sleep. It was about four o'clock in the afternoon. I hoped when I woke up it was the next day, and some part of me didn't want to wake up at all. I feared that if I opened my eyes, I'd see the dog standing on the end of my bed, it's broken nails digging into the duvet and that barbed tongue aimed directly at me."

I swallow, not knowing how much more I can share. It's all too raw, even thirty-five years later. My body seems ill equipped to deal with all the sensations running through it and I fear I might even piss myself right here.

"When I woke up only a couple of hours had passed. The sun poked beneath the curtains, but I had no interest in it. I turned to the wall away from the window and closed my eyes. I tried to think of happier times, like when our families went camping on the beach in Cornwall. Do you remember Dad being cocky about how he could put up a tent faster than everyone else? Then the wind blew it into the sea and he had to run in after it." I laugh, and it feels good. "Those are the memories that have kept me going all these years. I just wish there were more of them.

"Happier times gave me some renewed hope that this summer wasn't going to be total rubbish. All it would take was one great moment to lift everything.

"I tried to sleep again. But then something scratched at the door. I hoped my mind was messing with me and I covered my ears with my pillow and buried my head under the duvet. But it got more frantic, like something was desperate to get in. The tighter I covered my ears the worse the scratching got! 'Go away!' I yelled, falsely brave. I stared at the door as the scratching persisted. 'I'm not letting you in! Leave me alone!' I sat up and reached across to the bedside table, opened the top drawer and took out a pen." I shake my head. "What the hell was a pen supposed to do? I guess I thought it might be enough to put up a fight." I clench my fist at the camera.

"The scratching sounded all around me, as though something was trying to scratch its way through my skull and deep into my brain. This was an invasion in my senses. I rubbed my temples but it only hurt and I dug my nails so deep into my head I felt blood. 'Pissoff!' I yelled and leapt out of bed. The adrenaline hammered my body. I charged at the door, the pen now held up by my head, ready to stab the foul creature."

I hold my fist up to the screen in that stabbing motion from that day.

"I opened the door and shouted, only to see Dad stood there, pale as a sheet. The energy flooded from my body and I fell to my knees and dropped the pen. I sobbed and my dad sat by me and pulled me into a hug. He didn't say anything, he just hugged me."

I unplug the iPhone from the charger. I can't sit still anymore so I pick up the cleaver and pace the kitchen. I hate the darkness, so I open the fridge to get some light into the room. I check all the corners and keep the cleaver out of sight of the camera, but close to me.

"I curled up on the sofa in the living room and watched Dad

chop pieces of wood with the hatchet. The sofa had that old musty smell, as though dust had won the battle and the cushion covers would never recover, but it was somehow comforting. I wondered how many invisible bugs lived in the cushions and pictured a civilization of bacteria at war for territory.

"I stared at the fire, numb, hoping the flickering would calm my mind. The mind plays horrible tricks, though. I was sure I saw the fire form into the expressionless face of the dog. 'If there was a dog and it was damp, you'd see the paw prints or some dirt from its feet, so you've nothing to worry about, Ray,' Dad said.

"The sun had set and Dad chopped the last piece of wood. I nodded. What he said made perfect sense, but it didn't matter. 'We'll give your mum another twenty minutes and if she's not back we'll have dinner. He looked at the clock on the wall – 9:45pm. His shoulders slumped. At the time I thought it was from all that chopping wearing him out. I sat up on the sofa. 'Can I stay with you and Mum tonight?' I asked.

"I expected him to say 'yes' instantly. But there was a 'but'. That was the problem with this family, there was always a 'but'. I could stay in their room, of course I could, but he needed to meditate for an hour first. He said I'd be welcome to sit and watch him, though, but that I'd have to be completely quiet. I really didn't want to be alone, so when Mum didn't show up, we ate and then I watched my dad sit still and take long boring breaths."

I plug the iPhone back into the charger and scratch my chest. It's itching for some reason, maybe the polycotton from this horrible green boiler suit, but it feels deeper.

"I watched Dad for about five minutes and I tried my best to remain perfectly still, but I coughed. That's all it took, one cough. He didn't even open his eyes. He asked me to leave the room and said he'd come and get me when he was done. I couldn't believe it. He'd seen me shaken, disturbed, terrified, but all he wanted to do was re-align himself or whatever the fuck he was supposed to be doing. I stomped out of his room, making sure to slam every door and clatter whatever I could on my way. I got to the door to my room and froze. My heart stopped dead. A little mound of soil was perfectly placed in the middle of my doorway. It smelled of bins and burning. I called out for Dad. 'Dad there's soil! The dog, the dog!' But he didn't respond." I rub my forehead.

"I sped down the stairs, leapt over two at a time and I ran to the chopping block and grabbed the hatchet. I crept back up to my room, my chest rising so high it nearly touched my chin. I was ready to swing through that dog's expressionless face. But the pile of dirt was gone. I entered the room and checked every drawer, every crack, even the terrifying wardrobe, and then slammed the bedroom door shut.

"I buried the hatchet under my pillow and opened the curtains to close the window in case the beast could leap through the narrow crack. I tried to avoid looking out onto the dark field, but one flash across the emptiness was enough. Far in the field, silhouetted against the darkness, the outline of slimy fur caught in the moonlight. That's what I saw that night I tried to walk back to London.

"I shut that window and pulled the curtains across. I leapt into bed and gripped the hatchet. I grabbed the torch from my bedside table and shone it around the room, corner to corner, praying I didn't reveal the dog. I'd never been so awake, so alert. I hoped Dad would come and get me once he had finished meditating, but he never did."

I put the iPhone down a moment to scratch the backs of my hands.

"I kept the torchlight moving from corner to corner. I don't know what time it was, but I heard the front door close and footsteps. Then something smashed and my heart pounded. Armed with my hatchet, I walked towards the door and opened it a crack. Mum was back and she picked up pieces of a vase she'd knocked over. She swayed towards the fridge; the back of her dress covered in grass stains like she'd slid down a hill. I knew better."

I raise an eyebrow to the iPhone screen.

"She took a bottle of wine from the fridge, sat on the sofa and stared at the wall. She pulled the strap of her dress back over the right shoulder and drank straight out of the bottle. I caught a glimpse of Mum's face and her mascara was all over it.

"Every muscle in my body ached and I felt dull all over. I dragged myself into bed and turned the torch off. I put my head against the pillow and gripped the hatchet like it was my favorite childhood teddy bear. For a moment I wanted to stick the hatchet through my own face, but instead I cried. I was suddenly exhausted and fell asleep."

The hot feeling in my chest is overwhelming. "Hold on Becca. I'll keep talking but I need to get something." I put the iPhone on the floor and walk to the freezer. I open it, grab a tray of ice, take some cubes and wrap them in a kitchen cloth. I unzip the top of my boiler suit and press the cloth to my chest and take deep breaths.

"The next morning at the breakfast table was just cold. Mum's head was down the whole time and the stench of alcohol and regret poured out of her. And Dad's meditation must have not worked, because everything he did had a little bit more aggression to it. His fork hit the plate a little harder, he'd take a sip of juice and hit his glass against the table rather than place it. We were only eating omelets, but he cut it like he was trying to saw a piece of wood. I hadn't even touched my food. My appetite was lost along with my desire to live."

I walk back to the sink and sit in front of the camera again.

"I could barely keep my eyes open. I woke up about fifty times that night, sweating, shivering, and having muscle spasms. I was beginning to feel like my body was no longer my own and I was really irritable. Dad was chewing his food like he always did, you know, fucking slowly. It was like that time we had those homemade pizzas. We'd finished ours and he was still chewing his first slice." I mimic how Dad used to chew, slowly moving my jaw like a camel, chewing out of the left side, then the right side. "It was like he was trying to dissolve the food in his saliva before he could swallow it. This time, though, I didn't find it funny. I wanted to take the bread knife and slit his throat."

I raise a hand as though pleading my innocence. "I hated thinking that, trust me. I didn't even know I could have that thought. Maybe it was the lack of sleep. It scared me a lot. I wasn't seeing him as a father anymore."

I'm done with the cloth, so I take it out of the boiler suit, rest it on my lap and zip the boiler suit back up.

"Dad told Mum what happened the evening before. 'He was

acting weird yesterday,' Dad said. He, like I wasn't sitting right there. He wouldn't look at me. Mum finally looked up to glimpse my face. She turned back to Dad. 'Maybe you should take him on your walk today.' That was her solution, to work me into one of their activities, not to do something for me. I scratched my fork against my thigh, trying to distract myself from getting angry.

"Dad stood up. 'Why don't you take the kid? Or are you worried it'll stop you being as free as you can be?' He pushed his plate off the table. The smash made me jump and the omelet slapped against the wooden floor. Dad stormed up the stairs to their room. Then Mum threw her fork after him and followed him while chucking out every swear word she could think of.

"She slammed the door to their room behind her, and all I heard at that point were muffled shouts. I should've been sad or angry, but it was weird, Becca. I was almost catatonic. It was like I couldn't emote in that moment. Or my heart and my mind wouldn't let me. I didn't even notice I'd pushed my fork so hard it'd ripped through my shorts.

"I thought I may as well eat, just to fill the silence. I cut only a tiny section of the omelet and placed the forkful into my mouth. I chewed but I couldn't taste the egg. And the texture, it changed with each bite, from soft to rough. Rough like the grass I'd gotten a mouthful of the day before, but it was tougher. The more I chewed the tougher it got, and one bite released this hellish taste of rotten chicken, and a smell of rubbish and burnt sticks filled my face. My eyes watered and I retched.

"I fell out of my chair and coughed up this black slime. Something tickled the back of my throat and I reached in to pull it out. I pulled a stringy, black, slimy hair out of my mouth. Then another. And another. They kept coming and filled my throat. I tried to shout for help through the choking, but the muffled shouting in Mum and Dad's room drowned everything out. I pulled hair after hair until a pile the size of a cat was by my head. I looked around for that damned dog, but there was nothing. Why was it tormenting me? 'What do you want?' I yelled. But I was alone, shaking on the floor.

"I caught my breath, got up and poured as much water as I could down my throat and spat the foul taste into the sink. I swept up the hair and put it in a plastic bag, so I could show my parents. I walked up the stairs but stopped half way. I listened to more of their muffled shouts. Something smashed and I realized I didn't want to tell them, because they didn't care. I dumped the plastic bag of dog hair in the bin and went to my room. I sat and stared at the wall, waiting for one of them to reluctantly take me with them.

I wipe my hand across my nose. It's getting colder in here. I touch the radiator but the heating is on. I grip the cleaver and check the corners.

"Later, I walked through a field with Mum, but she didn't say a word. This was the most pissed off she'd ever looked. I reached my hand out, hinting that I wanted to hold hands, hoping she'd take it. I caught her glance at my hand, but she ignored my invitation. My heart couldn't take any more, so I just came out with it."

I slap my chest with each word. "Do you regret me?" I shake my head.

"In a flash and with the coldness of the stones she loved to touch, she simply said 'no'. That kind of question should hit someone deeply! It should make them think, not about their answer, but about why someone is even asking such a thing!"

I notice I've pressed the cleaver into my right thigh. I move the cleaver away and put it back on the floor.

"That question should've hurt her. Why would I feel so low that I needed to ask this? But she just said no, didn't look at me, and we walked on."

Tears creep into my eyes and I take a moment to dwell on that scene. "In that instant, my Mum became Laura and I became nobody. I don't remember the rest of that walk, but we got to a house and that prick, Lucas answered, smelling like he had a stick of incense burning up his arse.

"Mum ushered me through the house to the back garden. There was a tennis ball, and thankfully the fences meant I couldn't see any fields. Mum told me Lucas was going to do some healing for her and left me out there. Then they locked the door from inside and off they went. Three hours I stood in that garden kicking the tennis ball, alone. I had no drink even though the sun shone right on me, and I had to piss in the corner of the garden. I knocked on the glass door at one point but was left ignored."

I rest my head against the wall and take a breath. The tears stream down my face. "Have you ever felt like you didn't belong in this world, Becca?"

I get up and pace the kitchen again, trying to scratch the discomfort out of my left forearm.

"Back at the barn that evening, I sat in my room to the soundtrack of Mum and Dad shouting at each other some more. I imagined the rest of our lives. Would we go back home and become a happy family? Would I ever have any friends? Would Mum and Dad stay together or divorce? Who would I live with? Would I live with either or would they give me up? It seemed more likely they'd give me up. I started to think that I was wrong to think of myself as a trap, keeping them together. They didn't give enough of a shit about me to think of me as a trap. They were trapped by laziness, and not wanting to start from zero.

"I couldn't sit here anymore. I hated them, but I also loved them. I wanted this to work. I wanted to make more good memories to push the bad ones out. I decided to make them feel the love I hoped was still somewhere. I snuck out and I sat by a rock in one of the fields. It was six o'clock and I expected they'd notice I was missing in an hour when it was dinner time, worry and then come to find me. Then when they found me we'd have a family hug and at least feel a moment of togetherness. That's all I wanted. That feeling would be enough to tell me we mattered as a family. That I mattered as a son."

I stretch my legs out. My knee pops.

"But they never came. Eleven o'clock and nothing. Just me sat among the stones I hated in total darkness. I cried and I cried. I felt a slight chill and rubbed the goose bumps on my arms, but then was compelled to scratch my left forearm. I scratched and scratched, dug my nails right in until bloody lines formed. I stood up and I pounded the stone, wishing I could topple it. I kicked it, spat at it, swore at it. It took my parents, and now it had the blood from my fists.

"Defeated, I turned to go back to the barn of misery. At the end of the field there was the dog, silhouetted in the perfect darkness. The slimy sheen rose and fell with its breath."

I start to tremble and my voice quivers. I place the cleaver in my lap.

"That dull orange I'd seen in its eyes before, it was more of a fire now, and this time the dog walked towards me. That fucking walk, it was rigid and bitty, like its limbs were breaking out of a stone casing. But the thing is, you can't scare someone who no longer wants to be alive. I shouted at the thing. 'Fuck you!' And I walked towards it. It didn't run away, but it backed away, and I followed. Its stench hung in its path and I pulled my t-shirt over my nose.

"I was so angry. I called it all sorts of names. Before I realized, we were in the long grass and it jumped down into its pit. I looked down on it, that expressionless face, and I kicked some dirt onto it.

"It didn't even react. It felt nothing. I kicked more dirt onto it. I dug my hands into the soil and threw it in the dog's face. Still no reaction. It was numb. It was just a shell, walking the earth emptily. I shouted for it to leave me alone. I wished it would choke on the soil.

"I threw a stone and it was a great shot. Right in the dog's nose, but it didn't even react to that! I threw pile after pile of soil on it. It must have been hours and I'd barely covered its paws and I was exhausted. 'Leave me alone!' I begged. 'Just leave me alone, please...' It just fucking stared and I screamed into the sky. All the pain inside me came flooding out."

I lay on the floor of the kitchen and aimed the iPhone down at my face. My eyes were red from the tears about to burst through.

"Then I stopped looking at this dog like it was my enemy. I pitied it. It was rejected, living in a pit, misunderstood and ugly. Numb to feeling. My eyes stung and the burning I felt in my stomach became fiercer. I sat and swung my legs over the side of the pit and I jumped in. The stink no longer bothered me. I inhaled it.

"I extended my hand and the dog came and sniffed it. The dog opened its mouth and that nasty barbed grey tongue stretched out. It was like a snake and it wrapped around my arm all the way up.

"The barbs didn't sting; they comforted me and made my body warm. I stroked the dog's slimy head and it retracted its tongue. The scratches on my arm were healed."

I wipe the tears out of my eyes. "I know it sounds fucked up, Becca, but it's true." I check the corners of the kitchen.

"I pulled dirt down from the pit wall to give myself a way to climb back up, and I took the dog. He was coming with me and he was going to be the family pet. For some reason I though a pet would replace the lost little brother or sister I was supposed to have.

"We must've got back to the barn around two in the morning. I walked in and Mum was passed out on the sofa, two empty bottles of wine by her side. There was dried blood under her nose and the fire crackled. 'I got us a pet,' I told her. But she was out cold.

"The dog sniffed her and then followed me up the stairs. I went to my room and took my trainers off, then went to see Dad to tell him the good news. I opened the door to his bedroom and it was a mess. Clothes, a broken lamp, a drawer smashed on the floor. Yet somehow, at two in the morning, he was sat on his mat meditating! 'I got us a pet,' I said, and I noticed the blood on his lip and clumps of his hair on the floor.

I roll onto my side. My energy is completely gone.

"He didn't give a shit though. 'I think you should say hi to him,' I told Dad. But he cleared his throat. 'I've got a lot I need to process,' he said. 'Go back to bed and we can play whatever game this is tomorrow.'

"I stared at him. I couldn't believe he wouldn't even look at me. Then, without warning, the dog opened its mouth, swung its head and lashed its tongue half way through Dad's neck. Dad fell sideways and his blood pooled the wooden floor. The dog retracted its tongue, looked down at Dad, then swung its head back and lashed its tongue up and down, beheading Dad. With its fucking tongue!"

Coldness washes over my body. I can't quite believe the words myself.

"I didn't even try to stop the dog. I was paralyzed. The dog stared at me and I worried I was next, but he ran out of the room. I chased him and got to him right as he took a bite of Mum's face. He twisted and chewed and when he released her, the left side of her face was a fleshy mess, her eye squashed and bloody. I collapsed to my knees and screamed. But the dog took chunks out of her shoulder, her chest, her waist, and her legs... Fuck... When he was done that wasn't Laura lying on that sofa. I held her but I couldn't even grip her, it was all blood."

I run to the kitchen bin and throw up. I sip some water and

face the iPhone again.

"I swear it, Becca. I didn't do it. I looked back at the dog and he was gone. I don't remember anything after that. But from the police reports, I've been told they found me sat on the sofa, my mum's destroyed body in one arm and my dad's head in the other. They say the bloody hatchet was on the floor. But the dog must've put it there.

"I never told them it was the dog, because I was so traumatized. I barely believed it myself. I thought maybe I'd gone mad. Maybe I did do it. But I didn't. I know I didn't.

"The police searched the entire place and I hoped when they found the dog hair in the bin they'd ask more questions, but they never found it. Just a plastic bag full of spat out omelet."

I try to stand up but I collapse and sob onto the floor. I'm holding the iPhone but I don't even know where it's pointing anymore.

"I didn't do it, Becca. I swear it. The dog did it. The dog did it." I look up and see it in the corner. I haven't seen it in thirty-five years. I throw the cleaver at it and scream. It disappears but the smell of bins and burnt sticks remains.

My breathing calms and I look at the phone, still recording. The one black hair on my head shines with sweat. "I'm sorry, Becca." I stop recording.

I take a piece of paper from my pocket and type Becca's number into the phone. I attach the video. This is it. I'll send the video, go back to my cell, and tomorrow when I'm released, I'll kill myself. I've been thinking about the best way for a while. I tried hanging myself in my cell, but the makeshift rope was shit and it failed. I'm going to jump off one of those bridges that let people cross over motorways.

My thumb hovers over the send button. Why do I want to torment Becca? What is this going to do? It'll only hurt her. She's moved on, let her live in peace. I put the phone on the kitchen counter and scratch my arm. She'll only think I'm even crazier. I'm overcome with shame and I delete the video.

I look to my right and the dog is next to me, staring, expressionless. I put my arm around it and stroke it. I bury my tear-covered face into its slimy fur.

I get up and place the iPhone in the charger on the counter. I open the fridge and take out the sandwiches Danny kindly made - coronation chicken. I wolf them down, nearly choking. I walk over to the cleaver, pick it up and put it back on the hook. "I'm sorry, Danny," I tell the air. I wish it could be different, but I can't wait until tomorrow. I have no control over what I'm doing.

I grab the chef knife from its hook and thrust it into my neck. I don't even feel it. I'm numb. I collapse onto the floor and my blood flows into my fading eye line. The dog approaches, sniffs my blood and licks it. It faces me, expressionless, but then the fire in its dead eyes explodes. It opens its mouth and wraps its jaws around my head.

WILDFLOWERS BY MOONLIGHT

1.

When I was very young, my father had left home to find work elsewhere. Determined to succeed in the wide world and my mother believed him. She believed his quietly crooned promises in the soft, lamp-lit straw of the loft as they lay together in blissful ignorance and youthful delusion. She believed he would become famous and wealthy then return for her and I. He always promised to take us away to someplace where the ground wasn't covered in the colorless white of winter from the Beaver Moon to the Worm Moon. He was the one who named me Daisy, bringing the blooms to my mother when I was born. He was the reason the elder Keepers chose that name for me. I remember when I was young, she said my name with love. After he left, my name was spat at me like a curse. She despised me because I have his eyes. My aunts told me Mama was a very sweet and caring maiden who believed in romance and the promises of a handsome fool before being abandoned. Now she was as bitter as the winter wind.

I only have two faded memories of my father beyond him leaving for the fields every morning and coming home with flowers every evening. The first memory was when I was still a babe. We were laughing as he rubbed his nose into my neck by my ear, teasing me as I giggled. I remember it was early spring, and that day he showed me how to find the first dandelions. We savored the leafy vibrant green goodness together. The last memory; he was telling me what a beautiful maiden I would be someday, and how everyone would want me for their own, but I was his, and he would come back soon. The memory ends with him willingly climbing into a truck as my mother cried. He gave us a wink and a nod and then was gone forever.

It was high summer when he left. I was so young... I waited by the gate every night for him to return, but he didn't. After many bitter moons, I realized he lied. I swore if I ever met my father again, I'll hurt him... I plan to kick him until his eyes bulge out of their sockets, and his life's poppy red blood drains from his body. I hate him... I hate him almost as much as Mama hates him. He hurt Mama and I when he abandoned our family, but he also left her to a terrible fate.

Mama was forced to make children with another male, as was the way of our clan. She fought, she screamed, she even tried to run away. Then the elder Keepers bound her because she refused to submit and left her locked in with a chosen male until she was pregnant. Maisie's father was slain by wolves in the high winter before she was born. Maisie's twin died at birth, and Mama didn't even give him a name. Mama ignored Maisie from the moment she was weaned, except to criticize her or try to hit her.

Mama refused to show love to the lives her body produced. Because Father had left her to this fate, she vowed she would no longer believe sweet words or the lies of 'I love you'. She expressed her bitter coldness toward everyone every day. As eldest, I often felt the lash of her tongue or kick of her foot first; my half-sister Maisie was always hiding behind me.

In the next cycle, the Keepers chose another. He laid with her and she became pregnant again. This time she screamed when the babies were born. As soon as she could move after giving birth, she attacked them, trying to kick and kill them. The elder Keepers had to restrain her and force her to feed them. She wouldn't give my brothers names. She refused to acknowledge them or their father when he came in from the fields every night. He tried often to speak with her after she fed my brothers, but she would only lower her head, flare her nostrils, and bellow at him to go away. He was kind to Maisie and I, even though we weren't his. The twins were taken away one morning when they were very young, and their father left with them. My heart broke again, and it is still broken because I never saw them again.

While our mothers worked in the milking room or foraged in the fields, my half-sister, cousins, and I played in the late summer fields of the only place my family had ever called home. We were taught to always stay inside the fences. For beyond, the world became a dangerous place of predators and prey, of hunters and the hunted, of evil where no kindness or mercy awaited those who wandered. Being taught all this, I was timid and obedient, a fearful child. At the slightest unusual sound from beyond the fences, I would run for the longhouse and take Maisie with me.

One day during the time of the dry winds before the Hunter's blue moon, we found the fences down. My cousin Rosie ran into the unknown of golden grass and false freedom while I ran home. I never saw Rosie again, only her life's poppy red dripping from a stained canvas twisted around her body when they brought her back to burn. I will never forget how the red drops darkened the dry tan grass of autumn or glistened on the deep brown bark of pine logs before golden lily and marigold orange flames ate her. Beyond her pyre, I saw the moon rising, golden and perfect as the elders made us go inside the longhouse in obedience to the mantras. I will never forget Rosie's laughter or melodious voice, encouraging me to follow her on an adventure. I always thought she was so brave. For her courage, she was rewarded with a violent death for breaking our laws.

Two days later, a bitter winter began on Halloween with the wind bellowing like a bull, and there was no celebration of the harvest. The clan hurried to gather as much of the late grains and grasses before they were covered with snow as they could, leaving the carved pumpkins and tied stalks to be buried by winter's wrath. The Keepers led us young ones to the sheltered places out of the blowing snow while the adults worked in the open.

For days, the sky held the color of polished metal, and the sun was hidden. The biting wind beat on the longhouse and leeched the warmth from the world as the white snow buried everything of color. Foraging in the cold moons was hard. It was made harder in this land because the colorless winter just held on and on and on. Sometimes the snow would come as early as the Hunter's Moon or stay as late as the Flower Moon, or so I was taught.

VvvvV The beast...

He had never been in a place so cold, so horribly inhospitable. Only the strongest of beasts survived the search for food, for prey, for the one. He only survived because of the strength and fierceness of his beast. Even the wolves kept their distance now. Too bullheaded to flee to warmer climes, the beast refused to follow the herds south. Instead, he thieved wood and sometimes food from the little walled farming communities scattered in the mountains. He didn't know why he stayed, except that the longing kept him here. Sometimes, when his fire burned too low to stave off the frigid air before dawn, he mourned his loneliness in long low tones echoing off the mountains.

2.

The full moon passed... and then another moon and another... each cold moon more frigid than the last. Every day the Keepers sent us out to forage, so every day we searched the colorless, cold world for anything green or brown. By mid-winter, the snow was half-way up the walls of the longhouse, so we had no choice but to dig with frozen limbs to add to our meager rations daily. Mama bellowed at me to hurry up; as it was time to go in. Maisie followed closely in my tracks. The time of high snow was always hardest on the younger ones of our clan; many did not survive. But Maisie would survive; I would make sure of it. What I found as we foraged, I shared with her.

I led and she followed through the drifts, as high as my hips. Shivering and wanting only to get out of the bitter wind, we trudged back to the drafty longhouse we called home. I hated snow just like my mother, the freezing white that covered the world for over a third of the year. Every step reminded me of why I hated my father and his broken promises. It was the only thing Mama and I had in common, our shared desire to live someplace always warm.

At the end of the day, with our limbs numb from digging roots from the frozen earth, we huddled together and ate a flavorless meal. Occasionally, once or twice a week, we would have oats made with molasses. It was our only treat as the days ran together while we waited for the lush green bounty of spring. Tonight, would not be one of those nights.

The Keepers who protected and helped provide for us, walked through as we ate our evening meal and huddled together for warmth. They talked of having to sacrifice some to save us all if the winter didn't break soon. One had patted Maisie on the head. Mama didn't even lift her eyes in concern, but I was terrified for my little sister. That night, I prayed that the earth would shake off her cold white shroud and bless us.

The bitter winter held on. A few days later, the Keepers gathered the eldest of us. We could only watch in tearful silent horror as they were led away into the cold, dark evening. Maisie, not understanding what was happening, called out a cheerful farewell. I stepped between her and Mama before she could be struck by the one who had birthed us. That night as we huddled together for warmth, trying to sleep, Maisie murmured that she hoped the old ones had a warm place to sleep and that we would see them again soon.

The wind was blowing again the next morning, low and mournful. It mounded the snow around the longhouse up to the rafters and pushed the cursed icy flakes into any crack or hole it could find. The insidious breath of frost, making things miserable as the Keepers tried to keep the wind out with rags and mud.

The storm blew on, moaning and howling for so many hours, I thought I would go mad. We didn't go out that day or the next, confined in the darkness of the longhouse. Maisie and I spent the long, cold hours hungry or licking frozen water to slake our thirst and praying for the blessing of spring. Just eating some meager dry rations before bed, my guilt gnawed at my heart the way my starving stomach gnawed at my ribs when I didn't share my dinner with Maisie as I watched her licking her dish.

During the night, I woke to an eerie quiet. Sneaking out of our room and to the great door of the longhouse, I peeked out at a white world bathed in moonlight. The thin hoofprint of the moon hung over translucent puffy white clouds that looked more like the cottony fluff of dandelions than the source of our suffering. In the bitter winter, the stillness was haunting.

Never leave the longhouse before Dawn or after Dusk.

I took first one, then another tentative step out into the frigid air. My breath created glowing white veils of the proof of my life floating around my face.

Never go out in the moonlight.

Wandering toward the home of the Keepers, I noticed it was dark inside. The gate pushed open easily. The snow was so deep and as hard as stone. I walked over the drifts, where I knew the fences were. Walking around to the far side of the farm, there was a trodden down trail into the trees.

Never pass the fences.

I don't know why I followed that trail, but I did. I followed the path through the trees to a clearing. It had a sacred, beautiful feel in the moonlit stillness that I had never known. I wasn't even feeling the cold anymore as my awed tears froze on my cheeks.

Far away, I heard a strange sound, a low mournful tone as if night itself grieved the frigid grip of winter. It called to my heart, so I sang back to it, letting my pain carry out into the night through my voice. Only the silent night answered me. I waited, listening until the cold became unbearable. My feet ached to my knees in painful icy needles. Reluctantly, I turned and forced my frozen feet to return to the longhouse. The next morning, the wind was blowing again, but the storm had passed.

VvvvV The beast...

Another storm came, worse than the others. The wind tore the hides of his shelter, and he was forced to wrap his body in the scraps and crawl through the blinding white to a cave too short for his stature. Cramped, freezing, he tried to start a fire again to no avail. The pain from the bitter cold ran from the tips of his horns to the bottom of his hooved feet. He gathered what broken limbs he could and blocked the wind for some small protection. His thick fur and hide too cold to melt off the ice it had accumulated. Falling asleep, he feared his quest was for naught. He would freeze to death before he found the one meant just for him.

When he woke, the wind had stopped. The night was so quiet he could only hear his heartbeat and its echo so far away. He crawled out into the frigid stillness. His beast sang its loneliness, and to his amazement, the one answered. Shocked senseless, he stumbled down the mountainside to find her. Slipping and sliding, he almost went over a cliff and died. Clawing his way back to his pathetic cave, he collapsed and wept.

3.

The Flower Moon was only a few days passed when the winds changed direction. Warm and inviting, it carried the promises of spring as it blew around us while we foraged in the mud and slush. In the thinning snow, I found it, the first verdant shoots of a dandelion. No one was close, so I selfishly ate it all. The tangy green goodness reminded me of all the things I missed about the warm months. It was gone too quickly. The aftertaste made me want to cry as I chewed yet another frozen, old root, trying to fill my empty belly with anything that would keep me alive till spring arrived fully. As I searched so desperately for more, I heard it again; the mournful call of the winter night. Lifting my eyes from the frozen hole I was digging, I looked around. No one else heard it over the wind and the miserable moaning of the clan females and children.

That night, Maisie got very sick. She said she had eaten pine bark and needles. Her little belly bloated painfully, and her belches smelled like something was rotting inside her. I wondered if they had molded before they were frozen under the snow. My Aunt Bess had told me to never eat molded things; my cousin Betty had almost died of it. I went to Mama's room for the first time since winter began.

"Mama... Mama?" I called as softly as I could before stepping to her door.

"What, Daisy?" Her voice was like a whip against my flesh.

"I... uhm, please help me," I begged. "I don't know what to do."

"What nonsense are you spouting? You know what to do; the

night has fallen, go to your room." Her vicious tone almost had me drawing back, but Maisie's weak moan from our room gave me a strength I never knew I had.

"Mama, Maisie is sick. I don't know what to do," I repeated. "I think she ate something molded."

Mama looked at me with emotionless brown eyes as she refused me. "Too bad, she should have been more careful. You should have taught her better. Go back to your room."

"Please, Mama. Tell me what to do," I pleaded, desperate to help Maisie.

"There's nothing... Now. Go. To. Your. Room." Bellowing, Mama stepped toward me with the usual anger in her eyes, so I retreated, shaking in fear of the female who birthed me.

Back in our room, I pushed our bedding close around Maisie, trying to keep her warm. All I could do was rub her side and hope that she passed whatever was making her sick. By morning, she couldn't stand to go out to the fields to forage. Our mother had left without even looking in our door. I was shooed away as the elder Keepers came with the medicine man to check Maisie. I stayed close, peeking in to watch them give her medicine and taking the rancid air off her stomach with a tube. They seemed pleased with their work and left her. Ignoring my hunger, I snuck back inside our room to lie beside her. If she was warm, she would recover faster, or so I hoped.

But Maisie got sicker again during the night. At midnight, I rushed to the longhouse doors to get the medicine man from his home, but I couldn't get them open. They were barred against the monsters who stalked the night, monsters I had never heard or seen. But even as I tried to escape to get help, the mantras hummed in my mind.

Never pass the fences.

Never forage or walk alone near the fences or in the far fields.

Never leave the longhouse before Dawn or after Dusk.

Never go out in the moonlight.

Never let the monsters bite you.

"Open the doors!" Screaming as I kicked the door, I hated the mantras I was taught to keep us safe. Giving up, I ran back to our room, calling for help, "Please, someone help me." But no one heeded me as I rushed back to my sick sister.

"Hold on, Maisie, dawn will be here soon. The Keepers will come and bring the medicine man, and you'll be fine." I didn't know I was lying.

Maisie struggled to breathe and cried out in pain until she couldn't get enough breath to even moan. Her eyes looked at me in pained desperation as she opened her mouth, unable to speak. I could only kiss her tear-streaked cheeks repeatedly and try to soothe her.

"I love you, little sister, just keep breathing. It will be dawn soon." I promised in quiet desperation. Outside I heard the muted cry of the winter night, sharing my fear and grief. Before morning, my heart was broken.

"Time to go, Daisy," Mama said cruelly as she walked passed my door, but I didn't look at her. "Daisy! Get up and go outside."

"Leave her, Dora," Aunt Bess warned Mama, pushing her away from my door.

I refused to move or to leave Maisie when the Keepers and medicine man returned. They had to drag me out by my neck as I cried and thrashed. They locked me in a room. I hollered and kicked the walls until my strength was gone and I collapsed onto the cold, dirt floor. My little sister was gone. The only one in the world who loved me had left me alone to face the end of winter. I prayed to follow her. I wished I had died too and cursed myself for selfishly eating the dandelion shoots instead of giving them to her.

One of the elder Keepers came in, an older woman with hair as silver-white as the Wolf Moon. Emmie patted me and tried to get me to eat some oats and molasses, but I wouldn't. Day after day, she came back cooing to me in the sacred language of the Keepers about what a good sister I was. She told me I would make a good mother someday, a better mother than Mama. She promised that the pain would pass but said I needed to eat soon, or the others would kill me.

I couldn't make myself go outside, but many times before dawn, I heard the low, lonely moaning of the winter night's grief moving away until one morning, it was gone.

VvvvV The beast...

The winter never ended in this cursed land. He was wasting away, surviving only on scraps of frozen wolf meat and the bark he peeled from trees and boiled. Insanity and longing overcame all other needs as he sought the one. She had sung to him, and he was certain she was here in these loathsome white mountains. Time passed unnoticed. Days blurred together. Forage, hunt, search, sleep.

One day the wind finally turned warmer, bringing some relief from the bitter winter.

"Please, someone, help me."

He woke from a nightmare, but it wasn't his dream, it was hers. She was screaming; she was terrified. Trembling under the mass of hides and branches that was his moving shelter, his dark, beady eyes darted to and fro. The one needed help, and he was too far away to find her. He felt her heart breaking, her wish for death. Desperate to give her hope, he bellowed out his song before dawn every day and waited in quiet despair for her to answer. The spirit of spring came to life around him as her grief lured her soul toward death.

On the third day, a few hours after dawn, he was startled by his father's master-of-arms and a band of warriors. "My prince, it's time to return home."

His beast refused to even consider it and attacked them, trying to tear them apart as he had torn the wolves apart after they bragged about the female they killed. Unable to overcome them, he fled. They chased him relentlessly, but every day before dawn, he sang his song of loneliness and listened for her to sing back. Finally, they caught him and caged him, certain the trial of survival and the quest for his one had driven his beast mad.

4.

One day, the Keeper called Emmie brought me a bowl of dandelion salad.

"Look what I brought you, Daisy. The first of the spring," she claimed.

I ate it slowly, one leaf at a time from her hand. My guilt over not sharing my favorite food with Maisie made it impossible for me to thank her. I just cried as she rubbed my back. "I know you miss her, but as long as you love her, she lives in your heart."

I fell asleep, praying it was true.

The next day she coaxed me to follow. "Come outside, Daisy..."

The world had changed while I had grieved for Maisie. Gone was the barren and colorless white of the cold months. The fields were bright with green of every shade. Soon wildflowers would be blooming and sharing their sweet nectared blossoms with the bees and with us.

The warm sunlight felt so good, so healing, so hopeful after my days in the dark longhouse. She wept with me as we stood just beyond the door. My aunts and cousins came to greet me, touching their cheeks to mine, murmuring encouragement as I took my first tentative steps back out into the world of the living. The keeper left me with my family.

Walking toward the greenest new grasses and grain shoots, I saw my mother. Mama looked at me with her brown dead eyes and turned away. Something in me flashed like a lightning bolt igniting a prairie fire. I charged at her, knocking her over, first kicking then shouting at her as my Aunt Bess and Cousin Betty pushed me away. "I hate you! I hate you! I hate you!"

."Daisy, enough!" Aunt Bess scolded.

I stomped away from my family, vowing to myself to never speak to Mama again. I walked all the way to the fences and stood there, staring out at the green temptation beyond. So much food, so much bounty we couldn't reach. And for what reason? Those stupid superstitious mantras!

Never pass the fences.

Never forage or walk alone near the fences or in the far fields.

Never leave the longhouse before Dawn or after Dusk.

Never go out in the moonlight.

Never let the monsters bite you.

I hated every teaching of the clan at that moment. Maisie had first starved, then bloated and died because we couldn't forge beyond the confines of the fences. We couldn't claim the bounty that lay under the snow and now grew taller and untouched as spring bloomed. It wasn't fair.

"Daisy?"

"Daisy, please." It was the first note of softness I had heard in my mother's voice since Maisie and her twin were born.

"Go away, Mama! I hate you!" I bellowed at her without turning around.

"Daisy, you're all I have left. Please don't be this way." She sounded close to tears, and I felt the familiar sting in my own eyes. The sensation seemed to be my constant companion since Maisie's death, but I refused to share it with her.

"What about Maisie? You had her and you ignored her; you treated her like she didn't exist except when you wanted to kick someone. She was my sister! She died, and you didn't even care!"

My mother was silent for a long time. "I couldn't care about her. Not after what he did to me to make her. I am sorry she died though; I know you loved her as I love you."

"You don't know how to love, Mama, you never have. Maybe if you did, Father would have come back for us." I said the last just to hurt her. She had loved me once, just like we had loved him, but hate poisons love like foxglove poisons the body and kills the heart.

I listened to her heavy footfalls in the young grass as she walked away. Tears dripped off my face while I gathered ryegrass shoots, but no matter how hard I looked, I found no dandelion shoots.

As the days passed, I stayed away from everyone while I gathered the food that would have kept my sister alive. Everywhere I looked, my memory could see images of Maisie prancing and playing. In the distance, I could see there was still snow on the mountains. The bitter winter, clinging to the peaks the way it was clinging to my soul. It was as if the cold months hadn't ended, as if they still lived in my heart with the mournful cry of the night. I was so tired of being cold, but even standing in the golden warmth of sunlight and spring, I couldn't get warm.

Every time Mama tried to approach me, I turned and walked away. Every time she tried to touch me, I kicked at her without hitting her and shouted my hatred, always walking away before I attacked and killed her.

Today was no different, only I shoved Mama to the grass instead of kicking at her before my Aunt Bea scolded me, "Daisy, how dare you?"

"I'm sorry, Daisy," Mama whimpered as she stood.

My youngest sibling still grew in her belly, so instead of attacking her, I snarled at Mama, "I wish it were you instead of Maisie who died. I'd rather be an orphan than your daughter, and when my sister or brother is born. You won't have to care for them after they are weaned. I will do it so they will know love."

"I love you, Daisy," Mama insisted.

"Love, HA! You hate me for my father's eyes like you hated Maisie and our brothers for their fathers' blood. Like you will hate the child you carry," I snapped. "You don't know how to love." Then I walked away because Aunt Bea was staring at me like I had grown a second head. The sweet, mild, obedient Daisy had died with Maisy when no one in the clan answered my pleas for help.

VvvvV The beast...

Every time he escaped, they chased him down and caged him again, endeavoring to carry him home, but not this time. He had jumped overboard from the ship and swam ashore. Running for days through the birth of the season of plenty, he fled them. Never had any of his kind survived for so long, so far north. Never had one of their kind endured the winter like he had. They were fair-weather beasts, civilized as all men had once been before the great evolution, yet they were considered monsters or demons by the Northlanders. The agrarian purist had retreated from the change that had come over the world generations earlier, preferring their humanity over what they considered a curse. The Northlanders would kill him if they got the chance, but he didn't care.

He knew the pure soul made just from him was there, somewhere on one of the small walled farms. So, he pounded his hooves harder into the grass and fled back to the White Mountains.

5.

The sun was setting when the silver-haired Keeper Emmie came to where I foraged near the fences. Her kind smile warmed my heart in the way that only love could as she patted my cheek and rubbed my shoulder.

"Good evening, Daisy. Did you have a better day than yesterday?" She had taught me her name and always spoke to me in the sacred language. I understood the words like none of my family could, magic or miraculous; I didn't care. I only cared that she was my friend.

Bowing my head, I murmured in clan-speak, almost too soft to be heard, "Yes, thank you, Keeper Emmie."

"I am so glad." Answering as if I had spoken in her language, she showed me so much compassion and kindness, and for now, it was enough to soothe my spirit.

Her words in the sacred language made me wish I was worthy of her attention. "My dear one, I saw you with your mother today. You need to understand, she... she has always been headstrong and cold, but you are better than her. You have a kindness in your heart that I hope you don't lose. Your spirit carries a desire to protect those weaker than yourself. I know you will find your sweetness again after your anger and grief pass. Just don't give up your joyful, sweet spirit the way she did." The concerned tones of her voice and her words stole mine away. I couldn't answer her, I could only bow my head again and let my tears fall on the early grass.

Together, we walked back in silence and lavender twilight. A zephyr breeze gently stirred the grass around us. We didn't need to speak; just being together was enough. Halfway to the longhouse, a low mournful sound echoed from far beyond the fences; it was answered by several more. The elder Keeper looked over her shoulder in a panic; I was frozen in fear. Never had I heard anything like it, or had I? It was like the sound of the winter night, but it wasn't... it was something else. Something terrifying and desperate.

"Daisy, RUN!"

Emmie pulled me along as we ran for the longhouse. Huffing and wheezing, we made the doors. Another Keeper was waiting. He slammed the large wooden door and pulled the heavy blocking post through the upturned hooks that secured it.

That night the sounds came again and again, like the howling winter winds and echoing like thunder across the land. Everyone spokes in hushed tones, discussing what that sound meant. I didn't tell anyone that I had heard it before. It was the sound of the winter night. My aunts worried for those who had not made it back. There was no way to know if my uncle and male cousins were safe until morning.

Three of the Keepers kept watch that night. We could hear their steps on the stone tiles of the roof as they walked. The next day they kept us all inside, forcing us to eat the dry, flavorless rations of winter. Beyond the doors, the earth's bounty mocked our terror and hunger. Some of the males had not made it back to the longhouse from the farthest fields. I overheard the Keepers talking about how they had been torn apart, and their bodies trampled into the ground. Their vivid descriptions of how the verdant grass was stained vermillion and their bloody bones had been broken and scattered like so many twigs, haunted my nightmares.

The Keepers repeated over and over to each other, "They are back, and we can do nothing until they move on."

I didn't know who 'they' were, but I was scared. Everyone was scared.

The older ones began reminding the youngest generation of the five mantras.

Never pass the fences.

Never forage or walk alone near the fences or in the far fields.

Never leave the longhouse before Dawn or after Dusk.

Never go out in the moonlight.

Never let the monsters bite you.

Five days later, the Keepers believed it was safe and let us go out again. They followed us as we stayed grouped together, terrified we foraged quickly. Several times one of our more skittish would cry out in fright, and half would start to run before calmer heads prevailed, shouting the falseness of their flight after them.

Every day was the same as the full of the Strawberry Moon approached. I foraged quickly, staying close to my Aunt Bess and Cousin Betty. Scolding any of my younger cousins who strayed too close to the fence or far from the group. "Remember the mantras."

Mama was always nearby, but we had not spoken again. She just watched me with her large sad brown eyes as her belly grew. When I caught her eyes, I would turn away, I decided I would not forgive her. I would not forget her cruelty toward Maisie; I would punish her the only way I could. I would not love her, and I would make sure my siblings would not love her the way she had not loved our sister or brothers. Before they were weaned, I would take them and love them the way I loved Maisie. Dora would just be their birth giver, their milk provider, their cow, and I would be their mother.

VvvvV The beast...

So, close this time... He had made it back to the mountains, he could smell her on the breeze. But his father's master-of-arms hired a warlock to get them to the mountains ahead of him. They chased him into a canyon with walls too steep to climb with claw and hoof.

"My prince... please..." they begged. "If she is among those who live here, she is not one of us and not worthy."

Lifting his head, he bellowed in desperation and rage at being cornered again. The warriors of his homeland lifted their heads and echoed his anguish. The vibration brought down the loose rocks and as the more civilized, more sane monsters dived for cover, he charged out. He hooked horns with the master-of-arms and threw his weight into a twist, tossing the older beast onto his side. The chase was on again.

Just after sunset, he came across a group of males huddled in the trees at the edge of a field. One of them had touched her, others of them had been close to her. In a moment of insanity, he attacked them. Painting the green grass crimson while tearing the ones he caught into pieces. He ripped their flesh from their skeletons and chewed the bloody meat before stomping their bones into pieces. He heard them coming for him and bellowed a challenge. He needed to find her home. His one was so close. He just had to figure out which farm she was at and steal her away.

Days passed, and he realized they were chasing him away from her. He doubled back to the place of the massacre. Standing there, more rational than he had been that night, he regretted the madness and rage that had made him murder those males. He now realized they had been related to his one. Kneeling on the soft grass still spattered with dried blood, he grieved the actions of the beast within

him and wept for those he had murdered and eaten. She would make him sane again. She would soothe his every madness. Reaching up, he fingered the tips of his broken horns. He had been through so much to find her, surely, she would forgive him the madness that killed her kin.

He followed the path of the humans who had taken the bodies until he found the pit where they were burned to ashes. The cause of the evolution plague that created his kind was still unknown, and those who had remained uninfected lived in isolation, taking every precaution to remain pure and keep those with them the same. Kneeling in the ash, he could smell those he killed and wanted to be ill. He wondered what it would be like, to have a single form and to not have bouts of animistic madness. He tried to remember what his other body looked like, felt like, moved like... he couldn't. He ran his hands down his face; the long snout of his nose and wide flares of his nostril were so different from the features he once wore. The thickness of his neck and hunch of his shoulders made him a terrifying sight. He was trapped as a beast until he claimed the one.

Carefully, he circled the compound, studying the walls. Some were stone, some were rusting metal, and some were hewn wood. He found a place where he could look in and pried off a loose board, but the knoll of the hill showed him only the roofs of cottages and a longhouse. He could smell so many within; pure humans, pure animals... and her.

6.

Another week passed, and one day I smelled dandelions for the first time. I wandered closer to the fence. Beyond the slatted wood, dozens of the inviting yellow heads bobbed in the breeze over the bushy green of their savory leaves. My mouth watered as I stared at them. They were my favorite food in the whole world and this spring had been stingy with them. I stretched out, reaching for them, through the slats of the fence. This looked like one of the places where the winter had torn a few of the boards away and the Keepers had not repaired it yet. Perhaps they didn't know because this was below the hump of a hill.

The mantras of my childhood fear chanted, but I ignored them.

Rationalizing my efforts, I was safe if I stayed on this side fence and just reached through. It wasn't a very big hole, maybe large enough for a feline or a fox, but surely a monster would not fit through it. I managed to grasp just two of the plants. The flavor was so rich, the tart bite of the leaves with the sweetness of the blossoms. I groaned in pleasure as I chewed the flavor of my childhood's only happiness. Then I reached through again. Suddenly, I felt a chill that had nothing to do with the clouds passing over the sun. Mama pushed herself between me and the vision of delicacies.

In a hushed tone, she murmured, "Daisy, walk slowly away from the fences."

I pushed her away, shouting, "Leave me alone, Dora! What do you care what I do!"

She struck me hard across the face, "You are my daughter, and you will do as I say!"

Suddenly the sound of an angry bellow sounded from the other side of the fence and we ran for the others. The Keepers ran past us toward the fences, waving their weapons and shouting in challenge, as the whole clan raced for the longhouse.

As we panted for breath, safe in the darkness of the longhouse, Mama circled me and pressed close, sobbing her relief. "You're safe, you're safe."

"Mama, what was that?" I cried. In my terror, I had forgotten that I was supposed to hate her.

The eldest of the females of our clan answered me in a tone that sounded like blame, "It was one of the monsters."

Immediately the elders of the clan began to chant the mantras.

Never pass the fences.

Never forage or walk alone near the fences or in the far fields.

Never leave the longhouse before Dawn or after Dusk.

Never go out in the moonlight.

Never let the monsters bite you.

"Was she bitten, Dora?" the elder demanded. "Was she near the fences?"

"No... No, she was just gathering wildflowers," Mama lied for me.

Aunt Bess came to stand beside Mama. "Daisy has not broken the mantras. She is a good, young female who looks after the young and does all she is supposed to."

Cousin Betty pressed against my side, almost standing in front of me.

The elder eyed me suspiciously, "Put her in her room and

don't let her leave."

That night I heard my mother and aunts talking; actually, they were arguing with other mothers in the clan.

"I am sure they have chosen her. We have to keep her in the longhouse." Mama's voice was plaintive.

"If they want her, they will take her. They will bite her and change her, and we cannot stop it." Aunt Bea insisted, "We must put her out."

"For the safety of the clan and our daughters, they already killed my son. We must drive her out," Suzie insisted, her eyes wide and terrified as her daughter huddled against her side.

Siding with Mama, Aunt Bess disagreed with her twin Bea, "If we keep her locked up until the males return from the far fields, she can have a mate and they will leave her be. They never take a mated female. We will choose a male for her if the Keepers do not."

"Mating her is better than losing her." Mama nodded but that path also terrified me.

I had seen what happened when my mother was forced to take a male she did not love. I wanted love. I wanted to be loved. I didn't want to be relegated to life as a breeder, as my mother now was.

"That is ridiculous. They will kill us all to get to her, Dora. You are her mother; if you won't make her go, we should kill her ourselves," Suzie huffed.

"I won't let you hurt her," Mama bellowed, but Suzie's next words felt like thorns, "You never cared for any child you bore,

Dora. If you didn't bear children who are so beautiful, you would have been put out for the monsters long ago. You just don't want to lose the daughter who raises your offspring. Maybe her beauty is why they want her." Several murmured their agreement.

"My daughter's appearance means nothing to the monsters. Maybe we should offer them your ugly daughter who has failed to bear a child with her mate twice," Mama snapped.

They all began arguing in earnest and I crept away silently.

VvvvV The beast...

He waited and watched in silence, not wanting to alert those who dwelled within the walled farm. They would kill him and burn his body to protect what was there. To keep the infection that made him a monster away from them and theirs.

He could smell her as she walked within the walls, gathering grains and grasses. But she also walked to and fro as though she were seeking something. Her voice was the most beautiful sound he had ever heard as she scolded children, perhaps she was their caregiver. They smelled of her family, but none were hers.

They called her Daisy, like the flower.

Every night he pulled another slat away and pushed on the posts to loosen them. He was slowly going mad from her scent, but it was a clever kind of insanity. If he could lure her here, he could snatch her and be gone before they were caught.

His afternoon nap under a tree was disturbed. Smelling her so strongly he could almost taste her blood, he moved as quietly as a beast of his side could move. Crawling through the tall grass, he froze. Daisy was there by the holes he made in the fence, staring at the wildflowers. Her beautiful brown eyes darted to and for scanning for danger. She was the most perfect female he had ever seen. The color of her hair was like his grandmother's favorite toffee and so silky smooth it glistened in the sunlight.

Reaching through the fence, Daisy snagged two dandelions' roots and all, then oddly, she ate them. She groaned in pleasure as she devoured the leaves, slowly chewing the yellow blossoms last. He reached out and picked one, putting it in his mouth. It was tartly green in flavor but also had a slight sweetness he had never tasted. He lifted his head a little higher as he chewed another. Watching her trying to reach more, a cloud passed overhead. Glancing up at the sky then back, his eyes met the protective glare of one who could only be her mother.

Bravely, the other female slowly pushed herself between the fence and her child, murmuring something he did not hear, then he was shocked when his perfect soul shoved then shouted at her mother.

"Leave me alone, Dora! What do you care what I do!"

The mother hit her across the face, "You are my daughter, and you will do as I say!"

His angry bellow sounded before he could stop it and they ran away from the fences. He heard the shouting of angry humans and fled as fast as he could to the woods. All he could do was wait for another chance.

Hiding in the woods, he smelled his father's warrior with the warlock and knew he would not escape them again. As soon as the sun set, he retreated back to the wooden part of the wall. Pressing against the wood with all his strength, the section buckled and landed in the grass with a muffled thump. He cautiously crept into the field on his belly and peeked over the hill at the longhouse and cottages. The overgrazed state of the land shocked him, and suddenly he understood why she had reached through the holes he made for something to eat.

He spied on the human guards, and when one left his post to talk with the others, he started to rise to go and rescue what was his from this wretched place, then Daisy peeked out.

"Forgive us, my prince," His father's master-of-arms announced before a bolt of magic stunned him into immobility. "She's not one of our kind."

The warriors lifted him and carried him away as his mind and soul bellowed in anguish.

'My Daisy... My Daisy... My Daisy...'

7.

My own clan wanted to kill me. Only my mother and my aunt wanted to hide me, to protect me, but to be saved, I would be forced to become a breeder like Mama. The ache of betrayal clouded my thoughts as I wandered to the far end of the longhouse. The familiar cold that filled me since Maisie's death returned, hopelessness making me shiver. The Keeper who usually stood at this door was gone and the door was cracked slightly. I pushed it open easily and slipped out. The sky was as bright as a cloudy day. Everything, oddly clear and distinct. Two of the mantras scolded me.

Never leave the longhouse before Dawn or after Dusk... Never go out in the moonlight.

I ignored them. Creeping as silently as I could toward the sound of the sacred language of the Keepers. The air smelled of every fragrant bloom but also the reeking stench of fear. The Keepers were gathered in a tight group at the opposite end of the longhouse, talking in low voices.

"Emmie, she can't stay here. I know you're fond of Daisy. But those things are testing the fences every night. They want her." The medicine man was intensely serious.

The elder Keeper, with the silvery hair who had shown me such kindness, shook her head. "I won't let you do it. You've seen what they do to those they find. It is too cruel." I knew she was thinking of Rosie, she had cried when they carried my cousin's body back to be burned.

The other Elder Keeper rubbed his chin, "There isn't a choice.

I'm sorry. If they don't move on, we're putting her out for them."

"No... please... no." My friend wept and begged for me to be spared, and her heartbreak and helplessness had me running away from the longhouse.

Breathless, with tears still damp on my face, I found myself wandering back to the fences. Back to the place where I had seen the dandelions on the other side of the broken slats. The fence was laid down, pressing flat patterns in the tall grass. I paced back and forth in front of the gap. Staring out at the fields and the mountains beyond cautiously. There was no danger that I could see, smell, or hear. It looked just like the side of the fence I stood on, only more lush and inviting.

The gentle warmth of the world seduced my senses away from the cold of my hopelessness. The winter had been so long, so cold, and so colorless white. Springtime became like a vision of paradise, covering the world in the bright colors of wildflowers. Their perfume teased my nose. The spring night sang to me in the sounds of the night-birds and breeze, lulled my fears and heartache. It called to me to take just one step into the world beyond the fences.

Never pass the fences... never pass the fences... never pass... never...

The first mantra, the rule I had followed my whole life faded away like my sorrow and pain, like the cold of the bitter winter in the warmth of springtime.

I felt like my body wasn't my own, like my mind was floating beyond my body. I put one foot on the wooden slat. It felt hard and coarse under my sole, firm like the frozen earth of winter but not cold. The grassy meadow beyond the fence felt softer than the scrubby, over-harvested field I left. One tentative step was followed by another and another until I was surrounded by wildflowers. Their colors visible, but muted in the bright moonlight. The meadow swayed in gentle waves. My soul rejoiced in the vibrant life around me as I floated forward into a world I had always feared. But at this moment, all I felt was euphoria.

Never forage or walk alone near the fences or in the far fields...

The second mantra meant nothing to me. I stood still as the Strawberry Moon surrounded me in her light like a soft blanket. The tall grass tickling my knees in the slight breeze. Everything smelled so green, so alive. It was dizzying, so much so that my legs folded underneath me. I bent and picked a single stem; the slightly sweet and savory gold of the dandelion coated my tongue with its rich goodness. I chewed it so slowly. In my strange state, I marveled that dandelion blossoms had never tasted so good and I laughed. I picked another and another, nibbling as I rose to wander ever further from the fallen fence. I didn't care, I needed to fill the hunger that was growing inside me. To sate a craving I didn't understand, euphoria mixed with a terrible and liberating realization.

Rosie had been right!

I momentarily wondered who had really killed her. The monsters who no one had ever seen, or someone else? Did she die for breaking the rules? She said the fences were about control. The monsters were stories meant to scare us. There was nothing beyond the fences but the bounty of the earth, and yet we cowered and starved like caged animals inside them.

Never leave the longhouse before Dawn or after Dusk... Never go out in the moonlight.

The third and fourth mantras had stolen the beauty of the night from me for my whole life.

Never let the monsters bite you.

What monsters? I wondered about the fifth mantra, and I almost giggled. The five mantras screamed at me to go back to the longhouse in Mama's harsh voice, but I didn't. Leaping, almost dancing, I turned in a circle taking it all in. It was glorious, and yet it was also warm. So different from the last night I had gone out into. Then I had felt frozen to my core; now I felt warm to the deepest part of me.

Dizzy, I laid down in the softest grass I had ever touched and stared up at the Moon, stretching out every few moments to snag a cowslip, or white clover, or dandelion. Slowly, I chewed and savored the sweet goodness of the wildflowers. I felt full, almost happy as I lay in blissful contentment. I decided eating the succulent sweetness of wildflowers by moonlight was the most wonderful thing in the world. I wept silent tears because Maisie was not here to share it with me. I felt more alive than I ever had, then I heard it.

A low mournful tone that chilled my soul and vibrated my bones. It was the same sound I had heard the night after the blizzard, the night I had followed the moonlight and silence into the forest. The cry I heard in the before dawn twilight after Maisie's death and earlier today. Terrified, I realized it wasn't the sound of the winter night, it was something much worse. It sounded again, much closer this time, and was followed by a thundering of great feet.

Never pass the fences... Never leave the longhouse before Dawn or after Dusk... Never forage or walk alone near the fences or in the far fields... Never go out in the moonlight... Never let the monsters bite you...

There at the edge of the meadow, I saw the monster towering in the moonlight shadows of the forest. Hooves for feet, claw-shaped hands, man-like and yet not. Broken horns curled up from either side of the handsomest face I had ever seen. He grinned at me with pointed teeth. I suddenly regretted my decision to wander in the moonlight, to pass the fences, to leave the longhouse after dusk. I never should have broken the mantras. I rose and ran as hard as I could for the fences and the longhouse beyond. Desperately, I leapt over the fallen fence, not wanting to risk tangling my feet in it in my rush for safety.

Never let the monsters bite you.

The sound of my steps were whisper light compared to the footfalls of that which chased me. The monsters were real. All I could think about was Rosie's poppy red blood dripping from the stained canvas wrapped around her body. Would that be my fate?

Never let the monsters bite you.

A flash of yellow caught my eye. There was a dandelion only a few dozen steps from the longhouse. I faltered a step at that moment, and it caught me. I could feel the warmth of its breath and the heat of its flesh burning mine as it crushed me beneath its bulk.

Never let the monsters bite you.

I screamed, thrashing helplessly as its teeth sank into my neck, then blackness claimed me. My last thought was a fleeting plea for a quick death as my spirit cried out, I'm coming Maisie.

8.

VvvvV The beast...

He trembled, twitching against the magic that held him as they carried his beast back to their camp.

"Forgive us, Prince Tauran, but we cannot let your rutting madness break the treaty with the unchanged," the master-of-arms apologized.

Tauran's eyes twisted back toward the meadow of wildflowers as desperate tears escaped. Daisy would go there; she would go there to taste the slight sweet flavor of the dandelions and the succulent tang of their leaves. He panted, straining with his need to escape them and claim her, the pure soul meant to be his. After many minutes of being carried, they gently laid him down so they could rest.

"Master-of-Arms can the warlock make him change back so we can carry him easier?" one of the warriors begged. The small size of his horns showed how young he was.

The warlock refused, "It could harm him, and I don't want your king feeding me to his rabid goats."

"Can you at least make him a little lighter then?" Another warrior demanded.

While they argued, Tauran thought about everything he had been taught about magic restraints. The spell was to hold a creature the size of his beast, but would it hold something the size of his other body, or would it collapse? He decided there was only one way to find out. He tried to do something he had not done since the long winter had begun. To his horror he couldn't; instead, his body convulsed like it was dying. The magic blinked out, releasing him as his father's men gathered around him in worry. The clever monster inside him played weak and let out a low mournful bellow before pretending to fall unconscious.

"Get some water."

"Is the prince going to die?"

"Do something!"

When they were all rushing about, he rolled over and bolted through the trees, ignoring the startled exclamations of those who came to take him home. A blast of magic exploded against a tree he dodged behind.

"Tauran, stop!"

Panting, he bellowed again so she would know he was coming and ran straight to the edge of the meadow. She was sitting there in the moonlight surrounded by wildflowers. So deliciously beautiful, he grinned as she stared at him wide-eyed. Then she leapt to her feet and ran back toward her home. He had to catch her. It was the only thing that mattered as he ignored the shouts of his father's warriors. She leapt over the fallen fence with the gracefulness of a gazelle. Sprinting across the field at a full run, she stumbled. He wrapped his arms around her shoulders as they fell. She screamed and struggled as magic crackled in the air, so he bit her before it was too late. Bit her to make her like him.

"Sominatosa fortressa!"

Darkness overwhelmed him, but the taste of her blood on his tongue was worth every lonely night of the long winter, and falling asleep with her in his arms was the perfect moment before death.

"What have you done?" The master-of-arms shouted as he

bent over the unconscious humans.

"They only sleep, but we must hurry." the warlock announced haughtily. "Would you rather they be able to identify your prince as the one who broke down their fences, killed their males and attacked this female?"

"No," the old warrior reached up and rubbed his horn on one side. "Pick him up, we need to go."

"What about his mate? He bit her... if we leave her here, she'll be killed." One of the warriors demanded.

"She's not one of us, she probably won't even survive the evolution illness, and she's from... well, look around. She won't survive our world even if she changes into one of us. Leaving her here to say goodbye to her family is the only mercy we can give her before her death."

The master-of-arms grabbed one of his arms as the warriors grabbed the prince's other limbs. They carried him up the hill, then the warlock waved his staff. A circle of red magical fire swirled around them, then rushed toward the center and shot into the sky like a geyser before turning into a demonic-looking red fireball shooting to the south toward the sea.

"Wait!" Emmie was the only one awake. Her secret witch ancestry protected her from the sleep spell. "Oh no... oh no..."

She hurried toward Daisy. Kneeling, she examined the bite. Daisy was already getting the fever. Emmie hurried back to her house and came back with a poultice which she pressed over the wound and a vial of clear liquid which she poured down Daisy's throat. She sat up with Daisy, putting wet cloths on her neck to cool her fever until almost dawn, then she put everything away and went to lay down by her husband and pretended to be asleep like everyone else.

The red fireball looked like a demon's eye flying across the sky. It landed on the shore of an island kingdom. They all rolled across the sand except the warlock, who floated gently to the beach.

"You and your prince are home, my money please," the warlock demanded. "Your king has never been a friend to the witches, and I'd rather not be burned for bringing the prince home without his mate."

The master-of-arms snarled and pulled out a bag of emeralds. "Take your green and go."

The warlock bowed as the prince stirred, pushing himself up, "Where?"

The warlock turned and waved his hand. ***"Sominatosa minotaurus!"***

The prince collapsed back to the sand.

The warlock smirked as the Master-of-arms scowled, "How much is that going to cost?"

"On the wand. Nice doing business with you... I suggest you chain him before he wakes and tries to swim back to the continent. He marked that female; he's going to want to go back for her, she was beautiful." The warlock warned. "A dragon-fire forged chain would be best."

"She wasn't one of us," the master-of-arms snarled.

"She will be. You should retire and move far away. When he gets loose, his beast is going to eat you like he did those males."

The warlock waved his staff, and a red fire ring appeared before shooting into the sky

The master-of-arms ordered his warriors to each grab a limb and carried the Prince up to the castle.

Tauran woke up in his room overlooking the sea. His beast rose up and bellowed, rushing toward the terrace. His leg pulled, and he fell forward. His beast crawled across the floor to the wall and jerked on the chain holding his leg.

"Son?" The queen stood in the door. "You can't break those... you need to forget that common cow and choose one of the princesses in your stable. It's time to become king."

"Her." His word was garbled in this form, more of a rumbling growl.

"No." His mother denied him, holding her head up regally. "You have better-bred choices here."

"Her." He bellowed and charged her, but the chain kept her safe.

In his anguished rage, he began kicking and stomping the furniture with his hooves until there was nothing left. His claws shredded the silks of the bed and the tapestries. Then he rammed his horned head into the wall until the marble was cracked and chipped. In the end, he laid on the floor and whimpered in deep tones.

The queen watched him with sad eyes, then turned and went to the throne room. She went to the king and caressed his horns, looking into his dark eyes, a tear leaked from hers. A clawed hand reached up and wiped the glistening drop from her cheek.

"He's trapped as his beast like you are. It's the curse."

9.

The next morning, I woke to the sound of weeping. I was still lying on the ground outside the longhouse. The last mantra still drummed in my mind.

Never let the monsters bite you.

I was surprised that I wasn't dead, it had bitten my neck. The spot was numb, tingling like a leg laid on too long. My thoughts were floating, confused. I tried to lift my head, but it felt like it weighed as much as a bale of bound fodder. My whole body felt feverish, burning, and I wished for the freezing wind of winter. Those talking around me sounded like bees. I felt like I was melting as my body regained -the ability to move again. The silver-haired elder Keeper was patting my cheek.

"She has to go, Emmie. There's nothing we can do for her now. She has to go, and we have to fix the fences. We can't have them come back tonight," the medicine man put his arms around her and tried to lift her away, but she clung to my neck.

"You won't die. Go south... Find the one who bit you, Daisy... Run until you find him, run until you find your kind, then have a good life and lots of beautiful children," my friend whispered in my ear before the others pulled her away.

The other Keepers forced me to stand and walk back to where the fences were down. I stumbled more than I walked, but they wouldn't let me rest. "Keep moving."

"It will be okay, Dora, she's strong," My Aunt Bess comforted Mama, who moaned and cried, "No... not my Daisy... not her..."

Stumbling as she leaned on her older sister, Mama never

raised her head. The whole clan followed us slowly.

"Mama... Mama..." I tried so hard to get back to my mother, but the Keepers just pushed me away from her and the rest of the clan.

The Keepers forced me to crossover the fallen fence.

The medicine man spoke in harsh, threatening tones. "Go on, get over the fence, or we'll have to kill you. We don't want to, but we will." Then he made Keeper Emmie leave with him. Her shoulders shook as she walked away.

"Please, Emmie, don't let them banish me... I'm sorry... I'm sorry! I'll be good. I'll work harder. Please don't leave me outside the fences." My begging to be allowed to stay was ignored as the fence rose.

My pleading voice was drowned out by Suzie and Aunt Bea, who began chanting the mantras. The whole clan picked up the words.

Never pass the fences.

Never forage or walk alone near the fences or in the far fields.

Never leave the longhouse before Dawn or after Dusk.

Never go out in the moonlight.

Never let the monsters bite you.

Over and over, they chanted the words as the fence was stood up and reinforced. The Keepers left next. Then one by one, the clan walked away until only my mother and aunt remained. Finally, they turned and walked away too.

"Mama... no... Aunt Bess... come back... please come back."

Pressing my forehead against the fence, I had run out of tears. My voice was harsh from begging for mercy. Not knowing what else to do, I staggered down the hill among the wildflowers that had seduced me to my doom only a few short hours ago.

Before it chased me.

Before it caught me.

Before it bit me.

I never should have broken the mantras. I had cursed myself and was banished for it. The monsters were real.

Struggling to walk south, I stumbled, fell, and stood over, and over, dragging myself further from the clan. I didn't know where I would go. All I knew of the world beyond the fences was that it was a land of danger and death. I was unaware of where I wandered or how far I went, unaware of anything except the growing fire burning in my bones. When it felt like the branding iron the Keepers used to mark our clan, my legs gave out, and I collapsed to my knees, unable to continue.

I was in too much agony to even cry out. It felt like my bones were breaking as they burned. I convulsed, clenching my teeth so hard it felt like they were being crushed. I could taste blood in my mouth. I was alone, I was going to die alone, and I couldn't even cry out. I tried to draw a breath to scream, but darkness overcame me.

I dreamed of the monster's handsome face grinning at me with his deadly teeth. The Hunter's moon hovered over the horizon, golden and perfect, exactly as it had the evening after Rosie's death. But instead of a burning funeral pyre, dark turquoise water stretched to the end of the world, reflecting the golden lily and marigold orange colors of a fiery sunset. Those colors will forever remind me of fire and Halloween and grief. His embrace enclosed me with a gentleness I did not expect. It felt like love or perhaps the peace of death, and on my neck, I could still feel his breath burning me.

Shivering, I woke. The whole of me was feverish and aching. The sun was sinking toward setting. My body felt so strange as I dragged myself toward the sound of a stream. I gulped the water. Its icy goodness cooled my body, so I stuck my whole face into it, splashing myself. When I leaned back, I saw a girl sitting on a large rock across the stream. She was grinning at me and dressed unlike any Keeper I had ever seen. I tried to stand but fell over. My legs were strangely thin, my feet looked weird. As I stared at them, the girl laughed.

"Don't worry, you'll get used to it."

"What?" I croaked and froze; I had spoken the sacred language.

"I said, you'll get used to it. Come with me and I'll take you to our village."

"Village?" my muddled brain wasn't making sense as I stared at the changes to my body.

"You're one of us now, you're a shifter," she talked calmly and patiently as though I were too young to understand. She approached me slowly, holding out a large piece of cloth. "Do you remember what happened?"

"I... I was walking, the fences were down... There were wildflowers, they tasted so good..." It sounded strange to have the Keeper's language coming out of my mouth, but I couldn't stop talking. "It chased me, bit me..." I choked on a sob, "Then the Keepers of my clan drove me out after... After Keeper Emmie told me to go south... Even Mama walked away."

She held me while I cried, wrapping the cloth around my contorted body.

"It will be okay. We haven't had one of your kind in a long time, but you will learn to control your shift and get used to your new body," she said in a soothing tone.

"My new body?" I didn't understand.

"Yes silly, the one you are wearing now," She answered me in an amused tone. "I'm Kara, by the way."

"I'm Daisy."

"I'm a born horse shifter. So, I didn't get bitten like you or my mom, but it is fun to have two kinds of bodies. I'll help you. I've never met a bovine-shifter in person. You're so pretty and you have the most beautiful eyes. I'm so excited to introduce you to everyone, and on Halloween too, but first we need to get you to the village and get you some clothes." She talked very quickly in the sacred language, and my muddled mind struggled to understand, but one word stuck in my addled awareness.

"Clothes?"

Horrified, I realized the magnitude of what had happened to me. Looking carefully at my body, I suddenly deeply regretted my decision to eat wildflowers by moonlight...

I didn't want to be a human-shifter, I liked being a cow...

A/N: And I Made You Laugh - I WINZ! WERECOWS! Ha ha ha! - Mama Magie.

THE ABSOLUTE FURY OF HAGATHA BELFRY

Dawn bloomed on the sleepy town of Lilith's Hollow.

Just south of Newcastle and slightly north of Bristol (which is how the townspeople describe its location, even though practically all of England lies between), nestled inside a rather large forest that's home to many strange creatures, one would find the secret little town. Though, were you to come too close, an inescapable drowsiness would take you and sleep would be unavoidable. Waking up much later with no memory of the quest such were the protective incantations placed to hide the city and its occupants. For this town is special, and its citizens terrifying.

Mrs. Hagatha Belfry stepped out of her front door and onto the porch with a cup of tea in hand. Throughout the town, even though it was winter and snowy in the surrounding wood, autumn leaves sprouted from every limb of every branch of every tree, and the fallen leaves were replaced by new leaves overnight. Lilith's Hollow is graced by the autumn season all year round, thanks to a witch's spell from one who lived in town long before Mrs. Belfry's centuries of residency there. After all, this was the town that

Halloween built. Mrs. Belfry, along with all of the werewolves, zombies, mad doctors, monsters, ogres, and more mythical creatures that made up its citizens, were in-charge of maintaining the traditions of the holiday, keeping them alive and well.

A black cat sauntered onto the porch from around the side of the house. Slowly, he approached the witch and meowed what seemed like a question. Mr. Belfry looked down at the cat, her familiar to be exact, and patted the chair beside her. "Come, Renfield, join me for a rock."

The cat leapt up into the seat and meowed again.

"Well, how should I know?" Mrs. Belfry responded. "I don't go about talking to strange cats. That's your area of expertise."

Mrs. Belfry had met Renfield, the cat, nearly seventy-five years ago. He was a stray, wandering the streets of Paris, France, digging in the trash cans behind restaurants, chasing mice for snacks. He came purring around her feet when she sat in a café with a wonderful view of the Eiffel Tower.

Typically, a witch would only need a familiar as she was coming into her own powers. The familiar helps to guide her along the way. By the time the two of them met, Mrs. Belfry was well into her magic powers and the poor stray was washed up. An old familiar, an ancient cat. He wasn't even able to take human form anymore. She felt an instant kinship with him and brought him back to Lilith's Hollow.

Of course, as time is a little wonky in this town, the old cat had continued to live at pretty much the same age as he was when she'd found him. Now, he was a trusted friend and excellent company. She often thought it strange that she preferred the company of the cat more than anyone in town, but then she always had an affinity for animals.

Enjoying her morning tea on the porch while the cool autumn breeze wound through her hair, was a morning ritual for the witch. One of her few pleasures in life, for Mrs. Belfry was cursed with a short fuse. Her anger had been a hindrance her entire life. It was here amongst her fellow creatures of the night, where she found peace. Not that she could stand any of them, of course. But she so loved her house and her cat. And she valued the quiet times. She inhaled deeply, let out a relaxed breath, and just as she put her teacup to her lips, a loud crash forced her to jump and dribble her beverage down the front of her dress.

"Bloody hell!" she shouted. Renfield dashed back around the corner of the house. Up from her chair and out onto her front walk, Mrs. Belfry craned her neck over the gate in her broken-down picket fence to look down the street at the source of the ruckus. There, in front of the small market where the town turned for fresh fruits, vegetables and other groceries, was parked a rather large, ugly truck with dented fenders and a flatbed surrounded by makeshift walls made of slabs of plywood. The cab was painted an off-putting blue, but the damned thing was more rust than paint at this point. Mrs. Belfry watched as the owners of the store loaded their belongings in the back of the truck, taking no care whatsoever to be quiet about it.

Pushing through her front gate, the witch marched down the walk towards the store, ready to give her noisy neighbors a piece of her mind. "What's all this, then. Do you realize how early it is?"

The lone daughter of the family turned and backed away from

Mrs. Belfry. "Sorry ma'am. I suppose we didn't realize we were being quite so loud."

"I realized it," said the father in a defiant tone as he tossed a cabinet into the truck bed with as much force as he could muster. He was an aging man with thin, white hair and a large belly. "I'll be as loud as I please. I curse the day I ever stepped foot in this ruddy town and I'll make sure every one of you knows it."

It was only then Mrs. Belfry saw past her initial anger at the disturbance of her tea and realized the family was moving out of the store. "You're leaving?"

"That's right," the shop owner replied.

"You can't leave. Where will the town turn for our necessities?"

"Not my problem anymore. If you don't like it, take it up with that git Claymore. He's the reason we're leaving."

Claymore. These days she seemed filled with rage at the mere mention of his name. The vampire was the leader of their community, and in his days, one of the fiercest warriors she'd ever had the pleasure of fighting alongside. His sacrifices during the Goblin War and his family ties to one of the founders of the town, had helped propel him to his position amongst Lilith's Hollow's citizens.

When his wife was murdered just after the war, Claymore was left a shell of the vampire he'd once been. He cultured a phobia of the outside world and refused to leave his mansion, yet would not relinquish his position as the town's leader. How well could a community strive with an agoraphobic vampire in charge? The results were before her. Another shop had closed, and moved out of town. Something must be done about it.

She realized, with growing exasperation, the entire family that had owned the little shop, husband and wife, son and daughter, were now looking at her with disgust. "Well," she bit. "Don't stop on my account. The bloody truck won't load itself."

The father grumbled, perhaps tempted to say something but unwilling to have a vicious spell cast on him by the witch next door. They went back to loading their things and Mrs. Belfry at least took solace in the fact that she would get to cast a charm on them that would erase the memory of the secretive little town from their minds completely. She gave the family a fearsome smile that made them move a little faster.

Contrary to the typical idea of a witch's appearance, Mrs. Belfry was known for her great beauty. Her flowing, dark hair framed her face, drawing attention to the high cheekbones, full lips and stunning green eyes. Even though her lovely face was often painted with a hateful scowl, all who beheld her, praised the woman for her splendor.

The scowl was there as she marched down the street, and up the hill to Claymore manor. The witch was determined to give the Vampire a long overdue piece of her mind. The anger she'd felt that morning at another business leaving Lilith's Hollow had festered all through the afternoon and come to a boil. Now that the sun was down, she would let the vampire know exactly how she felt about his lack of leadership skills.

The house at the top of the hill was massive and castle-like in some of its architecture. Large towers were situated at either end and the huge oak double doors at the entrance boasted large cast iron knockers. The grounds that surrounded the house were made up of a vast pumpkin patch, where the town turned for most of the ingredients in its pumpkin related food and drink and pumpkin carvings as the sacred holiday grew nearer. A tall brick wall and a wrought-iron gate that was broken ages ago surrounded all of this and the gate was always open.

Mrs. Hagatha Belfry climbed the steps to the front door and used one of the knockers to make three thunderous booms that would surely be heard in every wing of the manor. After several minutes with no answer, the witch knocked again. The door swung open on the third knock and Claymore's ancient servant Shillingsworth greeted her.

"Ah, Mrs. Belfry," the old man said. He walked with a slight bend in his back. A wisp of white hair covered his head a thin, well-manicured moustache graced his lip, and he was so old that his wrinkles had wrinkles. "To what do we owe the pleasure?"

"You may dispense with the pleasantries, you old codger! I'm here to see Claymore and I want to see him right away."

"Of course," Shillingsworth replied, seemingly unfazed by Mrs. Belfry's rude approach. This only served to fuel her anger. "Please, step inside and I'll let Master Claymore know you're here."

Mrs. Belfry waited in the foyer as the old man climbed the stairs. The incessant click of the pendulum in the old grandfather clock against the wall only increased her foul mood. She was getting the sneaking suspicion that the vampire was making her wait. Games, all games with this one. A tragic sad sort; always brooding. Forever whiling away the hours of night, stuck in his mourning mansion. Afraid to leave. And why? What was he afraid of outside of these walls? Or perhaps there was something within the house that kept him here. What was he afraid to miss should he decide to leave?

"Mrs. Belfry," a velvety voice called from the darkness at the top of the stairs. "How kind of you to pay me a visit."

"Kindness is the last thing on my mind, Claymore."

As the vampire descended the stairs, a fire burst to life in the sitting room off to the left of the foyer and light fell upon his face, revealing a faint smile at her comment. "Yes, pleasant tides and warm greetings have always been foreign concepts to you."

Claymore reached the bottom floor, his dark suit without a crease, red satin lined cape flowing around him, and stood before her. His black hair hung loose around his perfect features. As handsome a man as she'd ever known, his red eyes seemed to glow and emanate the wisdom of his many years. Had she been a lesser woman, she'd easily succumb to his natural seductive powers. "I'm sorry if my attitude is a disappointment to you."

"On the contrary, I wouldn't want you any other way. You are as unique as you are beautiful, my dear Mrs. Belfry. May I offer you a drink."

Mrs. Belfry felt her anger buckle a little at the kind words of the vampire and she hated herself for it. In the end, she supposed she was at least a little susceptible to his charm. "A red wine would be nice. But actual wine, not the stuff you drink."

"Of course, come, let us sit by the fire and discuss what troubles you."

Claymore led the way into the sitting room and the two of

them sat in matching chairs near the fireplace, between them sat a short table occupied by a chessboard. Mrs. Belfry was glad for the warmth. The old house was frigid and the cold was made all the worse by the number of ghosts that called the place home. She couldn't abide ghosts and would never allow them into her home.

Shillingsworth appeared with a serving tray and held it out to Mrs. Belfry. She took the wine and sipped.

"Would you care for a match?" Claymore said, motioning to the chessboard.

"I've never had patience for chess."

"That's a shame. It's a rather relaxing escape from the things that haunt us."

As he said this, Mrs. Belfry thought she caught a hint of anguish in his expression. There one second, gone the next.

"Shall we get on to business then?" Claymore continued.

"The grocer has packed up and left town."

"Yes, I know."

"Claymore, this was once a thriving community. Town square was a place where the townsfolk gathered. We would socialize over tea or coffee at the café, enjoy fresh produce from the market, exchanged pleasantries over a drink at the pub. All of these places are gone now. Pete's Sweets is the only shop left in town."

"You're the last person I expected to see here complaining about a lack of community and commerce. Mrs. Belfry, you have never enjoyed socializing with people."

"That doesn't mean I want those things to go away. My neighbors and peers enjoy those things. What of the children? When the new school year starts and all of those children come here to learn about the traditions of Halloween, where will they hang out with their friends? For that matter, what about my children?"

Claymore looked amused. "I was unaware you had children."

"I will soon."

"What joyous news! I had no idea you were pregnant."

"Blast it, man, I'm not pregnant. I'd never put this body through all that. There are other ways to have children."

Claymore leaned back in his chair, wonder now apparent on his face. "Birth through witchcraft. Fascinating."

"Claymore, we are getting off topic. This once great town is losing its charm. In short, it's going to piss and this is all happening on your watch. Not only are we losing our businesses, but the town itself is falling into disarray. Signs are broken, walls are crumbling, we're being overrun by weeds. These things used to be kept up by outsiders who you have driven out of town, and now they need your attention."

The vampire stood and began pacing the room slowly. "Mrs. Belfry, I understand your concerns. Lately, I've felt the need for a change. I came to the conclusion that we have far too many outsiders living here in Lilith's Hollow. We used to be a small and tightly knit community, I felt that was slipping away from us. Growth is something we want to avoid. I have no desire to turn this town into a tourist destination or an industrial park. I don't want us separated by money and social status."

"Do you hear yourself?" Mrs. Belfry stood, her face flushed with anger. "You hide away up here in your mansion, far from the rest of us, and dare to talk to me about money and social status.

This tightly knit community, as you put it, was doing just fine without your interference. The good people who ran those shops weren't any danger to the secrecy of Lilith's Hollow. We were in no way, shape, or form ready to blow up into anything other than what we have always been. You speak as if we were on the verge of giving London a run for its money."

"My decisions were in the best interest of the town and the creatures in it. Surely you realize what would happen should it get out that this town is full of monsters. We'd be slaughtered. There are humans out there that hunt us for sport."

"Oh, please. They mostly hunt us for vengeance when we've wronged them. There's a reason we're called monsters."

"The citizens of this town are different. We are a peaceful community and I can no longer allow outsiders to live among us. We have hunters in the woods to supply us with meat, we grow our own vegetables, one solitary bewitched delivery driver can supply us with whatever else we need from outside of town limits. If a citizen of the town would like to re-open one of these shops, they are free to do so, but no more outsiders. My decision is final and it will not be swayed."

"Do you think Lilith would approve of these decisions?" Claymore flinched ever so slightly at the mention of the ancient vampire who had been one of the town founders and namesake.

"Irrelevant. Lilith abandoned us centuries ago."

Mrs. Belfry stepped closer to the vampire and stared up into his red eyes. "You are unfit to lead this community, Claymore. I will bring this to everyone's attention at the next town meeting and we will remove you from power."

"I'd feel more threatened, dear lady, if I thought for a moment, you'd attend a town meeting. For all of your bluster, your presence in this town is felt about as much as mine. The difference is, you choose to be distant and alone."

With clenched fists and enormous restraint, Mrs. Belfry turned away from Claymore and marched to the front door, where she turned to give her final word. "A change is coming, Claymore. Of that you can be assured. If I can't get this town to recognize your ineptitude and remove you from your position, I'll remove you with force myself."

Claymore smiled, showing his fangs, and held out welcoming hands. "I accept your challenge."

With that, Mrs. Belfry walked out into the moonlit autumn evening and slammed the door behind her. Down the hill and past her house, Mrs. Belfry walked to the fountain at the center of town. There, she sat on its edge and stared up at the statue in the middle. The black form only vaguely resembled a man, but a man it was. An old friend, from a long time ago. Though she only knew him for a brief time, he made an incredible impact on her life. Now, the sculpture was all that remained of him. She let the trickle of the water calm her, closing her eyes and breathing deeply.

"I wish you were here," she said to the statue. "I could certainly use your advice."

The statue said nothing. It only continued to filter water into the fountain through small holes in the stone. Mrs. Belfry would present her opinions to the other members of the town, though she knew they would not be supported. There was a complacency in the others she would never feel. They respected Claymore too much to go against any decision he makes. Still, she had to try. As powerful as she was, a physical altercation with Claymore would be a last resort. Going up against Claymore would be dangerous and it would be frowned upon. Hopefully, it wouldn't come to that.

Mrs. Belfry stood and walked back to her house with much on her mind. It would still be hours before her anger subsided and she was able to sleep. Until then, she would continue working on her most precious project. An ambitious project that, should it be successful, would change her life forever.

Renfield, the cat, joined her as she walked through the foyer. He meowed at her questioningly and Mrs. Belfry responded. "Oh, I'm alright. Just that blasted vampire at the top of the hill. So self-righteous. So self-involved. He can't see past his own issues enough to care for this town."

The cat mewed in a lower tone. "Yes, I'll be fine."

The Belfry house is a maze of mysteries and secrets. If one were to wander without the witch's guidance, they could very well end up lost among the moving halls, magic spells and living creatures that populate the vast number of rooms. It had taken Mrs. Belfry centuries to perfect the twisted cornucopia of magical mayhem and she prided herself on the fact that it was completely ghost free. One thing she could not tolerate was the presence ghosts in her house. Nosey things.

Through the kitchen, the back door led out into her greenhouse, where many of the plants were carnivorous and devoured the small gremlins that made their home there. Beyond this lay the back lawn, where Mrs. Belfry had set up her fire pit and cauldron. Renfield remained at her feet, purring as he rubbed his back against the heel of her boot. Her latest concoction would be key to her current project. The DNA she had procured from the ghost hunter all those years ago would finally serve its purpose. She was ready. It had taken her hundreds of years to get to this point, but she was finally ready to be a mother. Perhaps that was the reason she was so concerned with the direction of the town as of late. Maternal instincts kicking in. After all, if she were to raise children in this town, she'd want the very best for them.

It had happened only months ago. She'd had the sudden urge to have a child of her own. She had spent so much time with other children, teaching them magical potions and passing on the traditions of Halloween. It was time she had a daughter. Someone she could pass all of her wisdom on to. Even the dark magic she wasn't allowed to teach to her students. Along with all the secrets of her craft she didn't want others to know. Even though time was different in Lilith's Hollow and every adult aged at a very slow rate, she would eventually grow old and unattractive. Then she would die but take comfort in knowing that her gifts and knowledge had been passed on.

Creating a child was a slow process. Much like the old-fashioned way, the child would have to incubate. She would need nourishment and time to grow healthy and strong, before she was introduced into the real world. She supposed it was similar to the method humans discovered through their sciences, only they called it "cloning". The ancient process she used is called *Saothar Forsa Beatha* and her beloved plants are key for her success.

Mrs. Belfry spooned a bit of the bubbling potion from the cauldron and carefully poured it into a vial. She then removed a small pouch of powder from the pocket of her robe, reached inside, and added a pinch to the potion. Once she corked the vial, she shook it vigorously and put both vial and pouch back into her pocket.

"Meow?" asked Renfield.

"Well of course I remembered. It's the most important ingredient. This isn't my first broom ride you know."

The cat made a sound that was almost a growl. It had always amused Mrs. Belfry. With Renfield at her heels, she returned to the greenhouse.

"Hello, my lovelies," she sang to the plants. The vegetation responded to her voice with subtle movements as if they were turning to face her. Off to the left she walked around the Witch Hazel and Frog's Breath; past the Deadly Nightshade and Mandrakes, toward the corner nearest to the house where her precious ivy grew. "Dear sweet Ivy. Are you hungry, dear?"

The vines stirred with excitement as the witch pulled the vial from her pocket. She carefully pulled the cork and poured the contents into the soil, and the ivy vines seemed to perk up. Mrs. Belfry moved to the center of the plant and spoke in a soothing voice. "Come now, Ivy, show us the child. Come on, don't be shy."

Renfield leapt up on the large pit of the plant and watched with interest as the vines slowly moved aside to reveal a sac with a human baby curled up inside. "Oh, she's getting so big. It won't be long now. You've done so very well, love. Continue to keep her safe."

The ivy closed back over the small form and Mrs. Belfry

backed away, satisfied with the results of her potion. The nutrients that were fed to the girl though the ivy had ensured strong, healthy growth. The excitement about the child's impending birth was nearly enough to make her forget the rage still simmering beneath. The child would grow to be a powerful witch, and Mrs. Belfry would cultivate her powers as she saw fit.

Mrs. Belfry returned to the kitchen and made herself a pot of tea. Soon, she was back on her front porch with a steaming cup in hand, Renfield the cat sat next to her, she was content with enjoying the cool evening since her morning had been ruined. The half-moon shone across the town square and, with the help of the elegant streetlamps, illuminated the fountain and its statue. She could just hear the water trickling over the stone, a sound that had a way of relaxing her.

Movement in the square caught her attention. Mr. Crawley shuffled over the cobblestone street and up the steps of Lilith's Hollow Town Hall, closely followed by Miss Grey and several others. Mrs. Belfry stood and walked to her fence. There, she saw the pumpkin headed scarecrow Jack making his way toward the building as well.

"Jack?" she called. "Jack, what's happening?"

"Town meeting. Many of us are concerned with the shops leaving town."

"Really?" Mrs. Belfry pondered this. If she could turn the others against Claymore, perhaps she could take control of the town and help make things right. "Why didn't anyone tell me there was a Town Hall meeting tonight?"

"Well, most of the town is under the impression you don't like them."

The witch shrugged. "An astute observation I suppose."

"Is it true?"

"Of course not. I like old Crawley. And I like you."

The scarecrow's jack o'lantern mouth spread in an unsettling grin. "Thank you, Mrs. Belfry. I appreciate you saying so. Will you come to the meeting then?"

"Yes, I believe I will."

"Splendid!"

The tall scarecrow walked on toward Town Hall, with his long, awkward stride. It was Mrs. Belfry who had brought the strange creature to Lilith's Hollow. He was once human but nutty as a loon. It was a curse that transformed him into the scarecrow and, as calculated correctly by the witch, saved his sanity. The citizens of the town took him in with the same kindness and acceptance they showed to all new creatures.

Mrs. Belfry watched as the last of the townsfolk trickled into the meeting hall, before she stepped out of her yard and slowly took the steps up to the open doors herself. She looked in at her fellow creatures of Halloween. The Zombie, Mr. Shamus McLowry, with his decayed flesh and perfectly styled pompadour. Dr. Billingsly, the town's mad scientist, with his crazed eyes and bloodied apron. Pete, the cawing raven, who owned Pete's Sweets candy shop and employed Jack the scarecrow as a sales clerk, sat perched on a ledge in one corner of the large room. The meeting was filled with all manner of monsters.

Mrs. Belfry hung back by the door, content to listen as the meeting started. It was led by Mr. Farrell Crawley, who was a short, stout man with graying hair. Though he looked out of place with the various creatures that made up the town, by the light of a full moon he transformed into a vicious werewolf. To keep the citizens safe, old Crawley kept a careful eye on the phases of the moon and made sure to spend his nights as a beast outside of town in the surrounding woods.

"Alright!" the Scottish werewolf called over the chatter. "Alright, now. Quiet down. Let's get thing's started. We've called this meeting of the common folks of Lilith's Hollow to discuss the continued loss of businesses to the town, what impact it will have on our community, and what shall be done moving forward."

"Now, with the loss of Paddington's Market, the only remaining business in town is Pete's Sweets. Though, some of you have expressed concern about the candy shop closing as well, I can assure tha' will not happen. Not only is candy an integral part of the Halloween tradition, it's owned and operated by full time citizens of Lilith's Hollow."

Murmurs of approval ran through the crowd.

"Now, as for the impact of those other businesses leaving us, I have been assured by Claymore himself tha' other plans are in place tha' will limit the number of outsiders and mortals tha' will be made aware of our peaceful little town."

More sounds of approval and Mrs. Belfry felt an angered flush to her cheeks.

"I can't help but feel it's a bad move," said a large demon. Kazul wore a serape, for he looked upon the American Wild West as the greatest culture in the history of the human race, despite the fact his accent was somewhat cockney, and the oddly pulsating horns on his head and chin were off-putting to most. Adding to his already horrific appearance were the appendages on his hands. Each one consisted of a thumb, pointer, and a third finger that was long and whip-like. Kazul kept these coiled up, but from what Mrs. Belfry had seen in the many years she'd known the creature, those fingers had a great many uses. She had met Kazul in London over a hundred years ago and invited him to live in Lilith's Hollow permanently. She was happy when he returned a year ago, but displeased that he'd decided to work for Recluse, who had become the enemy of all things Halloween. "Without the shops, our little community becomes less like a community. Where will the children go to hang out when schools in session?"

Finally, someone who talks sense, Mrs. Belfry thought.

"Claymore has the best interest of the town in mind," replied Miss Grey. She was the other witch in town and polar opposite to Mrs. Belfry. Her blonde hair and bright clothes were in stark contrast to Belfry's black hair and love of dark colors. Miss Grey was sociable and pleasant, two traits Mrs. Belfry despised in people. The only thing they did have in common was that both were youthful and pretty. "Claymore will look out for us as he always has."

"I agree," Dr. Billingsly called out as he stood. The man had a mane of wild, black hair that was pushed back by a pair of goggles on his forehead. "Outsiders will only bring trouble. If word of our town got out to the wrong mortal, we could end up defending ourselves against an assault. Monster hunters are still out there, even in today's modern world. We should be leery of all humans."

Mrs. Belfry could hold her tongue no longer. "Are you all

daft? Honestly, do you even hear yourselves? Claymore will look out for us? How exactly? How is driving prosperity out of town 'looking out for us?' And what of danger? How will he protect us from Recluse or some other foul-tempered being who has designs on hurting the people of this town? Will he invite the fiend to his mansion for a showdown? — *'Sorry, old chap, but I'm terrified of the outside world, we'll have to settle this in my kitchen'.* It's laughable is what it is."

"Mrs. Belfry, please. The floor has not recognized you to speak," Crawley stuttered.

The witch started walking down the aisle toward the podium. "You think I give a damn about what the floor recognizes?" She pushed the old werewolf aside and took his place, now facing the rest of the townspeople. "This has gone on long enough. We blindly trust all the decisions a spineless vampire makes, yet those decisions so often are harmful to this town. It's starting to look like a bloody ghost town out there. Can you people not see that?"

"What do you suggest we do?" asked Dr. Billingsly.

Mrs. Belfry took a deep breath, preparing to press on, taking a chance in the hope she'd be able to make these people see the light. "I declare, I have no faith or confidence in Claymore's ability to lead this community. The responsibility is too much of a burden on his already fractured mind, I feel we need new leadership. I nominate myself for the position of town leader."

Several gasps and much muttering around the room.

Mr. Crawley nervously twiddled his thumbs. "Mrs. Belfry, I'm sure you don't mean that. If we just took a moment to talk this out."

"I always mean every word that I say," was the witch's retort. "Otherwise, I wouldn't say it. A change needs to be made, and I feel I am better equipped to lead this town into the future."

"Very well, then. Mrs. Belfry's proclamation means, according to town bylaws, tha' there will be a debate between the two candidates. A week from tonight. I'll handle everything and set it up so tha' we can hold this debate in Claymore Manor."

"I'm afraid not, Mr. Crawley." Mrs. Belfry interrupted. Here, she saw her first opportunity to gain an advantage. "The bylaws also state that the debate would be held here, in Lilith Hollow's Town Hall. You will not accommodate Claymore, and I will not pander to his insufferable needs. If Claymore really cares about this community and wishes to hold his position, he will come to us."

"Oh dear." This seemed to make Crawley even more nervous, he wrung his hands as if he expected water to drip from them. It was an action that only added to Mrs. Belfry's anger.

"Bloody hell, man, get a hold of yourself," she commanded. "You're a werewolf, stop acting like a child that needs to have a tinkle."

There were a few chuckles from the crowd, as Crawley's face flushed with embarrassment. "Fine. A week from tonight, here, at town hall. Everyone should attend and we will vote directly afterward. The votes will be counted and posted the following evening."

Mrs. Belfry pulled her robes tight around her, and left the hall with a pleased smile touching her lips. This would be too easy. When the debate came and the vampire didn't show, the town would discover just how little Claymore cared for them and the well-being of Lilith's Hollow.

Three days later, Mrs. Belfry sat on her porch, with a cup of tea and the autumn breeze moving pleasingly through her long dark hair. Renfield, sound asleep on the chair beside her. In her mind, she went over what she would say during the debate. Yet, she knew there was no point thinking too much about it. The vampire would not show. There was nothing that could pull Claymore out of his house. Surely, she'd be able to make the townspeople see that they were being led by a coward who in no way took the best interest of their beloved town to heart.

From time to time, Mrs. Belfry would study the two trees in front of her house and wonder why, in the entire town of Lilith's Hollow, with all its gloriously colorful trees, these are the only ones which appear to be dead. Was it something about the house, or perhaps her, that made these trees give up on living? She couldn't be sure. Once upon a time, she tried to return them to their former youth, but was unsuccessful in her attempts. Her mind had moved on to bigger and better things now and she no longer wasted her time on the stubborn things.

As footsteps resounded in the square, Mrs. Belfry watched with interest as Mr. Crawley walked up to her front gate, stopped and fidgeted with his suit, then reached for the gate. Seemingly wrestling with an internal struggle, the gray-haired gentleman released his hold on the gate, and turned away again, clearly unaware that Mrs. Belfry was watching all of this unfold with an amused smile on her lips. After watching him for a few minutes more, she decided to toy with him for her own entertainment.

"You know, for a werewolf, you certainly are docile," she called.

Mr. Crawley looked up at her, clearly flustered. Finally, he sighed and walked through the gate. "Well, Mrs. Belfry, you're not the easiest person to talk to. Some might even say you're rather intimidating."

"Are you amongst those who say such things?"

"Isn't that obvious?"

The witch chuckled. "What brings you by so early, Mr. Crawley?"

"I think you know. Mrs. Belfry, I beg you to reconsider this bid for control of the town."

"Why are you so content to keep things the way they are? Why are all of you so willing to go along with whatever Claymore says?"

"He's led this town for hundreds of years and his decisions have always taken us in the right direction. There's no reason to believe this situation is any different. Perhaps there's something going on tha' has prompted this change in letting outsiders operate in town."

"If that's the case, we should know the reason. And that's part of the problem. He stays locked up in his mansion making all these moves like we're all pieces on his ruddy chess board. Everyone is just so complacent that you all go along with it no matter what. I don't even know why you bother holding these town hall meetings, you just agree to whatever he says and call it a night. It's a joke. Claymore could tell you all to walk off a bloody cliff for the betterment of the town, and you'd form a line."

"Mrs. Belfry, tha' is a bit of an exaggeration."

"It's not! You especially bow to Claymore's every whim. You defend him to the others, and they listen to every word you say like they aren't capable of forming independent thoughts. Can't you see this town is fading under his leadership?"

"But would it survive under yours?"

Mrs. Belfry was taken aback. "What is that supposed to mean?"

"Well, it's no secret you have a mean streak about you. You keep your own secrets, your house is a death trap to frighten away any potential visitors, if it wasn't for the children, you begrudgingly teach during the school year, none of us would even know you were here."

The witch was quiet for a moment. Then, in a sheepish voice she said. "You know my house nearly as well as I do."

The werewolf climbed the steps to sit in the rocking chair next to her. Mrs. Belfry called to Renfield, and the cat reluctantly moved from the chair, only to curl up it the witch's lap and continue his slumber. "Tha's true. But if you expect the people of this town to vote for you over leadership they've known and trusted for several centuries, you're sadly mistaken Mrs. Belfry. I like you. I know, deep down, you have a good heart, even though you can sometimes be moody, but the others don't know you tha' well. If you are to stand a chance, you'll have to open up to them."

"Damn and blast. I hate opening up."

"I know you do, Hagatha." Crawley's voice had become comforting, understanding. She didn't like it. Somehow, he had turned the tables on her and the confidence she'd felt before his visit was replaced by doubt.

"You know, this is why I'm so distant with everyone. I don't like people getting involved in my personal life. I honestly don't know why this situation has rubbed me the wrong way as it has. Maybe I'm just bored."

"Or perhaps, and this is just a theory, you genuinely care about your neighbors and the community. You just want to do what's best for all of us. If you view this situation or Claymore's general lack of presence in leadership as an injustice, then you are just standing up for what you believe in."

"Perhaps."

The werewolf stood to leave but turned to her with one final piece of advice. "You know, all of this debate about the financial direction of the town, the future of our markets, it's secondary to our sole purpose here. To uphold the traditions of Halloween. We do tha' through the children who come here to learn, and tha' aspect of Lilith's Hollow has always been very successful. When the people of this town vote, they'll vote for who is best qualified to keep tha' going strong. Something you may want to keep in mind."

Mr. Crawley left her. The witch sat with her tea growing cold and her mind trying to wrap around the precarious situation, she had created for herself. Perhaps she should pull her name out and forget this entire thing.

No.

The werewolf had accomplished exactly what he'd come to do. Discourage her. She refused to be derailed. She would not let the old man, who was historically a sniveling yes-man to Claymore over the years, sway her determination. One way or another, Claymore would lose his grip on this town. Mrs. Belfry decided then, she needed advice. As much as she loathed the idea, she had to turn to the one being around that had butted heads with Claymore in the past and still lived to tell about it. Recluse.

The hour had grown late as Mrs. Belfry slipped out of her house and onto the square. She passed the fountain, the now empty market, and Pete's Sweets candy shop, which was closed for the night. Just northwest of the center of town lay Lilith's Hollow's own cemetery. A thick fog perpetually hung over the grounds, which at night took on a mysterious and eerie glow. The witch knew the fog was created by the restless ghosts that populated the old boneyard but continued on despite her strong revulsion of all spirits.

Quietly, so as not to alert the zombie, Mr. McLowry, who made his home in one of the large mausoleums inside to her presence, Mrs. Belfry entered through the gates and down the trail to the right. Some of the grave markers within the cemetery date back to as far as the 1300's, broken and decayed, the markings on their surfaces barely discernible now. Mrs. Belfry carefully stepped around the stones, taking the path toward the tomb that was located at the rear of the grounds.

The demon Kazul had told her of the tomb and where the door led and Mrs. Belfry kept it a secret from Claymore and the others. After all, she and the demon had a history that made him comfortable with confiding in her. He knew, she could keep a secret, and he kept a secret or two for her as well. Plus, she knew the knowledge of the tomb could serve her own interest one day, as it did now.

"Oscail," the witch commanded with a wave of her hand. The door of the tomb slowly slid aside with a grinding sound that would make most creatures cringe. Mrs. Belfry stepped into the darkness, unsure of what to expect on the other side.

Though she was aware of its existence, Mrs. Belfry had never stepped foot in the underside. It is a hidden part of Lilith's Hollow, most thought it only existed in legends. A mirror image of the town existing on the opposite plane. The first thing Mrs. Belfry noticed about the world was the lack of color. Every surface and object seemed to be a dull shade of gray. The tomb itself resembled the inside of any tomb. Three coffins were lined up inside along the wall, giving the witch a narrow path to cross over to another door opposite to the one she had entered.

"Oscail," she repeated. The second door opened for her to pass through. She exited to a dreary version of the cemetery she'd just left. Here, there was no fog. No glow. Somehow, this version of the bone yard seemed less lively.

Mrs. Belfry walked the same trail to the exit of the cemetery and came upon a crumbled, lifeless version of the town she knew and loved. The familiar statue at the center of the fountain was gone along with its water. The walls of Lilith's Hollow Town Hall were caved in; the library was no more than a pile of rubble. She couldn't see this alternate world's version of her house from where she stood and decided she didn't wish to. Off to the west, there stood a structure that did not exist in the real Lilith's Hollow. A devastated castle with an open front gate.

With a bit of reluctance, Mrs. Belfry walked toward the edifice, looking around at the strange world as she went. The colorful trees in the real town held no color here. The leaves were merely a lighter shade of gray than the trees they hung from. Not only that, but everything was perfectly still. No wind blew through the embers and carried the leaves away to fall on the ground. Not a sound was heard in all of the town. The witch found all of it rather unsettling.

This was the world Recluse chose to hide in. It was frightening in a subtle way, Spooky. It was fitting, really. She remembered the creature and the power he wielded. Fear was his ally. It was an ability he'd perfected over the years, to the point that the other creatures of the town feared him.

Mrs. Belfry entered the castle and walked a short way down a dim corridor. At the end, she found an open courtyard with more lifeless trees. A corridor split off to the right and a second to the left. The one on the left was covered in spider webs, the witch knew this was the way to take. Pushing past the thick, silk webbing, the witch soon came upon a staircase that spiraled upward to the second floor. There she found a set of double doors, in front of which sat the demon Kazul, reading a book with a toothpick dancing between his teeth.

He stood as she approached and seemed confused by her appearance there. "Mrs. Belfry? I didn't expect to see you 'ere. Matter of fact, I never expect to see anybody 'ere."

"I've come seeking advice from your master. Would you announce my presence please?"

"Uh…sure. Let me see if he's free," the demon opened the

door and poked his head inside, then looked back. "What do ya know, he's free. Little humor for ya. He really doesn't have much goin' on."

The demon chuckled and led Mrs. Belfry through the door and into the spider's throne room. Inside, the room shared the same gray atmosphere as the rest of the Underside. Situated near the rear, covered in cobwebs, seemingly forgotten by the spindly legged resident of the castle, there sat a large throne that could in no way accommodate the would-be ruler of this drab realm. Beyond this, was a massive tangle of spider webs with a hollowed-out center.

Kazul stopped once they reached the center of the room. "Wait here. He'll be right with ya."

The demon walked back through the doors and closed them as he exited. Mrs. Belfry was left to ponder just what she would say to the creature when he finally appeared. She heard the clicking of boney mandibles and a strange air filled the room. The webbing behind the throne swayed and a foreign fear moved in to settle at the nape of the witch's neck. The creature that emerged from the spider hole walked on four, long legs, the bulbous body of a spider at his rear which gave way to the muscular upper torso of a man, though with four arms instead of two. Each hand was made up of three thick fingers that ended in a sharp bone point. More bones protruded from his elbows and shoulders. His head was a mound of brown fur lined with eight shiny, watchful eyes. Below this were the mandibles that spread to reveal a mouth full of large, jagged teeth. In her entire long life, Mrs. Belfry was sure that she'd never met a beast as revolting as Recluse.

"The esteemed Mrs. Belfry," the half spider gave a hiss, followed by several loud clicks of his mandibles. "You honor me with your presence, do you like my castle?"

"It's charming," the witch managed.

"It was built by the goblins, you know, during the war." Recluse moved beside the throne and placed one hand over the top edge. "It's fascinating to me, really. The entire time that the war waged on with Claymore, Katrina, Lilith, even you and me, throwing our all into battle after battle against those foul creatures. And all the while, they were here; in this very realm, erecting this impressive structure and planning their every move against us. Right in our own backyard, as they say. Sometimes, I wonder, what if I had been on their side at the time? What if I had an army of Goblins at my command? How different things might be now. Perhaps I'd be the one ruling Halloween from Claymore Manor, while that spineless vampire was stuck here. Of course, I'd have to rename the mansion Recluse Manor."

Mrs. Belfry gave an impatient sigh. "I didn't come here to listen to the prattling of a nutter bent on world domination."

Recluse studied her with what appeared to be disdain, though it was hard to tell on the fiend's ugly face, the air seemed to grow thick with his presence. "Of course, what brings such a fair creature to such a desolate realm?"

The witch had to force the fear she felt away in order to gather her thoughts and speak. "I've come seeking advice."

Recluse's laugh was an awful sound, made worse by the echo in the large chamber. "That's rich. Surely, one as powerful as you, needs no pointers on scaring, even from one so gifted as myself."

"This isn't about tricks or treats. I'm perfectly capable of inducing fear in mortals. I may be heading for a conflict with Claymore. No one has gone up against him more than you."

The half spider moved away from the throne while he watched her with all of his eyes. "Interesting. I'm assuming you're aware of my success rate. While it's true I've faced the vampire on numerous occasions, rarely have I emerged victorious."

"Regardless, you must have some insight on how best to fight him."

"Indeed. I've learned over the years that facing Claymore head on is futile. I use fear and manipulation to get what I want. Claymore is far too powerful to fear me, so I manipulate."

"How so?"

"Even now, as we speak, I have several plans in motion to bring down his rule. I'll not divulge these plans, for I do not trust their secrecy with you, but suffice to say, the vampire is playing right into them. And if one should fail, I have a backup plan. I have backup plans to my backup plans. Time and careful planning are the only ways to break Claymore."

Mrs. Belfry pondered the possibilities. What could she do to manipulate the vampire?

Recluse moved closer to her. "Don't get me wrong, witch. Just because I don't have the power to defeat Claymore in a physical fight, it doesn't mean you should avoid it. After all, you are a highly skilled magic user. Plus, if you could remove Claymore from power, you'd be doing me a favor. Perhaps we could rule Halloween together."

The witch paused, then said, "Perhaps."

Of course, she was only humoring the half-spider. Being attached to the foul being is the last thing in the world she'd want.

Recluse moved closer still, and Mrs. Belfry could smell the stench of his breath as it hit her face. "Imagine the possibilities, my dear. We would bring terror back to the holiday. Do away with treats and make the tricks so much more horrible."

Another click of the mandibles drove a spike of fear into the witch's brain and she decided she'd had enough. With a wave of her hand, the half spider was forced off his feet and pressed against the wall. "Save your tricks for lesser beings, Recluse. If I take charge of Lilith's Hollow, I will use you as I see fit."

Recluse made a sound that made it seem as if he were taking some pleasure in the witch's punishment. "Of course, Mrs. Belfry. In truth, this is something I could get used to."

An awful laugh escaped the half-spider, Mrs. Belfry felt her stomach turn. She released him and turned to leave. "Thanks for the talk, Recluse. I'll let you know how things turn out."

She left without another word but felt the fiend's eyes upon her as she stepped through the door. Kazul stood and looked down at her. "Hope that went well?"

"Somewhat," Mrs. Belfry said with a shrug. "Kazul, why do you insist on working for this awful creature? When I invited you to join our community, this was not what I had in mind."

He shrugged. "I worked for Lucifer for so long, it's hard to do good at this point. And I'm not ready to retire and teach a bunch o' kids about trick or treating. I crave adventure."

"I understand. I suppose. Still, if you change your mind, we always have a place for you. But not him." She cocked a thumb at the door she'd just exited.

"I appreciate that, Mrs. Belfry."

With that, she nodded and took her leave. A long night of contemplation still ahead of her.

Sometimes, late at night, when Mrs. Belfry had a lot on her mind, she would wander the halls of her house, which was far larger on the inside than anyone would guess by looking at its façade; with her hands clasped behind her back and her mind churning away at the problem at hand. Renfield was often at her feet and tonight was no exception. In most instances, that problem would be complicated spells or concoctions, but tonight it was the upcoming debate. Even though she was sure the vampire wouldn't show, she still had to come up with a careful, impassioned speech that spoke to the townsfolk. The last thing she wanted to do was resort to violence to end Claymore's reign, so she worked to find a way to make the others see how wrong he was for the town's future. A way to manipulate the vampire or the situation, as Recluse recommended.

A scratch and a whine at one of the doors pulled her out of her thoughts. She opened the door and a spider the size of a French bulldog scuttled out into the hall. Renfield, the cat, hissed at it, and hurried into an open room three doors down. The halls of the house were color coded and right now she was in the red hall, named so, for the blood red carpeting that ran its length. The rooms were ever changing, the halls rotated to keep any intruders from finding their way out, not to deter visitors like old Crawley believed. Over the years, there have been people intent on stealing from her or doing her harm that were still lost in the confusing moving layout.

Precisely why she limited her students to the classroom at the front of the house. She had no desire to explain to an angry parent that their child was lost forever to the strange house, or that they'd become an evening meal to one of the creatures that wandered her halls.

Without realizing it, Mrs. Belfry had come to a stop in front of the pumpkin room. One of her favorites. She stepped inside, taking in the soft glow of candles burning from within the many carved pumpkins. The room (which could hardly be considered a room at all) consisted of a wrap-around porch that one might find off the back of a farmhouse in the American Midwest. Several jack o'lanterns projected their faces across the wood floor and ground in the early evening light. The steps off the porch opened up to a dirt drive, and beyond this a large cornfield with dry, late autumn cornstalks that swayed in the breeze. This was where she came to carve pumpkins, a favorite hobby, and to make a suitable replacement head for old Jack when his head started to rot.

She walked off the porch and across the drive, to the cornfield with Renfield by her side. Down one of the rows she went, slowly running her hands over the dry stalks. She loved the texture of them. The brittle fragility calmed her mind; she reached out with her natural air ability and pushed a gust of wind from the east. It rustled through the field and over her, whipping her robes and hair. Only through peace would the answers come. Only by calming her rage and fevered mind. After some time, she exited the field and returned to the porch.

Mrs. Belfry sat on the top step, staring out over the field as the setting sun painted the sky a vibrant purple and orange. From time to time she caught a glimpse of Renfield darting in and out of the corn stalks, hot on the heels of a field mouse. In all of her years, she'd only been to America a handful of times. This particular room, she had molded around a farm in Indiana that she found especially pleasing to the senses. With a temper like hers, spots like this were essential in keeping her calm. So, she sat there for many hours. After some time, Renfield emerged from the stalks with the field mouse in his mouth. He played with it for a while on the porch before growing bored and sprawling out for a nap. Ah! life of a cat. Finally, when all was calm around her, she formed her plan. And what a great plan it was!

Out of the pumpkin room, Mrs. Belfry walked over the red carpeting of the hall, bound for the staircase at the middle of the house. Rather than descending, she crossed the landing above and wound up in the green hall. Through the fifth door on the left, she found herself inside a magnificent library. She climbed to the second floor and moved a ladder over to the shelf she wanted, then climbed to a section of old books that had accumulated a thick film of dust over them. She cleared away a few cobwebs and ran her index finger along the spines until she found the exact volume she was searching for. Flipping through the pages, she finally found the spell she wanted. A malicious grin turned up the corners of her mouth.

The night of the debate came and Mrs. Belfry stood in front of the mirror in her foyer, adjusting her gown and robe. No matter what the townspeople's opinion of her personality, they couldn't deny her beauty. Her appearance, however, was only part of her approach tonight. The rest would lie in her words. Her hair was perfect, her eyes shone like bright green emeralds, her lips were just the right shade of pink. The gown she wore was a long, elegant black, accompanied by a bodice that pushed up and revealed two of her most ample attributes. The velvet maroon robes over her shoulders added a bit of class.

My looks alone may bewitch the audience, she thought. *A spell might not even be necessary.*

Mrs. Belfry's finishing touch was the pointed, maroon witch's hat that matched her robes. The people of Lilith's Hollow would appreciate her looking the part of a Halloween witch, even if not in the form of an old crone with large hairy warts on her bulbous nose. Some Halloween standards were just a little inaccurate.

Outside the house, the wind had picked up and fallen leaves scuttled across the cobblestone street as if racing toward some destination only known to them. Mrs. Belfry walked through the rickety old gate in her front yard and through the leaves, across town square, she took the steps up to the front doors of Lilith's Hollow Town Hall, where Mr. Crawley awaited her arrival.

"Mrs. Belfry, you look stunning," the old werewolf stated.

"Crawley, flattery will get you nowhere," she replied. "But feel free to continue."

This made Mr. Crawley chuckle and he seemed to relax a little for a change. "Good luck to you, my dear."

As he opened the door for her, she only nodded and thought, I make my own luck, old boy.

Inside the hall, the citizens had all gathered and turned to look at her when she entered. Some gasped at her splendor and when she smiled, even more gasps followed. Though she had a wonderful smile, it was something her fellow Halloween creatures had seldom seen. Usually, her expressions were painted with the aforementioned angered scowl or frustrated exasperation.

At the front of the room, two podiums were set up for the coming debate and Mrs. Belfry had to stifle laughter at the idea of Claymore showing up to stand at one of them. She moved down the aisle with all eyes on her, confident in her upcoming speech. Even more confident in the spell that would follow. Soon, every citizen in Lilith's Hollow would be under her control and more than willing to vote for a change in leadership. Taking her place behind the podium on the right, Mrs. Belfry looked out on their unsuspecting faces while she kept her radiant smile in place. The smile, reinforced by the knowledge that she was about to accomplish a feat Recluse had failed at for ages. The control of Lilith's Hollow, and in turn Halloween.

Mr. Crawley hurried to the small stage and stood behind the remaining podium. "Hello, all. We're going to give Claymore just ten more minutes to arrive before we begin."

Despite the old werewolf's best efforts to dress nice and come off professional for the event, he still seemed agitated and disheveled. He returned to the steps outside the hall and waited there, greeting the late arrivals and no doubt expecting Claymore to swoop in and save the day, while Mrs. Belfry waited patiently for the fiasco to start.

Ten minutes passed, then another ten minutes. Finally, Crawley returned to the remaining podium with a sheepish look on his face. "Well, it appears Claymore will not be participating tonight. Therefore, there will be no debate. Instead, Mrs. Hagatha

Belfry will tell us why she feels she would be a better fit to lead the town. Mrs. Belfry."

There came a smattering of applause as the werewolf turned the spotlight over to the witch.

Mrs. Belfry cleared her throat. "I feel Claymore's inability to show up to such an important debate is proof enough that he's not fit to continue leading our community. Nevertheless, I shall proceed."

"Lilith's Hollow, was formed on one solitary foundation; Halloween. It's what brought us all together here. That, and the total oppression of our kind from the mortal world. I'm sure some of you remember. For us, there were no rights. There were no privileges. There were some humans that hunted us down and slaughtered us. Why? Because of a few bad apples. Some vampires amongst us who left the drained husks of their victims lying around. A witch or two who kidnapped some babies. Certain zombies who insisted on eating the brains of townspeople here and there. These misguided souls have given the rest of us a bad name."

The creatures in the crowd murmured and nodded their agreement.

"This is our society," Mrs. Belfry continued. "Our town. As such, we should have the privilege of free enterprise. And yes, outsiders should be allowed to bring their goods to us from the outside world. Of course, we need protection from those who would do us harm, but at what cost? Under Claymore's leadership, we're becoming more like prisoners than citizens. Cut off from modern society and trapped in the dark ages. Hell, we just got bloody electricity more than a century behind the rest of the world. It's time for a change, I want to bring the change to you.

"When I came here, the town was still small, in its beginning stages. The school was just barely off the ground. I helped the town grow through invitations to others. Miss Grey, you'd have never known about Lilith's Hollow if I hadn't reached out to you. Same with you Kazul. And though you're here to represent Recluse, we all forgive you for that."

Laughter trickled through the crowd.

"And what about Recluse. He's out there right now, plotting and scheming, trying to come up with a way to take over our town and inflict his twisted vision of Halloween upon the entire world. And Claymore intends to do nothing. That's the protection he is willing to offer? That is how he shows he cares for us? I will bring Recluse to justice and make it so that he never threatens us or our way of life again. Claymore wasn't the only one who fought against the goblins for this town. I was there, fighting right by his side.

"On top of that, I have been instrumental in saving the world on several occasions. Our friend Jack, the lovable scarecrow, is a walking doorway to The Nightmare Tree, one of the most dangerous realms in existence. I brought him here over a hundred years ago to keep him safe and secret from the rest of the world. It was also I who ensured the Staff of Set was hidden away from those who would choose to use its power to take over the Earth.

"And what has Claymore done in this time? He's remained locked away in his mansion, where he continues to mourn the loss of his wife. Of course, what happened to Lady Katrina was a tragedy and my heart goes out to him. However, she was killed centuries ago at the end of the Goblin War. I was married once. My husband died. I grieved for him, then picked up the pieces and moved on because people relied on me. Children relied on me. I am the leader this town needs."

She had moved them. They were hanging on her every word. The time had come. In moments she would cast a spell on all of them and the town would be hers. The verses of the spell were on her tongue, but she stopped herself before she could speak them aloud. They all stared at her, listening intently to her speech and waiting to hear what she'd say next. She looked out on those familiar faces, the faces of her friends and neighbors, and knew she couldn't cast the spell. It would be unfair. It would be wrong. Instead, she would finish her speech and hope that they would come to the right decision.

"I know I can be hard and distant. I know, sometimes, I can even be difficult. But I love this town. I love the people in it. Allow me to show it. Let me lead you into a new era."

The crowd stood and clapped. She had done it. She had gotten through to them and done so without tricks or spells. The applause continued as she made her way down the aisle to exit Town Hall. Out onto the cobblestone streets, Mrs. Belfry turned and walked to her house, confident she would be the next leader of Lilith's Hollow.

"Two votes!" Mrs. Belfry bellowed. "After all the applause and praise, I got two bloody votes!"

"Mrs. Belfry, please" Crawley started. He had just nailed the results to the front of Town Hall and half the town had gathered to view them.

"Oh, spare me, you dried up twit," the witch screamed. "And to think I felt pity on you fools. I should have cast my spell and been done with all this."

"Spell? What-"

"I said shut up!" The force of her voice caused many in the group to step back. The clouds overhead began to churn and thunder rolled as Mrs. Belfry's natural elemental ability flared with her anger. "I tried to be civil about this. I tried to sway your opinion with sense and reason. Now, we shall see how well you respond when I turn your precious Claymore into a smoldering pile of ash."

Crawley stepped toward her, clearly hoping to calm her down with more words but Mrs. Belfry was done talking. She pushed her hand toward him, a gust of wind forced the werewolf and others that gathered off their feet, sending them tumbling away from her. The witch turned on her heel and began the march up the hill to Claymore Manor. The sun was setting and Mrs. Belfry was ready to unleash her anger.

Mrs. Belfry didn't bother to knock, instead, she pushed through the doors of the mansion and into the foyer where she was met by old Shillingsworth. "Madam, what is the meaning of this?"

The witch held out one hand and electricity danced between her fingers. "Step aside, old man. Your master and I have a few things to sort out."

"You'll have to go through me to get to him," Shillingsworth held up his fist as if Mrs. Belfry had challenged him to a boxing match. Was it not for her fury, she'd have cackled before striking him down. Just as she was ready to send a bolt through the servant, a familiar voice spoke up from the top of the stairs.

"It's alright, Shillingsworth. I have no qualms about entertaining our surprise guest." The vampire glided gracefully down the stairs; his red cape draped around his slender body. "Please, Mrs. Belfry, let us take our...conversation to the ballroom. There, we'll have plenty of space to work things out."

Claymore led the way through the hall and Belfry followed. "I've waited so long for this moment," the witch admitted.

"Well then, hopefully you won't be disappointed with the outcome. I'm guessing the vote didn't go as you wanted?"

Claymore's calm politeness only served to fuel her anger. "Of course not. You've got this bloody town brainwashed into thinking you're Halloween's messiah. They're all pathetic, and just as spineless as you are."

The vampire crossed the ballroom floor and removed his cape. He carefully draped it over a chair and turned to look at her as he rolled the sleeves of his shirt up. "Such harsh words, and here I thought you were one of us."

"Recluse was one of us as well. Now, I see he was justified in what he did."

At last, anger flashed across Claymore's face. The half man, half spider that had lived among them and betrayed Claymore in an effort to take over the town and Halloween, was a sore subject. Recluse was banished from the town, perpetually plotting to remove Claymore from power, and impose his will on the great holiday that he felt had become far too tame. "Perhaps, you'd like to join him. I hear he's always looking to add to his ranks. Build upon the number of followers that pledge their allegiance to him."

"I will follow no more. My power is far beyond anyone in this town and I should be the one to lead." Outside the walls of the towering ballroom, thunder rolled and a flash of lightening hit the roof, then ripped down the spherical façade, glass shattered and brick crumbled to the floor. Claymore's movement was a blur as he narrowly avoided being crushed by a large chunk of wall. She turned to face him as he moved behind her. Now, his face was contorted into a monstrous form as he bared his fangs and claws.

Another flash of lightening hit what remained of the roof and tore it away. The vampire quickly dodged more falling debris.

"The outside world, vampire" Mrs. Belfry screamed over the carnage. "I'll cripple you with your greatest fear."

A lightning bolt slammed down through the new opening in the roof and hit Claymore directly. Miraculously, he held out one hand and redirected the attack back toward Mrs. Belfry. The witch had to move fast to avoid being hit with her own powerful assault.

Mrs. Belfry stood and stared down the vampire.

Claymore straightened, casually brushing a bit of rubble from his shoulder. "A little talent, I possess. The ability to redirect magic spells."

"Very impressive."

"At last, I've impressed the great Hagatha Belfry. I'll sleep a little better in my coffin with the knowledge."

Enraged, Mrs. Belfry used a different approach. With a wave of her hand, she threw several chunks of wall at the vampire. Then tables and chairs from around the room. Claymore dodged the rubble and tore through the furniture with his sharp claws. While he was distracted with the debris, the witch quickly removed a pouch from her belt and threw it at his feet. The powder inside exploded on contact, sending Claymore reeling through the air. He hit the far wall hard and dropped to the floor.

Mrs. Belfry didn't let up. She dropped several bricks on his head and followed this with a volley of lightening that Claymore was unable to deflect. Still, as she stopped to examine the damage that was done, the vampire struggled up on his hands and knees. Before he could regain his feet, she sent more lightening.

This time, he was able to deflect it and Mrs. Belfry took the full force. The sensation of flying came to an abrupt end when she crashed through a window and tumbled over the ground outside. Her body was racked with pain and her mind was abuzz with fresh rage.

Mrs. Belfry rushed back into the ballroom through the window she'd come through. Claymore was just back on his feet, leaning at the wall to support himself. His clothes torn and tattered, cuts on his head and face that were instantly healing. She had him. It was over.

The vampire was too fast. A blur, as he moved past her and dragged his claws through her midsection. The attack tore through her flesh and left four deep gouges which bled immediately through her dress. Claymore swiftly moved by her again and slashed at her back. The pain was searing and shot through her entire body.

His speed was incredible. Another attack was coming. Mrs. Belfry sensed it more than saw it. She reached out with telekinesis and took hold of the vampire. She held him against the far wall and lifted several large pieces of rubble at the same time. Then, she pummeled his body with the brick and mortar. Shards of glass were next. The witch found the longest, blade-like pieces and sent them hurdling toward Claymore. They stabbed into his flesh and pinned him in place.

"Your feeble skills are no match for my power," Mrs. Belfry scathed. "This town is mine now, as is Halloween. You will bow before me or die."

"Then I choose death, witch."

The fury within Mrs. Belfry grew stronger and she pulled the vampire off the wall, then used her mind to fling him through the nearest window and out into the pumpkin patch that surrounded the mansion. Using telekinesis on her own body, she lifted off the floor and floated after him.

In the outside world, Claymore's phobia took hold. She found him lying among the smashed pumpkins, paralyzed and struggling to speak.

"You are weak and pathetic," Mrs. Belfry observed. "I know I should feel pity for you, but I find I lack the capacity at the moment. I will show you mercy, however, you will be around to see my success in leading this town. Only you will have the weight of your years to weaken you further."

Mrs. Belfry spoke the words of her curse in ancient Celtic. "Sean-Aoise!"

Claymore managed to move and held out his hand as the curse hit and an invisible force erupted around him. The windows that remained in the Ballroom tower erupted inward. Mrs. Belfry was thrown back once again, this time landing back in the ballroom and sliding over the floor until she came to a stop against the far wall.

In the silence that followed, Mrs. Belfry barely held on to consciousness. From somewhere down the hall that led back to the house, she could hear someone crying. With great effort, the witch stood and stumbled in that direction. She felt weak. Drained.

Mrs. Belfry glanced back out at the pumpkin patch to find Claymore was gone. She wondered if her curse had hit and turned the vampire into dust. Down the hall, Mrs. Belfry continued to follow the crying. Finally, she rounded a corner and found a servant girl lying on the floor, with Claymore crouched over her. How had he returned to the house? Had she passed out after all? The girl was a woodland creature and Mrs. Belfry looked on in horror as her body took on the form and characteristics of an old tree. Claymore looked back at Mrs. Belfry and she knew the curse had missed him. He looked as young and handsome as ever.

"Miss Darcy, my cook," he said. "Your curse hit her as well."

"As well?" Mrs. Belfry said, and realized her voice was no more than a croak. She looked at her hands in horror as they wrinkled before her eyes. Liver spots appeared on her skin and her fingernails yellowed and cracked. "No."

The witch refused to believe it. She looked further down the hall where a mirror hung on the wall over a table that held a vase full of black roses. She looked in the mirror and screamed. Her beauty was fading. The pretty, flawless face she'd grown used to seeing reflected back was being replaced by a weathered, wrinkled visage. She was turning into an old crone. The very witch that was associated with Halloween over the centuries. A wart appeared on her chin. Another on her elongated nose. Hairs sprouted from the warts.

"My face!" the witch cried. "My beautiful face! My perfect body!" She turned to Claymore. "What have you done?"

"I deflected your curse. Though you got what you deserved for your betrayal, poor Miss Darcy did not deserve the same fate. This is your lone chance to leave my house, Mrs. Belfry. We can consider your failed curse punishment enough for your actions." He stood and stepped closer so that their noses nearly touched. "If you do not take this chance, witch, I will drain your body of its blood and your hag-like appearance will be the least of your troubles."

Mrs. Belfry thought of fighting, but her great power had faded with her youth. Were she to attack Claymore now, she wouldn't stand a chance. "I will leave, Claymore. One day, my powers will return to me and I will have my revenge."

The witch turned, and limped toward the devastated ballroom, deciding to make her egress through the broken windows rather than walk through the house and face anyone who might see her lost identity. Her body ached. Arthritic pain in her joints and aches in her back that were new companions with her new form. By the time she reached her house and stumbled inside, she was in so much agony she could barely walk. To her kitchen and into the pantry, Mrs. Belfry rummaged through the hundreds of bottled potions there until she found what she was looking for. She uncorked the vial and swallowed the concoction, then breathed easier as the pain throughout her old body subsided.

To the small breakfast table in the kitchen, the witch dropped down in one of the chairs and stared into space. Her mind revisited the battle with the vampire. She had underestimated Claymore. He was far more formidable a foe than she gave him credit for. She had lost and had her power stripped from her. Not only that, her legendary beauty was gone. The only thing that comforted her, brought some semblance of purpose to this new life she would be forced to endure, was an old saying that she never felt was truer than in this case— *Revenge is a dish best served cold.*

In the days that followed, Mrs. Belfry searched tirelessly for a way to break the spell. Her crusade for the betterment of the town had been all but forgotten. Now, she was consumed with regaining her former beauty and vengeance. She studied her spell books and created potions that had no effect, though she was able to heal the wounds she'd sustained during the battle. Sleep had become a foreign concept. Her morning tea on the porch, the ritual that had calmed her so much, was a thing of the past. Even her rooms of meditation, the pumpkin room, the winter room, the craft den, all were forgotten. Much like Claymore and his search to find a way to contact his dead wife, Mrs. Belfry devoted all of her time to her library and research.

Poor Renfield was rather affected by it all, as well. He was so concerned with Mrs. Belfry's well-being that he could scarcely eat or sleep. Most of the time, he only looked on with worry as the witch went about her work. Sometimes, he would give his suggestions, but he too was at a loss on a way to break the curse. Though, she had been the one who cast it, and Claymore being the one to deflect, something strange had happened. She couldn't remove it.

The doorbell rang one day. It was a sound so seldom heard

that Mrs. Belfry didn't recognize it at first. She moved slowly through the house, toward the front door, cursing under her breath the soul who stood on her porch and interrupted her work. When she opened the door, she wasn't particularly surprised to see Mr. Crawley standing there.

"Oh Mrs. Belfry," he said, his expression one of pity at her appearance. "You poor thing."

"What is it, Crawley? I'm a very busy woman."

"Well, everyone in town, myself included. We've been worried about you."

"Why do you care now all of the sudden?"

"We've always cared."

Mrs. Belfry studied the man's face for a moment. Then, against her better judgment said; "I suppose you can come in, but only if you wipe that pity off your face. I don't need it."

"Of course."

She let him in and he walked past her to the foyer where he waited for her to speak.

"Would you like some tea, Mr. Crawley?"

"Yes, that would be lovely."

Into the kitchen, Mrs. Belfry filled a kettle and placed it on the stove. The werewolf waited in silence until the tea was ready and placed on the table in front of him. Mrs. Belfry took a seat with a grunt. The aches and pains of her aged body that were so foreign a week ago, now seemed to be a constant reminder of her failure.

"I suppose Claymore has been gloating about his victory," the witch said.

"Oh no. No one has heard from him since the fight. We heard

about what happened to you and Miss Darcy from Shillingsworth."

"Tis a shame Miss Darcy was involved. Wrong place at the wrong time. How is she?"

"Ashamed of her appearance. She refuses to have anyone in the kitchen with her as she cooks and takes the back stairs to her quarters to avoid the other servants and the master of the house."

Mrs. Belfry could relate. "Why on earth does Claymore employ a cook anyway? The man only consumes blood."

"Well, for the other servants more than anything. She also cooks for most of our events we have throughout the school year."

"Really?"

"Aye."

"Well, she's an excellent cook. I often wondered who was behind all that."

Silence fell between them. They each sipped at their tea.

Renfield appeared at Crawley's feet and hissed. It wasn't the first time the cat had seemed distrusting of the man, but Mrs. Belfry had noticed that this always happened when the full moon was close. She supposed the cat could sense old Crawley would soon turn into a dog.

The silence stretched on, and the cat and the werewolf seemed to stare each other down. It was Crawley who broke the staring game when he spoke up. "Mrs. Belfry, I just wanted to come by tonight to tell you, your impassioned speech did not fall on deaf ears. Many of us feel the same way you do about the direction of the town."

"I feel it necessary to point out I got two votes, Mr. Crawley."

"Yes, I'm aware. As much as they agree with you, the fear of change outweighs their concerns. Not only tha', but their fear of you."

"Of me?"

"Mrs. Belfry, I hope tha' one day you can see, how your anger sways people's opinions about you. I know, deep down, you're a woman with a great heart. I've seen it on many occasions. But I've also seen you do some things that were, shall we say, morally questionable."

Mrs. Belfry thought of the baby growing in her greenhouse, and more specifically, the dishonest way she'd acquired the DNA she used to create the life. Mr. Crawley had stood right next to her as she stole it from an unconscious ghost hunter.

"Beyond that," the werewolf continued, "When you lose your temper, it frightens people. I may see it as passion about your convictions, but others are hesitant to give someone with such anger a position of power. Imagine the possibilities, both awful and great, that one could accomplish with the title of Queen of Halloween."

"I suppose the people prefer their absent king."

"They take comfort in routine."

"I understand, Mr. Crawley. And I've also come to the conclusion that politics are not my area of expertise. Now, I have more pressing things to fill my time. Being trapped in the body of this old crone you see before you is not something I can stand for. You people can keep your failing town and missing leader. I'm content with living in my little pocket of Lilith's Hollow and letting all of you live in yours. And from my front porch, I'll watch with sick satisfaction as it all falls apart around you. Now, I hate to rush you but I have a lot on my plate."

The witch stood, and though Mr. Crawley looked as if he wanted to say more, he only nodded his head and walked to the front door. Mrs. Belfry watched as he stepped off her porch and down her walk. When he reached the broken old gate in her fence, she called out to him. "Mr. Crawley, out of the two votes I got, one was my own. You were the other, weren't you?"

"Aye. I may understand why the people in this town voted against you, but that doesn't mean I agree with them. Goodnight, Mrs. Belfry."

The witch watched the werewolf walk across town square to the south, where he kept his little hut on the edge of town limits. Tomorrow night was a full moon and she knew he'd spend it prowling the woods around the town with others like him. Of all the creatures in town, he had always been her favorite.

Mrs. Belfry closed the door and moved back to the kitchen to clean up. As she placed the tray and tea set on the counter near her basin, she heard a soft grunt from inside the greenhouse. This was followed by another, louder grunt and then a cry. Mrs. Belfry pulled a blanket from the pantry, where she had stored it in preparation for this moment, and hurried through her back door and to the ivy in the near corner of the greenhouse. There, among the vines and leaves, lay her newborn daughter.

The witch pulled out a knife to cut the vine that ran to the child's belly button, then wrapped her in the blanket and held her in her arms. "Shush, little one. Mommy's got you now."

Mrs. Belfry carried the girl back through the house and into her sitting room where she sat on a rocking chair and began to talk to the cooing baby.

"Hello, child. Welcome home. I shall name you…Blithe. It used to be my mother's name. Blithe Belfry. It really rolls off the tongue, hey? I am your mother." Mrs. Belfry looked down at her old, wrinkled hands and her heart dropped a little. "Well, I suppose that would be a little confusing to you as you get older. Let's just say I'm your grandmother. At least until I can find a way to reverse this curse."

Blithe looked at her with eyes wider than a typical newborn. It was almost as if she understood what the witch was saying. At least somewhat. Then, when Renfield, the cat appeared on the nightstand in the baby's line of vision, made an 'o' with her mouth, as if she were in awe of this new creature.

"Little Blithe," Mrs. Belfry sang. "With your father's gift of sight and your mother's magic ability, someday you will be more powerful than all of us. You will rule Lilith's Hollow and all of Halloween."

Blithe Belfry looked in the old woman's eyes and smiled

THE LONG SLEEP

1950 - The City of Angels.

It is at the suggestion of my long-time partner that I write down a few of my thoughts and actions. As the centuries tick by, even the best memory will lose things - like people and places, events and women and your keys. I admit these journals have proven useful over time; I just won't admit it to Amun, who's already a nightmare to walk beside in our long journey. I never do remember where I leave my keys.

One of the important lessons you learn over time is to keep an eye on your investments. There is big money in antiques and the like - live a few centuries, and you quickly work out you're going to need money. Stashing away cheap things to sell at a later date for a big reward – well, that just makes sense. It just helps to have a reminder where you have kept them.

Looking back, I cannot recall when Amun was first asked to investigate the murder of Shelby Lydekker, the fiancé of Jean McQueen, the only daughter of General Mark McQueen. The

General had made his name as commander of the US army forces in Japan after the war, before retiring and returning home.

The police had been hounded by Lydekker's family to find him - and in frustration Detective Dana Raskin had suggested Amun as a private investigator to look into the matter. Amun was busy with his usual thousand little projects and asked me to be his eyes and ears around the family until he could step in.

The McQueen's were old money, with a long tradition of the second-born son joining the army; thus, they were always positioned to take advantage of political and military opportunities. I only mention this because of the size of the house. I found myself walking up the long pathway decorated with every Halloween trinket the local five-and-dime had on the shelf to...well, I say house. I have seen baseball stadiums smaller than this mansion.

Beside me walked the guard from the front gate. Now, I won't say the shotgun the old man was cradling like a newborn baby was exactly pointed in my direction or that the scowl he wore on his face a result of my sudden appearance in his normally structured life. Still, I was pretty confident that if I made any sudden movements, he was ready to blow my head off. A man had disappeared from the estate, and the staff seemed to be taking the matter very seriously. As we walked, we passed a gardener hanging fake spider webs and someone I assumed to be the house's dog walker by the three dogs he was walking. All the men shouldered a weapon of some kind, and the trio of mutts nervously growled as I passed.

"Has something else happened?" I asked as we crunch our way up the stone driveway.

"Not my place to say," the old guard mumbled.

"A plague of pigeons?"

"What?" A furious storm of forehead rolled down his face.

"The guns - why is everyone carrying guns?"

The guard looked at the gun in his arms as though for the first time and seemed about to answer before simply harrumphing and continuing towards the house in silence.

As we approached the front door sporting the enormous face of a gargoyle with its tongue hanging out, I looked up and through a window along the top floor, I noticed a lovely face watching us. I fired off my best knee-weakening smile, and when that gained no reaction, I gave the vision a friendly wave. The guardsman looked at me like I was crazy, so I gave him the same winning smile. He just looked at me like I was deranged. A less confident man would think there was something wrong with his face by these reactions; luckily, I was not that man. My heart sank a little when I returned my attention to the window as that lovely face was gone.

Once inside, I was shepherded by another servant, who never spoke a word. We passed through an enormous front entry hall containing a winding staircase with burning candles and a grinning jack-o-lantern perched on every step, rising into the upper floors. On the far side, I was led into a library full of books and photos. By the monkey suit the man wore, it was a safe bet he was the butler.

Above a large fireplace festooned with bats, black cats, and grinning skeletons was an enormous portrait of a stern man in military uniform adorned with enough medals hanging off his breast to smelt down and build a new battleship. Once I was seated, the butler left the room, reappearing a few minutes later with a balding, older version of the man in the portrait. The only real difference between the two was the man before me wore a forest of eyebrows that made him look constantly unsympathetic, a fearsome trait I dare say an army general would happily cultivate.

"You're the fellow Detective Raskin sent to look into the disappearance of Lydekker?" he asked.

"No."

"No?" General McQueen turned on the butler as though the man had allowed a snake to find its way into the house.

"No," I repeated. "I was sent by the man Raskin asked."

"Explain," The general ordered.

"The detective asked my partner to investigate so he could get the Lydekker family off his back, something he is very serious about, by the way. Amun is busy for the next few days when he has every intention of arriving and bringing his considerable talent for this sort of thing to the mystery. Until then, he has asked me to do the initial leg work."

"And why should I allow that?" the General asked firmly, those eyebrows lowering like a thunderstorm over a mountain.

"Well - I have my own set of unique talents, but that's not really the point. I do believe I mentioned detective Raskin and the LA police department are very keen for us to start investigating to get the Lydekkers off their backs? From everything I have heard, Lydekker junior was a wastrel, unworthy of his family name, which is why they cut him off from their sizable fortune - one that's sizably larger than yours." I pointed out, hoping the old man would catch the threat.

He did. When the General looked like he would start bellowing or whatever it is Generals do to mouthy subordinates, I added. "I only bring this up to point out the political pressure they can assert on the Mayor and Governor, which is far more than what your own family can bring."

The General's anger grew, and he looked as though he was about to say something like 'toss this garbage out', so with nothing to lose, I kept going. "I'm only saying this to highlight that I did my homework before I came here. I am asking your permission to talk to the household, thus keeping the Lydekkers happy and the LA police from initiating a full-scale investigation and pulling apart the lives of you, your family, and anyone attached to this house. There is always the chance that a well-greased police officer will sell anything they find or even anything they don't find, to reporters who'd gladly crucify everyone to sell a few hundred thousand newspapers. Feel free to turf me out if you want, but I really am here to help."

General McQueen was not a stupid man, and his entire life was built around his ability to devise long-term strategies. After some thought he nodded, indicating I was likely correct, turned back to the butler and said, "Put this man in one of the guest rooms and ensure the staff understands they are to answer his questions, as long as they only relate to the missing man."

I opened my mouth to argue but just as quickly closed it. Staying inside with access to the house was not the worst idea, and there was always a chance I would bump into the owner of that lovely face in the window.

The General must have seen that I'd been about to argue and

added, "Policemen are not the only ones who can sell information to the newspapers, so you staying here will be as much a protection for us as to us."

"Loose lips sink ships," I smiled.

"Exactly."

My room was large and well furnished, almost cheerful in décor with none of the ghoulish ornamentations so prevalent everywhere else. Conveniently it was at the rear of the building. I was not sure if I should read something into this. Was I only a guest given a fine room or an invader quarantined from the rest of the household?

After a few minutes, there was a knock at the door. The butler carried in a tray with a jug of water and a single glass. He placed these on a table in the middle of the room, then turned and explained, "I have alerted the staff that they are to answer all questions about Master Lydekker."

"Why the guns?" I asked, trying to catch him off guard.

"I'm sorry?"

"Since my arrival, I have seen three men carrying guns, and everyone seems to be on edge. So again, I ask, why the guns?"

"A girl went missing from the grounds two days ago."

"A girl - just any girl?"

"One of the housemaids', a pretty young thing called Laura. She had only been working here a short time before she vanished."

"And the guns?"

"Did I mention 'pretty young thing'?" The butler glared. "The General is concerned she was abducted, and as there are a lot of other girls working in the house, they could be in danger too."

"No," I said.

"No?"

"Young girls are more likely to run off with a young boy or a thousand other flighty reasons that take their fancy, so a simple disappearance does not explain the guns. What is really going on? And please do take that as a direct question about the disappearance of Shelby Lydekker."

"I am not sure…"

"I am assuming you have worked for the General for some years. Is there any time in your lengthy employment that the General did not mean what he said? For example, when he specifically ordered you to answer any of my questions if they involved the disappearance?"

"There have been threats," the butler relented. "We are just taking precautions."

"There are precautions, and then there's an encamped army walking guard around the house. To me, this indicates you guys are taking this threat a little more seriously - so spill!"

The butler seemed to deflate a little as he took a seat by the table. "The General was the highest officer overseeing the occupation of Japan after the war. You have to remember things were extremely bleak and chaotic then, and the changes the US imposed on the culture of the country meant a lot of people were very unhappy."

"Are you saying we might be attacked by ninjas? Because that would be seriously fun." I grinned.

"How do you know about ninjas? No one outside of Japan has

heard about them."

"I've been around. Now answer the question."

"We are not sure who sent the threat. The General helped develop the new voting system designed to empower Japanese women, and many traditional Japanese men were angry over this decision. He later oversaw the investigation into war crimes, so families of the men sent to the firing squads were angry about that. He closed down a number of the more aggressive military companies to ensure they could never begin the country's rearmament process, so a lot of formerly rich Japanese businessmen became upset about that. He also oversaw the trials of American troops accused of crimes such as theft and rape, so..."

"Yeah, yeah, I get it. The General has enemies on both sides of the Pacific."

The butler rose and headed towards the door. As an afterthought he said, "Dinner is at seven."

With two hours to kill, I left my room and climbed the stairs to the top level. I could kid myself that I was being sleuthful and looking for clues, but the truth is that I was hoping to find the owner of the face I had seen earlier.

There were fewer rooms on the top level due to the slope of the roof, and curiously, all showed little use, including the one I believed the girl had been occupying. This room was the largest, and all the furniture lay under protective sheets. There was thick dust on the window sill and the wooden floorboards, and though I am not the investigator, my partner, the old snake is. Even I could see there were no footprints or traces of anyone walking through the chamber in this dust. No one had been here in years.

Walking over to the window, I was keen to check if this was the room I had seen the girl in, and sure enough, along the floor behind me, I left a trail of footprints, confirming my earlier observation. Looking out the window, I saw the same girl down in the garden watching me. When she was sure I had seen her, she ran off around the side of the house. My natural instinct was to give chase, but I realised by the time I got downstairs, she would be long gone. I had other tricks I could call upon later to find her if need be.

This triggered a thought, and around the window, I began inhaling deeply through my nose to find any trace of the girl's scent. When I detected nothing, I cocked an ear towards the house and listened carefully. When I was sure nobody was nearby, I changed.

Amun has asked me many times what it feels like to transform into my wolf form, and I have to admit I have never answered him truthfully. The pain as bones warp, enlarge, skin splits and regrows as my body transforms, the reshaping of teeth and organs, the enlarging of the jaw...honestly, it's like being torn apart by wolves.

But the pain lasts for only a moment, and then...well, then there is total freedom. When the wolf takes over, the world becomes a different place. Vision is less important, and the planet becomes an enticing kingdom of scents and sounds. Heightened senses reveal paths that are totally invisible to humanity. Scent trails last for hours and appear like the proverbial yellow brick road to the wolf, drawing me further and further into the mind of the predator.

The problem is the wolf has its own agenda, to feed, to hunt, to mate. This is useful at times, but not in a house full of strangers. As my usual backup to keep me under control was not here, I had to be very careful about how much I allowed the wolf to take over. Thinking of the girl, I realised Amun could not get here soon enough.

Instead, I only partially turned. Half the pain for half the abilities, but these were still enough to follow a scent that was only hours old. This change was also easier on my clothes. I watched my hands transform until they were slightly larger and hairier than normal, with curved claws replacing fingernails. My vision also became sharper, as did my hearing. I could perceive almost everything in the house, including the birds nesting in the ceiling and a family of rats behind the wall. These I could smell. I also recognised the dust of age, the scent of the butler on my clothes, and I knew there would be roast lamb with rosemary for dinner. The only thing I could not smell was the lovely young lady who had been standing by this window just hours earlier.

Changing back, I waited until the wolf was entirely gone before heading downstairs. There was no one on the stairwell or the foyer, so I headed out and curiously unlocked the front door into the garden beyond. At the far end, a gardener worked on a flower bed, with a gun propped next to him. The man gave me a long, hard stare before returning to his toil. It would seem the General was true to his word, and all the staff had been forewarned of my presence. Otherwise, that gun would be currently aimed at my head.

Crunching along the white pebble path lined with paper mâché witches' heads and hissing black cats, to the section of the garden where I had seen the girl, I looked for any sign of her. There was nothing, but as my senses were currently only a little better than a normal human's, that did not really mean anything. As it was too public a space to try anything else, I gave up on searching for her now, storing the idea away as something for later when it was dark and perfect for skulking.

I could not help but chuckle to myself that I had come looking for a missing fiancé and was now chasing a mysterious, disappearing woman.

Dinner turned out to be a strange affair. The General was positioned at the head of a large dining table, and about him sat the estate's staff. I was surprised how many there were; but it was logical that such a large estate required a lot of upkeep, especially if there were any commercial enterprises going on here such as farming, horse breeding, or any of the other 'hobbies' rich people have to either remain rich or spend their way into destitution.

I did not see the cooks during the meal, only the waiting staff. I assumed they ate once the household meals were finished. Notably missing from the table was Miss McQueen. The general's daughter and bride-to-be was not eating with us it seemed, and though I wanted to ask why, with so many curious eyes turning my way, then diverting when I caught them, I felt it was a question that could wait.

Eating was a sombre affair. No one conversed, possibly because the General had no time for the small talk of those who worked for him. I was happy to go along and made sure I sat, ate, used the correct utensil for the proper course, and even managed to chew with my mouth closed. I will admit to waiting until most people had been served, leaving only the bloodiest, rarest slices of lamb, which I piled on my plate. Once a wolf, always a wolf.

As I was sopping up the remaining blood on my empty plate with a piece of bread, and the serving staff started bringing out pots of tea and coffee, the General finally spoke.

"Chase has informed me that he told Mr. Vulk here about the threats we have been receiving. I have been contemplating the possibility that these are connected to the missing Mr. Lydekker. If anyone has any idea as to why all this has been occurring, or by who, understand I am telling you it is your duty to inform Mr. Vulk."

I raised my hand as a child would in class.

"Yes, Mr. Vulk?" The General asked.

"Who is Chase?"

Night had well and truly fallen by the time I walked outside and into the garden to do a little primeval investigating. Instead, I found the General, who was puffing on an enormous stogie like it was the last one on earth.

"Mr. Vulk," he said.

"Sorry General, I did not mean to disturb. I was just taking some air."

He took a lengthy drag, and the glowing tip illuminated a face deep in contemplation. As he exhaled a long column of smoke, he said. "Your theory is a bit of a stretch, but I admit it does fit."

"How seriously do you take the threats you have been receiving?"

The General took a long pull on his cigar and then let the smoke out into the night air. "How do you take any threat seriously? Some would argue the loudest and most demanding are the least likely to follow through as they have already vented much of their frustration. It is the quiet, less insistent that you need to watch out for as they are holding on to their fury until it one day explodes."

"So you…?"

"…have learnt over a very long career fighting my country's enemies that you strategize for what you can do, plan for what they might be able to achieve, and keep vigilant and ready to react to whatever you have not thought of."

"I will take that as you are concerned about at least some of the threats."

In the window on the top floor, I noticed that lovely face looking down on me once again. Though it was dark, I was sure she was scowling. "That reminds me, I will need to talk to your daughter at some stage."

"That may take some doing, but I will try and arrange it. Ever since Shelby disappeared, my daughter has isolated herself from the rest of the household. The staff was kind enough to decorate the house in all this," he said, gesturing to the Halloween ornaments all about us. "Halloween is her favourite time of year, but nothing has worked. I tried to sneak a doctor in to see her a few days ago to check her wellbeing, but she discovered the ruse and flew into a rage, demanding we all leave her alone."

"I assume she has to eat?"

"The only person she was talking to was the girl Laura, who brought meals up to Jean's room, stayed and chatted while she ate, and then brought down the empty plates. Since Laura went missing, anyone who tries to talk to her now gets something thrown at their head."

"Sounds like you're talking from experience."

The General laughed, more at the memory I believe, than my question. "Softball. Jean always had one hell of an arm."

He then dropped his cigar to the ground, crushed it with a heel, and walked inside without another word. I looked up, and the window was once again empty.

Walking deeper into the dark garden, I waited until all was clear and then crept over to the spot where I had seen the girl earlier. Checking to see if I was watched, I lowered myself into a shadow behind a large rosebush and transformed into my partial wolf form. The garden cloaked in night was suddenly as clear as on a bright sunny day, and the scents of the world flooded my senses. I could smell the flowers, the birds sleeping in the distant trees, a number of rodents here and there, and even a rabbit eating the General's lettuce. I winced at the overpowering smell of fertiliser on the roses, as well as the General's foul cigar. What I could not detect was the girl, not her perfume or any special aromatic soap, nor the detergent that kept that dress oh-so-white. I could discern many other scents, but none of them belonged to a young woman.

I changed back, stood up and walked inside. It was useless to head back upstairs to the window. Twice now, I had not found the girl's scent in the places I knew she had been, so there was little chance of a third time being the charm.

When the staff was not working, they spent their time in the mansion's game room, shooting pool and playing cards. Entering the room, I received several dirty looks, some curious glances, and a blank stare or two. Some of the maids were in the far corner, listening to the radio, so I headed over. From the large cloth cover speaker, I heard the distinct voice of Orson Welles.

"...in the early years of the twentieth century, this world was being watched closely by an intelligence greater than man's and yet as mortal as his own. We know now that as human beings busied themselves about their various concerns, they were scrutinized and studied, perhaps almost as narrowly as a man with a microscope might scrutinize the transient creatures that swarm and multiply in a drop of water. With infinite complacency, people went to and fro over the earth about their little affairs, serene in the assurance of their dominion over this small spinning fragment of solar driftwood which by chance or design man has inherited out of the dark mystery of Time and Space. Yet across an immense ethereal gulf, minds that to our minds as ours are to the beasts in the jungle, intellects vast, cool and unsympathetic, regarded this earth with envious eyes and slowly and surely drew their plans against us."

It would seem the local station was replaying the Mercury Theatres infamous version of War of the Worlds for Halloween. When the program went to an advertisement, I approached the ladies and gifted them with a smile. There were four of them, and judging their uniforms, two worked in the kitchen, one was a maid and the other possibly in the laundry, her still-pruned red hands and the scent of detergent on her clothes was a dead giveaway.

"Mind if I join you lovely ladies?"

"Please do," the youngest said, indicating the empty chair next to her.

"If any of you were responsible for dinner, my heartiest congratulations," I said, planting myself deep in the offered seat.

The smiles that spread on the cooks' faces gave me the answer to that.

"The lamb wasn't that good. What do you want to know?" This question came from the oldest woman in the group. She gave me a stone-dead glare as she picked up a mug of tea and sat back, continuing to eye me over the steaming liquid as she blew across its surface to cool it.

"Actually, the lamb was great, but fair point. I am here to dig up the dirt, or get the skinny, or however they say it on those radio private eye shows."

"Then get to it, so we can start talking about you once you leave."

This woman was a tough one. "Were any of you close to Laura?"

The ladies all shook their heads while looking about to check the answer of the others. The younger cook said, "She had not been here that long, though she did strike up a pretty quick friendship with Miss McQueen."

"That girl has never had any friends," the second cook

admitted. "Sheltered from the world here, with a domineering father who was never home, along with a mother who died when she was a child - is it any wonder she attached herself to the first person her age she had more than passing contact with?"

"Hey!" said the younger girl.

"Please, Charlotte. You're so desperate to find a husband that you scare me sometimes."

Well, that was information that could save me some trouble in the future.

"What killed Mrs. McQueen," I asked, trying not to make it sound too invasive of a question. Clearly, I was not subtle enough as the ladies looked around, threatening each other with silences and killer stares. It was obvious besides the order from the General to answer my questions, a second instruction had been issued on what subjects were strictly not to be talked about. It was time for a retreat, so I wished everyone a goodnight and headed for bed.

Over the next two days, little happened. Halloween came and went with barely a recognition, yet no one seemed ready to remove all the decorations. I questioned the staff members I could find, and they all said mostly the same thing. All agreed the relationship between daughter and father was messed up. Jean had grown up while her father, the world-famous general, was overseas fighting, making them now less of a family and more two total strangers living in the same house sharing a last name. The daughter had been raised by nannies, and the General had done little more than command men, so they had nothing in common and very little chance of connecting when the General finally returned home.

I did receive a phone call from Amun during this time. My

absent partner had finally arrived in LA and was about to head out to the house. I asked him to hold off and use his numerous connections to find any background on the house and staff. Something was definitely going on here, and we likely needed an outside source to figure it out. Why you ask? When a dozen people give almost the identical answer to a question, it's time to investigate. I have clearly spent far too much time around Amun, who is suspicious of the sun's motives for rising every day.

My partner agreed and promised to come to the estate the instant he had anything of use. Meanwhile, I got to work at what I did best. I waited until everyone was asleep, except for the guard stationed at the front gate, who would be in no position to see what I was up to. I walked outside and was about to turn into my partial wolf form when the hairs on the back of my neck stood up. Most people ignore or misinterpret this sensation, claiming 'someone had just walked over their grave' or some other odd adage for what they were feeling. They forget humans are animals at their primitive core, and animal senses are hard-wired to alert their owner when something is wrong.

I turned about and saw the girl at the far end of the garden, next to a large equipment shed. This time I decided to take control of the situation and gave her a friendly wave. It was hard to tell at this distance, but the girl seemed at first to be taken aback by this - and then her right hand slowly rose, and she gave me a short, quick wave back. I swear she was smiling.

We both stood there like two idiot children in the playground who liked each other but were unsure if they should try for a kiss or strike out with a kick to the shins. The spell was finally broken when the girl raised a finger and gave me the 'come hither' sign.

As I walked over, that object of all men's desire disappeared around the corner of the building. By the time I reached the spot she had been standing, the girl had made her way to the way to a grove of young trees, likely being grown to create a privacy barrier between the street and that side of the house.

The minx had the nerve to give me a cutesy little wave when I saw her. I wanted to believe it was a 'come-and-catch-me' wave, but I really was trying to keep my mind on the job until Amun arrived. Once the old snake was here, I would be free to answer as many come-hither looks as I wanted, but until then, I was a rock.

The small pebble path had recently been raked, and the grass on either side was slightly wet with dew. The paper mâché witch that had been populating this part of the garden was looking rather soggy and worse-for-wear. I mention this because I am not exactly slow, and still, the girl had just covered almost twice the distance I had walked, yet the pebble path was still perfectly manicured, and there were no footprints in the grass. If she had run, which she must have done, there was no evidence of it.

I will admit I had been starting to think everyone had been lying and that the General did not have one daughter, but twins and both were playing the old bait-and-switch prank on me.

Yeah, I did not believe it either.

I looked hard at the girl, who returned my earlier surprise move with one of her own. She did a little pirouette, ensuring I got a good look at her from all angles. I laughed as she next lifted her right leg before her left thigh, cocked her elbows, dropped her head backwards and in an 'exit-stage right' gesture, ducked behind the trees.

I jogged down the path, searching for any sign of her passage, but found nothing. It took next to no time to reach the exact spot the girl had been, and-surprise-surprise, she had disappeared again. I do not mean that she was standing somewhere else. I mean, there was no sign nor scent of her at all. Stranger still, there was nothing she could be hiding behind. There were no buildings, and as far as I knew, no gate anywhere near the distant wall that revealed the border of the garden some hundred feet away. Even if there was, this meant a wisp of a girl in a long flowing dress had run this distance and ducked out of sight in the short time it had taken me to move from the shed to the trees. And all this without leaving a footprint or any scent whatsoever. This girl could either fly or tunnel like a mole.

Now, there was a thought. I had been thinking like a predator, not like prey. Old houses like this one often had older foundations, sewers, water pipes, secret corridors, and the like. Perhaps there was nothing supernatural about this at all, nor the need for a mystery, until-now the never documented twin. Maybe the girl was simply playing a very good game of hide and seek.

I stood in the shadow of the trees, hiding my outline from anyone looking this way and shielding my eyes from the low light filtering into the dark garden. Once sure I was not being observed and that no one was about to walk down the path, I initiated the transformation into my part-wolf form.

Once again, everything became crystal clear and the scent of the night flooded my nostrils, hitting my system like a direct bolt of adrenaline. I detected no scent of the girl, so there was no path to follow to some hidden tunnel entrance. That, of course, did not mean there was not one to find.

I began systematically searching the garden for the girl or a hidden tunnel entrance. I was almost certain I would pick up the musky, partially rotting smell of a submerged tunnel filled with damp dirt and foliage, yet again, I found nothing.

Well, nothing was not exactly true. What I did find was a very old blood trail. It was faint, and if there had been rain in the last week or so, I doubt even I would have been able to find it. The blood that led towards the distant wall was so old and indistinct that I could not discern if it was heading from the garden to the wall or from the wall to the garden. Why would anyone drip a line of blood into the garden or towards the wall though? I could understand if it was towards the house, as this could be explained by someone injured looking for help - but into the garden or away from the main house?

Snuffling my way to the estate's boundary, I easily found the spot where whoever had been bleeding passed over the wall. I looked around, made sure I was still alone, then leant back onto my heels and sprang over.

I located the blood trail on the other side, inspected the lay of the land with a predator's eye, and looked straight into the face of the girl. She stood some distance away, her eyes - almost hidden under her brown, curly hair - were wide, a hand covering her mouth in a gesture of shock at my werewolf form. Before I could react, she took a step back into a distant tree line and disappeared.

As the scent of old blood led directly to where she had stood, I trotted over and again found no sign of the girl - well, not that girl anyway. About ten feet into the trees, I found what was left of the blood trails owner. By the scent, state of decomposition and her clothes, I assumed the body belonged to the missing maid, Laura. Though animals had dug up the body from its shallow grave and been feeding on the carcass, I could see that her throat had been cut.

I sniffed around the corpse, and though there were a number of other scents associated with the body, none seemed to be specific enough to point towards the killer. A cold shudder ran down my back when I started to think about what had just occurred. My mystery girl had just led me directly to this murder or at least pointed the way for me to follow and find it.

If she knew about the body, why had she not said something earlier or reported it herself? There was definitely something going on here, and until I knew what, I would have to be on my guard.

After gathering the information, I turned and loped back, leapt over the wall and re-entered the garden. I transformed and walked up the path to the house. I took the front steps as quietly as possible and opened the still unlocked front door slowly, making sure it did not creak on its hinges. I had noticed most of the windows had gone dark since I had left, meaning many in the household had gone to bed.

Once inside, I closed the heavy door as quietly as possible. Before moving, I stopped and listened. In the distance, I could hear the baker hard at work baking bread and rolls for the coming day.

I did not want to invite any unwanted attention to my nightly hunt as there was likely a killer in this house who I did not want to know what I was up to. I headed up the stairs and back to my room. As I turned to close the bedroom door, someone came out of the shadows and hit me in the head. Though I had not smelt anyone hiding in the room, they were unlucky as my hearing was sensitive enough to detect the weapon swoosh through the air.

Thanks to this warning, I managed to duck enough to be struck only by a glancing blow, but this was still hard enough to stagger me. My stomach churned, my knees wobbled, and I dropped to all fours. I tried to suck in a deep breath to get some oxygen into my blood, hoping to focus and stay conscious. With a great deal of effort, I managed to raise my head and looked into the face of a demon. My mind froze on the image of horns on the head and a big, almost sympathetic smile as the demon grew closer, raised something high above its head, and brought it down with great speed. A bright light exploded behind my eyes, and then I fell into a pool of darkness.

I woke up to windows full of sunlight and the old guardsmen from the front gate sitting in a chair along the wall. Across his knees was the shotgun he always carried.

"That for me?"

"This," he said, hefting the weapon, "is in case whoever tried to give you a second mouth on the back of your neck comes back."

"You mean the...." I stopped and held my head as though I was overcome by a sudden pain. It was probably not the best idea to start spouting about demons and evil twins and hidden tunnels and a dead body on the other side of the fence until I understood more about what was going on. "They really did a number on me."

"I thought you were going to die. I've seen men during the

war that had lesser wounds never come back to the land of the living."

"Was that the American Revolution you fought in there, old-timer?"

"Smartass. And to think I was about to go and get you some water. You'd thrown up a few times before we found you, so that must be a terrible taste you have there in your mouth."

"Water would be great."

"I'm sure it would," the guard said, getting out of his chair. "Me, I'm going to report to the General that you ain't dead."

I sat up slowly and felt my head. The wound was gone, and in truth, I felt perfectly fine. If anyone came in for an inspection, it could prove a little tricky to explain why the gash had healed so quickly. I decided to waddle out to the toilet located down the corridor and along the way, bumped into the young maid. Charlotte gave me a beaming smile and asked if I was ok. I admitted I had a bit of a headache and a bump under my shaggy brown mop of hair, but otherwise, I was right as rain.

After washing my mouth out and rinsing away as much dried blood from the back of my neck and shoulders as I could, I headed back into the corridor. Here I found Charlotte still waiting. She had placed a tray of water and food in my room and had an armful of blood-stained sheets from my bed. The amount of blood and the look on her face told me that she was concerned. So before she could launch into anything, I tried a subtle ancient form of distraction. I asked her a question she was not expecting.

"For the last few days, I have seen a girl around the house and gardens wearing a white dress. For a while, I assumed it was Miss

McQueen. As of yet, I haven't the chance to meet the young lady. I don't want to assume too much."

"Miss Jean?" she said, thinking hard. "I suppose it could have been. She does get around the house, and we never really know where she is or what she's doing."

"The disappearance of Laura hit her that hard, huh?"

"Oh, I doubt that, I mean they seemed pretty friendly at the beginning, but just before Laura went missing, things had cooled between them."

"Laura did something?"

"Not so much Laura as Mr. Lydekker…" Charlotte did not get to finish what she was saying as a voice bellowed her name. '…it's Estelle."

The older maid, who had been less than pleased to chat to me in the game room, walked to the top of the stairs and began pointing back down in the direction she had just come from.

"You got work to do girl, so get to it and leave Mr. Vulk alone."

"There is no problem, we are just talking," I said.

"Downstairs Charlotte," Estelle demanded, ignoring me.

The girl looked as though she was about to curtsey, but instead, she gave me a quick smile and ran down the stairs.

Estelle turned her attention back to me. "You should be in bed."

"I'm fine, just needed to clean up. I intend to go clean that tray of all the food and water on it and see how I feel then."

"Good," she said and turned to leave.

"Before you go, a question. Who is the girl in the white dress running around the estate?"

I swear the woman turned pale. She looked at me for some time, as though debating whether to answer or not, before following Charlotte down the stairs.

There was definitely something wrong in this house.

After I ate and drank, I did feel a lot better. My metabolism was fired up - having repaired what was likely a fractured skull - so it needed sustenance to get me back to peak performance.

I was determined to no longer stumble around in total ignorance, so I headed for the library. Previously I had seen a number of photos on the wall, and now I wanted to get a closer look at just who was in those images.

No one was downstairs, though I could hear people at work in the distance. I walked into the library as though I owned the place and began my search. The first photo I saw was of a much younger general with his arm around a woman that looked remarkably familiar.

I kept searching and found a second photo of the girl. This one was a studio shot of her looking her best - her brown, curly hair framing a warm, almost playful smile I found haunting. Next to this was a third photo containing the General and the girl holding a young child in her arms.

"You really are sticking your nose everywhere," the old guard said from the library door.

"The McQueen family, I presume?" I took the photo off the wall and carried it over.

"Happier days. The General had not been burnt out by the war, and both were excited by the arrival of their first child. The world really did seem to be a brighter place back then."

"War and death have a nasty habit of making people see the darker side of life. When did Sharon McQueen die?"

"The General was not a general in the late 20s. He was a captain and stationed in China, then later Nicaragua," the guard said, recalling his master's biography. "Mrs. McQueen died about a year or so after he returned."

"Of...?"

"Car accident," he said quickly. "She was driving home when some idiot ran her off the road."

"So, Jean must have only been..."

"...about three at the time."

"And Miss McQueen, today she is about this tall, brown curly hair, looks a lot like this?" I asked, holding up the photo of her mother.

"I had never thought much about it, but yes, Miss Jean does look a lot like her mother."

I returned the photo to the wall. "I assume you came looking for me for some reason?"

"The General was pleased to hear you had not died last night, and he has asked when you might be finished with your investigation?"

"You can tell the General I will be done once my partner has arrived and tells me that I am done. He is the real investigator; I'm more of what you would call a leg-man."

"I'm a leg-man myself," the old guard said, giving me a leery wink. It seems I was not the only old dog in the house.

It was after dinner that night that I saw my mysterious girl again. I was standing at the top of the bannister in the main hall, and down below there she was, smiling and swirling about in her dress as though on a beach somewhere warm. She looked up and once more gave me the come-hither finger. Two can play at this game, so in return, I raised an eyebrow and looked quizzical.

She skipped out of the hallway, then suddenly peaked back around the corner and poked her tongue out at me. I admit it; I could not help myself. I laughed out loud. This girl was real trouble.

I followed downstairs and into the hallway. She was nowhere to be seen, but there was a door at the far end that I was positive as I headed out to the back of the house.

Outside there were a number of buildings and the young woman beckoning me towards a different section of the wall. No surprise, by the time I reached the same spot, she was gone. What I found instead was a young houseman acting as guard and walking the perimeter.

"Did you see a young girl run past, about yea tall and wearing a white dress?"

The lad looked at me like I had grown a second head. "Recently?" he asked.

"Yes, like in the last minute. She likely climbed over this wall," I said.

"Why would she climb over the wall? There's a gate just over there."

I looked where the guard was pointing, sure enough, there was the gate.

"So, she went through there?"

"Who?"

I gave him my dirtiest look. "The girl...and before you say what girl, forcing me to punch you very hard, I am going to leave now and walk through that gate over there." I turned and walked through the gate.

On the other side of the wall, I found the girl. She was dancing around a tree, flicking her dress around like a butterfly. When she saw me, she gave me a little wave. I was smiling like a loon when the guard, who had followed me through the gate, asked:

"Why are you smiling?"

I looked at him, then back into the very empty field containing trees and exactly zero pretty women dancing around them.

"Just...recalling someone."

I walked over to the tree the girl had been dancing around and stubbed my toe on a rock. Frustrated and confused at what was happening, I kicked at the stone.

A piece of bone went pinwheeling through the air.

"What the hell?" the guard yelled as the projectile sailed past his ear.

The General stood by, chomping his cigar like a dog with a snake as he looked at the box of bones the staff had dug up before I asked them to stop and call the police. These had arrived about three hours later and started barricading the area.

"Any idea who she is?" he asked.

We had figured 'she' was a woman by the clothes and the

small locket around the neck. I looked at the General and shook my head.

"Is that an 'I have no idea' shake of the head, or an 'I have an idea, but not one-hundred percent sure' nod of the head?" This was from my long-absent partner, Amun Galeas, as he walked over to the grave. He was a darkly handsome, impeccably groomed man who somehow looked younger than me, yet he had walked the earth forever…well, I say 'walked'.

"It's an "I have no idea' nod," I said, taking my oldest friend's proffered hand and shaking it warmly. "About time you got here."

"Seems you have been doing alright without me. I assume it was you who found this body?"

"Yeah, this body," I said. I was worried Amun might miss the subtlety of the exactness of that. I need not have worried as he gave me a 'we shall talk later' look.

Having never said a word, the General returned to the house in a puff of cigar smoke, leaving the police technicians to exhume the remains. I took Amun aside and explained, "There's another body hidden amongst the trees on the other side of the estate, a body nowhere near as old as this. I cannot be sure, but I think it might be the missing maid."

"Missing maid? How many people have disappeared from the house?"

"Well, I am hoping you are about to tell me that. What did you find out in your search?"

"The police do not have the missing maid story if that's what you're asking. They, of course, know about the missing Lydekker boy. I did find a report about the disappearance of another maid around fifteen years ago, just a few days after the murder of Sharon McQueen."

"The General's wife was murdered?" I was taken aback by that news. It seems people had been lying to me about that important little point, leading me to ponder what else they have been lying about.

"We calling Detective Raskin and his investigators in yet?" Amun asked.

"Not just yet, I have a plan to try and shake this all up."

Dinner that night was a sombre affair. The food was good, but no one seemed to have much stomach for it except for the men, many of whom were veterans of the war and had learnt to eat no matter what gruesome activities were going on around them. The General did not eat with us, and again there was no sign of his daughter, but the old man did appear later to take tea - a habit I daresay he picked up while stationed in England. Though I was still investigating, I had agreed that Amun should take the lead when it came to the General. It was Amun that had been asked to investigate the disappearance of Shelby Lydekker, and things would likely go a little smoother if he dealt with the Lord of the Manor, leaving me free to continue interrogating the staff.

I am pleased to say what came next was my idea. Before everyone departed for the evening, Amun asked the General if we could interview them one at a time. The interviews would not take long, but they were going to be important.

The General did not like the idea and liked it even less when we explained we could not tell him why. He looked as though he was about to refuse when Amun reminded him Raskin had yet to be informed about the dead body we had discovered today. With a murder on the estate, the Detective would likely camp in the General's life until he found some answers. The old snake is subtle when he wants to be and more than capable of bludgeoning someone between the eyes with the truth when he needs to.

Needless to say, the General agreed.

We set up in a small room off the library, displaying the most recognisable parts of the clothes and the locket from the dead woman on a table. One by one the staff came through, and one by one they left, admitting they did not recognise the items.

I had told Amun to leave the old guard and Estelle Porter for last, as they were the only staff members who'd been here before the war. I will be fair and say the guard gave the items a good look before admitting he had no idea who they belonged to. Grumpy Estelle, however – well, she was a different story.

When the maid walked in and saw the clothes, she gasped, but the clincher was the locket. When Estelle saw that, she burst into tears and slumped to the floor. We helped her into a seat, and once she had managed to calm herself, she admitted everything belonged to her sister Agnes.

The dead woman had been Jean's nanny, and she had disappeared a few days after the death of the girl's mother. The General originally explained that Agnus had run away with the estate's chauffeur, a man called Troy Hemsworth, along with a substantial amount of McQueen's money. When confronted with this, Estelle explained she had always doubted the story because, even with the guilt and shame of the theft, Agnes would have contacted someone in the family, yet in all these years, no one had ever heard a single word from her.

I was keen to press for more, but Charlotte entered the room to tell Estelle she was needed upstairs. This was clearly code for something likely to do with Miss McQueen and was bound to be the only thing that would have called her away immediately from her sister's remains.

Looking back on things, I wish we had been more insistent on getting all we could have before Estelle left.

Chase the butler had placed Amun in the room next to mine, and once everyone had gone to bed that night, I was at his door, tapping gently. He answered, fully dressed, and we both headed downstairs and into the garden. We slipped over the wall behind the shed and ducked across the field to the treeline beyond. Here we inspected the first body I had found by torchlight. Once Amun was done having a look, I asked him to keep an eye out for anyone and changed into my partial werewolf form.

The world was likely about to end because I'd had more than one idea.

Once the transformation was done, I ran about the grove, sniffing at every tree and bush like a dog in a desperate need to pee. Once I had covered this area, and having found nothing of interest, we walked around the outside of the wall to the back of the estate, where I had found the older body. I led the way as pregnant clouds overhead threatened to drench us and shrouded the moon. Amun had decent eyesight in the dark, but nothing compared to my wolf vision, and we needed to ensure we did not bump into anyone as our presence would be hard to explain. A man taking his werewolf out for a walk was likely not an excuse anyone was going to believe.

Encountering no one, we made our way to the second grave and again, once Amun was satisfied, I made a systematic search of the area. This time it took no time to recognise the sickly-sweet smell of decaying flesh.

With clawed hands, I dug at the ground and soon had a number of bones unearthed. These were from someone far larger than Agnes, and Amun agreed with me they belonged to a man who had died maybe 18 years ago. It would seem Troy Hemsworth had not run away with the General's money and Agnes after all. Not that this news was surprising.

I changed back, waited until the desires of the predator had cleared my head, and then turned to Amun. "So, we began with a missing fiancé and now have four murders."

"Five," Amun said.

I thought about that number for a while. It hit me like a sledgehammer. "Mrs. McQueen."

Amun nodded. "And five is the number we know of. It's not at all obvious what is going on here, a killer who strikes every 18 years, now that is a very strange quantity of time."

"I have not told you the half of it," I finally admitted. "I have been keeping this to myself, but I think there is something happening with the daughter."

"You better explain that," Amun said.

"I have been seeing a pretty young girl everywhere." He gave me the evil eye.

"Not like that." I snarled. "This girl showed me where the bodies were hidden before disappearing."

"'Went into hiding,' you mean?"

"No, I mean totally disappeared. I thought there might be hidden tunnels and passageways between the house and the outer buildings, but I have found nothing. Also, not once I have been able to detect her. She leaves no scent anywhere."

"Well, that is unusual?"

"Not if there is something magic or supernatural going on. Often, whatever or whoever has been cast invisible and kept hidden from the supernatural as well as the natural."

"You think she's...actually...I'm not sure what you're thinking."

"Neither am I, just informing you about another strange mystery in the house."

"Anything else?" Amun asked suspiciously.

"Yeah, I was attacked by a demon last night. It almost took my head off."

My partner looked at me as though waiting for the punchline. I did not offer one. Any further conversation was then ended by a piercing scream from the main house. We were both up and running along the grass path beaten flat by those working on the second grave, through the gate in the backyard fence, and into the house. I saw my girl again as we ran, still dressed in white, but this time I was too preoccupied to wave hello.

Inside we found Estelle on the marble floor in the front foyer, the blood pooling under her body evidence she had likely fallen from the top bannister. I tried to get close to the body, but the concerned staff flooding into the stairwell kept me well back. I looked up, right into the eyes of the girl. She looked heartbroken and gave me a pleading gesture that I could not interpret. I fought the urge to run up the stairs, grab her, fold her in my arms and shield her from the world. This woman I had never said a single word to was the closest thing to a relationship I'd enjoyed in years, and yet I remained rooted to the spot, watching as she backed away from the bannister and disappeared into the gloom of the house.

I looked at Amun, who was watching me with concern. I nudged my head towards the top bannister, and he followed my gaze before giving me a weird little nod.

I am not the investigator Amun is. He can take the thousands of small threads and snippets of information we uncover and tie them into a bow and point out who, why, and where the criminal is. My nature is more wolfish, a predator that hounds and charges and snaps with fang and claw until its prey is subdued - yet I felt I finally had an idea how to find our killer. If, and I do stress 'if', the killer had pushed Estelle off the bannister, it was almost a certainty I would be able to detect their scent on the body unless of course, my girl was the murderer.

An ambulance was called for, and the police arrived to investigate. This time Detective Dana was with them and upon arrival, he took us both aside once the technicians started fussing about the body. The policeman asked us straight out if it was murder.

"I'm pretty sure it was," I said.

"And you?" he asked Amun.

"Hey, I've been here less than a day. If Vulk says it was likely murder, it likely was. He knows what's going on here more than I do."

"I need to ask a favour - actually two, now that I think about it," I said to the Detective. "Keep the suggestion of murder under your hat and the body here for a time. I think if the murderer believes they got away with it, we may have a chance of finding out who they are. The pressure of the body still on sight may also cause a paranoid reaction to the situation."

"That's a lot to ask," Dana said with a stern look.

"It's all I have right now." I had considered asking about the chance of being alone with the corpse for a while, but having just watched the policeman's reaction to my first suggestion, decided against it. It did not help that I could not come up with an angle better than 'If you give me five minutes alone with the body, I will slip into my werewolf form, sniff the corpse and hopefully catch the murderer.'

"What is the second thing?" Dana asked.

"Can you use your badge to get us an interview with the General's daughter? We have a few questions to put to her, and the household seems keen to keep us away." See, I can think quickly when I need to.

Dana had a word with the technicians. Afterwards, instead of bagging the body and taking it away to the morgue, they erected a tent around it and claimed they had tests to perform before disturbing the scene. The tent was to keep the gruesome scene out of the view of the people who knew the dead woman.

I felt a ping of guilt, as Estelle deserved better than to be used as a chess piece in this game, but the thought that this would hopefully help find her murderer, not to mention the possible killer of her sister, meant it would be all worthwhile.

After hearing about the weird situation of the McQueen family, Dana agreed with our last request and the three of us headed upstairs.

Jean McQueen's quarters took up the entire third floor of the four-floor mansion. Apparently, she had taken over this section of the house after her sixteenth birthday, when she no longer wanted to live in her small, childhood apartment on the second floor. That happened to be the same room I was currently occupying.

We knocked on the main door to Jean's quarters, and Charlotte answered. Dana flashed his badge, and we were shown into a large waiting room filled with chairs, artworks, and a number of statues. We all took a seat, and the girl bustled off into a back room.

I was struck by how impersonal the room was. I admit to having sat in many ladies' waiting rooms, and none felt as sterile as this one.

It wasn't that it was lacking in feminine charm, which it wasn't, but the room just did not feel very personal. There were no photos of family, friends, nor frills, flowers, or anything that would really give the space warmth and a sense of home. Instead, it was stark, as though the furniture and fixings had already been here when the girl moved in, and she had never bothered to change any of it.

After what felt like an hour of communicating with each other through eyebrow raises, nods of the head, and flicking eye lines, the door to the inner sanctum finally opened and a familiar face stepped in.

Jean McQueen was a beautiful girl and wore a flowing, white dress. My breath caught in my throat, but it quickly became evident this was not the girl I had seen everywhere. She had the same face, the same curly brown hair cascading wildly down to her shoulders. It was the eyes - there was absolutely no humour in them, and in fact they were as cold as a shark's; black, deep, haunting. The girl also did not seem to recognise me at all.

I watched Jean closely as she entered the room and shook everyone's hands. Amun looked at me expectantly, probably because I had been the one to suggest we needed to talk to the girl. The only problem with my plan, this was the wrong girl.

Luckily Amun was quick enough to cover my hesitancy. He began by asking Jean about her relationship with Estelle, who it turned out had been more of a mother to her over the years, having taken over looking after the young girl after her nanny, Agnus, had disappeared. The way she talked, it was clear Miss McQueen was unaware of Estelle's death, and we informed her, the news had little effect. She didn't seem to care.

We asked Jean about any noises she may have heard at night, as well as any suspicious people she may have seen hanging around the estate. Did she think an intruder could sneak through the house, and if she'd seen anything unusual over the past few days? The answer was no, yes, no, and no. The suspicious people hanging around the house – well, that turned out to be me, so no help there.

After fifteen minutes of mostly useless questioning, a policeman appeared at the door. He told us the technicians had loaded the body onto a gurney and were ready to transport it to the waiting ambulance outside. We gave our thanks to Miss McQueen for her time, and this lonely, strange girl returned to her rooms.

It was as she left that Amun figured it out. Actually, that's not quite true.

He had been watching the girl carefully, and his questions had been a lot more specific than I realised. He had noted her responses were abnormal, each and every one. She was either evasive or way too specific, both classic avoidance techniques.

When Jean left the room, Amun turned his attention to the young maid. He began asking questions.

"Has Miss McQueen gone through a personality change recently?"

Charlotte thought about this for a while before answering, "I had only been working here a short time before the General came home, so I did not have much contact with Miss McQueen before then."

"But?" I asked. There is always a 'but'.

"The other girls who work here talk. Apparently, she had always been something of a weepy girl, wrapped up in her own little world. But once the General came home, she changed and seemed to get stronger, less emotional. She no longer cried herself to sleep and seemed capable of standing up to her father - something she had never been able to do before he left."

"Where was the General stationed before he came home?" Amun asked.

"Japan," I answered. "He was in charge of a lot of different things, including dealing with crimes against the Japanese by the allied occupation forces."

"Contraband?" Amun asked.

Dana answered. "I would say so, I saw a pretty expensive samurai sword in the library while I was looking around." We both looked at the Detective, who shrugged his shoulders and explained. "I was an MP with the army in Japan. I saw a lot of weapons like that."

Amun turned back to the maid. "Have you ever seen a mask somewhere around the house, one that looks something like a demon, with a big smile and with two little horns on top? It was likely brought home as a souvenir by the General. Maybe someone was wearing it for Halloween?"

The girl looked like we had slapped her in the face.

"How could you know about the mask?" she asked.

"Where is it?" Dana asked, catching on that there was something unusual about the war trophy.

"It went missing about a month ago," Charlotte admitted. "The General was angry and threatened to start firing people until it was returned."

"And it was never found?"

"No."

"Was this about the same time the girl's behaviour changed?" I asked.

"It could not have been that far off. The General returned, and not soon after, things started to change in the house."

"The General, did he get along with Shelby Lydekker?"

"They played chess every night."

Amun stood up and said to Dana and me: "We need to find that mask." He then turned on the girl. "Get the staff. Have them pull this house apart for that damn thing."

The girl ran off, and Amun began to explain. "If I am right, we're dealing with a Hannya - a Japanese demon mask that traps the souls of obsessive or jealous women."

"You mean it was Jean wearing the mask who attacked me?" Dana looked at me with surprise at this news. "Wait, if this Hannya is raised by jealousy, does that mean she also killed her fiancé?"

"Probably."

"So why would she have killed Estelle?" Dana asked.

"That may not matter at the moment," I said, peeking through the girl's slightly open door. "Did anyone see where Jean went?"

We checked her back rooms first. They were as sterile as the waiting room, yet we found no sign of the mask. We then headed downstairs and instructed the staff gathering in the foyer. I noticed someone was missing, which gave me an idea. I turned to Amun and whispered, "You have to cover me."

"Cover you for what?" he whispered back.

Ignoring him, I snuck over to the screen the morgue technicians had erected and stuck my head inside. There was no one there except the body of Estelle on the gurney, so I pushed all the way in. Then when Amun stood between the curtain and the gathered crowd, did a quick change.

The transformation only took a moment, but while it did, I managed to reach out through the pain and unzip the body bag. Once this was done, I shoved my snout into the bag and took a big sniff. The answer hit me like a hammer, so I changed back.

I pushed out from behind the curtain. "We need to find the General."

Up on the next balcony, I caught a glimpse of Jean and then shook my head with the realisation it was not the General's daughter. My girl had returned, though she no longer had the glint of mischief in her eye. She gestured for me to approach, and this time I was not going to ignore her. I ran up the stairs, leaving everyone well behind. By the time I got there, my girl was now standing at the top of the next flight of stairs.

On and on this went until I reached the top floor. Though I could not see my girl anymore, I did hear the sounds of a struggle. I ran into the room where I had first seen her lovely face looking down on me through the window, and there was Jean and the General. The daughter was wearing the Hannya mask and had a knife to her father's throat. From this angle, it looked as though the mask was sad, but once I entered and she faced me, the mask's face became furious.

Amun was next through the door, followed closely by Dana and the rest of the household, who had chased me up the stairs.

"Please let him go?" I asked. The mask looked at me, and I could see the eyes through its drilled, round holes. If it was possible, the eyes were even more lifeless than before. The girl inside the mask was not there anymore; in her place was something older, something far more dangerous. I looked at Amun, and he was clearly seeing it too. Live long enough and you get to recognise the signs.

"Do you know which demon it is?" I asked.

"I think so," Amun admitted. "We have a problem though, traditionally you can only get rid of it with an act of compassion or love."

A movement behind father and daughter caught my eye, and I watched as my girl walked up to the pair. When I saw one of the police officers moving to get behind Jean, I raised a hand to stop him. Everyone began watching me for the reason why, but I was watching as my girl, who I could see the policeman clearly through, leant in and ran a caressing hand down the side of her daughter's face.

The murdered Sharon McQueen, for some reason had remained in the house, watching as her daughter was tortured by indifference and neglect. The fear and protective instincts toward her troubled daughter likely fuelled whatever power was keeping her spirit tied to the mansion. And the appearance of the Hannya mask possibly increased this power to the point that she could physically appear, though I surmised, only to one person.

I watched as my girl lowered her face to Jean's, so both were at eye level. Sharon leaned forward and laid kisses on both of her daughter's eyes; at the same time, she pulled at the mask's horns.

At first, I thought I was seeing things, but after a moment Jean's grip on her father began to loosen, and the mask slipped from her face. There was no stopping my comrades this time, and a number leapt forward, pulling the knife from the girl's hand and her father from her weakening grip.

The police quickly had the girl under control.

Dana reached down and began to help the General to his feet.

"It's ok sir, we have the murderer under control," the detective said.

I looked about but could not see my girl anywhere. I then felt someone holding my hand and looking to the side, there she was, at least the ghostly image of her. Looking back, I like to think Sharon was smiling because she was holding my hand, but instead, I was pretty sure it was because she knew what I was about to do - I was about to save her daughter for the second time today.

"You do have the murderer, Detective. You're holding him."

Everyone looked at me in surprise. This, unfortunately, gave the General the chance he'd been waiting for. In one swift motion, he pushed Dana away and grabbed the Detective's revolver from its holster. He then raised the weapon at me, and I noticed he had picked up the mask with his other hand.

Instantly the sound of gunfire echoed throughout the room, and the General pitched backwards to the floor, stone dead.

We left the distraught Jean crying into Charlotte's shoulder and made sure the General's body was loaded into the morgue wagon. Once we were alone, I turned to Amun, who looked as though he was about to explode.

"Spill!" he growled.

I smiled and launched into my tale. "The General killed Estelle. I could smell him, or more specifically, the cigars he smoked all over her back. The only reason he would have killed her was to keep her from talking."

"About what?"

"How he had murdered his wife and her lover, who also happened to be the father of his daughter, I assume."

"How did you figure that?" Amun asked.

"I can count. He'd been stationed down in Nicaragua in the late 20s, then he came home for a few months before heading overseas to help with America's insertion into the Philippines. His daughter was born a year later."

"Ok, but that does not explain the deaths of Laura and Lydekker."

"No, you explained that. The mask is fuelled by jealous, vengeful women. When Jean got her hands on the mask, she was taken over and her rage fuelled the demon into killing Laura, who had been getting close to her husband-to-be. She later killed her fiancé when he grew close to her father."

"The chess games? Why would that trigger such destructive jealousy?"

"One thing about daughters, they are always looking for the love of their fathers, even estranged ones. Jean had been raised by the mansion's staff, and finally when her father came home to her, she found the General developing an interest in the one person alive that she loved. The mask guaranteed he was dead from that moment on."

"So, we saved her from the mask only to condemn her to prison?"

"I don't think so. I said the General was the murderer; I never specified who he had murdered. His attempt to escape means he will never have to answer for his crimes, and I do mean ALL of his crimes, even the ones he caused but did not physically commit.

"General McQueen caused all of this when he killed his wife. Everything, the hate, the fear, the loneliness, and most of all, the jealousy, it all stems from this one act. And now the only people alive who know the truth are you and me."

Well, what do you know, it turns out I am the kind of investigator that ties it all together at the end after all.

"So, the mask affected him as well?"

"No, he's the true demon in this sad tale. McQueen killed his wife and her lover, Troy Hemsworth, years before he ever went to Japan, where I assume he received the mask as contraband. I am pretty sure he killed his daughter's nanny just a few days after his wife because she had somehow learnt of the murders."

Amun looked at me for a long time. Finally, he asked, "How do we get paid?"

I walked into the library and took the framed photo of my ghost off the wall.

"I have all the payment I want from this family."

Amun must have sensed the dark mood growing inside me as he placed a friendly hand on my shoulder and steered me outside. We walked together, down the white marble stairs and across the stone driveway to his car.

Before I got inside, I took a final look at the window on the top floor, and there she was. Sharon's outline was faint, likely having used up whatever energy had been keeping her tied to the house, but she was there. Sharon McQueen looked happy, and when she blew me a kiss, worded 'Thank you', and then slowly faded from sight, my heart skipped a beat.

When I finally turned and looked at the road before us, the world indeed seemed to be a brighter place.

Author's note.

In my first novel, I wanted to tip my hat to a very influential story, Raymond Chandler's the Big Sleep, and though many elements of this hardboiled detective story made it into my tale, the one thing I could never seem to make work was the romance story. So, when I was asked if I had such a story that could be entered into this collection, I realised here was my chance to fix that omission. There are also elements from other classic noir/romances here, such as Laura. Many of these old movies lay forgotten, and it's my hope people may go back and have a look at these classics and begin to see them for the gems they truly are.

Wherever possible, I try to cement my tales in actual historical occurrences. The career of General McQueen is based on the very real General Matthew Ridgway, who began his career as a soldier in Mexico during WW1. He then followed this with a command in China before heading down to Nicaragua in 1927 to supervise free elections there.

In 1930 Ridgway moved to the Philippines to become an advisor to the US Governor-General there before completing a number of internal army positions back home. Growing in rank, by the time the US entered WW2 in 1942, Ridgway was a major-General with the 82nd Airborne. He fought with his men throughout Europe before being transferred to the Pacific to serve under General Douglas Macarthur. Ridgway eventually assumed the role of military governor in Japan and Supreme Commander for the Allied Powers after Macarthur. In this role, he oversaw the restoration of Japan's independence and sovereignty on April 28,

1952.

The General's crime is loosely based on one Captain Jeffrey Robert MacDonald committed in 1970. This American Green Beret was convicted of murdering his pregnant wife and two daughters, though he claimed a bunch of hippies broke not only into his house but the secure military base the family lived on. These hippies then killed the family, Manson style, before mysteriously disappearing without a trace. It's believed MacDonald actually killed his wife, and then later both children over a domestic fight, possibly over one of his daughters wetting the bed or perhaps from his numerous infidelities over the years.

The Hannya mask is used in Noh theatre and indeed represents a jealous female demon. The name actually means wisdom and is believed to come from the very first artist to perfectly create one of these odd, scowling, grinning masks. It is also just as likely the name explains that an artist would need to be very wise indeed to create one of these masks.

FIRST NIGHT OUT

"On the last of October
When dusk is fallen
Children join hands
and circle round me
singing ghost songs
and love to the harvest moon."
Carl Sandburg "Theme in Yellow"

1.

Rose

Maddie smiled up at me, her goofy grin making her look even younger than she was, fresher and more...not innocent exactly. None of us were, but cleaner somehow, less soiled. After all, this Halloween was her first night out.

It was a tradition among us to take the new recruits out on Halloween night once they had been properly prepared and proven themselves capable of not making a scene or putting themselves in danger. It is often a night of fond memories for us. Every childhood birthday wrapped into one orange and black night. Sweet memories full of falling leaves and ominous fields of corn, paper decorations and costume parties. Every year on October 31st, the world becomes an endless macabre fairy-land, seemingly just for our young.

Halloween was always a special night for us.

I smiled back as Maddie entered the van, taking in her tight black clothing, silver jewelry- her pale makeup with its dark hi-lights. She wore her hair shaved on one side. The other side dyed and striped in red and black, brushed, so it covered one of her dark brown eyes.

I wondered what her real hair color was.

It struck me at that moment how funny it was that so many of us dressed in ways that were considered "odd" or "outsider" before we were taken in. And how many of us kept to the looks we had favored, well past the time that society had moved on. Replacing the new and outre' with something else. Taking our little rebellions and making them either a relic of past times or absorbing them into the woof and warp of the mainstream. I remembered being in Maddie's position, with my short hair and straight dresses, arms exposed. I had been called strange then, and a bit dangerous. But now that look was nothing more than a costume young girls would wear in plays, movies, or parties on nights like tonight when being anything but yourself was praised.

Even though Maddie made me happy, it made me a little sad to look at her, so I turned away.

"How are you doing back there, kid?" James asked from

behind the driver's seat. We had a rule that whoever was driving got to select the music, so the air was full of the chainsaw guitars and bratty snarls of classic punk rock. Once I had gotten used to it, I rather liked James' music, as it reminded me of the energy and rebellious jazz of my youth. Like youth fashion music transformed, but somehow stayed the same.

"I'm great!" Maddie shouted, pumping her gloved hand in the air along with the incessant drums. "I'm so ready for Halloween!"

"Right on!" Michael shouted, matching Maddie's enthusiasm. He had discarded the fashion of his youth as I had, realizing that being "dated" would make us stand out to those who were looking for us, those that meant us harm. He had kept the long hair, though, and the beard. Hippie had become hipster, another change that changed nothing.

"So, what do you want to do tonight?" Shirley asked timidly. She too had toned down from her "before look," but she was still fond of crinolines and saddle shoes when she could get away with them. "Hmm," Maddie said, giving it serious thought.

"We could hit up some parties," James suggested as usual.

"Or maybe see if we can't find a corn maze?" Michael asked.

"Of course, we have to start with the parade.", Shirley chimed in. "It is, after all, a tradition."

She was correct, of course. Since the Village parade started in 1974, we had always begun the night there, among the dancers, brilliant costumes, and giant puppets that filled the streets from Sixth Avenue to Sixteenth street every October 31st.

Maddie nodded, chewing on one of her black-painted nails. I wondered how long she would keep that particular habit.

"Let's go to some haunted houses!" She said, smiling widely, showing off her new teeth. I had cautioned her about that many times during her training but figured that I would stay silent just this once. After all, if there was any day that we could let our strict rules on blending in fade a little, it was Halloween.

2.

We were on the subway when I noticed we were being watched. We had parked the van in Brooklyn, in a neighborhood that we knew would remain safe, among the mischief-makers of Halloween. Even on a normal day, it was far easier and faster to take the B-line train than drive in city traffic, and tonight the roads would be even more of a mess than usual.

I saw our watcher on the other side of our train-car, past a crowd of festively dressed tourists. He was dressed simply in a pair of black camouflage pants and a t-shirt, which lay tight against his muscular frame. He wore a backpack and was pretending to read from an 80s horror paperback, the sort that always had leering skeletons and creepy children on the cover.

I nudged Maddie, using the train's shaking to disguise my movement. I'm sure the others have been at this game long enough to see him, but I wanted to make sure that our newest recruit would not be caught unaware if there was to be trouble.

I see him. Maddie mouthed, turning her head to face me. Eventually, she would be able to communicate with the rest of us psychically, but that was a gift that came with age. It was part of our job as Elders to be patient with the limitations of the young ones.

We kept an eye on the man for the duration of the twenty-minute train ride, hopefully being less obvious than he was. He rarely even turned a page in his book, simply glancing down at it every few moments and staring blankly, then shooting one of us a glance. He seemed especially interested in Maddie. I wondered if we had done something wrong, bringing her over, somehow drawing attention to ourselves.

I hoped not, but it was always a risk to bring in a new one. Children, even adult children, were often missed.

Finally, the train stopped at our station, and we fought through the crowd onto the platform. Since the confusion made our surveillance impossible, we waited until the train was pulling away to search for our friend in black. Quickly, we discovered him, now seated behind the window of the departing train. He hadn't followed us off.

I wondered if this was a good thing.

3.

The parade was fantastic this year, one of the best I'd seen. Costumed people of all stripes cavorted, marching around us while giant puppets danced and twirled through the air. Everywhere we looked, there was something to catch our attention, to engulf us in the Halloween spirit. Here a skeleton played guitar for a group of succubi, there a clown doll bounced on a pogo stick, while a man in leather pants and a chest harness juggled balls shaped like Jack-O-Lanterns. It was a scene out of Ray Bradbury, and I could tell from the permanent smile on her face that Maddie was eating it up.

If I'm being honest, I got drawn in as well. Our enemies had to shroud themselves in almost as much secrecy as us. It would be totally foolhardy of them to strike in a crowd like this. Even if they were inexperienced (and from the man in black's performance, I assumed they were), they wouldn't dare. I wished, for a moment in the chaos, that we too had dressed up for the occasion. To this day, I'm not sure why we didn't. Maybe we recognized deep down that we were already Halloween spooks, and no amount of latex or grease paint would make us more so.

Finally, the insanity moved on, making its way to another group of waiting onlookers further down the road.

"What do you think, kid? Time to see if some costumed teenagers can make us pee our pants?" James asked Maddie. I noticed he was smiling as well though obviously doing a better job at hiding his teeth than our newcomer.

"Yeah!" She said, clapping. It amazed me at how different eighteen was now from when I was a girl. The world may have changed in many dark ways, but it had also altered in a way that allowed us to hold on to our youth a bit longer. If you ask me, that's a good thing, and I would know a thing or two about preserving youth.

4.

The haunted houses of New York ranged from cheesy to genuinely upsetting, and it was clear that Maddie loved every last second of it. We spent the next few hours facing down zombies, werewolves, and seemingly endless killer clowns in building after building. Making our way through mazes and ducking into crawl spaces to escape pursuing nightmares. Somewhere along the line, we found ourselves back in the van, driving beyond the confines of the city into the relative quiet of the suburbs, seeking even more thrills.

I had traded places with James, and was now driving. We were only a few minutes outside the city limits when we noticed that we were again being followed. A black van was keeping pace with ours, about three car lengths behind. It lacked any sort of markings, and due to the dark tint to the windows (far beyond what was allowed by state law), I was unable to make out anything of its passengers.

We've got a tail. Michael's voice said in my mind. I nodded and looked to Maddie, who was watching the road through her window, taking the occasional casual glance at the other van. I was proud of her.

Yeah, I'm going to try to lose them. I said, turning down the radio, cutting off Bessie Smith mid-song.

I had to be careful. If I responded too aggressively here, they would be on to me and probably do something dangerous. However, If I reacted too timidly, they would follow us to the ends of the Earth, and who knows what would happen when we got there. So, I sped up a bit, altering my mental route to our destination to take a few of

the more twisty confusing side roads that the suburbs were so known for.

The van followed, straddling the line between blending in and keeping pace like an expert. I imagine that if there was any connection to the man in black, he was not the one driving, as they were showing basic competence. If these people were more like the unseen driver, I reasoned, we might be in for a bit of trouble.

Finally, I either lost them, or they got tired of following me in circles because none of us could see them. After driving around for a while longer just to be sure, we arrived at the next haunted house. We had driven quite some time by then, and the bustle and light of the city had slowly been replaced with multi-colored leaves and small farmhouses.

"This place had better be good." James muttered, "after taking us way the hell out here."

It didn't look like anything special from here. The building was just another small farmhouse, with only a few drugstore decorations and a hand-made sign reading *Demon Dwelling,* marking it as our destination. Still, it had gotten good reviews online, and I was hopeful.

We never found out if the *Demon Dwelling* was any good because, at that moment, the black van pulled out of the darkness and into the spot next to us.

5.

We sat still for a moment, unsure of how to proceed. Maddie's eyes widened as the van parked; I noticed that she had grabbed Shirley's hand without even thinking about it. Shirley forced a smile and squeezed back, though I could tell that she was just as tense as the rest of us. These people could be a lot of trouble, and if we weren't careful, they could cause serious pain.

The van's passenger door swung open, and a figure stepped out slowly, calmly sauntering toward us, absently swinging a wicked-looking machete through the air as he approached. I quickly recognized him as the man from the subway and noticed that he had added a bullet-proof vest to his urban commando outfit since we had last seen him. He had also donned a silver crucifix, which meant they weren't playing around.

I should probably explain that crosses don't affect us, not in the way it shows in the movies. A person with significant faith could turn us away by brandishing a holy symbol, sure (and it didn't need to be a cross; Star of David, a Buddhist lotus talisman would work just as well), but that spoke more to the power of will and innate, untapped psychic ability of the wielder than any otherworldly power. Most of the time, brandishing a cross would have the same effect on us than it would on a normal human, namely nothing.

Still, the fact that these people had come at us with religious symbols meant that they knew full well what we were, and it would be difficult to surprise them.

Let me handle this guy. Michael said into our minds, and

before we could really react, he stepped out of the van to face down the man in black. Maddie looked at him, her eyes wild, and opened her mouth to speak. Shirley placed a hand on her leg, however, and she stayed quiet, though she didn't seem to calm much.

The man stopped walking forward but continued to swing the machete, occasionally tapping its broad-side on his leg. I could tell that he was one of those people that could never stop moving, not even in sleep.

"Can I help you, friend?" Michael asked. Next to me, James tensed, and I could tell that he didn't like this whole situation.

Neither did I, if we're being honest here.

"We aren't friends," the man said. "We don't make friends with your kind." The man took another step toward Michael.

"My kind?" Michael asked, still keeping his voice calm and friendly. "Look, we're just taking a friend out to see the sights of Halloween. We aren't looking for any trouble. I think you might have us mistaken for..."

"We don't make mistakes," the man said. "And we don't talk to bloodsuckers either."

With that, the man rushed forward. He attacked awkwardly and without much finesse, making moves of a man who was used to raw force and intimidation to win his battles. I imagined he was some sort of a bar-room hero in his other life, quick with a right hook and unable to fathom anyone being a bigger dog than he.

Michael smiled and sidestepped the attack effortlessly.

The man in black reeled around. He didn't seem surprised at Michael's sudden burst of preternatural movement, but then again, he wouldn't be. He knew what he was dealing with, at least on paper. All he seemed to lack was the experience, and I was confident that Michael was about to make sure that he would never get that.

"Die, bloodsucker," the man snarled, leaping forward with another swing of his blade. Michael sidestepped it again, this time also shifting his body, so his useless human nails were replaced with wicked talons.

Oh yes, we can shapeshift just like the stories say. We can become bats, wolves, mist, and all that (though I've never met one who could become a pile of rats like the big Drac supposedly could), but we can also change parts of our body, making them bestial if needed. That's how we see in the dark. The only thing we're unable to change for some reason is our fangs, which we're stuck with from the first change forward.

Don't ask me why. It was just the way things were.

The man in black eyed Michael's claws and, for a second, showed fear. Then he redoubled his attacks, swinging viciously at Michael's ever-moving form, trading what small modicum of tactics he had been using for utter violence, screaming and yelling the whole time. It was a small wonder that the workers in the haunted house didn't hear us, but it was my experience that those places piped-in sound effects so loudly that you couldn't hear anything that was going on beyond their walls.

Finally, Michael struck, digging his claws through Kevlar and cotton and then flesh. The man's stomach unzipped, spilling its contents onto the dirt driveway, where they steamed in the relatively cold air. The man died with a look of confusion on his face, unable to fathom, even in his final moments, losing a fight.

"Leave now." Michael shouted to the van, letting his fangs glint in the moonlight. "and we'll only take out one of yours."

It happened all at once. Once second, Michael was taunting whoever was in the van, and then his look of defiance was replaced with one of shock. His body slumped to the ground, a look of stunned panic on his face, a steel bolt piercing his chest.

They must have had someone hiding in the trees with a crossbow, watching the proceedings. I wondered if the man in black was like our Maddie, young and out on some sort of rite of passage. That would explain his mix of lore and lack of actual field time. The others just wanted to see what he could do against us.

I was almost sad for him.

Maddie screamed beside me, pulling away from Shirley and trying to get out of the van, to strike at the people that took her friend. Faster than the eye could see, Shirley pulled her into a bear hug, holding her struggling form as though she was little more than a child. Finally, she slumped into the older woman's arms, crimson tears staining her face.

Yes, we cry blood; some stories get that part right.

We can also die. There is no special way to kill us, no magical ritual or special tactics needed. We heal frighteningly fast, but if something kills us quickly enough, we don't have time to repair ourselves. That's why we're usually dispatched with a strike to the heart or blow to the head. Fire also does a number on us, overwhelming our systems so thoroughly that we don't know how to fix it. Sunlight won't kill us, but it does, like Stoker said, take our powers away. Also, when we do meet our final curtain, we don't become dust, or revert to our "true" age, or burst into flames. Nothing fantastic and cinematic-like that occurs at all. We just go from being a living, moving thing to a shell, an empty vessel that gives up its battle against the relentless pull of gravity and slumps to the ground, which claims us all one day anyway.

Like Michael just did.

Mist? James asked in our minds, and I turned to Maddie, repeating his word out loud.

She nodded, her breath hitching with sobs. She was still in the habit of breathing, though we only need to do so to speak. It could be a hard habit to break, and because it sometimes added to our human camouflage, I didn't push.

We turned into mist, seeping out of the van and into the surrounding forest.

6.

They won't be able to trace the van back to us, so it was okay that we left it behind. I did feel bad for the cast and crew of *Demon's Dwelling*, who would end their undoubtedly stressful night running around amidst fake dead bodies to find two real ones waiting outside. When all of this was over, I would have to anonymously send them some money. Such gestures don't fix everything, but I've found that they do help quite a bit.

We reformed in a corn maze, hoping that its twists and turns would deter anyone who may have found a way to follow us. I could tell from the sparse (but clever) decorations that filled this maze that it had once been a haunted attraction as well, but like many of the smaller examples, it was not open for business on Halloween night itself.

Lucky us.

I shot a glance at Maddie, who was currently sitting with her back against a pumpkin-headed scarecrow, her fingers rapidly tapping against the screen of her cellphone. From the rapid movement of her digits and the look of concentration on her face, I assume she's playing some sort of video game, which is a realm that I have never quite gotten around to exploring. I remembered how there used to be rooms full of video games in parts of New York, pulsing with noise and light, and was taken once more with how quickly things changed. I wondered if Maddie would still be playing these games in twenty years, fifty even, and how different they would be, the new technologies as alien and amazing to her as the current state of things would probably seem to me.

It made me smile and feel sad at the same time.

"We're sure Upstate now," James said, appearing next to me. He had taken to patrolling the maze in mist form, though I suspect it was more due to boredom than vigilance. "I can tell by the smell."

I nodded. It *did* smell different up here, less human. I knew that a lot of people in these parts liked that, liked the quiet and tranquility that only living far from the teeming masses that were part and parcel of city life. I never really understood those people. Even when I was still alive, I preferred to be surrounded by a sea of motion, and my current state made it almost a necessity. It was easier for us to hide in a throng, not to mention the over-abundance of food choices.

"How's the kid holding up?" James asked.

"She's alright. Distracting herself right now." I replied.

"I'm sure Shirley will put her head on straight when she needs to," James said. He was right; she was good at that. Even though I was the oldest, her calm, quiet strength was the heart of our little group.

"Damn it, Rose, why did it have to get so fucked up on her first night out?" James kicked at an errant stalk of corn, which cracked under his boot, falling to the dirt below. "It ain't fair."

I nodded again, and we stood in silence. Finally, more to break up the moment than out of curiosity, I spoke. "Have you seen Shirley?"

"Yeah, she's walkin' around, exploring, doing that processing thing that she does where she paces about and sorts everything out."

I nodded once more. "You did a good job guiding Maddie today," I told him. It was difficult to coordinate while traveling in mist form, especially when one of your numbers lacked any psychic connection to the others. Still, James had really risen to the challenge, making sure that Maddie would join us at the end of our journey.

"Yeah." He said modestly. "I didn't wanna lose the kid."

At that time, Shirley appeared, holding a lit Jack-O-Lantern in her arms. She must have found it tucked away in one of the maze's many displays. For some reason, Shirley never quite developed the cat-like night vision the rest of us had, and I realized that she was using the flickering of the pumpkin's jagged grin and triangular nose to light her way.

"How goes it?" James asked her.

"It goes." She replied. "I found this and thought that Maddie might like it."

James and I agreed, and we went back to where she was sitting, watching as her eyes lit up just as bright as the Jack's.

"That's so cool." She said. She then stood and walked over to where Shirley had set the pumpkin, dropping to her haunches to inspect it further. "Just like the ones I made as a kid."

The rest of us shared a smile, glad that such a simple thing could bring joy to the odd, gothy/punky kid that we had picked up and taken as one of our own.

We all knelt down then, surrounding the glowing Jack-O-Lantern, something like a family once more, even though one of ours was taken away. We would go on.

We   always   did.

7.

"So, who are those people?" Maddie asked. I tensed a little bit and realized that I hoped that she wouldn't bring up what had happened, at least not for a while, but realizing that it was all part of her process, all part of how she had to deal with things. I was pretty impressed with how she was doing and knew that her reactions would bode well for the girl's future. This would not be the last tragedy in her long life, after all.

Not by a long shot.

"Vampire hunters," I told her simply, not wanting to dull my explanation with fancy words.

"Seriously?" She asked, her surprise making her look far younger than her eighteen years.

"Fraid so," James said.

"Like Van Helsing?" Maddie asked.

"Yes. "I said. "Like him.""

"He was a real person, you know." Shirley offered the flickering candlelight making her look wise even though she wore a face as young as the rest of us. We had all been eighteen at inception, after all.

"Really?" Maddie asked. "So was Dracula real too?"

"Sort of. But he wasn't anything like he was in the book. In fact, he was afraid of vampires."

Maddie thought about this for a second, chewing on the tip of her pinky nail, getting a bit of black enamel on her front teeth. "So... these hunters...are they just people? Or can they do things? I mean things like we can do."

"Mostly, they're just people," Shirley said. "But some of them do learn tricks, little bits of magic."

"Wait...So you're telling me that magic is real too?" Maddie's green eyes narrowed.

"Yeah," James said. "But it's not like flying and throwing lightning bolts at people. It's little things."

"Like what?" She asked.

"Like stopping the flow of blood from a wound or making a crop grow in a blight, finding underground water or lost things, folksy stuff like that," I told her.

Suddenly a look of worry crossed her face.

"What's the matter?" Shirley asked.

"Finding lost things?" Maddie said, a slight waver in her voice.

"Yeah, so what?" James asked.

"Aren't we...lost things?"

8.

The Hunters

A bowl of water sits on a mass-produced map, ripped from some long-forgotten almanac. A needle carefully cleaned and kept rust-free floats lazily. The water is clear and still, and one could see its surroundings reflected on its surface. All at once, the needle bobs and dips, as though it were being pulled by an unseen magnet. Finally, it begins to spin wildly, disrupting the water's calm surface.

Beyond the bowl and map sit two figures. They are scared and angry, having lost one of their own, but they know that loss is a part of their lives now. They had, after all, chosen this path. The one that was lost was young and stupid, prone to letting emotion lead him, which is how the enemy had bested him in the end. He just could not fathom being beaten.

He would still be missed, but now was not the time to mourn. They both played their teacher's words in their minds, again and again.

We are soldiers.

This is war.

They watched the needle, their four eyes tracking its spin, waiting for it to reveal something useful, a path that they might follow to continue their duty, which they held sacred. The needle spun more and more violently, causing the water to lap at the side of the bowl, an almost literal tempest in a teapot.

Then it stopped.

Guided.

Pointed.

"We got them." One of the voices said.

"Damn bloodsuckers." The other replied, fury in her voice. "Damn them all to Hell."

9.

Rose

"We can't stay here all night, you know," James said.

"Thank you, captain obvious," Maddie replied, rolling her eyes. She had always given us proper respect but also never took any flack. I respected that a great deal.

"What do you propose?" I asked James, who was eyeing Maddie like he was about to start something. Even if it was half playful, I didn't want us to erupt into a fight right now. We needed to be a unit if we were going to survive to see November 1st.

"I'm not even sure where the hell we are," James muttered to himself. "Or how long it's gonna take to get us back to the city."

"We can't be too far out," I said. "We only traveled by mist for a few moments. Besides, the sun isn't even thinking about rising yet, and it was already pretty late for the hunters...when we had to flee."

James nodded and, while he was looking at me, Maddie stuck her tongue out at him. It took every ounce of my willpower not to laugh and was still losing the fight when Shirley returned. She had again picked up the Jack-O-Lantern, and its eerie light made her seem more ethereal than usual.

"What's the news?" Maddie asked. She smiled as she said it, making sure to shoot James an innocent glance as she did so. I almost lost control anew.

"I heard an engine," Shirley said. The unlaughed laughter died in my chest.

"Van?" Maddie asked.

"I couldn't tell. I came to tell you as soon as I heard it."

"How far?" James asked.

"Not." She replied simply.

Maddie muttered something that sounded suspiciously like "Lost things."

"How do you want to run this?" James asked. I was happy to see that he spoke aloud instead of telepathically, so to include Maddie.

"Why not bring the fight to them?" Shirley asked, surprising all of us.

"We could," I said, pondering.

"Or we could sneak away. If we're careful and quiet, I bet they won't be able to find us in all of this, and we can slip out. Go back home." Maddie sounded tired as she said the last part, longing.

"I don't want to run anymore," Shirley said. "Not after Michael."

Many people would be shocked to hear this coming from Shirley, but not me. She possessed an intense loyalty to her family; a killing spirit when it came to those she deemed close to her. It was this trait, in fact, that first caught my attention, first made me consider bringing her into the fold when she became an adult.

She was a lioness.

We all heard the engine die, leaving the night silent once more. Shirley was right; it wasn't far away at all, probably only paces from one of the entrances to the maze. The time for discussion had ended.

I brought a finger to my lips and nodded to the others, then pointed deeper into the maze, away from where we heard the engine stop. They nodded, nearly in unison. The serious look on Maddie's face almost broke my heart. The first night out was supposed to be fun, a way to reward the young one's hard work and training. Instead, it had become yet another trial.

We moved into the maze, a pack again. Shirley left the still glowing pumpkin grinning in the center of the maze. Perhaps it would be a decoy for our enemies, drawing them away from our location and buying us some time. We had decided without discussion that Shirley would just have to rely on our eyes for the time being. As we walked away, I noticed Maddie give the pumpkin a final look over her shoulder, her chest heaving in an unnecessary deep breath. Somehow, her reaction made it all the more real.

Then it was tears I was holding back, not laughter.

10.

None of us was particularly good at shadow control, but we all tried to shroud ourselves nonetheless. It was a small thing, something that, if successful, could give us a bit of an edge against our opponents. We wrapped the shadows around us like jackets, twisting them and molding them to disguise us as we waited. Slowly, we made our way to the other side of the maze, stopping here and there to regroup. If we went on undetected, we decided to slip out without conflict, leaving Shirley unfulfilled but very much safe and alive. However, if we were detected while we hunkered down, we would use surprise and our superior physical abilities to strike, making damn sure that they would never hurt anyone ever again. If I was being honest with myself, I wasn't sure which outcome I hoped for.

It wasn't long before we saw one of them. She was a few inches taller than me and I'm far from short- with auburn hair pulled into a no-nonsense ponytail. She wore the same black camouflage as her fallen compatriot, accessorizing it with a golden cross and some sort of night-vision goggles that gave her the look of a giant, bipedal insect. She also carried a Bowie knife in one hand and a fancy looking crossbow on her back.

Seeing the crossbow, I was filled with a rage so venomous that I had to bite down on the inside of my mouth to not bolt from my hiding spot, throttling the hunter where she stood and throwing our plan to the four winds. Unless they all carried crossbows, which I somehow doubted-this was the woman that killed Michael. I turned and looked at Maddie, who seemed to be having the same problem as me and was handling it just as well.

The woman turned her head and quietly muttered a series of numbers and letters that, I assume, was picked up by some sort of communication device and meant something to whoever was listening. This told me that there was at least one more hunter out there, and we had to be even more careful.

Strike or keep moving? James asked telepathically from his hiding space.

We can take her. Shirley responded. *If we do it quickly.* Clearly, she hadn't calmed down a single iota since Michael's death.

Wait. I said. *Stick to the plan.* As I sent this message, I held my hand up, palm out, for Maddie to see. She nodded from her spot.

Another voice, crackling with static came from the woman, giving its own coded message. Between the quietness of the voice and the distortion, it was impossible to tell anything about its owner. The woman nodded to herself, and then, with a muttered "ten-four." began to leave.

It's a waste. Shirley said with her mind. *We can drop her right now without alerting her friend.*

What transpired in the next few moments happened so quickly that I'm not sure how to explain it and for the sake of telling this story, I'm going to try to put the images I remember in some sort of order and put a sense of continuity to the events that I just don't feel was really there. I'm going to try to build the same illusion that countless writers before me (with much more talent in tale-craft, I'll admit) have built. The illusion that something as chaotic and insane as a battle could ever be put in ordered, measured words.

The woman's head jerked up suddenly, reminding me of a cobra, her body shifting automatically into a battle position, knife at the ready. I could tell by how she moved that we were dealing with someone exceptionally trained than the last hunter, far more dangerous.

I'll never know what alerted her to our presence, or even which of us she noticed. Did Maddie make some sort of mistake in her inexperience? Did I, more taken in by my anger than I thought I was, move in a way that alerted her? Or did...and I hoped this wasn't true, I really hoped it was not... Shirley intentionally drew the hunter's attention so it would erupt into the fight that she so desired? No matter how it began, it quickly turned into chaos.

"Come on out of there, Hemmy." The woman said. At the time, it seemed like she was looking directly at me, but she was most likely doing the old public speaking trick where you look between multiple points to create the illusion of eye contact with several people. "We know where you are."

Careful. I transmitted. *She's trying to goad us, make us angry.*

It's working. James mentally replied. *Callin' us Hemmies...*

Hemmy was short for Hematophage, literally "eater of blood" and something that hunters have been calling us for years, a sort of preternatural slur if you will. It didn't bother me much, but I've met some of our kind that would fly into a killing frenzy just hearing the word.

I looked to Maddie, who was leaning forward, claws out. She realized that she had the hunter's back and was preparing for a sneak attack. She also kept stealing glances in my direction, hoping for some sort of sign, some signal that she should take her shot. I don't know what I did to become the leader in her eyes, and I wasn't sure I liked it.

I nodded. Whatever god looks over creatures such as us protect me, I nodded. What happened was, at least in part, my fault.

The hunter opened her mouth, most likely to taunt us further, but was interrupted as Maddie flew from the darkness, knocking the woman's goggles from her face with a well-aimed claw strike, causing them to hit the ground with a surprisingly loud crash. It was a good move, blinding the woman like that, and none of us were going to let the second of disorientation go to waste.

We surrounded her, a pack of night-wolves surrounding their prey. The woman pointed her knife at us in turn.

We struck as one.

This should have been the end of it, there were three of us vs. one of her, and we were far faster and stronger than even a well-trained human. It should have gone about as well for the hunter as in went for a gazelle in a nature documentary about lions.

It didn't.

Instead, the huntress struck out, nearly as fast as us, slashing wildly with her knife, which was quickly becoming covered in our blood. She pushed us back, and somehow (I still don't know how) managed to straddle Shirley and began to drive her knife, again and again, into my friend's eye socket.

James screamed and redoubled his efforts, driving his claws into the hunter's head, piercing both temples simultaneously. He pulled, and the woman's head tore free of her body with a ripping sound that sickened even me. I remember looking into the hunter's stunned eyes, still blinking, as James threw her severed head to the ground, where it lay, its gaze still filled with sharpened hatred.

11.

There was nothing we could do for Shirley. The knife had pierced too far into her head, too many times. We were now three.

Our existence is, by its very nature, a lonely one. The secrecy that we must keep, forces us to play everything close to the chest, an endless life of lies and deception that makes closeness difficult. Not to mention the fact that we, if left to our own devices, never die, which makes any sort of relationship with normal humans a tragic and pointless affair. This is why we make others of our kind now and then, creating our own pack that makes our special lifestyle more livable. We have to be careful with this, however, for if we choose lightly, we may end up living for an eternity with someone that we grow quickly bored with, if not outright detest.

For instance, there was a young, upstate woman that caught our attention before Maddie. She was rich and beautiful, a potent combination for our kind. She was also dissatisfied with life and willing to uproot everything if it meant being given a second chance, which is the one thing that we look for above all else. We quickly found out, however, that she was as cold as the mirrored sunglasses she wore, as distant as the noisy electronic music she preferred.

We voted to pass her by, and a few months later, found our dear Maddie.

I tell you this now, so you'll understand how hard those hours were for us, how painful. You might have lost someone once, maybe many someone's, and I'm sure it hurt. I'm sure that it tears you apart during the day and makes it impossible to sleep at night.

Imagine, however, if you had a literal psychic bond with this person. A connection that went far beyond that of family, even beyond the link that is said to exist between twin siblings. It's like losing a part of one's self. Now I want you to realize that we had, as a group, as a unit, been through it twice this night. The one who chose me, who pulled me from my mortal life and made me the creature that stands before you now, was gone.

I understand why a wolf that loses its pack goes insane. I have yet to have this luxury, but I understand it.

We returned to the city as mist, discussing a rendezvous point with Maddie so she wouldn't get lost. It was a lot quicker than walking or traveling by vehicle, and there was less chance of being spotted by the voice on the other side of the hunter's communications. Hopefully, they would have to find us all over again, a process that -gods willing- would give us some time to rest.

We re-converged outside of a Brooklyn brownstone, one of the many places we kept paid for and vacant to use as a base. With our lifestyle, it pays to have many of them throughout the New York metro area, so if events required -as they did right now-we move, it would be an easy process.

We were careful to return to human form separately, so no onlooker noticed three figures suddenly blinking into existence. The city was busy, and even in this relatively quiet residential neighborhood, you have to be wary of prying eyes.

I unlocked the door and ushered everyone in, carefully locking it behind me. If anywhere in this whole world was safe, it was here. We settled into the main sitting room, which though small, was very comfortable. I had made sure, over the years, to make it so. To me, a sanctuary shouldn't just be safe, but a place that you could call home without reservations.

It was James that broke the silence first.

"Does anyone wanna talk about what just happened?"

I turned away from the book I had been halfheartedly reading and looked at him, and Maddie looked up from her handheld game.

"How about the way that hunter fought us?" He asked.

"What do you mean?" Maddie said. She had set her game down on the small end table next to her chair. Things were getting serious.

"I mean, did you even see that girl? She squared off with Shirley and freakin' won. She fought like a goddamned vortex..."

"She fought like one of us," Maddie said, her voice wavering slightly. I reached out my hand, and she grasped it tightly. "How can a human fight like one of us? Can magic do that?"

I shook my head, giving her hand another reassuring squeeze, trying to give her comfort that I wasn't feeling. James had a point.

"No magic I've ever seen," James said. "They must have some sort of new trick up their sleeves."

"She wasn't one of us, right?" Maddie asked.

"Did she feel like one of us?" I responded. "Did she have an aura like one of us?"

Maddie thought for a moment, chewing absently on her painted pinky-nail. "No. She felt like a human. Only...a little different. I don't know how, but she felt different."

I couldn't have said it better myself.

We lapsed into silence once more. I picked up my book and tried to continue reading, but found it impossible to hear the author's voice-over James and Maddie's, which were ringing in my ears.

Did you even see the girl...

She fought like one of us...

No magic I've ever seen...

When Maddie spoke again, I could tell it was just to change the subject.

"I'm hungry," Maddie said, patting her stomach.

"I bet you are, kid," James said. All the misting we had done, as well as the speed and strength we pulled forward during the confrontations, was taking its toll on me, so I could only imagine what it was doing to her younger body.

"We can go out for food in a bit," I said.

"We ain't got much longer," Maddie said. "Before the sun comes up."

"She's right, you know," James said. "We're gonna be humans here pretty soon, and I'm already wiped."

All I wanted at that moment was rest, time to recuperate and mourn, a few moments to myself where I could start to process and recover. I realized, however, that the others needed a distraction, something to take their minds away from the horrors of this night, a mental setting-aside until they could approach their issues on their own terms. Though I had little doubt that Maddie was hungry, I could tell that her needs went beyond physical, and what she was asking for had little to do with blood-drinking. I think, in those final hours of that Halloween night, we all just needed something other than death to focus on.

"Alright," I said. "We can go on a quick hunt. But I want to be back by sunrise."

12.

There is something that the more recent stories and films have gotten right. Night clubs are, by far, the best hunting grounds for those such as us. Something about the atmosphere made humans docile, easily led. They were places where people went, tired and weary of the "normal" world, to escape their troubles for a few blissful hours. Though the threat of human evil was never too far from their minds (due to the endless fear-mongering and sensationalism of "news" programs that were more blood-thirsty than we are), they came to these places to not worry anymore, to be carried away by music and light, movement and connection. Basically, clubs made humans docile and therefore were ideal places to shear off a few sheep from the herd.

I wore a simple black dress; my hair pulled up into a complex series of braids, a look that I've noticed is timeless. James wore a pair of leather jeans and a zippered leather jacket over a plain black t-shirt, each article of clothing tight enough to show off his lean musculature. Surprisingly, Maddie put the least amount of effort into her "hunting clothes", putting on a black skirt, a pair of Doc Marten boots, and a shirt that advertised some band called My Chemical Romance, her innocent face hidden behind black and white makeup that made her a parody of what she truly was. I guess that of the three of us, she was the one most naturally attuned to modern nights.

At that moment, I missed being young.

We settled on a place in Williamsburg called the Vanguard. Though she had never been, Maddie had insisted that we visit this place since early in her training. It was no Studio 54 or Limelight, but I had to admit that it was still a sight to see, with state of the art lighting and sound, and, more importantly, a gaggle of young, hip people for us to choose from. I liked the place and hoped it would survive the curse that caused most "hip" city clubs to close down in their first year.

"We should have worn costumes," Maddie said, raising her voice to be heard over the jackhammer bass that filled the air.

She was right. Almost everyone in the club that night had come prepared for a grand masquerade. Even in its waning hours, the sacred night of Halloween was being observed and commemorated by the people of the Big Apple. I silently hoped that our apparent youth and timeless beauty would be enough disguise that night.

James and I made our way to the largest of the club's three bars, while Maddie slipped onto the crowded dance floor and began to writhe and gyrate to the music. She wasn't much of a dancer in any technical sense, often off-beat and jerky with her movements, but I imagined that her utter enthusiasm more than made up for it in a place like this.

I smiled, remembering the dance floors of my youth. For a second, I was transported back there, back to the then-dangerous Jazz that filled the air (along with a fair amount of smoke from illicit cigarettes), all of us on the floor Fox Trotting or Texas Tommying with partners, or moving alone in the bird-like sequence of movements that made up The Charleston. As I observed the young people in this club, it occurred to me that I was feeling the same energy that had so enveloped me as a human.

Nothing ever really changes, does it? James said in my mind. I thought back to the violence and barely contained chaos of James' favorite human haunts and agreed.

Kids will, always and forever, be kids. Especially, it seemed, on Halloween.

I watched as Maddie bopped along with the electronic din, amazed that even with our losses, even with the horror of the past several hours (so different from the faux horror that we had sought), the kid could still make me smile. She slid and bounced through the crowd, stopping briefly to dance with one "lucky" partner or another before finally seeming to latch onto a particular young woman.

Maddie had chosen her night's meal.

Another thing that a lot of stories get wrong is feeding. We don't need to kill to eat, in fact, it's a bad idea to do so. If a lot of dead bodies pile up without their blood, even in a city as crowded and strange as New York, people start asking questions. Also, just biting someone doesn't make them one of us, a zombie, or any other silly thing. We just take what we need and send the victim on their way, a little bit lightheaded, but otherwise unharmed. There are humans that seek to do far worse with the people they pick up in places like this. Also, it has nothing to do with sex at all, though we so often use that as a pretense to get our meals where we want them. We chose our targets based on a preternatural feel for how the blood would taste, not the gender or physical attractiveness of its owner. In fact, the change into what we are pretty much killed those feelings. We could still love, as my feelings toward Maddie showed, but we could not, to put it bluntly, lust.

I never really missed it, not sure if the others do.

Anyway, the girl that Maddie picked out was tall and thin and almost pure muscle. She was dressed in a black bodysuit and cat ears, a wire-frame tail waving behind her as she danced. Her hair was shorn down to the skin and this, along with her build, made her costume less cute and more deadly, a kitty with claws without a doubt. She also wore a simple black back-pack that matched her bodysuit well enough that I almost didn't notice it at first.

She and Maddie conversed, their mouths moving excitedly, though even with our special hearing, we had no chance of making out their words from where we sat. It was clear, however, that whatever was being said was having the proper effect. As I mentioned before, I had no idea what Maddie's sexual preference was as a human, but she sure knew what to do to get a girl's attention on a crowded floor.

After a few moments, Maddie grabbed the girl's gloved hand and led her to where James and I were seated. I would have to praise her later on how quickly she could move when the time was of the essence.

"Hey, guys. This is Chole." Maddie said, patting her new "friend" on the shoulder. Chloe smiled and nodded to us both as we were introduced. "She wants to come hang out, have a couple of drinks, and ring in November the right way."

Then Maddie began to spin quite the tale. Apparently, we had a grand and wonderful party planned at the start of this October the 31st, only to be thwarted, again and again, by events that, quite simply, defied all belief, until there were only the three of us left. There is refuge in audacity, and Maddie seemed bound and determined to use it to her greatest advantage. Chole, for her part, seemed totally taken in and charmed by Maddie's wild story, whether she believed it or not. I imagine that the fact that the girl was acting like she had had more than a few drinks that night had something to do with it. Still, my senses told me that the girl's blood would be tasty and filling, and that was really all that mattered with so little time left in the night.

Maddie talked the smiling Chole's ear off the entire way home.

13.

The Hunter Remembers

The hunter stared at herself in the mirror. If the redness in her eyes was any indication, the injections were taking their toll. She feared that if she took much more of the potent cocktail, she would lose something of herself in the process. Still, there were more important things in this world than self-hood, and she had taken an oath.

She saw her first vampire as a little girl in West Harlem. She had spent the day along with the rest of her third-grade class at the Sugar Hill Children's' Museum of Art and Storytelling, a place that she had always loved. She wandered away from the group and had somehow found herself in a dark corner of the place devoid of classmates or museum staff. There she saw two men, the taller of the two bent over the smaller one.

She had been a precocious child and at first, figured that she had walked into one of those mysterious things that adults got into when alone, but then she saw the blood dripping down the smaller man's neck. No, it had been clear even to her small eyes that the bigger man was drinking...the other man.

She knew what vampires were, of course. She had seen Dracula, both Bela Lugosi's and Christopher Lee's versions. Had even watched The Lost Boys (behind her parent's back; of course, they would never allow such a film to pass through the eyes of their "innocent" daughter). However, she didn't think that they could walk around during the day. Even so, there could be no question of what she was seeing.

She did the smart thing then and ran as fast as she could back to her teacher, who was so frazzled dealing with thirty other kids. She didn't even notice that the young huntress was missing.

She had spent the next ten years absorbing anything and everything she could get her hands on pertaining to the thirsty undead. From fiction to nonfiction, romance to anthropology, she read, watched, and listened to it all, adding some facts to her repertoire and dismissing others as fabrications as she went.

It was these studies that had brought her to the attention of the other hunters. She had requested an obscure book from her local library, and it had somehow sent up a flag for their organization, who quickly tracked her down. She was investigated thoroughly, her knowledge about the vampire threat scrutinized again and again. Finally, when she turned twenty, they took her in. Training her to fight, to strategize, and when they realized how clever she could be, to lead.

Returning from her memories to the current moment, the huntress reached into her backpack and pulled out a vial and syringe, looking at them with hatred and disgust.

"This is a necessary evil." She muttered quietly to herself, drawing the dark fluid out of the vial and into the transparent body of the syringe. When your enemy was faster, stronger, more resilient than you, able to do things that you had never fathomed even in your most fantastical childhood imaginings, you needed an edge. No matter what gaining said edge did to your body or your soul.

It had been her mentor, long killed by his prey, who had first discovered this trick. He had found that if you injected vampiric blood into a human host without first draining theirs, said host would gain some of the attributes of the damned. They couldn't shift their shape or do some of the more bizarre tricks that the Hemmies were able to do, but they did become much faster and stronger and able to heal wounds in minutes that would take a normal mortal weeks. Combined with the element of surprise ('suckers always underestimated humans), it was a potent trick that had led to many victories over the past few years.

The problem, however, was that the side effects were unknown. Some of those who "dosed" as they had begun to call it, reported sudden bursts of aggression, causing them to react far too violently to otherwise mild stimuli. Others had said that they craved the blood in the night, shaking and even vomiting as they yearned throughout cold sweaty nights. She had not felt either of these things yet, but she had noticed a strange shadow of ennui covering her heart for a few hours after taking the blood. Which, if you combined it with the troubling redness, spelled trouble. She wasn't sure if she still believed in a soul. And was fairly sure that if there was such a creature, it was absorbing most of the negative effects of the dose, leaving a lasting impression well after the other effects of the 'dose wore off.

Sighing, she pulled a third item from her backpack. A cheap leather belt, which she wrapped around her arm and tightened it until a vein popped under her skin.

Just like a junkie, she thought to herself, as she plunged the needle into a said vein, just like a damned junkie. She turned her mind away from what she was doing; instead, she focused on the music that was blaring from the other room, the punk rock thud and slam, the singer wailing about monsters and demons, and even funny enough, vampires.

Rose

"She's been in there a long time," James said, drumming his quick bitten nails against his leather pants almost to the beat of the Misfits song screaming from the radio. Ever since I changed him, it had been a tradition to listen to Horror Punk in the final hours of Halloween night. At first, it was a bit grating, but I grew to actually enjoy it as the years wore on.

"She is pretty hammered," Maddie said. She was humming along with the song while slaying dozens of alien soldiers (or whatever those awful looking things were) in her game.

"Yeah, but I don't hear her pukin' or anything," James replied.

"I don't think you could over this din," I said.

"You wound me," James responded, putting a hand over his heart. In truth, it was possible that James would be able to hear the girl vomiting over the music, as he had the best hearing of all of us. It's funny how our powers differ, and I wondered what special hand Maddie would be dealt as she grew and matured.

"Maybe we should go check on her," Maddie suggested.

"I'll do it," James said. He stood up at the precise moment the music's crescendo peaked. He always did have a flair for the dramatic, even as a human. It had only amplified, it seems, with his unlife.

I suppose that was true of us all.

14.

The Hunter remembers...

"Vampires are monsters, pure and simple." Darnell's deep, resonant voice boomed as he observed the young hunter in training's every movement. She had admittingly chosen to fight with paired hatchets because she thought they looked cool, but Darnell noticed that she had gotten quite good with them, far surpassing where he was at her age. He smiled slightly as he continued his lecture.

"They have no feelings, no emotions, nothing to hold them back in a fight. You can't reason with them, can't appeal to their humanity, can't even hurt them to slow them down. All they are is hunger and rage. Their hearts are as cold as their dead bodies."

"I hate them!" The young huntress screamed, driving her axes into the neck of the training dummy in a maneuver that would have decapitated any living target, sending wooden splinters into the air.

"Good." Darnell rose from his chair and made his way to his young ward's side, placing his hand on her shoulder. "Then you too will strike with no feelings. It's the only way we can defeat them."

As he squeezed the young girl's shoulder, Darnell noticed that though she was breathing heavy covered with a sheen of sweat, she was far from exhausted, even though he had pushed her far harder than necessary that night.

Not only is this kid ready to hit the streets, Darnell thought to himself, she's ready to lead a hunt.

"I'm proud of you, Chloe," Darnell said, giving her shoulder one last squeeze before walking away. "Now, hit the showers."

Rose

"You alright in there, little bird?" James asked, rapping on the bathroom door. Despite not being British, he had picked up terms like 'bird' from some character from a TV show from the 1990s and made them part of his new identity. I didn't blame him for the affectation, however. We all wear masks, and not just on Halloween.

"Yup. I'm fine." Chole's perky voice chimed from the bathroom. "Just finishing up in here."

James turned and nodded, mouthing the girl's words back to us as if we didn't hear.

"I'm glad I don't have to deal with that anymore," Maddie said, just loud enough for me to hear under the music.

"Me too." I laughed.

Then the bathroom door exploded.

James' reflexes were fast, and his reactions very often true, but he was caught as flat-footed as a human when Chole tore through the wooden door like a dervish, two hatchet blades flashing in the dim light like the glow-sticks she had been waving around at the club.

"This is for my brothers, you bloodsucking scumbags!" Every ounce of the bubbly, slightly tipsy girl we had brought home was gone, replaced with pure fury and hatred. She had become, not to put too fine a point on it, a monster.

James dodged and weaved, but somehow the hunter's blades were quicker, burying themselves again and again in his flesh. The fight went on for only a few seconds, and before we could even begin to move in assistance, it was over. James fell to the ground, disgusting fluids dripping from his head wounds. Chloe pulled the hatchets free with a sickening slurping noise and turned to face me.

She took her stance.

I drew my claws.

The Hunter Remembers

All Chloe ever wanted was a place to call her own, a group of people that cared about her unconditionally. She had thought she had found that the hunters, with Darnell as a father figure and the other young ones as siblings, had even begun to drop her guard (just a little) around them. It was, however, not to be, a fact that she had discovered when she was sent out on her first ground mission.

"Your opponents are cold machines. No matter how much they look like human beings, don't be fooled. I have told you many times. What I am going to tell you now, however, is new and it gives me no pleasure to have to say it. We are not The Army. We are not bound by "no man left behind." All of that sentimental nonsense went out the window the moment we realized that dead bodies could get up and kill us.

Every time you leave for a mission like this, every single time, you have to realize that some of you may not come back. In fact, it's the most likely outcome. You must be cold about this, as cold as the Bloodsuckers. Don't ever let me hear that you let one of them go because of some misguided brotherhood nonsense. The men and women standing next to you can not, and I repeat can...not...matter more than your oaths."

These words found purchase in Chloe's mind. Rarely did a night pass where she didn't think about them, shaking and tearful in the night, like the nightmare-ridden child that she had once been. As she went on more and more ground missions (and lost more and more of her compatriots along the way), her hopes of community, of home, faded. The hunters could never be what she wanted.

And yet, she continued on burying ally after ally without being given time to properly mourn. At first, her heart grew light with every new recruit. Each fresh young face that came to her, full of the same hope and feelings of duty that she had begun with. However, as they, one by one fell before her, that began to fade. She had hardly allowed herself to learn the last one's name.

And yet, she continued on. Even as her heart which her daddy had told her was "bigger than the whole world" first broke and then became stony.

It was, when all was said and done, all she had.

Having comforted herself in the darker times with the thought, no matter how cold she had to be and how much one must deny themselves simple companionship, she was better than the Hemmies. They, after all, felt nothing but hunger.

But...

Sometimes when one of them died, there was a look on the other monsters' faces...

Sometimes they even seemed to mourn.

It was almost like...

    Like...

        Like...

            The reaction one would have losing....
            A member...
                Of a family.

15.

Rose

The young huntress struck like lightning, and it was all I could do to defend myself from her endlessly slashing hatchet blades. Normally, when faced with a battle, I was able to rely on my fast movements and vicious strength to bring down my enemies. Therefore, I am a bit ashamed to say I never properly learned to fight. Faced now with an enemy that matched my physical prowess but also possessed combat training, I found myself horribly under-matched. Again and again, the girl's weapons found my body, leaving gaping wounds. The fact that I had also landed a few strikes with my claws meant nothing and I, like James before me, began to falter.

Maddie rushed from the sidelines, her claws also extended, her normally dark brown eyes flashing red. She drew her claws down the huntress' back, raking away flesh and fabric alike. Leaving three ragged, bloody stripes, but for all it was worth, she may as well have smacked the girl with a pillow.

Without breaking her stride or even turning away from me, the huntress grabbed Maddie as though she was no more solid than one of the glass dolls I had played with as a little girl and threw her roughly into a corner. Maddie slid down the wall, the impact wound on her head, leaving a crimson trail, laid still.

I knew she was fine, that even if part of her skull had been crushed by the impact, it would not be enough to end her unlife. Even so, the sight of her lying there as pathetic as a discarded toy filled me with rage. I redoubled my efforts but was still woefully unable to turn the tide of the battle. Before I could even react, I found myself prone on the hard floor of my once safe brownstone. The huntress straddled me, holding her hand-axes in a crossed formation, reminding me somehow of a Jolly Roger in a children's pirate book.

"Goodbye, bloodsucker." The girl gasped. I took some solace in the fact that I had put up enough of a fight to make her breathe so raggedly. Forgetting myself, I sent the psychic signal for the others to run, not realizing in my dazed state that there was no one left to hear the message. I opened my mouth to scream the command out loud when I heard a piercing scream from the corner of the room.

Maddie had regained consciousness (or whatever our kind has that replicates consciousness) and was now using her endless lung capacity to create a din so powerful, so hopeless, that I was reminded of my family stories of the Banshee that supposedly heralded death.

Maddie's head wound had already begun to heal, but blood was still dripping down her face in little rivers, and it took me a moment to realize that much of it was coming from her eyes. She was crying for me, for the others, for everything that had happened on this day that was supposed to be a special, wonderful rite of passage.

This awful weepy scream saved me.

The Hunter Remembers

"...And hanging from the car door was a bloody hook!" The teacher whose name Chloe had lost to the ravages of time stage shouted. Sadie, who sat rapt next to Chloe, twitched and grabbed the young girl's hand. All around them, boys and girls, dressed as monsters and super-heroes, began to titter and giggle, the tension from the story leaving their little bodies.

Chloe wasn't afraid of the story; in fact, she had read it before, as well as many others. She didn't have many books at home, but one that she did have was a cheap paperback collection of scary stories that she read over and over again, becoming immune to their quaint shocks.

"Alright, kids. I hope that wasn't too scary for you," the teacher said. The class, as a single unit, assured her that it was not, in fact, too scary. However, several of the children's faces said otherwise.

"Now, we need to get ready for the Halloween parade." The teacher said. "And then we will have candy and cider and watch Hocus Pocus."

The class cheered and began to fix their costumes for the big event. This would be the last year that Chloe would participate in the school parade. Next year she would age out, becoming an observer. Already, several of the younger kids had stopped being peers and had become "cute." Somehow, this made her feel a little bit sad.

"That was a pretty scary story, wasn't it?" Sadie asked, adjusting her witch hat. She had been having a hard time keeping it on her tangled thick mass of hair all day.

"I guess," Chloe said. "I wasn't scared at all."

"Me neither," Sadie said, smiling. It was clear to Chloe that her best friend was indeed scared, but now wasn't the time to push things. Instead, she grabbed the other girl's hand once more.

"I'm glad you're my friend," Sadie said.

"I'm glad you're mine," Chloe responded.

"We're always going to be friends, right?"

"Of course, dork."

They made their way, still hand in hand, to the row of cubby holes in the back of the classroom, where they detached long enough to pull out the bits of their costumes that had been deemed "classroom inappropriate."

Sadie, who was now holding a plastic molded broom, glanced nervously around the room. When she was content that the other students weren't paying her any attention, she spoke, her voice barely above a whisper.

"You know, Halloween is my favorite holiday."

Chloe understood her friend's hesitation. There had always been those, especially in this neighborhood, who felt that there was something wrong with All Hallow's Eve, something forbidden and outright evil. Not to mention that they had reached an age where it was becoming a bit uncool to be taken in by plastic bats and spiders much to Chloe's chagrin. One had to be careful in speaking of such things, especially when one was surrounded by peers.

"Me too," Chloe whispered.

"It's like, Christmas is nice and all and Easter too, I guess, I mean I love the food on Thanksgivin', but there's something extra special about Halloween."

Chloe nodded solemnly. Even with the existence of vampires

somewhat muddling things, she agreed.

"And I'm glad I get to spend it with you," Sadie said, before tearing off once again connected at the hand with Chloe, to join the Halloween parade.

Chloe's memories were shattered, leaving her back in her adult body. It was unlike her to slip into nostalgia, especially amidst a battle for her life. It went against every single grain of training and self-discipline that she carefully honed for years. She wondered, axes still poised for the killing blow, what had caused such a lapse. With something edging on horror, she realized the culprit. It was one of the bloodsuckers themselves.

It wasn't the taller one that was struggling beneath her that had caused it, but her compatriot, the smaller darker-skinned girl who currently sat, slumped in the corner, her face covered with an ever-flowing crimson sheet. Though they looked nothing alike, something about the little sucker reminded Chole of her old friend, the girl she had, promises to the contrary and left behind in childhood. For just a moment, she could imagine that it was Sadie there, wounded and screaming like a monster.

All of this happened in seconds. Pulling herself kicking and screaming out of the sudden bout of emotion, Chloe tensed for the killing blow.

16.

Rose

"No! Please don't!" Maddie screamed through her tears. I'm not sure what about her cries had caused the huntress to freeze, but clearly, she had been affected. She had me, as I stated before, and had she not frozen for a moment looking at Maddie, I would be a headless mess, not fit to be telling this story today. But the girl did, in fact freeze for just a second, sealing her fate (as well as mine).

All too soon, however, the young huntress snapped out of whatever reverie she had fallen into, and I sensed her muscles tense for the final blow.

It never came.

I don't know if I would have been able, even with the distraction, to get the killer off of me. She was still very strong, and I would have been acting from a position of disadvantage, to say the least. Thankfully, however, I never had to find out.

A wolf came and knocked the huntress off of me.

It was small (at least for a wolf), its fur a reddish-brown, its brown eyes so dark that they became black in the dim light of our refuge.

I recognized it as Maddie at once.

Shifting form is, as I'm sure I mentioned before, tricky. You have to make sure that all the important parts come apart and back together in the right order, or you may find yourself wearing an internal organ as a hat. Because of this, it could take some time to pull off a full transformation from man to beast, especially the first few times.

Maddie pulled it off not only quickly but flawlessly. Once again, I was impressed. She had finally found the thing in which she excelled.

The hunter, as surprised as I was, found her fortunes reversed. Now she was the one on the floor, with something vicious and terrible atop her. I saw her eyes grow wide with terror, her mouth working silently. *It's not fair;* I'm sure her mind was screaming. *I was winning; I'm supposed to win! After all, aren't I the good guy? Aren't I the hero?*

"Sorry, Chloe." I found myself saying out loud. "There are no heroes in this game."

The wolf brought its mouth to the hunter's neck, its teeth white against her skin. I knew that if I did nothing but lie here, Maddie would tear free the girl's throat, gorging herself on her lifeblood. It would serve the hunter right, I reasoned. After all, she and her merry band of fanatics had taken away our friends, our brothers, and sisters. Still, something about the way the girl had frozen stuck with me. It made me see her not as a monster, a faceless killer from one of those slasher films that had been so popular in James' time, but as a young woman with the same fears, problems (I guessed) and loves that everyone has.

Wait. I said in my mind, forgetting that our young ward was not yet receptive to psychic communication. Still, the wolf stopped, teeth poking into Chloe's neck, but not breaking the skin. Maybe she heard me after all, or perhaps she was struggling with the same emotions I was. I never asked her and, therefore, may never know.

I pulled myself into a standing position and walked over to where they lay, Chloe too primally frightened to move, Maddie unsure how to proceed. I placed my hand on the wolf's shoulder and patted it softly. The second I removed my hand, the beast had become a girl again, mouth still against the hunter's neck, no doubt feeling and being teased by her life pulse.

Maddie and I locked eyes then, and I smiled in understanding. Normally I am very careful when I smile, making sure that my teeth remain human so as to not draw suspicion. This time, however, I let my fangs grow. This was not a moment two humans could have. It belonged only to us bloodsuckers and should be treated as such.

"Happy Halloween, kid," I said out loud. Then I plunged my teeth into the other side of Chloe's neck. In perfect synchronization, Maddie also applied pressure, breaking the girl's skin and getting to the sweet vitae below the surface.

17.

Comedy and tragedy. Today, as it was in my time, the difference is a matter of emotion. The comedy makes you laugh, frees you of your mundane problems, or (forces you to laugh at them, rendering them powerless) or shows you a good time. Tragedy, however, makes you tear up, makes you realize that other people have problems that are probably greater than yours. It gives you a cathartic release where you can safely succumb to your darker feelings.

This was not always so. The difference in times before mine, before anyone but the most ancient of my kind, was in the ending. No matter if what had passed was funny or tragic, action-packed or sedate, the thing that places a tale somewhere on the axis was simple. If things end well, it was a comedy. If it does not, it becomes a tragedy.

This may seem like a segue, a pointless history lesson. It may seem like I am swaying from the story I set out to tell. That I am simply talking to hear myself speak, but trust me, this is a very important distinction to this storyteller. And what is important to the storyteller is, almost always, essential to the story.

Learning of this distinction, back in the halcyon days where I still breathed and subsisted on solid food, changed my entire outlook on things.

A comedy can be tragic.

A tragedy can be funny.

The difference is simply in how things play out.

I'm telling you this because I want you to know, despite the awful things that happened to me in this story, the loss of almost my entire family, the fear and rage and paranoia, the story that you're hearing is not, in fact classically a tragedy.

It is a comedy.

I remind myself of this a lot.

I was on a boardwalk before I came to tell you this story, just like in that flashy movie that James had so loved (though there was no muscular man playing saxophone). I've always loved places like this. Places where people went to get lost in lights and sounds, activities and events beyond the minutiae of daily life. Though I will sometimes engage in such festivities, the fun for me was more a matter of getting lost in the chaos, feeling myself become one with something bigger than myself. I have never been a religious person, and I often wonder if the fairs, carnivals, and festivals that I so love fill that spot in my soul, or whatever passes for a soul in my kind.

I wandered through the crowd of cotton candy eaters. Of children and child-like adult dreamers, and found Maddie who was watching a performance on a tiny stage only slightly taller than she. On this stage, a long-nosed puppet did battle with a series of adversaries, first a police-man, then an alligator, and finally the devil himself. I recognized the show, though when I was still alive, it would often begin with the murder of said puppet's wife, played for laughs. Sometimes the way the times change is a positive one.

I slid through the crowd of onlookers, mostly children, and stood next to Maddie, placing a hand on her shoulder.

"Are you enjoying the boardwalk?" I asked. On the stage, the puppets were coming out one by one and taking their bows. The puppeteer was quite skilled, imbuing the simple stick puppets with something almost like life.

"Totally." She said, a smile lighting up her face. Though she was the same age as me when I was turned, she still seemed younger to me, especially when she smiled.

I wondered if that would last.

"And how about you?" I said, turning to the dark, intense girl standing next to Maddie.

"It's great. I love it."

I removed my hand from Maddie's shoulder and placed it on the other girl's. Even though she was new, she felt older than Maddie, older than even me. She had explained to me, during the training and transition, what her life had been like before. But I could never understand it, not fully.

It was hers and hers alone.

"Do you want to stay here for the rest of the night?" I asked. We had already seen the traditional parade, so the rest of the evening was totally at her whim.

She pondered for a moment, squinting her eyes and absently fingering the plastic sword at her waist. She was dressed as a pirate. We were all in a costume that night. The new girl had insisted on this.

"Maybe a bit longer." She said. "But we should probably visit Ami before sunrise."

I nodded silently. You see, even then, we were thinking of you, Ami. That is how things are with us, the way things could be for you if you want them to be.

"We haven't done the haunted house yet," Maddie said. She still loved those things even after all of these years, after all that had happened on her night out.

"Do you think it's any good?" The new girl asked.

"Oh, Chloe, Chloe, Chloe," Maddie responded with mock derision. "When will you realize that that doesn't matter."

We shared a laugh into the illuminated, magical night.

Do you enjoy the tea? I ordered it special from Morocco when I heard how much you enjoy mint. Don't think for a minute that we're trying to buy you or that we've put ourselves out on your behalf. When you live for as long as I have and very few physical needs (at least needs that money can sate), you find yourself buying all sorts of strange things on a whim. The choice is ultimately yours. That's why I'm telling you this story, the tragic comedy (or comic tragedy? No, never that!) that tells how I lost one family and began to build another. That is also why I had Chloe fill you in on the parts that I'd only heard second-hand, the parts that I could never tell as well as she could. I imagine those are the parts that are of most use to you in your decision.

Oh.

You want me to tell you the rest?

I thought it was obvious.

Alright, because you insist, I will finish the story, though I think you'll find that the interesting parts have already been told.

18.

So, we drained Chloe's blood until she paled, her brown eyes rolling back to the back of her head. Part of me wanted to keep going, to drain this huntress, this killer, dry. It would serve her right to be left there, an empty shell. For the human authorities to puzzle over and her people to fume about. However, I remembered the look she gave us at the end, the moment, the second of vulnerability, of (for lack of a better term) humanity.

I placed my hand on Maddie's shoulder, and she stopped drinking, looking at me with feral eyes as of the wolf! For a fraction of a second, I worried that she was going to lash out, strike at me, the one that she so fiercely protected for denying her meal. Instead, she calmed the fury leaving her and being replaced with the young woman I had taken under my wing once more.

We spoke with Chloe between us, her head lolling as if in sleep or drunken torpor.

"What do you wanna do with her?" Maddie asked.

"It's entirely up to her at this point," I replied.

"She killed James."

"I know."

"And probably others."

I nodded. Chloe muttered something in her sleepy fuzz state, something soft, like the coo of a dove.

"And yet..."

Maddie nodded. "Let's give her a choice, then."

We had to abandon the brownstone. There was just too much

death there now, too much destruction. Not to mention the fact that if Chloe followed us there, she might have been in contact with others of her kind, somehow transmitting her location like an ant back to its colony. Thankfully, I wasn't the type of girl to put all my eggs in one basket and always had a second safe haven already lined up.

It was a small warehouse in Red Hook, not far from The Old Rhinebeck Aerodrome Museum. I remember sitting on the roof with Michael, watching the planes fly overhead as the museum put on airshows. It's a good memory and the right place, if a little bit less glamorous than our Brooklyn digs.

We expected Chloe to wake furious, expected to have to do battle with her once more. But much to our surprise, she came to and was sedate, calm, her face an unreadable mask. She knew she had been bested, knew that she was at our mercy.

"What are you going to do with me?" She asked.

"That is entirely up to you," I told her. Maddie nodded her head, standing by my side, close enough that I occasionally felt her shoulder brush mine.

"Are you going to kill me?" Chloe asked.

"No," I replied.

"Why not?"

Maddie shrugged. I said nothing.

"There are things I can do," I explained. "Things I can do to your mind to make you forget you ever saw us, even forget that you even knew that things such as us exist. I can put you back in Brooklyn, with whatever memories you want me to leave you with."

She listened carefully nodding, and occasionally drinking the orange juice we had picked up on the way here.

I continued on. "You wouldn't be a threat to us anymore, and you wouldn't have to keep fighting this stupid war. But you would lose anyone that you have become close to in your...little circle."

"I'm not close to anyone. Not really." She said, something like sadness in her voice.

Neither Maddie nor I knew what to say to that.

"You're talking like there's another option," Chloe said.

I nodded again. Maddie smiled a bit, hiding her fangs this time.

"And you said you aren't going to kill me unless I do something stupid like attack you again, right?"

"Right."

"So, what's my other choice."

And I gave her the same choice I'm giving you right now, dear Ami, though your circumstances are quite different, I think you'd agree. Chloe has had you picked out for quite some time now, and since, after tonight, she will be a full-fledged member of our little club, she gets to decide such things. We wanted to tell you this story tonight so you could choose with a full understanding of what it means of the "life" you will live if you agree.

If you do not agree with this, no harm will come to you. You will forget my face and those of Maddie and Chloe. Your life will continue as it had before, free of memories of things that stalk the night.

Halloween is sacred for us, always has been, always will be, but I think it's even more special for Chloe. It would mean a lot to her if you made this choice on her first night out.

Remember, dear Ami, that no matter how sad parts of this story are, how dark and scary some of the things that happened. It is not a story that ended badly, at least not for those that still move and speak.

For Maddie, this is not a tragedy, nor is it for Chloe. And though I lost those dear to me and think of them often, it wasn't a tragedy for me either, classically speaking.

It was, you see, a comedy.

Ah.

Good.

The night grows old now, and we do need to get back and have some rest after the festivities of tonight.

We do need our rest.

Happy Halloween, dearest, and we will see you again soon.

THE RECORDINGS OF DR. FREYMAN

I cannot believe how treacherous some of these kids' lives have been. Do the parents not see how their arguments and abuse at the hands of another are scaring them? That's why I took it upon myself to get them through their ordeals. Why do you ask? Cause I've been there. I've lived through the arguments. The alcoholic binges from both of my parents. It's devastating. I try to give these kids hope for a positive future. I try to teach them there's hope beyond their troubles.

So good people believe me when I say, "I hear you." I understand what you're going through and I'm here to help. Parents, if you read my books, let them be a guiding light to you. Let the children see how much you love them, don't make them regret having you as parents; make them trust you. Don't be spiteful against dad because he bought a lottery ticket instead of saving money. Don't be spiteful against mom because she bought a new pair of shoes instead of that razor you'd been eying for months.

Children see that, and they mimic your behavior. They are

anything but fools and know when their parents are having trouble. Kids know when you blame them for it; they know everything. All I ask is that you be mindful of your children and yourself.

It was one of his most famous speeches and probably one of the reasons he was attacked early this morning. The Officers played the speech on an old tape recorder. Old technology, but one Doctor Edgar Freyman preferred over the newer methods. Also, the one Officer Ned Pullman and Officer Wes Steyer could do without. Pullman hiked up his pants as forensics combed Dr. Freyman's house from top to bottom.

The old recorder they discovered was bagged for evidence along with the tapes. Steyer sighed as he watched the bags being carried out of the house. They'd be dealing with this from now until night-fall.

"I wonder who'd attack him in broad daylight no less," Steyer contemplated tapping his glove against his hand.

Pullman snorted. "Someone who's got balls, I know that much."

Officer Jack Lee appeared around the corner. He was the first officer to respond to the call. Pullman adjusted his belt and went over to him, maneuvering his way around the crime scene photographer huddled on the floor. The flash illuminated everything around a forensic team that dusted the place.

"Alright, Lee. What've we got?"

"Dr. Freyman was attacked in his bedroom while he slept and then hit in the head with a blunt object. So far, we've had no luck in securing it."

"The upstairs bedroom?" Lee's positive nod led Pullman to his next destination.

Pullman went upstairs, finding the blood trail starting in the back of the bedroom. Upon entering the room, he saw pictures were knocked off the wall and sheets dangling off the bed. Contents Pullman assumed belonged on the nightstand, were thrown to the floor and a lamp turned over. Whoever the attacker was, the Doctor made his escape downstairs. Pullman followed the trail of blood, which ended on the living room floor where a table was knocked sideways and the chair turned over.

"He made his way down here to call for help, as you can see."

Officer Lee followed Pullman's gaze to the spot on the living room floor. Pullman nodded. He would have passed out after making the call or tripping the alarm. Then again, the alarm was disabled meaning the attacker knew him. Pullman scoped out the house for a long time. Another briefing with Lee confirmed his suspicions. Nothing of value was taken, which was odd.

Dr. Freyman was famous in his field of child psychology and even wrote a few best-sellers. He was the encyclopedia of children's wellness and behavior. Well, the parents believed this to be true about him, Pullman wasn't sold on the idea. Dr. Freyman was nothing but a money-hungry psycho who basically used his expertise in child behavior to stick his nose where it didn't belong. A whistle across the room brought his attention to an antique vase. Steyer was tossing the thing gently from hand to hand.

"How much do you think this is worth?"

"More than we can afford. Put that down and let's get back."

"Fine."

Besides, it was starting to get a little crowded here or it could be he felt confined. Most crime scenes brought out an eagerness in him; the eagerness to solve the case and to put it behind him. He wanted to put these bastards in jail, put his feet up, and enjoy an ice-cold soda. He couldn't get out of the house and into the driveway fast enough before reporters surrounded them.

The flashing of the cameras invaded his personal space was enough to make Pullman sick. The reporters' shoes crunching on the gravel beneath their feet, with an itching for a good story no matter how tense the situation. He rolled his eyes seeing the hunger for news before a microphone was jammed in his face.

"Officers, we've some questions."

"Obviously."

"Do you know why Dr. Freyman was attacked?"

"If I knew I wouldn't be here, would I?"

The questions continued and Pullman swerved around the cameraman who leaned back to keep his precious equipment in place on his shoulder. Steyer, on his heels, pulling the same swerve technique but with less grace. The reporter who shoved the microphone in his face was pushed forward by the others resulting in the microphone slipping from her grasp.

Pullman watched as she tried to grab the thing, trying to keep herself from being trampled at the same time. He would have helped her cause he had a thing for the damsels in distress, but she had gotten on his nerves. She would have used his courtesy for the ladies as a way to get a story out of him.

"That's all the questions for today, ladies and gentleman.

Now, if you'll excuse me."

Turning away, he ducked into the police car. The reporters made no move to get closer and he was glad about that. He couldn't guarantee their safety. Steyer didn't get all the way into the car before it pulled away. He let out a yelp while struggling to get his leg in. Pullman slowed down not wanting to hear the same song and dance from the citizens of this great town, 'Cops were there to enforce the rules on citizens and yet they don't follow the rules themselves.' As Dr. Freyman's house became a distant memory through the rearview, the phone rang. Steyer was quick to pick up the receiver on the first ring.

"Steyer here."

Pullman craned his neck, trying to listen to the call and concentrate on the road at the same time. An 'uh-huh' was muttered along with nods of the head in his peripheral view before the call ended with an okay.

"The good doctor lives."

"And?"

"He's still out cold. They think it might be a while before he wakes up but they're not entirely sure, his vitals look good along with everything else. Now it's the waiting game."

"Hope he wakes up soon-" Pullman parked into the police station drive- "We've got to get to the bottom of this."

Steyer nodded. "Let me know how it goes."

"Will do."

Steyer didn't stay long at work but he had a good reason. His wife was due any day now, a baby girl and the miracle baby they'd been waiting for. Pullman was immediately given the role of

Godfather, something he would thoroughly enjoy. He has children too, but they're all grown up and out of the house with families of their own, leaving just him and his wife now.

They were greeted upon entering the station. Pullman made his way back to his tiny office. It housed some sort of comfort for him.

"Good evening, Ned, Wes."

"Same to you, Henry. How's your case coming along?"

"Pretty good. Almost got her wrapped up."

Pullman wished he could say the same. His case was just beginning and might take a while. The tapes were dusted for fingerprints and left on his desk. He figured the only prints found on the tapes belonged to Dr. Freyman. The old recorder was set up by Steyer before he left to be with his wife at the hospital. Since it was the same hospital Dr. Freyman was carted off to, Steyer promised to let him know when the doctor woke up.

After getting a doughnut from the box on Henry's desk, he closed himself up in his office. The paperwork on Dr. Freyman's case sat on the corner of his desk; the flimsy file paper clipped with perfection and not a single document out of place. There wasn't enough evidence as of right now. He called in Officer Ryan to assist in case he missed some important clues involving the case. Although he was pretty sharp, it did well to have another set of ears.

"Let's see what we've got."

"Sure."

Ryan did a slow countdown before he pushed the button, to which Pullman raised an eyebrow. It must be a pre case ritual for him, it was something he always did when they came across new evidence. Pullman caught him doing this mostly when they had footage to watch or tapes to listen to.

The date is March 4th, and I'm speaking with Adelaide Watson. Addy, as she likes to be called, is 15 years old. She's having bad dreams; in them she's chased by an unknown assailant. He is never quite able to catch her before she wakes up. Addy, can you walk me through it?

I don't know if I'm ready to talk about it. Dr. Freyman, are you sure this will help me? I'm still a little freaked out by this whole ordeal. Sitting here in your office, I still don't feel safe.

It's a sure-fire method. I've never had patients come in and say talking about it made the dreams worse. Often they tell me talking about it has made them feel a lot better and their problems less scary. My office is the safest place you can be right now. There's nothing to fear here, please tell me your story.

Okay, I'm walking through the forest, it's something out of a fairytale. Beautiful flowers, butterflies fluttering around and all the animals friendly and lively. All of a sudden, everything grows quiet. The animals disappear and I'm there alone. Then this man comes running out of the bush.

He's wearing a clown mask, but it's a scary clown mask. He's about 7 or 8 ft tall, but his height changes from time to time. He charges at me while carrying hedge clippers, and I run as fast as I can but he is always right on my heels. No matter how far I run, no matter how many shortcuts I take, he's always right there. I can't get away from him.

Addy gasped as if trying to breathe, then continued the story in a high-pitched tone.

Then I fall into a pit. The pit is filled with ice. I can't get out, it's too slippery. I claw until my nails chip and break. I claw until my hands bleed but to no avail. The next thing I know, he's right behind me. He slides down into the pit and-and-

Addy's words were enough to make Pullman and Ryan's blood run cold. The tape ended. Both men wiped the sweat from their brow. Pullman gestured toward another tape. With hesitation, Ryan removed the tape from the recorder and replaced it with another one.

The date is March 12th. Addy and I have decided to try hypnosis. She claims that meeting her attacker this way may help her. I must admit I'm questioning the reason behind her sudden boldness but she reassures me. It's true, she's gotten bold but she won't confront him alone. I plan to be her shield in case the situation turns deadly. I suspect there will be no such thing considering the man is in her dream. So far, so good with Addy is fast asleep. Let's see what I can get out of her.

Addy's words were slurred and almost robotic. Pullman didn't approve of using this kind of method. All the results for this kind of method were inconclusive. He didn't believe in hypnotherapy. The doctor could implant things into Addy's head, but he was silent the whole time as she explained her ordeal.

Why did I come here? For whatever reason? I don't know if I'm strong enough to confront him. Dr. Freyman? Are you there? Please tell me that I'm not doing this alone. Answer me!

It's alright. I'm here for you, I'm right beside you. There's no reason to be afraid, just listen to the sound of my voice, let it be your guide. Where are you right now?

I'm in the forest. It's the same place where I met him for the first time. There are no animals here this time. I'm all alone. There's no sound.

Is the sun shining? Is it nighttime? Tell me everything you're seeing; I would like to see it too.

It's night. The moon is full and hangs high in the sky. It illuminates the forest. To my left, there's a broken tree, it's been hit by lightning. The grass is frozen but it's not cold out, the moon makes it glisten. In front of me, there's a small cabin, but it looks abandoned, there are no lights on. This scene would be beautiful if it wasn't for that cabin.

Okay. Go towards that cabin. I'm right there holding your hand. We're going to confront him together. Put one foot in front of the other and go towards that cabin slowly.

I feel you here with me, Dr. Freyman. I think it's working. The grass crunches beneath my feet and it's starting to get cold now that I'm walking towards the cabin. I'm at the front door. Should I go in?

Yes, go in there. It's his place of dwelling. It has to be. Don't bother knocking. Walk inside and confront him. Let him know that he can't terrorize you anymore. You won't stand for it. You're strong enough now to fight him.

There was a long silence that seemed to stretch for twenty minutes or so. Pullman wondered if the doctor really believed this would help the patient. He didn't think she was strong enough to confront the dream yet in just one or two sessions with him. He cursed under his breath; he wasn't exactly a medical expert.

The silence was damning and he figured she went into the house to confront the dream man. Ryan sucked in a breath and Pullman glanced at him. He clasped his hands together on his lap so tight, they were white as a sheet of paper. He felt the same way Ryan did like they were there at the scene.

I'm in the house. There's nothing much going on here. The only light is from the moon. Is this really his place of dwelling? As I said before, the place looks abandoned. What if I don't get the chance to confront him?

It's fine. Usually, nightmares are locked up at the scariest places for us. The abandoned cabin must have been a scary place for you. Perhaps you saw it in a movie, or you are afraid of being left alone. Don't focus on that right now, what's more important than being afraid is to be aware of your surroundings. Describe to me what you're seeing.

Chains, Rusted chains, on the floor and hanging from the ceiling. There's a rack with tools on it. I see something that looks like zip ties. There are missing person fliers on the bulletin board. There's dust everywhere. It smells like old fabric in here. Oh god! There's dried blood on the floor.

I don't know how old that stain is. As I get closer to the stairs, I see a rack of dolls. There's a clown doll in the corner and another doll. I think they're watching me! As I move, their eyes follow me. Doctor help me!

Addy, you know for yourself that dolls are just inanimate playthings, they can't see or hear you. The bloodstains could be animal's blood, don't let that steer you from your goal. You want to confront him; remember I advise you to keep going. Go towards the stairs. Get out of that place and see what else you can find.

I don't know if I can. I'm sorry, Doctor. I'm not ready to do this, I shouldn't have done this. I need to get out of here before he returns. Oh no. He's here. I hear footsteps upstairs. He's back. He's going to kill me; I need to get out of here.

Addy, calm down, it's only a nightmare. Nightmares can't hurt you, they're only manifestations of your deepest darkest fears. Confronting your fears, facing them head-on is the only way to cure them.

Wake me up, Doctor. Get me out of here, I don't think I'm going to survive this.

Alright, alright, run if you must. I'll wake you up, just listen to the sound of my voice. This might be our last session. There isn't much I can do for you. All you're good for is running away. You'll never be rid of-

A loud bang sounded throughout the station. Pullman cursed; he didn't have the volume of this damn thing up too loud. The bang was enough to make him and Ryan jump up from their seats. From the movement coming through on the other side, Addy had tried to make a run for it. She no longer trusted the doctor could do anything to help her. Dr. Freyman tried to calm Addy down but to no avail. The tape ended when a scream erupted from her.

"What in the hell was that? Why did he make her go through that?" Ryan asked shivering. "Did he really think that would work?"

"That was hypnosis and something that won't hold up in court. I don't know what he or his patients are thinking but let's move on to the next one."

Although Pullman wasn't sure he wanted to hear any more of these tapes. Addy's ordeal was enough to make the hairs on the back of your neck stand on end. Ryan removed Addy's tape swiftly and shoved in the next tape. His finger slammed on the play button without his infamous countdown. Pullman couldn't blame him. He was ready to get this over with just as much as he was. At first, they heard nothing, then Dr. Freyman's voice emerged through.

The date is April 4th, and I just spoke with 16-year-old Ginger William. Our conversation on this particular day wasn't recorded. The reason being Ginger believes that she'll upset the entity she worships. Recording in the month of Easter is a sin to her. I don't really understand, but I'm here to help my patients and do whatever it is they desire.

On that note, Ginger requests something odd of me. She wants me to burn candles every time she visits. She claims the light from bulbs burns her eyes. I comply with her when she comes to my office the next day.

She's dressed in all black and wears a hat with a veil covering her face. Upon her visit, Ginger tells me that she's having trouble getting along with her parents. They don't seem to understand her. From the way she talks about them, it sounds like she utterly despises their guts. She calls them ugly names and talks about how they want to take everything away from her.

I decide to make a house call without letting her or her parents know. When I arrive, I discover that her parents are pretty nice folks. Her mother was rather charming. I see a dog house in the backyard but no dog. When I ask the parents, they are almost chilled to the bone. I find that the dog was sacrificed in some kind of ritual.

Apparently, Miss William likes to delve into black magic. It's the reason for her odd behavior every time she visits my office. I suggest to her parents they should send her to a specialist. Delving into black magic and the occult isn't a good thing. It usually leads to dire consequences but they refuse.

They want me to continue my treatments with her. They think I have all the answers, claiming they've read all my books and they can see that I know how to handle wayward kids.

I'm flattered and I will take up this task with the utmost importance. They claim since Ginger has been coming to see me that she's getting better.

She does seem a little brighter than before. Her clothes aren't as dark, and now she shows me her beautiful face. Her eyes look lifeless, and that's what I'm worried about. The child has no emotion whatsoever. It's not enough to convince me she's getting better. I'm going to have to do further analysis of her case.

The tape ended and Pullman remembered how that turned out. A few days later, Ginger tried to sacrifice her parents to the devil. Mom and Dad both were found bound and gagged in her dad's basement workshop. Dr. Freyman was there to save the day. He claimed he felt something was off when Ginger came to visit him that morning.

She had requested her visits be at night, but there she was. Once the police got there, the parents were sitting in the yard. They both had several cuts and bruises. Part of the dad's ear was missing and the mom would have been decapitated.

A long gash was present on her neck. Luckily, Dr. Freyman was there to talk Ginger down and keep her busy long enough for the cops to arrive. It was one of the biggest and most famous trials in history. Pullman remembered Ginger's demeanor that day. Emotionless, unresponsive, uncooperative.

When she was sentenced, it was the same. She wasn't an adult at the time of her crimes so she was sent to a juvenile detention center. She was to get counseling from a different doctor while there. Her parents forgave her, they chose to stand by their daughter through thick and thin. Dr. Freyman was labeled a hero and the police incompetent for not seeing through Ginger's behavior a long time ago.

Dr. Freyman soaked up the good press like a sponge. He made sure everyone knew he was the one who saw through Ginger a long time ago. And was the one that warned the police to keep an eye on her after she was caught stealing with a boy from school. Dr. Freyman made sure he was captured in every shot and made sure he was available at every police briefing of the media. Their words were ignored by the public with him present.

The tape was removed and replaced with a new one. This time a young male voice came through.

Hello, I'm Eric Meyers filling in for Dr. Freyman, I'm 18 years old and made to see this quack at the suggestion of my parents. He claims he can cure anything, I mean A-NY-THING. I don't believe him. I mean my problem isn't something that someone like him can truly understand. I asked him if he could cure Cancer or call for world peace.

He told me that I was pulling his chain and he didn't

appreciate it. And you know what I said? I said he was full of himself. While he's trying to cure "child behavior" or whatever the hell he calls it, he should take a look at himself. He only laughed at me, but I know the truth. His wife left him for a younger man and his kids want nothing to do with him.

He spent the rest of his miserable life butting into everyone else's business because he couldn't handle his own. He claims to understand us, but what does he understand? Who made him our savior? I just see him as a glorified TV doctor. He's only after fame and fortune. Personally, I think he's- oh shit! He's back, Eric out!

Footsteps, along with the opening of the door were heard before Dr. Freyman's voice cut in. He reprimanded Eric for tampering with his equipment. Eric whined before stopping abruptly. It was a mystery as to why he didn't erase the tape of Eric Meyers' conversation. Judging from the tape, Eric was the prime suspect. He based this on experience, but he didn't want to count his chickens before they hatched. There were still a lot more of the tapes to listen to.

"Let's take a break." Pullman rubbed his eyes. It might be time to hit up the coffee pot. Ryan was dismissed to return to his tasks. He didn't want to keep him from his work. Steyer would be back in the morning if his wife didn't give birth. Pullman wished he just took time off. He wasn't the only one on the force who thought this way.

He was cutting it close, considering his wife was due any day now. Steyer wanted to get in the extra hours up until the birth. After filling his cup with the latest decaf, he headed back to the tapes. Upon seeing how much of the pile he had left, he sighed. He'd listen to a few more before getting himself a late-night snack. Glancing at the clock, he hadn't noticed it was almost eleven, an hour until midnight. He placed another tape in the recorder.

The date is September 27th. I paid a visit to relatives in the suburbs. It had been a long time since I went home. I thought I'd go there and get a little bit of rest. My relatives were happy to see me. They suggested we go out for something to eat. You know, catch up on some old times. We chose this restaurant that was a little way out of town.

As I waited for my meal, there was a kid at the restaurant. I hate to say this, but he was a brat. I couldn't enjoy the meal the way I wanted. The child practically cried and screamed the whole time he was there. I wanted to give the parents a good bop upside the head for not doing much to contain their child. One minute he's sitting there and the next, he's running all over the place. I told my relatives I had to go. There was a case that needed my attention. It turns out it's the child's family. They have a teenage daughter who was in serious need of my attention.

I went to their house and we talked for a while. Having to babysit her brother and the breakup with a boyfriend took a toll on her. She broke down crying. She told me she was on drugs and any attempts to quit were for naught. This went on for hours and I was able to convince her to check herself into rehab.

This was different. The doctor was in the business of even recording his own life. The visit with relatives was fair game for his recordings. He stopped the tape and inserted another one. Dr. Freyman talked about being displeased with one of his patients.

Eric Meyers to be exact. He didn't want to counsel him again, nor the other patient who's recording Pullman didn't find yet.

He practically insulted them and their parents for not raising them well. Pullman smirked. Apparently, Eric was onto something. The good doctor wasn't so good after all. According to his rants, their kids wouldn't have made it through without him. He picked and chose his patients. If they didn't follow his rules to the letter or didn't believe in his form of counseling, he wanted to end things. He turned off the doctor's rants and went on to the next one.

The next tape housed some of the doctor's treatment methods. Some were inhumane, to say the least. Under hypnosis, one of his patients recalled her sexual acts with a would-be lover. From the way Dr. Freyman addressed the woman, Pullman would go as far as to say the doctor was the lover she talked about. The scenes they both described were a little too explicit for his taste.

He turned off the recording after clearing his throat one hundred times. Another recording led to the old method in which to treat a patient and one he bet the parents had no idea he used. Dunking someone in ice was a rather old method. The method was outdated and inhumane.

The good doctor got away with some of the things he did, which was nonsense. It was beyond his comprehension. How the parents didn't notice if their son or daughter came home shivering or soaking wet, they didn't bother to question the methods used to treat him. He had enough with the treatment methods and moved on to the next tape.

It's September 30th, and I'm at the police station with Kyle Draken. Kyle has just been arrested for a string of serial murders going on around town. Not that it was Kyle who confessed to me but an alternate that lives inside of him. An alternate that goes by the moniker doll.

Another voice comes through. Pullman swallowed. It was a cross between a male's voice and a female's voice. The doctor dealt with a lot of weird patients, didn't he? How many freaks of nature did the doctor run into on a daily basis? The voice giggled. A cough came through along with the clearing of the throat.

I'm more than just a moniker Dr. Freyman. You know that. I'm practically Kyle's shadow. The one he leans on in his time of need. The one that's always going to be there for him. No one has ever done that for him except me.

My apologies. I didn't mean to offend you. I know how much you've done for Kyle. I'm sure he appreciates it as we all do. Thank you for being there for him. He had no one else in the world except you.

It's fine. You're forgiven. As long as you know now how important I am to him and his life. He needs me you know. He wouldn't have lasted this long without me. I protect him from anything and everything looking to do him harm.

Yes, yes, I understand. Let's get down to business, shall we? According to my colleague Dr. Rappaport and the files I have on your condition, you emerged after Kyle's dad walked out on him, correct? While under hypnosis Kyle admitted this. His dad leaving took its toll on him.

That's just the half of it. He left Kyle's mom and Kyle for another woman. Left her while she was pregnant with Kyle too. He told Kyle's mother he never wanted her anyway. They weren't

even married. It was just a fling.

He leaves the family and goes off to marry this other woman. I'm pretty sure the mother feels a sense of betrayal. She's carrying his kid. So, the dad leaves the family and what happens after that?

Kyle suffers because of it. His mom turned her hatred and betrayal at the hands of Dad to a hatred of all men. They're liars, cheaters, and betrayers. She prayed every day that she'd have a girl. Girls are sugar, spice, and everything nice. Girls don't lie to you. They'd never betray you.

Imagine her surprise when she gives birth and it's a bouncy baby boy. His mom was anything but delighted. She promises to make him into the perfect girl. He will be the most beautiful girl in town and there's nothing anyone can do about it.

So, she basically subjects her hatred out on her son. If the dad left the way he did, then Kyle could do the same. She sees Kyle as his father. There's no escaping it. All men are evil and to curb this evil within my son, I must change who he is. How am I doing so far?

You're right on the money, doctor. She taught Kyle that men are evil. She reminded him that he was impure. He needed to do whatever he could to get rid of the impurity. She wanted a daughter and she tried her best to make Kyle her daughter. Dress like a girl, walk, talk and act like a girl. If you don't, you're punished severely.

Gasps were heard around the room along with hushed whispers. A gasp emerged from Pullman's own lips. He didn't have to be a doctor to know where this was going next. Her abuse shattered Kyle's mental state. He didn't understand how the mom could do something so vile to her son. It echoed back to the speech that contributed to Dr. Freyman's fame.

Kyle was beaten or starved for days if he so much as mentioned he wanted to be a boy. If he mentioned, he liked being a boy. Poor Kyle endured so much. Luckily I was there to help him. I was the most beautiful girl for Kyle's mother and Kyle could be the boy he wanted to be. Everybody's happy until Kyle meets a girl prettier than I.

You were created to be the perfect girl. Kyle wanted to live life as a male because that's what he is. So, the mom's happy because she thinks she's confirmed him to her ways, but what do you mean until Kyle meets a woman prettier than you? Kyle's not allowed to meet beautiful women?

Have you ever seen Kyle's mom in her younger years? A true beauty among many. All the men would fall at her feet. How could she not expect his dad to fall in line? When he didn't is when the trouble started. I took it upon myself to protect Kyle from their trickery. If she could hurt Kyle the way she did, other beautiful women could hurt him as well.

I must stop them. Kyle can't ever have another woman come into his life. They're all the same. I can't let him go through that pain again. After cleansing him of those that could hurt him, we got rid of his mom. She was the only link left to Kyle's horrid past. I had to get rid of her.

Pullman ended the tape. If Kyle was already in police custody for the serial murders of the hotel women, there was no point in hearing anymore. Plus, his case was one of the freakiest cases he ever worked on. It was one of the cases he couldn't get out of his head.

Young, beautiful women found in a basement and encased in ice. Their features were forever frozen in time. Their beauty was captured like some horror portrait. It was something they couldn't unsee no matter how they closed their eyes. The mother was found locked in a cage and her head twisted completely around. It was enough to give the department nightmares for weeks. He took a moment to glance at the TV. He forgot he turned it on. Dr. Freyman's attack was all over the news.

His cases were brought to light. One of the cases mentioned was about a supposed wolfman. The young man came to the doctor for treatment. The wolfman was arrested when two police officers were found dead in his neighborhood. Their vehicle wrapped around a tree. It took the officers a long time to pry the bodies out of the vehicle. Dr. Freyman went to visit the supposed wolfman, but that was all he heard of the case until tonight. Pullman turned the recorder back on after muting the volume on the TV and changing out the tapes. It was Eric Meyers again.

Hello, it's Eric back again at the beginning of this lovely month. I know, I know. The doctor doesn't rest, does he? Already calling me back in with another session. I don't get him. He gave up on me. I heard the recording where he badmouthed me and others who came to see him. We didn't ask him for his help. It isn't like our parents put a gun to his head and made him help us.

It goes right back to what I said before. He's only in it for fame and money. This doctor doesn't know shit. He's as fake as a plastic rabbit. He must have realized that his career isn't shit without us. I guess he realized that without us, there would be no

Dr. Freyman. There would be no fame, fortune, nor success. He needs to realize that. Asshole. Anyway, while I got you here, let me tell you about a game I'm working on.

This game is called Creator. Since I'm into that horror shit, I made this game to follow a character named Edgar Sorrow. Yeah, I named him after that piece of shit doctor. Anyway, Edgar wakes up in a lab having no idea who he is or why he's there. He exits the container he's kept in, only to find that his legs and arms don't work that well. After getting feeling back in his limbs, Edgar proceeds to look around the lab. He notices he's got two choices. He can see what sadistic artwork the doctor has done on him or he can leave his place of dwelling.

If Edgar chooses to look in the mirror, he will have a major freak out upon seeing himself. He'll see glowing red eyes and long dark hair and breaks the mirror. Causing Edgar to cower in the corner of the lab until he's comforted by his creator. The creator will tell Edgar about how he was near death and saved his life. Edgar will hear some bogus lie about the creator being his father. As a father, he couldn't let him just die. You know how it goes. Edgar will then have the choice of trusting the creator or going out on his own.

If Edgar decides to trust the creator, the creator will put him back in his container to sleep so he can calm down. This is where the game will conclude. If Edgar decides to not trust the creator and leaves, the creator will let him explore the lab. Edgar will find out clues about his past, and he will leave the lab to find his former partner. If Edgar chooses to try the door, he will leave the lab and find clues to his past.

He will then find out he used to be a cop and that he was supposedly killed in the line of duty. He will find an article where it tells the location of his gravesite and sees a picture of his former partner at his funeral. Edgar must choose if he'll go visit the gravesite or locate his former partner.

If Edgar chooses to visit the gravesite, he'll see his mom and brother there. His brother is now a cop and works for the department. He vows to catch Edgar's killer and make him pay for what he's done. Mom cries. You know how women break out the water-works. Edgar watches his family from afar and decides not to confront them because he doesn't want to shock them. He instead returns to the lab.

If Edgar decides to locate his former partner, they'll wind up going to the police station. Edgar waits for his partner outside of the station, where he confronts him after his shift is over. Of course, he's shocked to see him alive and explains to him what happened. Edgar finds out that the world is in a state of disarray, and he was supposedly attacked and killed by an unknown assailant. That's not the only shocker. He learns that all of these events were orchestrated by none other than the creator. The end.

Yeah, it's one of those choose your path kind of stories, but it sounds cool doesn't it? I pretty much told you most of the storyline. I didn't mean to. You know how once I get excited about something I can't stop talking.

Anyway. I got this idea from someone I visited while on my nightly excursions. He's a game lover like me. I told him we should play sometime but that's impossible. Well, I better disappear before the good doctor returns. Eric out.

Pullman never saw the game. It was probably something Eric made up to pass the time. If the doctor left the recorder alone for even a minute, Eric was there to shine. He had a feeling the doctor did this on purpose. Perhaps he felt it helped Eric in some way. Another tape down and a long list of more to go. On to the next one.

It's October 4th, and I'm here with Spencer Davis, age 18. Spencer has been away from home for two years. He claims that his parents have been acting strange ever since his return. He claims they rarely acknowledge him at home. They have replaced him with another kid. One that he doesn't particularly like.

Pullman perked up at the name. He knew Spencer Davis. Well, he knew Spencer's parents. Spencer ran away from home at the age of 16. The parents never bothered to look for him. The only way he found out was from Steyer's wife. The Davis family were planning to keep this under wraps. It wasn't a good idea. He wanted to help them, but they never came forward with the news. They were either ashamed or didn't care. Where did Dr. Freyman find him? How did he find him? Pullman turned up the volume. He grabbed a notebook and pen.

Spencer, you can begin your story whenever you're ready. You're wasting my tape here. If you don't want to talk about it now, I can turn off the tape and we can talk some other time. The choice is up to you. I won't force you to do something you're not ready for.

There is a bit of hesitation on Spencer's end. The tape continued to roll, accompanied by silence. Pullman leaned forward, his ear almost touching the machine. He tampered with the volume again, but the tape ended. The doctor probably cut it short Cursing under his breath, Pullman rummaged through the pile of tapes.

He hoped he could pull another one of Spencer's tapes. There had to be a reason the kid turned up after two years. He found a tape that was littered with scratches at the bottom of the pile. This one had a date on it. Pullman picked up another tape and noticed small numbers etched on the tape. Why were they dated like this? Wouldn't it be easier to use a slip of paper? He went back to the previous tapes he listened to with officer Ryan. The dates were scratched into the surface of the tapes. Pullman sighed. To say this was a dumb error on his part was an understatement. He should've paid attention.

Not wanting to waste any more time, he pulled all the tapes dated after October 4th from the pile. Starting with the one dated October 6th, he placed it in the recorder and listened.

It's October 6th, and I'm back with Spencer Davis. After a lot of convincing from both his parents and me, Spencer is ready to tell his story now. First things first, we need to address the reason you ran away from home.

Mom and Dad were too much. They argued all the time. I was always in the middle. Spencer, who do you think is right, mom or dad? Spencer, what were you doing when dad did this or mom did that. They didn't even care about my problems. They never took the time to listen to me. They never understood how I felt. I couldn't stand it any longer so I ran.

Did you believe this would make them listen to you? Did you think they would stop fighting if they had something else to concentrate on? What did you hope to gain by running away from home? Perhaps they would focus on their son for once, right?

I just wanted them to understand me. I missed our outings and spending time with them, they don't do that anymore. They're always fighting, I thought if I ran away, they'd apologize for being so hard on me.

In other words, your parents should feel bad not for putting you in the middle of their arguments but for disciplining you when you're in the wrong.

Dad hit me. Their arguments turned on me. I tried to voice my opinion and he would hit me. I was so shocked I could barely speak. How could he slap his own son in the face?

And that's a reason to run away? There's no right or wrong way to discipline children. There's no rule book on parenting, and some of them have a hard time but that doesn't make them bad. Parents hit their children all the time. It's nothing to act like a spoiled brat over.

I thought if I came here you'd help me. I heard you were the best psychologist in town. Is this how you help your patients? By making them feel like shit? Is this some form of reverse psychology? I don't even know why I need to see you anyway.

A violent scraping of a chair being kicked across the room can be heard. Static came through as Pullman lowered the volume a little at the chief passing by the room. The chief nodded in his direction and kept walking toward the break room.

Your parents have said you're not yourself lately is why you're here. They want to figure out if there is something else going on with you since you've been away so long. Your claims about them seem to be you acting out. They're concerned and I'm here to help.

I didn't think they noticed. I haven't heard a word from them in two years. I haven't seen my face printed on milk cartons, Nor have I seen missing flyers with myself posted around town. If I didn't go home when I did, they never would have found me.

And that's supposed to make them kiss up to you? You make it sound like they owe you something. If they didn't care, they wouldn't have sent you here to talk with me.

What is your deal, man?

My deal is, you are a spoiled rotten kid. I don't have the slightest bit of remorse for your predicament. You made the decision to run away from home. You decided to act like a child and take your ball and run off to god knows where. If your parents didn't look for you, perhaps it was they weren't going to waste their time looking for a spoiled rotten kid.

Screw you, I don't have to sit here and listen to this. I'm leaving. You obviously don't know what you're talking about.

Items were knocked over along with the breaking of glass. Pullman chewed on his lower lip. Dr. Freyman was relentless with his insults. The way he talked to Spencer could have led the young man down a bad road. He was another prime suspect. Then again, it could be another one of the doctor's many tactics. Sometimes insults were used to get a reaction out of the patient. Rather it was to release repressed anger or get them to let out everything they kept bottled inside.

The frustrations of society, along with the overwhelming

struggle to hang on, was enough to make anyone lash out. Pullman remembered reading this in a book that involved a D.I.D. patient. According to specialists. The patient had a personality that was angry no matter what happened. When the patient finally had the courage to get angry on their own and speak up about the abuse that plagued them for so long, the other identity was no longer needed.

That didn't seem to be the case with Kyle Draken. He practically did away with the problems that angered him. Pullman didn't feel sorry for the mother though. It was cruel of him to say, but she got what she deserved. He could never understand how a parent could treat their child so badly. They were supposed to protect them, not blame them for the problems in their lives.

Spencer, calm down. Let's think about this with a cool head. I know you're angry, but you've given me nothing that suggests your condition and stress is from your parents' arguments. Tell me the truth. You're angry with them because it's like they don't care. They fail to see what's ailing you.

I don't have to listen to your crap. You're nothing but a quack. First and foremost, you have no idea what's going on with me. You have no idea how wretched that place is. I admit I ran away at the time because I was frustrated, but do you know what's more frustrating? The fact my parents didn't bother to look for me.

That's not even half of it. When I returned home, they replaced me. They replaced me with another kid. I felt so betrayed and hurt, but you wouldn't understand. They act as if they don't know me. Two years hasn't been that long. I haven't

changed that much.

That's perfect, Spencer. See? You addressed the problem. Your frustrations spilled out of you after feeling ignored and neglected by your parents. You lash out at anyone who tries to lecture you on your way of doing things. It's one of the reasons they wanted you to see me. So, you have a new sibling and you feel ignored. Is this sibling nice to you? Do you get along well? Let's talk about your relationship with-

He's not my brother, and I've talked to you all that I've wanted to. You better change the way you cure your patients because the way you talked to me makes me want to bash your head in. Have a good day, asshole. You better watch your back. Stupid, fake TV doctor.

The door slammed and the doctor murmured that Spencer needed more counseling. After ranting on and on about his session with Spencer the tape ended. Pullman sighed. The doctor made it sound like he was filming a YouTube video and asking for subscribers. His methods were unorthodox indeed.

Pullman stacked the October tapes in a pile. Spencer was the prime suspect ahead of Eric. The fact that Spencer went as far as to threaten the doctor on tape during a session was damning. To think that the doctor recorded the whole thing. His phone buzzed on his desk startling him.

It could be the chill in the room, but hearing these tapes was kind of freaking him out. He stared at the caller ID. It was the call he'd been waiting on all night. He grabbed the phone and cleared his throat.

"Pullman here."

"Ned, he's awake. I'll wait for you before I head over there to see him."

"Steyer," Pullman grabbed the keys from the desk. "So far you haven't been able to question him yet?"

"Negative. I tried to question him but he had trouble focusing. He fell asleep. His family's visiting with him now. I guess the daughter still maintains contact with him although the parents are divorced."

"Okay. Make sure you stay near him. If the assailant figures out he's alive, they may try to finish the job."

"Okay. There are officers stationed outside his room, so getting in there will be difficult. Plus, they have cameras all over this floor. Oh, and watch out for the reporters. They pretty much camped out the place."

Pullman wasn't going to even entertain that idea. He knew criminals who found a way to get past the officers stationed to protect the victim. Some of them didn't even care if there were cameras present. The methods they used weren't always a slip of a drug in their coffee to get them to sleep. Sometimes it ended with murder.

"Okay, I'm on my way."

Pullman arrived at the hospital in no time flat. The reporters briefed the media on the case. Pullman groaned; these guys never missed an update. He made sure to pull his car around to the back of the hospital. He wasn't up for being mobbed by them. He didn't have the patience nor the answers for their twenty-one questions.

Steyer waited for him near the entrance. Pullman parked the

car and cut the engine as his partner came quickly to greet him. Steyer opened the driver door before he had a chance to wriggle out of his seatbelt. He held onto the door and saluted playfully.

"Has he said a word yet?"

Steyer shrugged, shutting the car door once Pullman climbed out. "I haven't been in there yet. I tried to give him some time with his family as I told you over the phone."

"Right."

The two officers took their time getting back up to the second floor where Dr. Freyman rested. They were greeted by a nurse and doctor here and there. By the time they made it upstairs, his family stood outside the door. The daughter looked in their direction. She offered a small smile but it barely reached her eyes.

"Hello Mrs. Freyman, it's nice to meet-," Pullman started to say.

"It's Mrs. Lancaster now, officer."

The ex-wife moved on and didn't look back. She was a striking beauty. Dark brown hair and beautiful brown eyes. Tall and slim with perfect posture. The daughter was just as lovely. Mrs. Lancaster sat in one of the chairs. She placed her head in her hands and sighed.

"How's he doing," Pullman asked.

"Better I guess. He didn't exactly say how he felt," she eyed them with distaste. "Doesn't want to talk to any cops though."

"Well, it's not exactly his call."

Pullman went into the doctor's room while Steyer stayed behind to question the wife and daughter. Upon entering the room, Dr. Freyman clucked his tongue. The balding man pushed his glasses up his nose. The remote was held in his slightly wrinkled hand. He placed it on the lunch table in front of him. He looked a little worse for wear, but it seemed like he would pull through.

The wound to his head wasn't deep enough to cause major brain damage, but it did require a lot of stitches. He pulled the lid off the tray and winced at the contents in disgust. He took a better liking to the tea and took a long sip. Pullman pulled out his notebook and pen. Dr. Freyman shook his head.

"Dr. Freyman, welcome back," he said, bringing the pen to the paper. "I have some questions for you."

"About?"

Pullman frowned while clearing his throat. Either he suffered memory loss because of the blow, or he was being sarcastic. From the look in the doctor's eyes, he'd say it was the second one. Pullman moved closer to the bed. Dr. Freyman's arctic blue eyes never left him.

"The tapes for one. There's a lot of incriminating evidence on there. I found some interesting things on there. I plan to use some of it as evidence if you don't mind. Never mind, I have already secured a warrant."

Dr. Freyman didn't seem fazed by this latest revelation. Pullman knew the man was putting up a front. It was enough evidence on those tapes to arrest him for his inhumane treatment of some of his patients, but he wasn't going to make a big deal of it yet. First and foremost, he'd handle his case first.

"I've done a lot for this society over the years and you want to talk to me about some private conversations that you had no business listening to? Do officers follow a law that we citizens have no idea about? Who do you think you are going through my patient's private files?"

Pullman smirked. "When a crime happens, where it happens is evidence. Everything involved in or around that crime scene becomes evidence. You know that."

"Doctor-patient confidentiality. Ever heard of it or does it not exist in the rule book cops made up for themselves?"

"Heard of it but it doesn't matter when a crime's involved. Now cut the bullshit and tell me what you know. Don't try to give me this righteous citizen crap. You are anything but."

"I don't know anything and I won't put my patients in harm's way just to help you with your case. They have nothing to do with this. Go somewhere else to find your criminal and leave me alone. You won't get anything out of me."

A lie. It was obvious with the doctor's shifting eyes. If he cared so much about protecting his patients' dignity, then he wouldn't use such practices. There was nothing he could do to protect them. They were criminals, simple as that.

"Eric Meyers and Spencer Davis. These two seem to have it out for you."

Dr. Freyman sat up and straightened the pillows behind him with a wince. Pullman eyed him curiously. The painkillers must be wearing off, or the doctor was ready to confess the truth.

"Eric would never do something like that. He's a good kid. He talks a lot. If you heard our conversation, you'd know that."

"According to your tape, you couldn't get rid of him fast enough."

"Doesn't make him a suspect, officer. Eric's not even in town now. He went on a fishing trip with his parents. You can check it if you don't believe me. He won't be back for another day or two."

Pullman jotted it down for reference. He placed a call to Steyer to check on the kid's alibi. Once it was confirmed, he checked him off his most-wanted list. That just left Spencer. He still had the other tapes to sift through, but he'd take it one step at a time.

"How'd you meet Spencer Davis. He ran away from home two years ago."

"He returned, he wasn't satisfied when his parents didn't look for him," Dr. Freyman frowned. "Of all the cases I've dealt with in my career, his case is the strangest."

"What do you mean?"

If the doctor thought Spencer's case was strange, what in the world did he think of the others? Some of them talked about things that he never heard of from patients. It was weird, to say the least.

Dr. Freyman slumped down on the pillows and closed his eyes. "He told me his parents recently brought in another kid who looks exactly like him."

Pullman paused with his pencil tip on the notepad. "I heard some of it. Can you give me more details?"

"Spencer told me his parents replaced him with someone else. I thought it was weird. His parents are older now and have no energy for the hanky panky. At first, I thought he meant they adopted some kid from an orphanage but that wasn't the case. Spencer kept telling me the same thing over and over. They replaced him. The kid looks exactly like him."

"What did his parents say?"

"He's imagining things. There was no one else there. So they made him come see me, to figure out why he was seeing something like that. Spencer's story never changed. He insists that his parents act like the kid is him and even took pictures with him."

Pullman thought about the conversation between Spencer and Dr. Freyman on the tape. The doctor thought Spencer had a new sibling but it was deeper than that. The young man felt replaced by this new person in his home if there was one.

"I remember on the tape you asked him about this new sibling. You asked them if they got along."

"Yeah and he adamantly denied this kid was his sibling."

"Did you ever see this new sibling?"

"No. Well, I didn't at first."

"What do you mean?"

Dr. Freyman placed a hand to his chin. He hesitated, and Pullman knocked on the table to get his attention. Dr. Freyman glanced at him and snorted. Pullman sat on the chair near the bed. The thing was uncomfortable, making him twist this way and that before he could get into a position where it didn't feel like his ass was on the ground.

"Well," Dr. Freyman started. "I met with his parents at home and didn't see this look-a-like kid. I was starting to believe Spencer made this kid up to get back at them, but then he came into my office on a stormy night in October."

"Did he look like Spencer?"

"Yes, the spitting image of him. I thought he was Spencer for a moment until he spoke. The language in which he spoke and the things he said didn't make sense. His eyes were different; they were a lot colder. His mannerisms and everything was scary."

"It could be Spencer. Maybe he has a split personality disorder or something."

Dr. Freyman shook his head violently. "Oh no, officer. The way this kid came off, he was possessed by demons. He may look like Spencer, but trust me, it's not him."

"And you believe that?"

"Of course, there are strange things in this world. That kid is the devil. I'm telling you. That kid is not of this world."

Pullman didn't know what kind of game the doctor or Spencer was playing, but he didn't like it. Spencer attacked him, that was all there was to it. There was no reason to talk to him any longer. He didn't believe in ghosts, hobgoblins, or whatever you wanted to call it. Crime was crime and having some supernatural entity in the picture was just another story Dr. Freyman cooked up. Either to gain sympathy from the unsuspecting populace, or he wanted to be famous above all else, and this was the perfect way to do it.

"And you expect me to believe that this Spencer look-alike is possessed by demons and the demon attacked you?"

"I'm telling the truth."

"Spencer is the prime suspect whether you like it or not. I'm going to have a lot of trouble proving a look-alike did it and I might lose my job in the process."

"Spencer wasn't the one who attacked me. It was someone or something else."

"Who or what was it then, the devil?"

"Go back and listen to the rest of the tapes; everything will make a great deal of sense. If you arrest Spencer, that thing will take over his life. It's already eating away at him and his parents."

"Have a good day, Doctor."

Pullman left the room as Dr. Freyman called after him. He didn't want to listen to the rest of the tapes. Spencer Davis committed a crime and he hadn't been back that long. It was time to wrap up this case. He too wanted to get home and rest if only for a little while.

Pullman returned to the office and laughed at himself. Was he really going to believe Dr. Freyman's hocus pocus nonsense? Or that he was trying to convince himself there was no such thing as ghosts and demonic possession? Perhaps this case was making him lose his mind. He pressed the button and sat back with another doughnut and some freshly brewed coffee. He laughed at his typical cop snack of choice. Well, he found the tape with the wolfman.

Pullman listened to the young man explain his troubles with changes he experienced. Of course, Dr. Freyman chalked it up to the young man going through puberty. The young man was sure it was more than just puberty. He was hungry all the time. The moon made him feel uneasy.

The conversation went on and on until the tape ended with the young man feeling reassured that hunger and the moon weren't out to get him. There was no such thing as werewolves. He listened to another tape.

It's October 16th, and I'm sitting here once again with Spencer Davis.

I'm not Spencer.

Spencer sitting in front of me claims not to be Spencer. I'm having a hard time adjusting to this. Spencer, what do you mean?

Exactly what I said. I may look like Spencer but I'm not. Come on you're the doctor. Figure it out.

What does that mean? You look like Spencer. You walk, talk, and act like Spencer.

Walk, talk, and act?

Pullman shivered at the low growl that came from Spencer's throat mixed with static. He was hot upon entering. Did they turn the heat off? He lowered the volume as the growls continued. Growls that rumbled the table, or it could be his imagination. This kind of work played tricks on you.

Spencer, calm down. Let's talk about your relationship with your family.

Do you mean Spencer's family?

Yes.

The voice lowered to a hushed whine, sounded nothing like the Spencer Davis he remembered.

He left his family. So much negative energy surrounding that place. They fought all the time and left Spencer to handle things on his own. They were interested in their own grievances that they didn't think about the wellbeing of their child. About the things he could become involved in.

Okay. What kinds of things did Spencer get involved in?

Maniacal laughter emerged in a high-pitched tone. Pullman undid the first few buttons of his shirt. It was funny. This shirt was never so tight around the neck before. It was choking him. He wiped at a bead of sweat on his brow. Weird, now he was hot again.

Drugs, alcohol, and my favorite summoning the undead.

Excuse me?

Another loud noise like feet being placed on the coffee table. Pullman followed suit. He placed his feet on the table next to the recording. A sip of coffee that burned his tongue a little. More laughter ensued.

You see, Doctor, Spencer bought an Ouija board. You know what it is, don't you? You know what it can do?

Ouija boards are used to talk to ghosts, right? I'm sorry, but I don't think that has anything to do with his treatment. Are you saying he summoned you?

Yes. Spencer lost a very dear friend. Did you know he used to have a girlfriend?

This is new. Did his parents know? How do you know?

Well…it's not really a secret. When he left home at the age of 16, it was to be with her. She talked him into running away with her, you know how kids are. They voice their concerns to other friends and the next thing you know, they're kindred spirits.

So, he meets this girl and what happened?

She was killed and the police never figured out who did it. Her death wasn't normal either, but we won't get into that. Spencer's so distraught that he buys an Ouija board. He wanted to communicate with her from the other side. He goes to the last place she was found alive. She was at the bus stop, waiting for him.

It still doesn't explain why he stayed away for two years. If she died, why didn't he return home to his parents?

He blamed them for her death. If only his Dad hadn't held him up. If only he hadn't gotten into a fight with his Dad that night. If only he had been there on time, she'd still be alive.

That's when the argument happened. When he said his father struck him. He was late meeting her and as a result, she was killed by an unknown assailant.

Correct. Spencer's devastated, and he stays away for two years. We met around this time. I pretend to be his long-lost love. In return, I escape from my realm into the human world.

What do you mean, 'you pretend to be his lost love?' How can Spencer not know you from her? She's dead.

Do you not understand how the board works? Unsuspecting victims call us from the other side and before you know it, we're in their world.

How? Are you saying you're from the board?

Come on, Doc. You're not that slow. Let me put it in simpler terms. If you don't end the conversation, we come for you. If you don't say goodbye, it's an invitation for us to step into your world. Don't you know that?

Spencer didn't close the conversation. You took it upon yourself to enter our realm. I don't believe you.

What do you believe?

You're Spencer and you're lying to me. You are a deeply disturbed young man. I think it's best you seek treatment elsewhere.

Leave to you and scientists to think there is an answer for everything supernatural. Spencer believed the same thing you

did. He believed this was all a game until he came home and saw me sitting in his living room.

What did he do?

What else? He freaked out. I mean, it's not every day you see someone with your face. You have to be crazy not to freak out. He doesn't have a twin now, does he?

The tape ends abruptly. Pullman wiped the sweat off his brow. He might need another coffee break by the time this was over. He jumped out of his seat at the loud rapping on his door.

"Come in."

Steyer stepped into the room with furrowed brows. "You okay?"

"Yeah, this case has me a little on edge."

Pullman rubbed his eyes as Steyer sipped his own cup of coffee. His presence here echoed to Pullman; his wife hadn't given birth yet. Steyer pulled a chair up to the front of the desk and took a seat.

"Find anything?"

"Just some hocus pocus by Dr. Freyman and Spencer Davis."

"Spencer Davis?"

Pullman raised an eyebrow. "Why'd you say it like that?"

Steyer smirked. "No reason, but my wife did tell me something weird about him while I was there with her. She said Spencer changed a lot. He wasn't acting like his usual self and get this, his parents seemed to be afraid of him."

Pullman didn't doubt it. From the way he sounded on the tapes, one would believe he was possessed by demons. What was he thinking? There was no such thing. Could he really say that for sure?

"Well, you should listen to these tapes. The kid's obviously on drugs or something."

Pullman rewinds the tape. Steyer's expression was the same one he was sure he wore when he listened to the tapes. Like him, Steyer also undid the first few buttons of his shirt. This was going to be one case that the two of them would probably never forget.

"So, what do we do now?"

"I say we pay Mr. and Mrs. Davis a visit. Perhaps they can explain this in more detail to us."

"I can't."

Steyer had a good excuse as any, but Pullman knew the truth. After hearing those tapes, he didn't want to go anywhere near the kid nor his parents, but they didn't have a choice.

Pullman sat at the small gate of the Davis residence. In the yard, Mr. Davis collected some trash. He seemed to be lost in thought as Pullman got out of the car. The man paused and looked at him with the trash still in hand. Pullman smirked and pulled out his badge, although he and Mr. Davis were anything but strangers.

"Ned, what brings you here?"

"Hi, Larry, how's it going?"

Mr. Davis shrugged. "Could be better but I'm hanging in there."

"I would like to talk to your son if you don't mind. Is he home?"

Mr. Davis nodded. He motioned for Pullman to follow him. The house was how he remembered. Nothing out of the ordinary. It was clean and tidy, just the way Mrs. Davis liked it. The pictures lined the stairs. Pullman took a seat on the couch, not wanting to disrespect them by walking around their home. He hadn't brought a warrant anyway.

"Would you like anything to drink?"

"No, I'm fine. I had plenty of coffee before I arrived."

Mr. Davis offered him a smile. He sat on the couch facing the steps. From the look on his face, Dr. Freyman had the right idea of it. They were scared of someone or something in the house. They waited in silence.

"He should be down in a minute."

Pullman didn't understand it. He didn't see him go upstairs to get the boy, nor did he call out to him. His phone buzzed. He excused himself to take the call from Steyer. He went out to the porch where he saw vines growing up the side of the house.

"Pullman here."

"Hey, just wanted to brief you on what Mrs. Lancaster said about some of the doctor's patients."

"Sure."

"Well, the doctor specializes in a certain kind of patient, if you know what I mean."

"The rich and famous?"

"Not quite."

Pullman thought about the recordings he heard. Well, he mostly specialized in the creepy but true types. He had about two patients on the tape who had problems that weren't related to some supernatural event of some kind but he didn't bite the bait. He wasn't sure if these people were truly going through these experiences or making them up.

"Most of the patients have some kind of supernatural happening going on around them."

"Except for Eric Meyers and the wolf kid."

"Well, Eric believes he can leave his body at will. Claims, he helped lost souls cross to the other side while on his journey."

Were any of them normal? Pullman rubbed his eyes. Eric was another supernatural occurrence. This was starting to get on his nerves.

"Okay, and how'd you learn that?"

"Mrs. Lancaster said she was there on one of their visits. Dr. Freyman put Eric under hypnosis and he mentioned this, but while out of hypnosis, he was confused as to why he told the doctor such things."

"Hmmm. Perhaps he wanted it to be a secret or something?"

"Maybe."

The conversation continued as Pullman studied the neighborhood. The houses next to The Davis's and across from them were empty. There was no going to the neighbors for news about Spencer's arrival back in town. Steyer announced his wife went into labor.

"Call me whenever you get the chance."

"Sure thing. I'm sorry I can't be there to work the case with you."

"It's fine, I'll talk with you soon," Pullman ended the call.

Mrs. Davis emerged from the house. She appeared haggard. She ran a hand through her tangled hair, offering him a tired smile. Dark circles were present under her eyes. Pullman was offered a cup of coffee.

"No thanks, I'm fine."

"What brings you here?"

"I wanted to speak to your son."

She laughed. "Is this about Dr. Freyman?"

"Yes. I just have some quick questions for him."

"Come on in."

He returned to see Spencer sitting in the chair, facing the door. The smirk on his face wasn't friendly. He hadn't changed that much since the last time he saw him. He was taller and his hair a little longer. The dark strands were curly and bangs in his eyes. He tossed them away, revealing his own dark circles.

His eyes, which were usually teal blue, were tinged with red. Pullman took the seat across from him with caution. The kid's gaze never left him. Pullman cleared his throat, the feeling of being strangled was present again. With trembling hands, he pulled his notebook from his breast pocket.

"Spencer, I would like to ask you some questions concerning Dr. Freyman."

"Ask away Officer."

It was the voice from the tapes. It didn't sound like Spencer at all. It could be just a trick, but he didn't think so. Where was the real Spencer Davis? There was no time to wonder about that. He had to figure this out.

"Where were you the night Dr. Freyman was attacked?"

"I was there in the flesh. I was the one who attacked him."

Pullman didn't expect a confession that quick. He didn't bother dragging out the case any longer. He pulled the handcuffs from his belt but didn't get the chance to get to Spencer. He was flung into the wall. Spencer's parents screamed at the top of their lungs. Pullman tried to catch his breath, crawling to the foot of the stairs.

He crawled up, leaving the parents to comfort the boy as he raged and screamed. Across the hall, Spencer's door was open. He didn't bother to try the other doors. He crawled into the room and shut the door. It was another case for the ages, a supernatural entity or something like that.

Another kid emerged from the closet, Pullman gasped. It was the real Spencer. The fear was present in his eyes as he crawled over to him. The noises grew louder. Pullman stood up then ran to the window. They were on the second floor but it didn't matter. He'd rather jump to his death or break a leg than die by something not of this world.

"Now do you believe Dr. Freyman? I told him there was something here that looked just like me," Spencer whispered.

"How in the hell did this happen?" Pullman checked his firearm. "This stuff doesn't happen in real life."

"I think it was the Ouija board. I didn't say goodbye and I let him in. I thought all this time I was speaking with Alice. I swear, I did."

"Alice?"

"She's my girlfriend. She died in a car accident. I didn't want to let her go. I bought the board after my friends told me it was a way to speak with the dead."

"Some friends. Didn't they know this would happen?"

There were footsteps outside their door. A loud banging shook the door to the point it cracked. Spencer screamed while Pullman looked out the window. He would get Spencer out first. He opened it and grabbed the kid's arms.

"What are you doing?"

"Go, get out of here."

"Are you crazy? We're on the second floor."

"Would you rather die by this doppelgänger's hand or try your best to escape? It's up to you."

"What about mom and dad?"

"We'll worry about them later."

Pullman helped Spencer climb out the window. He was relieved that he got him out first. Spencer carefully made his way to the edge of the roof. Pullman wasn't so lucky. Before he even got a leg out the window, he was dragged back in. Pullman screamed. He tried to fight off the entity. He was swung over the bed and onto the floor.

Pullman wrapped a hand around his gun, but he wasn't fast enough. To his surprise, Spencer's parents were there to aid the doppelgänger with capturing him. They pulled him to his feet. Mr. Davis snatched the gun out of his palm.

"What in the hell are you two doing? This thing isn't your son."

"It's our Spencie. He's come home," Mrs. Davis echoes.

She laughed, showing her dingy teeth. Mr. Davis's breath was on his neck. They smelled like they hadn't taken a bath in ages, he couldn't believe it. He hadn't noticed it before. As he was led downstairs and into the kitchen, he prayed Spencer didn't try to be a hero. He hoped he got far away from here.

Pullman was tied to a kitchen chair. He tried to fight his captors but it didn't work. Spencer's doppelgänger smiled. The outcome looked helpless but he wasn't giving up. The fridge opened and Pullman gasped. Most of the food had rotted away and was surrounded by maggots and flies. The smell was enough to make him gag.

"Let me go, you bastards."

"No, we can't. There's no telling what you'll do."

He couldn't believe the Davis's went along with the Spencer look-alike. The reason they hadn't looked for Spencer was they believed this thing to be their son. Did they send the real Spencer to Dr. Freyman to cover their tracks? When he left home, they'd already ruled him out. If they were going to kill him, his death wouldn't just be swept under the rug.

"You can't kill me. I'm a police officer. They'll notice my disappearance."

The doppelgänger smiled at him. "Kill you? Who said anything about killing you?"

He wasn't going to die. Pullman struggled against his restraints. Mrs. Davis peered into his face with a wide grin. He turned away. Mr. Davis patted his shoulder and sighed.

"I'm sorry, Ned. I can't let you turn my boy into the police, we just got him back."

"He's not your son," Pullman screamed. "That thing is not of this world. You have to believe me."

They chose to ignore him. If they had any conscience at all, they'd know this was wrong. Spencer's look-alike spoke in a language that sounded similar to Latin. Pullman tried to go over the recordings in his head. He prayed he learned something valuable about the look-alike but he was drawing blanks. Dr. Freyman's recordings played in the background. Pullman listened.

The date is February 4th, I'm speaking with Marsha Hamon. Marsha is 18 years old. She tells me there's a ghost haunting her room. She claims no matter how she tries to make it leave, it won't budge. He sticks to her like glue. Go ahead, Marsha.

Well, it happened one night while I slept. I don't know where it came from or how it got there. I just noticed it one-night staring at me.

Staring at you? Could it have been just a trick of the light? Did you watch any scary movies or shows the night before? You know, our mind tends to play tricks on us at times.

No. I'm positive it wasn't a trick of the mind.

Describe it. Was it a boy or a girl? Did it wear any particular style of clothing?

It was a boy. He dresses like you and me. I guess he's from this era. Sometimes he can make himself solid and other times, I can see right through him.

Make himself solid? Can ghosts really do that?

I don't know. I'm just telling you what I saw. I don't think about the details. Anyway, he's staring at me. I shoo him away. I'm not scared of him, but he doesn't go anywhere.

So, he watches you the whole night and then what?

And then I fall asleep when I see he's not going anywhere. The next morning, I wake up and he's gone. I noticed he only appears to me at night. Sometimes he even brings me gifts.

Gifts? Like flowers and things like that?

Duh. It's stupid. Why doesn't he find some other girl to haunt-?

The tape was cut and replaced with another one. Pullman closed his eyes. This whole situation was a nightmare.

The date is April 4th, I'm speaking with 17-year-old Robert Frank. Robert tells me he's having trouble getting along with his parents. They don't seem to understand him. From the way he talks about them, it sounds like he's desperate for their attention. I decide to make a house call without letting him or his parents know. When I arrive, I discover his parents are pretty nice folks. The dad was rather charming.

I see a dog house and a dog playing in the garden. When I go to converse with the parents, they are happy to see me. I find Robert sitting in the garden. He's taken up origami. A hobby he tells me he enjoys a lot. If only he could make people as easy as he makes birds and frogs. I don't see anything wrong with it and tell him to study the hobby more. It seems to please his parents. The next time we have a visit, he tells me he's found a new hobby.

This one is taxidermy. He catches a lot of animals and like he said with origami, he enjoys it a lot. If only he could stuff humans instead of animals. I found this comment to be rather disturbing. Further treatment is needed to curb this behavior.

Pullman remembered this case. Robert found a new hobby alright. He went from stuffing animals to stuffing humans. The taxidermy murder case was another high-profile case where Dr. Freyman became more famous than what he was already. Robert confessed to the crime and complained about Dr. Freyman's treatment of him. Another tape was played.

Hello, I'm Eric Meyers filling in for Dr. Freyman, I'm 18 years old and made to see this quack at the suggestion of my parents. He claims he can cure anything, I mean A-NY-THING. I don't believe him. I asked him if he could cure Cancer or call for world peace. He told me that I was pulling his chain and he didn't appreciate it. And you know what I said? I said he was full of himself. While he's trying to cure "child behavior" or whatever the hell he calls it, he should take a look at himself. He only laughed at me but I know the truth. His wife left him for a younger man and his kids want nothing to do with him. He spent the rest of his miserable life butting into everyone else's business because he couldn't handle his own. I think he's- oh shit! He's back, Eric out!

Pullman frowned. It was Eric's case again. Why were they listening to this? The words echoed in his mind.

"Dr. Freyman claims he can cure anything. I mean, A-NY-THING."

The answer was there, Dr. Freyman couldn't cure anything. He couldn't cure the patients who faced problems that weren't solved by therapy or science. Eric's therapy was a test along with Spencer's, Addy's, and Marsha's, to name a few. The parents went to him because the doctor was a braggart.

Pullman laughed to himself, it got him in trouble. The reason Spencer's doppelgänger attacked him was clear. He couldn't cure Spencer. There was no cure for demons who emerged from another world. Spencer's look-alike attacked him to prove this to the parents. A broadcast confirmed this. Faith in the doctor was lost along with faith in the police. His blood ran cold at the response.

He was next. He didn't brag like the doctor, but he didn't

believe in supernatural occurrences at first. Now, he was going to be made an example of. Thrown back to the police after they failed to solve this crime.

"Let your sacrifice be an example to all the ignorant. Let them know the error of their ways. If you don't see it, you don't believe it. That's your type officer. Doctor Freyman's type is bragging about your success when you can't solve everything."

Pullman screamed. He clawed at his face trying to remove the object jammed with force into his eyes. His restraints were loosened and he collapsed to the floor.

"Since you don't believe unless you can see, feel, and touch it," the doppelgänger snarled in his ear. "What about if you can't see anything ever again? Does that change the rules?"

The Davis' danced around him as he screamed in pain. The tapes ran together. The recordings he listened to played over and over.

It's October 16th, and I'm sitting here once again with Spencer Davis.

I'm not Spencer.

Spencer, sitting in front of me, claims not to be Spencer. I'm having a hard time adjusting to this. Spencer, what do you mean?

Exactly what I said. I may look like Spencer but I'm not. Come on you're the doctor. Figure it out.

What does that mean? You look like Spencer. You walk, talk, and act like Spencer.

Walk, talk, and act?

The date is March 4th, I'm speaking with Adelaide Watson. Addy, as she likes to be called, is 15 years old. She's having bad dreams in which she's chased by an unknown assailant. Addy, can you walk us through it?

It's September 30th, I'm at the police station with Kyle Draken. Kyle has just been arrested for a string of serial murders going on around town. Not that it was Kyle who confessed to me but an alternate that lives inside of him. An alternate that goes by the moniker Doll.

It's October 4th, I'm here with Spencer Davis, age 18.

"Shall we make a recording of our own, officer? I made one with Dr. Freyman before you came here."

On cue, news of Dr. Freyman's attack at the hospital appeared on the screen. The doctor's tongue was cut out and his lips sewn together. Pullman screamed at the news. The doctor won't utter another word again. The shock from the attack sent the entire hospital into a frenzy. Pullman's shoulder was patted along with a recording device slid closer to him.

The date is October 25th. I am here with Officer Ned Pullman. Ned tells me he doesn't believe in the supernatural. Spencer's ordeal is a figment of his imagination. It's something he and Dr. Freyman cooked up to garner fame and fortune. I can't tell you how wrong he is.

The good doctor will never poison another child or parent's mind again with his honeyed lies. It's over for him. Now he'll spend the rest of his life wondering why this sort of thing happened to him. Isn't that right, Officer? I mean, there's no point in sugarcoating the truth. You believe or you don't, it's fine, but be prepared to face the consequences.

Pullman uttered a groan. And just like Dr. Freyman would utter no more words, he would never see the light of day, ever again.

MITHRAVATHI
THE LEGEND OF MUSSOORIE

Prelude

November 25, 1995

Pari Tibba, Mussoorie, India.

Hiss…

The unsuspecting rodent never saw it coming. A squeak escaped its mouth as it took its last breath. The snake slithered through the bushes, satisfied with its meal, and blended wholly with the surroundings, but another hiss slipped out of its mouth when someone stepped on it.

The person in question cursed and hurriedly jumped out of way, barely avoiding its bite. "Shit, that was close."

"Shh." The other one silenced him, pushed to move forward. The two figures silently moved through the thick vegetation. The silver glow of the moon infiltrated through the gaps of the tall trees, guiding them through the darkness of the jungle. Dead leaves crunched under their feet; sweat coated their brows, their chests heaving. They had been walking for almost two hours now, trekking through the uneven path that stretched ahead.

The older of the two staggered when his foot caught on a fallen log. His free arm shot out to hold something for support.

"Careful, dad." The youngest caught him.

"I'm fine," Grabbing his son's arm he steadied himself, his eyes darted from side to side as he caught his breath. "Are you sure this will work?"

"Yes," His son's determination rang louder. "Let's keep moving. Time's running out."

Andrew Garrison nodded, and they resumed walking again. His fifty-year-old body couldn't keep up with the twenty-eight-year-old's pace. Heavy breaths huffed out as they ambled their way through the fallen logs, rocks, and slippery slopes.

As they went deeper, the sullen clouds covered the moon, drowning them in utter darkness. With only the dim flashlight and the sound of the chirping crickets as a company, they advanced toward their destination. Andrew had to stop several times to look around before walking again. The odd sounds unsettled his nerves. Something flew to Andrew's right startling him for the umpteenth time that night. The flashlight fell from his hand as the oldest clutched his chest. "What was that?"

Jean Garrison, his son, hastily grabbed the flashlight, "Must be an owl or a bat."

They were deep in the belly of the deodar forest. The sight of coniferous trees with the conic crown, level branches, and drooping branchlets in different shades of green would have been a treat to the eyes in daylight. However, at this time of the night, the permeating scent of cedar accompanied by the dark silhouettes of trees was nothing but ghastly.

Andrew nodded, calming his heart, only for it to thunder again when he heard something. His son moved closer, sensing his discomfort, and placed a hand on his lower back. "Dad, you okay?"

He eyed the towering trees around them in apprehension. No. He was far from okay. Shaking his head, he held his son's hand, registering the slight tremble of his fingers. If Andrew had a choice, he would be at home in the comfort of his couch with his beloved wife. But that wasn't an option. If the bastards were caught and punished as they deserved, he didn't have to be here. If... if only the mother fucking monsters had stopped with his daughter—

Andrew's mind reeled and he swallowed a sob. His left hand raised to pat the newspaper sat nestled in the safety of his jacket's pocket. Three weeks ago, when he saw the mauled body of the barely eighteen-year-old girl, he knew it wasn't a one-time thing. Later, Jean's deep research pulled a list of five girls murdered over the past five years, including his daughter.

"Dad," Jean shook him again. "It's close to eleven. We have to be there before the clock strikes twelve."

Andrew shoved the thoughts aside, turning his gaze to Jean. "O-okay. Are we close?"

"I think so."

Darkness reigned as far as their eyes could reach. They started before sunset, stopping only to catch their breaths. Exhaustion slowed them, but determination kept them going. "Let's go." He patted on Jean's shoulder.

"Water?"

Andrew grabbed the plastic bottle wordlessly and took a few sips, just enough to nourish his throat. "Are you sure that we're not lost?"

"Yeah. We're—" His demeanor changed when his flashlight fell on a tree.

"What's that?" Andrew held his breath as Jean approached the enormous tree.

The flashlight illuminated something red. On close inspection, they noticed the sacred silk clothes, threads, and a few other items they didn't recognize tied to its branches and trunk as some sort of offering. Vermilion coated the trunk as if it were a second skin. Jean reached out, touching the scarlet pigment, rubbing it between his fingers. Andrew recognized the powdered mineral cinnabar widely used by the villagers. He deduced it must represent something important to them.

"This is it. The sacred tree," Jean's words hauled him out of his observation. His son turned the flashlight off and secured it in his backpack. The moonlight illuminated the side of Jean's sharp jaw, "It starts from here."

They weren't allowed to use any form of light in these parts of the woods. It was the first warning from the villagers. With only the moonlight as guidance, they moved forward, unsure of the outcome, and hoping to find their destination on time. Fear gripped their hearts, but desperation kept them moving. It brought them all the way from a small town of Wyoming to this infamous village in India.

After what felt like an hour later, the trees thinned out leading them to a clearing. The temperature suddenly dropped. An ominous chill crept through his spine. Andrew bent, resting his hands on his knees overcome by fatigue, and beside him, Jean sucked in a sharp breath. Goosebumps erupted all over his skin as the sensation of something unknown crawled over him. Something moved around them. His heart beat faster. Jean latched onto Andrew's arm out of fear.

His breath hitched when his gaze noted the rocky structure in front of them. Now that he looked closer, he realized it wasn't just a pile of rocks, but more like a cave. The moon highlighted the ancient ruins that appeared scarier than the one they saw in the old paintings at the village.

"We're here."

With a thundering heart, Andrew nodded, his grip tightening on the shoulder bag he carried all the way from his home. As they approached the ruins, the structure seemed to grow in size. His son marched forward with outstretched hands as he searched for the entrance. A couple of minutes later he called out, finding it hidden under a huge rock—a manhole.

"It's small," Jean stated, inspecting its entrance. "We have to crawl inside."

Andrew swallowed his fear with a bob of his head and crouched with his heart leaping to his throat. With a grunt, he followed his son inside. Darkness swallowed them whole. With only their senses to guide, they proceeded.

"Dad, hold my leg," the young one whispered.

Andrew did as he was told. He gripped Jean's ankle for guidance as Jean maneuvered through the tunnels. The rough edges of the rocks abraded Andrew's knees, palms and scratched his sides. He hit his head on the wall a few times. Pain shot through his body, but he ignored it. The stale air and lack of oxygen made him dizzy. He struggled to swallow through his parched throat but kept going.

"We're almost there." His son's encouraging words drifted to him but only the dark tunnel stretched farther and farther.

Andrew swallowed a hiss of pain when something cut into his palm. His back bothered him because of his uncomfortable position on all fours but still he continued to crawl his way in. His eyes grew heavy and he didn't think he could keep up longer. He fought the urge to surrender and give into his body's demand for rest because they were running out of time.

Turmoil churned his mind. The bloody, broken image of his daughter flashed in his memory; the painful reminder still fresh like it happened yesterday. His baby girl never got justice. Most of the nights, he lay awake imagining thousands of ways to kill those bastards who ended her dreams. *I can't give up.* Motivated by the memories he pushed his debilitated body forward, ignoring the soreness of his limbs and throbbing pain that continued to grow.

Just as he thought he was going to collapse, the cold air hit their skin. Their movements grew urgent as a dimly lit space came into view. They entered what appeared like a chamber. Moonlight seeped through the cracks of the rock from the roof ahead. The room was normal-sized, perhaps the size of his living room back home. He couldn't tell the shape of the room, but his gaze traced the dark line of things littered on the floor.

Andrew squinted his eyes to get a better look and felt goosebumps erupt on his skin for the second time that night as something whisked past them. This time it was definitely not a bird or an owl. His body shuddered involuntarily. A sinister feeling crawled over his spine. With his eyes adjusted to the darkness, he thought he saw someone or something in his peripheral. His heart catapulted against his ribs, a silent scream leaving his mouth.

"It's okay, dad." He felt a gentle squeeze on his shoulder, but didn't miss the slight tremor of the touch. "Give me the bag," Jean's voice wavered despite the gentleness and determination.

Andrew's gaze swept around as he handed his bag to Jean and closed his eyes on impulse when a gust of wind blew past him. *Was that a whisper?* The maliciousness he sensed right then was something worse than his nightmare.

"Please," he whimpered as his knees gave up. He didn't know what he was pleading for. Andrew knew it was foolish to beg a malicious entity considering their reason for being here at this ungodly hour of the night. However, he was desperate. The mourning father couldn't care if he was selling his soul as long as his baby girl got justice. Tears stung his eyes as his son pulled out the materials from inside the bag. Jean hurriedly drew the pattern he had been practicing for over a week on the ground. He then arranged the items around the drawing.

"Give me your hand."

He numbly extended his hand, only to stiffen when a small

gust of wind blew in his hair. Andrew locked his jaw, trying to calm his hammering heart. His neck prickled with awareness. The small sliver of air moving along his exposed skin resembled the breathing of a person. His heart thundered in his chest.

The sharp cut on his palm shot daggers of pain into his system. He clenched his jaw and bit the inside of his cheek tasting blood, but didn't make a sound. Jean squeezed his hand causing more blood to fall into the clay bowl they brought. The son then proceeded to cut the inside of his hand, filling the second bowl.

A chill ran through their spine as a deep growl reverberated around the chamber. Andrew's breath caught in his throat. Nothing had prepared the father and son for this. He caught his son's hand on impulse and held tight as he tried to remember the words of the villagers.

"The entity senses your fear. It relishes in it. Never show your fear."

But he couldn't help it even if he wanted to. The pounding of his heart continued to grow louder as a sudden non-existent wind blew around them. He felt a squeeze on his hand and held his breath. It was his cue to start the chant—a four verse mantra taught by a temple priest. Together they chanted the prayer. They must chant for a hundred and eight times without any mistake.

Loud inhumane noises ricocheted across the eerie walls of the cave. Leaves and dust circled them, and the heavy wind tried to knock them off balance. Andrew shut his eyes tighter, chanting with a fervor fueled by his pain. Their lips never stopped the words. When the hundred and eighth chant left their lips, the chaos stopped. A deafening silence fell upon them.

Andrew opened his eyes, his breathing was coming out in pants. If the ritual was successful, the ancient oil lamp in the cave would light up. However, darkness still shrouded them. *Did they do it right?* He almost opened his mouth to ask his son when he caught a slight movement in his peripheral vision.

A dark, insidious shadow crawled toward them. He pursed his lips, his body trembling like a leaf. Beside him, Jean shuddered. Their grip tightened around each other as the shadowy figure, more apparent now stopped in front of them. Andrew didn't know if he should thank the darkness because he didn't think he would survive if he saw the entity in the clear light.

Andrew's eyes shut on instinct, silently praying. The villagers never mentioned this part. A nasty breath hit his face with a slight accompanying growl. "Please…" he pleaded with a cracking voice. "My daughter… my Alina was only seventeen." Words stuck in his throat as he whimpered. "Help us…"

The silence stretched for what seemed like minutes before he cracked open his eyes. The golden yellow glow of the old oil lamp in the center of the room greeted him. A small square-shaped stone painted in red stared at him. Several bowls and personal belongings littered the small room. He swallowed noticing the now empty bowls that earlier contained their blood.

The men cried in relief as they grabbed their belongings. Without another word, they hurried out of the cave hoping justice will be served soon.

1.

April 31, 1996

Pari Tibba, Mussoorie, India.

The evening was still young when the 1986 red Contessa
Classic rolled through the unpaved roads of the Pine Valley Estate.
Fog covered the grounds despite it being late April, unseasonable
and unreasonable. Joe Martinez swore he could almost sense
something deadly lurking in those fogs—hiding, waiting.

The famous tourist destination situated in the northern state of
Uttarakhand, India was a paradise for a nature lover. Thickets of
oak, pine, and deodar forests covered miles of the region; long
trekking trails offered a breathtaking view of Mussorie peaks, and
a wide range of traditional Indian cuisine that aimed to please the
taste buds—it was definitely a traveler's dream. The locals entitled
it the land of fairies and Mussoorie was also called the Queen of
Hills for its luscious green hills that lay at 1900 meters altitude.

As warm and welcoming as it sounded with a promise of
lifelong worth memories, Joe knew it differently. It was one of the
top most haunted places in India. He'd heard several stories about
the abandoned Lambi Dehar Mines during his very short stay in
Mussoorie. But he was here for something worse than the haunted
mines that took the lives of countless workers.

"We're here, sir."

Joe was so immersed in his thoughts that he didn't notice the
car had stopped in the sheltered driveway. He exited the vehicle,

Beyond the Hallow Grave

shuffling in his feet as he smoothed a hand over his creased shirt and adjusted the shoulder bag.

"Mr. Singh is waiting for you."

Joe switched his attention back to the driver who was already climbing the wide stairs. Throughout his three days' stay, he learned the young man's name as Narayan, a handyman of the sort around the Pine Valley Estate. He stared at the young man's wide back disappearing inside, his mind is churning. He drew in a shaky breath as he followed Narayan inside the modest cottage that was nestled in the belly of a private estate in Pari Tibba.

His nerves were haywire when he stepped into the threshold of the small reception area. The cottage with ancient stone walls and recent upgrades that infused modern interior came with a central heating system and Wi-Fi. It wasn't the best or luxurious like a few other estates he had perused but this particular property was relatively close to his destination and had stroked his intrigue.

Once inside, Narayan gestured him to the large living room before turning toward the kitchen area. Joe strode to the corner table that overlooked the forest and dropped to the cushioned wooden chair unceremoniously scrutinizing the elderly man with a long white beard. He had a book in his hand. He settled the bag on his lap and leaned on his elbows.

Vishwanath Singh, retired professor and the owner of the lavish three-bedroom cottage lifted a bushy brow, peering at him from under his glasses. "I thought I told you to stay away from the forest," the older man grumbled under his breath before focusing on the book again.

Right. He thought that was made clear to him when Narayan

came to fetch him from the village almost abruptly, cutting off his chat with one of the elders in the village.

"I wouldn't have gone if you had answered my questions in the first place," the former answered nonchalantly. His eyes narrowed at the male immersed in the book. The older man heard every word Joe spoke, but he didn't react.

The silence stretched between them—uncomfortable and tense. None of them attempted to speak.

Pari Tibba was sure a spooky place. The unspoken legend of Mussoorie had caught his attention a couple of months ago when his friend had traveled all the way from Wyoming, United States to the tiny village of India, seeking justice for his daughter's untimely demise. It was so unlikely of Andrew to do something as reckless and stupid. As a paranormal investigator, it interested Joe Martinez in the bona fide to rest his case.

The Garrison and Martinez families had been friends for over two decades. They were neighbors who happened to live in the same community before Andrew moved to live in the city to be close to his work and children's school.

Andrew's action surprised Joe because something like this was too adventurous for the Garrisons. Something Joe thought Andrew or his son Jean was not capable of doing. But it was until an unfortunate event had forcefully taken the youngest daughter, Alina, from them. Joe knew why Andrew did what he did.

Alina's untimely demise left the Garrisons devastated. The girl was so lively, so full of promises and dreams. Joe's heart tightened at the memory of Alina and his daughter playing in their backyard as children. They called themselves soulmates, exchanged identical bracelets and had sleepovers every weekend.

With the help of Joe, Jean, and the few other friends, the middle-class father had tried everything in his power to bring his daughter's murderers to justice. When weeks rolled into months, the media attention they received had died down and the police with no further clues to move on had left it to collect dust.

Suddenly, Andrew started contemplating something Joe deemed as insane and out of character. Andrew didn't believe in paranormal stuff and often made fun of Joe's career of choice. So Joe had laughed at his friend when he showed that smudged letter he received months after his daughter's death. But little did he know that Andrew had kept that letter safe, and another incident similar to Alina's death would push him to follow the most unimaginable path.

Jennie, Andrew's wife, had panicked with all the planning going on in their home and called Joe right away to help her knock some sense into the father and son. Joe tried warning both Andrew and Jean about the risk they were taking. He had been in this shithole for years with no way out. Once in his early twenties, he had dipped his toe into the world of paranormal as an adrenaline junkie and got stuck for life. He wasn't even drunk that night when he decided to summon the spirits in that abandoned cemetery. Joe hadn't been able to stop it, though he tried to get out of it with all his might; but they always found him. That was how it worked.

Despite his fair warnings, the Garrisons had been adamant. They argued about how police hadn't found a piece of single evidence and Alina's killers were still out there killing more girls. With no option left, Joe had agreed to let them go with condition that they tell him everything upon return.

However, when Andrew refused to speak of his trip on his return Joe knew something was up. The fearful look on the faces of Jean and Andrew spoke a million words. As days passed by, he saw Andrew and Jean grew more and more restless. The signs were all there. Andrew's wife informed him about both having nightmares but still they were not ready to utter a word about their trip.

Joe was sure something had happened to them during their visit. They were now tainted with the first taste of the paranormal world. He understood the meaning behind the dark circles under their eyes. One night, Jennie had called him saying Andrew and Jean were behaving strangely. Joe immediately knew what went wrong. Well, that was what happened when someone waddled into uncharted territory with no knowledge and oblivious to the risks involved.

Now they had brought the evil home, and that evil was feeding off their souls. It took a while for Joe to realize whatever they stumbled upon was no ordinary spirit he could shoo away with simple rituals. This one was far too powerful and dangerous.

When Joe tried to help his friend, he got the taste of Andrew's grueling nightmares filled with screams, gory images, and everything sinister. He had to find a way to stop the entity from destroying the Garrisons and had to do it soon. For that, he needed to find the roots of the problem and what he was dealing with. Whatever was the outcome, he was keen to find the answers to this mystery.

At his request, Andrew's wife had slipped that letter to him and Joe started digging. His investigation landed him in Pari Tibba.

"Here's your tea, sir."

Narayan's presence hauled Joe out of his thoughts.

Vishwanath Singh was still silent and Joe didn't think he would get any information from this man. He looked outside the window. The sun had already settled and for some strange reason, all villagers were already inside their homes. Narayan had been jittery during their entire drive to the estate.

Somewhere a window fluttered and the man lifted his gaze from his book again. "Narayan!"

"Forgive me, sir!" The twenty-year-some-old boy who worked at the cottage ran upstairs.

"I'll find the truth," Joe said, ignoring the tea and determination tightening his features, "I always do."

Mr. Singh closed the book and rested it on the table. "Good luck with that." He stood and reached for his cane. "Keep your windows and doors shut for the night. I don't care what you do in the morning."

"Is there something I should know?" Joe lifted a brow because the villagers seemed ridiculous. It was obvious they were afraid of something because all reacted the same when he inquired about the unspoken legend that originated from the deep valleys of this small village.

"Some things are better left unsaid." Mr. Singh turned to pin him with an intense look he couldn't decipher. "It's for your safety, Mr. Martinez. I don't care if you're a paranormal investigator or a tourist or whatever you like to call yourself. You should leave this alone and go back to your country."

Joe opened his mouth to retort, but Mr. Singh had already left the room. He clenched his fists before standing, grabbing his bag, and spun on his heel to climb the wooden stairs that led to his room. The windows in his room were bolted and he grimaced, noticing the small red-colored threads tied around the latch. He also noticed some unique patterns drawn on the glass. He'd seen similar symbols on the doors of almost all the homes at the village, though he didn't know what it meant.

A long sigh drifted past Joe's lips as he settled into his bed for the night. The room was spacious and looked exactly like the photos on the travel blog. The evening was still young, and his attempts to find the truth went futile. He stared outside to the dark sky through the glass window thinking about the letter. He pulled it out from his bag and traced the anonymous letter for the umpteenth time. If it was printed randomly, he wouldn't have bothered to look at it twice but the handwritten letter screamed so many things at him. Why would anyone go through the pain of writing a letter about something like this?

Joe had experienced a fair share of paranormal activities in his career. But none like this one. The mystery surrounding this one had pulled him in like a magnet.

Fingers tapping on his knee thoughtfully, he took his journal to summarize the events of the day. He was re-reading his journal entries since his arrival when suddenly the wind picked speed outside the window. He glanced up with a frown. The weather had been quite pleasant all day. Tall trees danced in the wind. The windows rattled as the wind sent twigs and leaves flying in the air. Perhaps, they received a storm warning. It made sense why Mr.

Singh warned him to stay in tonight.

The lights flickered twice before immersing him in the darkness. A glass broke somewhere. He patted his bed searching for his bag only to stop when the familiar chill spread through his spine. The temperature in the room dropped just like the night he brought that letter home. His heart cartwheeled when his brain vaguely registered the sudden cold grip on his hand. Fuck!

He couldn't deduce if the presence inside the room was malignant or peaceful. It hadn't attacked him yet. So far it had only indulged in warnings and nightmares. The years of experience didn't make these rare encounters any better. Every entity was different. No two entities were the same. He forced a breath through his mouth.

The grip on his hand tightened and he closed his eyes instinctively. A wisp of breath teased his skin. *Shit.*

Nausea churned in his stomach and his head reeled. Suddenly, cold wind brushed against his skin. The fresh scents of the forest pricked his nostrils. Joe opened his eyes to realize he was no longer inside the room. *What the—*

Darkness surrounded him just as his exposed skin registered the unnatural chill. There was a minute difference between the natural cold weather and the one caused by the spirits. A difference only people who have encountered the otherworldly things could tell. This chill reminded him only of death, despair, and unfinished business. The wind whipped his face. He waited with bated breath, eyes scanning his surroundings, ears listening for any odd noise.

It took a while for his eyes to adjust to the night. Once he did, he saw the ancient ruins standing tall in its glory illuminated by the waning moon. Damn.

Something moved past him. He whirled around, finding no one. He placed his right hand over his chest just above his heart. The spirits or malevolent entities fed on one's fear. Joe forced his body to relax and took deep breaths to calm himself.

He eyed the ancient ruins again. Should he head inside?

But he couldn't bring himself to move a muscle. Never in his lifetime Joe had encountered something like this. He couldn't tell apart the reality and nightmare.

A thick white fog crept towards him. He wanted to move, but his knees were locked. A ghostly whisper made him jump out of his skin. A peal of musical laughter followed, more like mocking at him.

"W-who's that?"

The tinkling of bells resonated in the distance. Bells? He'd heard them before. Joe ran a hand over his weary face. He suddenly remembered. Every woman in the village wore a silver anklet on their legs. It produced a beautiful clinking noise when they walked. He ran in the direction of the sound, running into a few trees as the fog barred his vision. He fell down a couple of times, scraping his knees and palms. The sound continued to grow farther.

"Wait...who are you?"

He climbed to his feet dusting off dirt from his pants and followed the sound blindly. He needed answers. Who was this woman? What was she doing out here in the night? But then he already had an idea of what she was. *The legend.*

With his palms outstretched to avoid bumping into the trees

and low branches, he advanced cautiously. A few minutes into the walk, the fog thinned suddenly and he saw her. Walking at least ten feet ahead of him, the moon shone her form.

"Stop! Who are you?"

She stopped but did not turn. "I'm the one you came here to see tonight." Her voice was gentle yet radiated authority.

Joe swallowed and inched closer. He couldn't decide what color clothes she wore, but he could tell she wore something similar to those women in the village. This was it. "What's your name? Why did you send that note?"

She slowly turned to face him and he gasped. A strange aura radiated off of her and she seemed to glow even in the darkness. Her commanding presence and the way she held herself was more regal than any other entity he had encountered in the past. She wore a traditional ghagra, choli with rich embroidery design and stones that glittered under the moon. A long piece of light patched fabric, heavy with embellishments covered the upper half of her face, showing only her straight nose and perfect bow-shaped lips. The intricate choker necklace adorned her neck reminded him of the ones those Indian brides wore at their weddings.

Royal. That was the first thought that crossed his mind. She looked like a royal.

"You're not welcome here."

Her voice though soft and breezy, not more than a whisper rang with finality and instilled an unknown fear in him.

"I just wanted some answers," he sounded slightly brittle. He shifted from one foot to the other. Her presence unsettled his nerves and for the first time in his career, he didn't know how to handle the situation. He couldn't decide if she was good or malevolent.

"Men speak nothing but lies," she hissed disappearing from his view.

Joe whirled around, searching blindly before a hand grabbed his neck pinning him against a tree. His feet dangled in the air as he struggled to breathe.

"They'll die..." she snarled, her voice now taken a dangerous edge that shot cold shivers down his spine. He still couldn't see her face. She had a perfect row of pearly white teeth and the nose ring she wore a diamond embedded nose ring.

"Andrew did nothing," he said weakly. "They killed his daughter. He only wants justice."

The woman dropped him to the floor. "Why should I believe you?"

"Please...don't hurt Andrew. He—"

The woman boomed with laughter. "Hmm..." She turned to walk away. "What can a peasant like you do for me?"

Joe knew the moment the words left his mouth there would be no turning back. But he was desperate and the entity brought him here for a reason. If his years of experience taught him anything that they always needed something. Their purposes vary, but their actions always had a reason. She wanted him here for a reason. A reason he was hell-bent on finding out. So he steeled his resolve and straightened his posture. "Please...I'll do anything. Just leave him."

The woman turned. "Anything?" she demanded.

"Anything," he felt compelled to say, gaze never wavering.

Her lips stretched forming a full-blown smile. "Good."

The fog surrounded him again and Joe woke on his bed drenched in sweat. The power was back in the room and he was still in his bed. He looked down at his arm, noticing the dark handprint, and knew right away he made a deal with the devil.

2.

The next time Joe woke up the room was still dark and the windows still closed—everything intact. He blinked and tried to make sense of his nightmare. Was it even a nightmare? Years of experience had taught him better.

He glanced down at his wrist, where the entity had grabbed him last night before pulling him into the woods wherever that was. A dark purple bruise, the shape of a human hand, glared at him. The contrast of it against his pale skin was a painful reminder that whatever happened was real

One thing Joe learned during the time he dabbled in this side of the paranormal world was not to take things lightly. Everything mattered, even a tiny harmless warning. Who was she? What did she want from him?

He tried to analyze their conversation and came up with more questions than answers. Joe rubbed the bruise thoughtfully. With a sigh, he jumped out of the bed and decided to confront the estate owner again. He dragged his legs to the attached bathroom to freshen up and wash off the sweat. Vishwanath Singh cannot hide anymore. Not after last night.

Half an hour later, Joe went down dressed in a pair of comfortable jeans, a white short-sleeved t-shirt and his favorite worn-out leather jacket. He adjusted the ball cap as he slung the bag on his right shoulder.

Narayan was in the living room, dusting the furniture, and barely looked his way. "Narayan, is Mr. Singh in his office?"

The younger man looked over his right shoulder before pointing a finger toward the closed door that held a steel plate with black shiny letters that read Dr. Vishwanath Singh, followed by his accolades. Joe mumbled a thanks and strode to the door, entering with a simple knock.

"Good morning, Mr. Singh."

Joe let his gaze sweep around the tidy place. Mr. Singh's office was modest with oak wood furniture—a medium-sized table and a leather swivel chair positioned in the center. A vintage bookshelf with glass doors lined the entire back wall; a four-foot cabinet sat on the right side of the room filled with awards and photos taken on various occasions; a huge four-door window opened on the left side of the room and a small tea table with two bamboo chairs covered in soft red cushions completed the look of typical office space.

Mr. Singh was sitting on a bamboo chair, looking out of the open window, sipping his tea in silence. He didn't look at Joe or bothered to acknowledge him when he stepped inside. It bothered Joe to no extent. The man had been anything but cordial ever since he learned Joe's purpose. He bit the anger and closed the door before marching to the old man, collapsing on the empty chair that faced the door. That was when his breath hitched.

Beside the door were several paintings, but one stood out from the others. Before he could examine further Mr. Singh cleared his throat demanding his attention. "What do you want?" His eyes narrowed at Joe.

Joe took several deep breaths, forcing his body to relax and organize his thoughts. He needed answers. And Mr. Singh was going to give that to him.

He turned to face Mr. Singh. "I know you're not being completely honest with me here, Mr. Singh." The old man's lazy gaze fell on him briefly before he looked outside again. "I don't think you realize how grave this entire scenario is for me. My friend is in danger and I need to end this madness."

Mr. Singh let out a humorless laugh. "End..." he trailed off before fixing sharp eyes on him. "You don't even know what you're dealing with."

"Enlighten me then." Desperation rang loud in Joe's voice. He leaned forward, focusing all his attention on Mr. Singh.

"I warned your friend and his son. I told them to stay away." Mr. Singh placed the teacup on the table and leaned forward, resting his elbows on his knees. "They shouldn't have meddled with this. There's nothing you can do to help them now. I'm saying this again, you must leave and never return." He reclined in his chair and crossed his leg.

Joe scoffed. "It's too late for that." He was a paranormal investigator for fuck's sake. If there was one thing he was sure of, there was no running now. They were in too deep. His face was void of emotions when he pushed the sleeve of his jacket, revealing the bruise on his skin. He watched in satisfaction as Mr. Singh's smug expression morphed into horror.

Mr. Singh jumped to his feet, his breathing faster and eyes wider. "That... That's—"

Joe flicked his gaze to the painting, making sure that Mr. Singh followed his gaze. "Wanna tell me the truth now?" He slowly climbed to his feet.

Mr. Singh blinked. "Leave!" He stumbled forward, pushing Joe as he mumbled something in his mother tongue. It sounded like a curse, but Joe wasn't here that long to understand the language.

Joe, still in his early forties, was stronger than Mr. Singh. He didn't budge from his position. "I'm not leaving this place without answers."

"Do you want to die?"

Joe narrowed his eyes at the man and laughed bitterly. "Running isn't an option anymore. We both know that. I crossed that line last night." He lifted his hand. "She has already marked me. There's nowhere in this world I can hide now, can I?"

Mr. Singh swallowed harder as he stared at Joe before collapsing on the chair and the paranormal investigator knew right then Mr. Singh had cracked. He will get his answers now.

October 31, 1996
Halloween Parade, Wyoming, USA.
"Happy Halloween!"

Cheers filled the air, drowning her muffled cries behind the goat mask. She had stopped screaming a while ago. It was useless anyway. People mistook her screams for enthusiasm. No one realized the real horror the monsters behind the wolf masks had subjected her to endure.

The Halloween parade was so full of life and joy. It was something she enjoyed as a kid. Only she never thought she would become a part of it in such a manner.

Sweat soaked her underneath the goat costume. The three men

in wolf costume honked as they howled at the top of their lungs. Their jeep wrangler, roared across the street, passing ghoulish animated figures, haunted house props, and cute little ghosts. They had exited the crowded street now, driving onto the long highway she recognized so well.

Tears welled up in her eyes. With her hands tied behind her back, she was helpless. This wasn't how she had planned her Halloween night. She had a masquerade theme party planned at her parent's extravagant home. She wouldn't have stepped outside if she knew what awaited her. What should have been a simple trip to the grocery had soon turned out to be a nightmare.

Did her friends realize she was missing? Would someone call the cops?

She sank into her seat as she contemplated her fate. Will someone find her?

She didn't know what was more painful— waking up butt naked surrounded by unknown men in freaky masks staring at her; or the horrible realization of violation on her body and mockery she had to endure as they forced her into a ridiculous costume; or the helplessness she experienced while they paraded her like prey.

She was a laughing stock in front of hundreds of people. Would they still be laughing and waving when they learned the truth?

The fear of the unknown clawed at her chest. More tears flowed down her cheeks as the men clinked their bottles, drinking and talking rubbish. From their conversation, she figured didn't intend to let her go anytime soon. They were already making plans for the night. What they planned to do with her, she didn't know.

The uneasy squeeze inside her chest made it harder to breathe. Whatever awaited her cannot be good.

Were they going to kill her? Or keep her locked and rape her for days? What if they were human traffickers?

Her hopeless mind conjured every possible scenario. As a sheltered child of wealthy parents, she had nothing to worry about in her life. She always thought she was safe. Things like this would never happen to her because it happened only to the most unfortunate ones, wasn't it? Oh boy, how wrong she had been.

One of them reached for the radio. New Edition's *'Hit Me Off'* started playing with the drunkards slurring along. The memory of her dancing to this song with her friends and boyfriend at a birthday party only a few days ago clenched her heart.

Her entire life flashed in her mind. Her very first princess dress, that beautiful crown she still adored, those precious family vacations and fun-filled trips with her friends, her first kiss and her perfect boyfriend. More tears trickled down her cheeks. She had been mostly on the fortunate side of life. Guess she woke up on the wrong side this morning.

Every tiny achievement she ticked off in her diary suddenly seemed ridiculous. Her life would end today. She'd never get to go on the road trip next week with her boyfriend. She even packed her bags a week prior because she had been so excited. Will she ever see her family or friends again? Oh, how much she wished this was all a nightmare and she was still under the comfort of her thick purple blanket back home.

The cold wind whipped against her mask entered through the small slits they left open for eyes and nose. She lifted her gaze to stare at the night sky. This wasn't a nightmare. This shit was really happening but she shouldn't give up easily.

A blind hope bloomed in her chest. Maybe if she could act calm, she might get a chance to escape when they least expect. They were drinking. Maybe if they got too drunk, she could use the opportunity to outsmart them. She bit her bottom lip, trying to think of ways to escape. Jumping off the vehicle wasn't an option.

Relax, Sophie. Think of those thriller movies you watched. This was no time for a pity party. Every passing second brought her one step closer to her doom. Relax! She forced a breath and tried to calm her racing heart. *Think!*

She regarded each man trying to deduce his weakness. Two were at the front seat and one was in front of her at the back. There should be something she could use. All she needed was a moment of carelessness.

Sophie was lost in her thoughts when the jeep halted with a screech. Her body was jolted from the seat at the unexpected halt. Her head would have taken a hit if not for a pair of calloused hands that grabbed her, pushing her roughly back to the seat.

"Fuck!"

The men cursed, as she looked around flabbergasted. The one beside her grabbed her arm tightly, earning a whimper from her.

"Did we hit that thing?" The man who was driving the vehicle, wolf number one asked.

"I don't think so." The one on the passenger seat answered.

"Go, see if that thing is dead," the man beside her said, keeping his tight grip on her.

Dead?

Her heart cartwheeled as her gaze fell on a figure curled in the middle of the road. Who was that? Wolf number two, the burliest of them all slammed the passenger door shut and marched out of the vehicle. The headlight illuminated his ass that hung out of his tattered jeans. He crouched in front of the figure and brought his meaty hand to its nose.

Was it a woman?

"She's alive!"

"She?"

Sophie could sense the excitement bubbling inside the jeep.

"Bring her over," wolf number three in front of her, ordered.

The burly grunted as he threw the woman over his shoulder. Sophie's breath hitched. She couldn't see the face yet, but she could tell this one was shorter than her. Her lithe frame stayed limp, swayed on his shoulders. He walked over to her side and deposited the unsuspecting female beside her.

"What a day!" Wolf one mused as the jeep jerked forward.

"You." Wolf three loosened the grip on her and removed her ridiculous mask. "Here," he thrust a first aid kit she never knew existed in the vehicle. "Clean her up."

"Yeah, I don't fancy fucking a corpse," wolf one chimed.

Sophie swallowed hard as her captor untied her hands.

"Don't try anything funny," he growled.

Her hands shook uncontrollably as she set to work on the unconscious female. It was too dark to see her face clearly or make sense of her injuries. She pressed two fingers to the latter's throat and sighed in relief when her strong pulse thrummed against her index and middle finger.

"I…" Sophie cleared her throat, "I need light."

Someone turned the light inside the jeep on. But it wasn't enough. It was still too dark to see in the back. The lankiest dude with a tattoo on his right sleeve, wolf one thrust a flashlight just as wolf three who stayed beside her lit a cigarette. He deeply inhaled the smoke, closing his eyes. She could barely make out the outline of his clean-shaven face. Too afraid to look further, she quickly fixated her glance on the female. Her small head lolled to the side, warm blood coated her hands.

Sophie exhaled slowly and bit into her lower lip. The girl looked like she was in her late teens. So beautiful with a small oval-shaped face, pink full lips, straight nose, and almond-shaped eyes. Her well-groomed eyebrows were thick and curved, the one that made Sophie envy.

She brushed the brunette hair off her face and pity immediately filled her. The poor thing had unknowingly fallen into the arms of the wolves tonight. Their luck couldn't have fucked up anymore. With the limited resources, she tried her best to clean the blood and patch her up. Once she regained her consciousness, perhaps they could both escapes. *Strength came in numbers, right?*

Worry gripped her heart. Will the girl wake up in time? What if she can't make it out on time? She gnawed at her lip again. They might probably get no chance to run. But the captor's attention will now be divided. There was no way to predicts what they would do next.

"You finished?" Wolf three's annoying question came after a while.

Sophie scooted to her seat with a nod. The girl was fine except for a few scratches on the side of her head and arms. She had checked her head and did her best to inspect. There were no bumps or cuts. Why was she still unconscious?

Her train of thoughts broke when the jeep suddenly left the highway, swiveling to the side and onto a dirt road that threw her off balance. The guy in the back barely paid her any attention. He had kicked his leg on the seat beside the unconscious girl and sat as if he owned the world.

Sophie's heart hammered inside her chest. *What do I do now?*

3.

The night had grown chilly, announcing the early arrival of the winter. Halloween marked the end of summer, a joyous occasion where families spent time together before the dark, cold winter arrived. In the ancient days, when winter was filled with deaths from famine, people used to believe the boundary of the worlds between the living and dead blurred on this day. They believed the otherworldly spirits slipped into the human world as the veil came down at nightfall.

The witches used this day to communicate with the spirits and predict the future or perform deadly rituals they believed would benefit them in some way. These rituals often demanded human sacrifice which eventually led to people hunting down anyone that practiced witchcraft and killing them in the sixteenth-seventeenth century. However, with time, Halloween became a festival of neighborly get-togethers, ghost costumes, and pranks.

As much as Sophie wished this to turn out to be a horrible prank, it didn't, which only cemented the gravity of the situation. Sophie held her breath, whimpering quietly as the jeep approached the fenced private property in the middle of the forest. Her heart clenched at the sight of the steel fence surrounding the whole area.

There's no escape.

Her heart plummeted to her stomach when the fenced gate closed behind the vehicle. She tried to study the surroundings, but soon gave up when she saw the thick vegetation shrouded in the darkness. The headlights cut through the night, advancing through the bumpy road, and a Victorian-style house looked like it came right out of a horror movie. It stood massively illuminated by the moonlight.

The burly jumped out of the vehicle, patted down his pants, and then fumbled with the keys. The third guy dragged Sophie out of the vehicle while the lanky one with tattoos moved to hoist the unconscious woman over his lean shoulders but stumbled on the steps.

"What are you doing, asshole?" he shouted at the burly. "Turn the lights on."

"I can't find the switch," burly aka wolf two yelled back.

"Then fucking use your flashlight, idiot."

Burly fumbled some more before pulling his flashlight out. He struggled with the lock two more times before succeeding. He opened the door and quickly jumped inside, turning the lights on.

Sophie's heart cartwheeled inside her ribs. The lights did nothing to lessen her fear. If anything, it only brought her one step closer to her doom. She weighed her chances of breaking into a run and getting as far as possible, but the steely grip on her arms said otherwise. There was no way she could break out of that hold.

The man behind her shoved her forward and soon the door shut behind them with a bang, sealing her fate with the monsters surrounding her. Her foot caught on the edge of the dusty old carpet and she fell. Pain exploded from her knees where she landed hard. Sophie sucked in a breath, fighting the tears while peering at her surroundings.

The place was enormous with a grand fireplace to her left. An ancient-looking chandelier hung above their heads and in front of her was a staircase with a white wooden railing. A long Carpet lined the dark stairs where there was no light.

A few old paintings hung on the wall and she barely had time or mood to register the artifacts when the third guy carrying the unconscious girl walked past her and dropped her unceremoniously on the couch. The girl's head lolled to the side, her hair covering her face and her body slumping to the side like a rag doll.

Is she dead? The girl showed no signs of waking up. She didn't even stir throughout the ride.

Sophie tensed when the burly walked to her, grabbing her elbow and pulled her upright. A surprised squeak left her mouth. She tried her best to put as much distance between them as possible. "What's the plan?" he directed the question to the wolf three who was now standing in the middle of the room watching the unconscious woman intently.

Wolf three with the clean-shaved face removed his mask. Sophie gasped. He looked far from a killer. *Fuck.* If she hadn't been in a dreadful situation like this, she'd have taken him for a model or an actor. The guy had a square-shaped face, a killer jawline, a straight nose, and hooded pale blue eyes with flat, groomed eyebrows. He was well built and at least six feet tall, maybe someone from a wealthy family.

"The usual," he casually murmured, taking a seat on the couch and crossed his leg, resting his right ankle on his left knee. He lit another cigarette and took a long drag, and exhaled through his nose smoothly.

Her heart cartwheeled when the burly and lanky removed their masks following suit. The burly one with dark eyes, had his long hair secured in a band at the base of his neck, his facial hair covered his round face and most of his unremarkable features. The lanky had an angular face with round eyes, a slightly big crooked nose, and thin lips with a five o'clock shadow.

Sophie stood in her place, trembling in burly's arms. Now that she had seen their faces, her worst fear was confirmed. They were going to kill her. She swallowed a sob as the lanky dude marched to her right disappearing through an archway she didn't notice was there. Her knees locked as she fought to stay upright, only to sink to the floor as soon as the burly removed his hands from her.

The lights flicked once, the buzzing crackle caused her to jump. An exploding sound reached her ears shortly.

"What was that?" Sean boomed.

"It's the fucking bulb," Lanky yelled in response.

She bit her lips, stifling her sobs waiting for the verdict. The lanky returned with more alcohol and placed it on the small table in front of the couch. The handsome one just grabbed a bottle, opened the lid and took a generous gulp straight from the bottle. The other joined lifting the bottle to their lips.

Sophie drew her knees closer, hugging them to her chest as she rocked back and forth. Her gaze trailed around her. She weighed her chances of survival, and so far, it was zero.

"I can't believe this one came right at us," the burly said after a few more sips and moved to grab the unconscious girl. "Looks pretty."

Lanky laughed. "Sean, which one do you want?"

Sean, the clean-shaved guy, whom she assumed must be the leader of the trio, looked at her, scrunching his nose. Sophie squirmed under his scrutinizing gaze. "I already had that one, nothing special." He sniffed, wiping his mouth with the back of his hand. "I'll take the new one."

"Then she's all ours tonight." burly and lanky laughed. Sophie swallowed, her eyes widening and her skin crawling by the way they looked at her. They continued to drink leisurely as if they had all the time in the world. Her stomach churned.

Sophie's heart beat erratically when Sean rose to his feet first, hoisting the unconscious girl like she weighed nothing onto his shoulder. "Have fun with that one." With a grunt, he walked off, climbing the stairs two at the time, and disappeared from her view.

Her heart ached for the unknown girl. She didn't know how to help that one while she herself was locked here.

"Are you ready to play with daddy?" The burly grinned, making her skin crawl again. Above their heads, the lights flickered again before going off and immersing them in the darkness.

Calloused hands lunged for her in the darkness. "P-please..." She forgot her resolve to not give what they wanted the most as she squirmed out of his reach, crawling away with all her might. Perhaps if she could make it to the door, she might have a chance to escape.

But destiny worked against her tonight. A flashlight was clicked in an instant and this time one of the guys grabbed her ankle, dragging her to him. Sophie kicked out with a scream but the hold only tightened.

"This one is a screamer." The burly chuckled, a dirty sound that made her shudder with disgust and the lanky laughed in the background. "I like her." He let go of her briefly and she scrambled back again.

"S-stay away. D-don't come near me." Sophie looked around her for a way to escape. They both were drunk. She could run and hide somewhere. The lights flickered back to life, crushing her hope. But she wasn't going to give up. Her eyes darted around, analyzing her options. The burly took another step and Sophie jumped to her feet, ducking under his meaty arms and bounding for the steps.

She bounded through the dark corridors, falling a few times but never stopping to rub her scraped knees or palms. Her thoughts raced, searching from room to room for a hiding place. Loud laughter followed her, making her realize they would soon catch up.

Stumbling into their leader was the last thing she wanted. She paused briefly in front of each door, listening for any sounds coming from the inside. However, the sound of her own heart beating loudly with heavy footsteps bounding upwards had drowned any other noises she could have heard. Her frustration mounted, all three rooms she came across were locked. Her luck couldn't have been better. She suppressed the urge to scream and continued with determination.

Sophie was once afraid of darkness, but today the fear for her own life kept her going. She still had two rooms to check. With that thought, she ran to the far end of the corridor, tripping over something twice and stubbing her toe once. Sophie almost cried in relief when she reached the last room to see it was open. She lifted a hand to push the door only for the door to open wider with a creaking sound that made her heart leap to her throat.

She however, had no time to contemplate as she heard the footsteps growing louder. Sophie rushed inside the room and the door shut with a loud thud, deadbolts locking itself into place. *What the—*

She slapped her cheeks twice. *I certainly did not imagine that.* The sound of the footsteps grew closer. Sophie turned around, noticing the room was mostly bare except for a chair and a dresser by one wall. The windows were open, white curtains danced lazily with the light breeze. Moonlight seeped through the windows, illuminating the peeled wallpapers on the wall.

She almost jumped out of her skin when someone banged at her door, there was no other place to hide in this room if they entered. She crept to the far end of the room, pressing herself to the wall as her heart hammered loudly. Her brain quickly processed the situation. At least she was in no immediate danger. She thought of climbing out through the window but fear again clouded her mind.

Sophie slid to the hard ground, finally getting time to breathe and thinking about what happened from the time she entered this place. The memory bring tears to her eyes but before a sob left from her mouth a cold hand covered her stopping from making any sound.

"Shh..." Her heart almost exploded at the soft whisper brushing over her ears.

She whirled around on impulse, seeing no one.

What was that?

"This door is locked," she heard the burly say, hauling her out of her stupor. Her head whipped to the door.

"Break it."

Someone tried hammering the door and she covered her mouth with both her hands.

No. No. Please, God, no.

She swallowed the sobs, shutting her eyes tight.

I don't wanna die. God, please, help me this one time.

The faces of her family and friends flashed in her mind. Someone kicked the door this time. The door rattled but the bolts didn't budge. How long will the door hold?

"What are you doing, Mike? Sean will be pissed."

They had lowered their voices. Sophie quickly crawled to the door, pressing her ears to the wood, trying to listen.

"How do we get her out?" Burly growled. A sound of a fist connecting with a wall echoed through the door.

"Shit!"

The voices continued, barely audible to identify the speaker.

"Does this room have windows?"

Sophie clamped her mouth shut, more tears running down her cheeks.

"I guess so. And there should be a ladder in the garage outside."

"Okay. Let's get her before Sean finds out."

"Come on."

Blood rushed to her head. Her vision blurred as she stumbled to the windows to lock them but before she could reach them, they shut by itself, once again the locks sliding into place. An unknown chill crept on her spine. Warm air puffed out of her mouth and goosebumps erupted on her skin as the temperature in the room dropped. The room grew colder and she wrapped her hands around her waist, shivering slightly. It was then she noticed a sense of being watched. She looked around finding nothing, but that feeling twisted her gut. Cold sweat trickled from the side of her head, down her cheek and then to the floor. She bit her lower lip, breathing faster as she sensed it. A shadow moved from the corner of her eye.

What the fuck was that?

Sophie stumbled back. She can't leave the room but fuck whatever was in her. She did not imagine that. Fear clawed at her chest.

She choked on a scream and whirled around when she felt someone grab her ankle. The sudden movement caused her to fall face first. She hit her nose hard on the floor, moaning in pain. With her head swimming, she twisted her body, slowly rolling on her back.

Her heart stopped when she saw the unconscious girl from earlier hovering above her, their faces so close that she could feel her breath on her face. *How did she get inside the room?*

"Sleep, sweet Sophie…" The girl said in a sing a song voice. A strange sound clouded her senses, soft and eerie yet hypnotizing. She didn't recognize the foreign language as it slowly pulled her into darkness.

4.

"Where do you think you're going, Johnny?" Mike hissed. They were at the top of the winding stairs that led them down to the living room. "You stay here and keep an eye."

"Whatever." Johnny folded his hands across the chest. "Yo, Mike…"

"What?" Mike whisper-yelled.

"I've heard the garage is haunted. You won't piss your pants this time, will you?"

"Say that again and you'll be the one pissing your pants." The lights flickered as if on cue and Mike stilled on the stairs, eyes widening.

Johnny burst out laughing, and Mike suppressed the urge to choke the bastard before pivoting on his heels. It was a one-time thing where the idiots thought it was okay to pull that nasty prank on him. The bastard was still laughing.

"You better watch her, Johnny. I won't stop Sean from putting a bullet in your head this time."

That shut him up. The last time had gotten quite messy when their prey escaped into the woods. He definitely didn't want a repeat.

They had been in the underground for too long. This wretched mansion belonged to Sean, who supposedly inherited it from his great aunt. Sean, the leader of the trio, had immediately made this place his base. Situated in the outskirts of Wyoming, approximately five miles from Kemmerer, this was the most secure spot for their illegal activities.

The keys jiggled in his hands as the lock clicked open, the clinging sound permeating the otherwise silent surrounding. He hated silence. Mike couldn't wait to get back, to start what he was craving for all night. He traced the foldable cold metal blade in his back pocket in anticipation. As much as he loved to play hide and seek, he was already on edge and couldn't wait to get his hands on her.

The strong scent of pine invaded his senses as soon as he stepped outside. He shut the gate behind him, turning on the flashlight he carried. His foot hit the gravel path as he headed to his left, navigating the narrow road that led him to the back of the mansion. Sweat trickled down his forehead and the moist in his palm caused his grip on the flashlight to slip. The chilly wind that blew in his direction did nothing to lessen the humidity. As he wiped his hands on his jeans something moved in his peripheral vision, his lazy gaze flitted across the dark tree line quickly ignoring it for a cat or something else.

Sean was one lucky bitch. Mike thought, running his tongue over his teeth as the concrete structure that stood out like a protruded belly from the mansion came into view. He lifted the flashlight, gaze sliding across the recent addition—the metal shutter. He found the lock at the right bottom and crouched to unlock the padlock.

Mike grunted, fumbling with the numbers on the lock. He planted the flashlight against the shutter, only to yelp when he saw a shadow move. He quickly flashed the light in that direction, finding no one.

"I swear, Johnny, if you pull a prank on me again, I'll kill you," he grumbled under his breath, set the flashlight down and continued his struggle with the lock. It opened after a few tries and he heaved open the heavy shutter with a loud grunt. He fucking hated the legwork. How did the bitch open that room? It was always locked. They used only one room whenever they stayed here. The other rooms are locked because of the precious cargo and things only Sean knew. Who the fuck opened that room, anyway?

Just as he was about to slip inside the shutter came down, hitting his shoulder.

"Ah, fuck!" Mike cried out at the impact but soon regained composure, pushing the metal up and securing it in place so it won't come down again.

"When I get my hands on you..." he gritted through his teeth. "I'll fucking make you scream so hard that you'll regret ever running from me." He found the switch and pressed it. Light flooded the dingy garage, illuminating the array of crates stacked inside. It was one of the things he hated about this place. Sean's old bitch never bothered to upgrade the place instead she stuck in the rut until death. The mansion needed more upgrades to make it comfortable for dwelling, but they were hardly here. Sean preferred to keep it away from the knowledge of the others involved in the business.

Mike swept his glance around the place and found the foldable aluminum ladder. How was that supposed to reach the window? He frowned and looked around, finally finding a wooden ladder with twelve rungs. *That should do.* The problem—it was buried behind all sorts of garbage and he was left alone to clear it.

The only bulb in the garage flickered with a buzz and he let out a curse upon seeing his shadow. He contemplated calling Johnny to give a hand, but again they couldn't risk the girl running away while they were down here. That left him alone to work. *Fuck that bitch!* Mike took a few steps to where the ladder was and froze. The shadow, his shadow did not move.

"What the fuck?"

Something fell with a loud thud and he whipped around catching a glimpse of golden-brown locks running away. *What the–*

Light footsteps grew distant. With a clench of his jaw, Mike chased. He ran out and toward the sound.

Johnny bounced the stress ball in his hands. He crushed it in his palms a few times before throwing it up in the air and catching it. He was sprawled in front of the room in the corridor, illuminated by the moonlight.

No sound came from inside the room. He kept silent, hoping the bitch would step outside and he could use the surprise factor to subdue her. But so far, he had no luck. He strained his ears to listen to the sounds from the other room—the one Sean usually occupied. *Nothing.*

He frowned before realizing the girl was unconscious. Johnny scoffed. What was the point in fucking the unconscious one? He preferred fucking while they screamed and begged under him. The more they cried, the more aroused he became. Just the thought of that new girl screaming turned him on.

She was a remarkable sight with creamy thighs, flaring hips and decent sized boobs. It had been a while since they got a decent one like that. Earlier, when he undressed her to put her into that goat outfit, he couldn't control himself. Soon Sean and Mike had joined him. But it was nothing close to the euphoria he felt when they were screaming while he carved those beautiful marks on them.

A wistful sigh left his lips. *Where the fuck is Mike? What is taking him so long?* His patience was waning thin as he heard footsteps. His head whipped to his right, noticing the silhouette of someone. *About time.*

Johnny jumped to his feet. The shadow was shorter than Mike and as he approached, he noticed the feminine curves. *What—*

He blinked and the silhouette was gone.

"Hey!" He shuffled on his feet, rushing forward. A mop of golden-brown hair slipped outside the main door that was now ajar. *Why the fuck did Mike leave the door open?*

Shit!

Sean was going to kill them if he found out. The last time this happened, they spent the entire night hunting through the woods. If it wasn't for one of the old hunting traps their prey would have escaped. He rushed outside without another thought, fully intent on catching the girl.

"You!" Mike yelled. "Stop right there."

The girl kept running. His chest heaved, and face heated with the effort. Mike staggered to a stop, bending down and resting his hands on his knee. *Fuck!*

When he straightened, the girl was nowhere in sight. He turned off the flashlight and listened to the sounds around him.

Crickets chirped as if they were having their own Halloween party; leaves rustled above his head, but nothing else. The wind gently ruffled his hair and pine scent was thick in the air.

He spun on his heel choosing a direction and palmed his flashlight when he felt a feather-light touch on his neck.

"Giving up already?"

The ghostly whisper had him jump out of his skin. "Hey!" he shouted, swiveling around. His heart hammered in his chest, breathing erratic as he stumbled on his feet. He fumbled with his flashlight to turn it on, hitting it twice in his palm when it didn't turn on immediately. "Stop fucking with me," he grunted and let out a relieved sigh when the light flickered back to life. Mike twisted his wrist, scanning his surroundings and seeing no one. "Stop being a pussy," he growled. "Show yourself!"

The light wavered as he circled the spot, eyes flitting from one side to the other in search of the damned girl. The light fell on someone, just for a second, and he quickly backtracked to the place. There… standing in between the gap of two trees was the girl. Darkness covered half of her face, but he could see her lips curl into a smile.

"There you are." He lunged forward with renowned strength. "You won't escape this time."

She moved again, this time running slow as if to taunt him. Her chuckle drifted to him.

"You like playing, don't you?" he jeered. "Stop now and I will go easy on you." He traced his teeth with his tongue in growing anticipation.

More laughter could be heard as the girl careened through the trees. Mike kept up, his own laughter tumbling out, almost maniacal as he closed in. Only a few more feet and she would be in his hands. He stretched his arm, missing her by a beat. Her hair brushed against his fingers and he felt an odd sensation tingling his fingertips. He ignored it and continued the chase. The sound of her laughter infuriated him. "You're gonna fucking pay for this, bitch," he gritted through his teeth.

The girl quickened her pace, leaving him breathless then slowed down only to run faster when he caught up with her. She was toying with him. He stopped briefly to catch his breath and leaned on a tree for support. The muscles in his legs burned with exhaustion. He wheezed, smacking his chapped lips. The thirst was killing him and it pissed him so badly. When he straightened, ready to give a chase, realized he had lost any sense of direction now.

The girl, however, was waiting for him with a head tilted to her side. Mike scowled. Did the girl really think she could outsmart him? She fucking had a death wish. A wish he didn't mind fulfilling.

"I'll make you regret every fucking second of your life," he promised in a dangerous voice, anger tightening his features. His gaze narrowed at the girl and he pushed his lanky legs faster, determined to get her. The girl only laughed before pivoting on her heel and running. He won't spare her, he vowed. Suddenly, she stopped. With her back still turned to him, she froze in the middle of the forest.

A lecherous smirk stretched his lips when he realized it was a dead end. Tall bushes blocked her path and she whirled around in dread. His flashlight illuminated her fear-filled gaze.

"It's not fun anymore, is it?" he growled, his breath heaving. His lungs burned with exhaustion. He spat as he closed the distance.

The girl yelped when he lunged forward, grabbing a fist full of her hair.

"I'll make you pay for this, bitch." He quickly pocketed his flashlight, slapping her across the cheek. Her head lolled to the side and he caught her before she fell down. "Now you don't have anywhere to run, huh?" He shook her, spittle flew out of his mouth.

The girl didn't make a sound, which infuriated him further. He grabbed her neck, squeezing it between his palms. "Does that hurt, bitch?" He dragged her to the nearest tree, slamming her head on it.

"Cat got your tongue, bitch?" He slammed her head again. Sticky liquid coated the tip of his fingers that were secured at the nape of her neck. "Scream for me, bitch!"

He shook her violently before throwing her on the ground. She lay there without moving. With a growl, he pulled the metal blade out of his pocket. "I won't let you die without giving me what I want."

The blade sunk into her flesh, blood splashing on his face. Mike opened his mouth to say something, only to gag at the putrid stench now penetrating his nostrils. He covered his nose and stumbled back when it smelled worse.

What the fuck?

He wiped his hands on his jeans looking around. The girl was still on the ground, unmoving. He dropped the knife, covering his nose with his elbow and directed the flashlight to the girl with another hand.

Fuck!

The dim flashlight flooded the girl and his stomach churned at the sight. Mike stumbled back on his feet and tripped on something, falling backward and scrambling until his back hit a tree. His heart hammered inside his chest. The flashlight still trained on the girl, he gaped. The decaying stench was coming from her deranged body festered with maggots. Mike's gut wrenched, he twisted his body, emptying the contents of his stomach, almost seeing the stars as his head reeled.

Fuck!

His hands clenched at his sides. Mike plodded away from the mess he made, grabbed the tree for support and tried to steady himself on his feet. He had to get away. Perhaps, he was seeing things. His knees locked and he almost fell. He ran out of the place, lost in his thoughts. This can't be true. It must be the booze.

A sudden scream halted him. It was a girl. Mike swallowed the heavy lump in his throat, his eyes darting to the sides. He patted his pant pocket only to realize he left his knife back. Another scream to his left had him bolt in the opposite direction.

"Scream, bitch!"

The eerie whisper and the ghostly laughter widened his eyes. His foot caught on something and he fell down with a gasp. "Fuck!" He caught his knee, pain exploding as he tried to catch his breath.

"Does that hurt, bitch?"

Mike stiffened. The voice teased the outer shell of his right ear. A sliver of cold crept onto his spine. "W-who's that?" It was no longer fun.

He whipped his head side to side. The atmosphere suddenly grew cold and the silence suffocating. The crickets no longer chirped and the leaves did not rustle. Absolute silence. His heartbeat grew louder in his ears.

"When I'm done with you, you'll look fucking gorgeous."

The blood froze in his veins as his throat went dry. Terror washed over him. This is a fucking nightmare. That's it. He slapped his face to clear his haze. "Wake the fuck up, Mikey."

Her laughter grew louder.

"Scream for me...that's right, babe. Scream for daddy."

Those were his words, he realized a little too late. Words he used to taunt his victims. His Adam's apple bobbed. "W-what do you want? Who are you?"

"Please...Let me go. I swear I won't tell anyone. Please..."

The voice turned into that of a helpless woman, one of his victims he vaguely recognized. He clutched his chest, feet tumbling back.

"H-hurts..."

"Don't hurt me."

Flashes of tear-stained faces slipped into his memory. Mike clutched his head, swallowing audibly.

"Beg me more, bitch. Maybe I'll show you some mercy."

"S-stop." His chest heaved. "Stop that."

His head hurt badly. *What's happening to me?*

A sudden shrill of the scream caused his body to go rigid and before he knew what he was doing, he had bolted blindly. Mike didn't make it too far though, because he stumbled in front of the same woman with golden brown locks.

"Giving up already?" Her feminine sound was like a nail on the chalkboard.

"G-get away from me."

"Don't you want me to scream, daddy?" She advanced. *"I can be a good girl for daddy."* Another step. *"I can scream."*

Mike paled, taking several steps back. *He's definitely seeing things.* His back hit something. He jumped and turned only to see her face up close, now shining with a rage that sent cold shivers all over his body. Something shifted in her eyes and he screamed.

5.

"Well, well, well… aren't you a pretty little thing?"

Sean circled the girl on his bed, unconscious and still like a sleeping beauty. He planted a knee on the bed, slightly hovering over her as he pushed the hair out of her face. The soft glow of the light highlighted her delicate features—angular face, high cheekbones, almond-shaped eyes, straight nose, and bow-shaped lips. He licked his lips in anticipation and traced her lower lip with a calloused finger.

"We're going to have a lot of fun today." He tapped her chin. "Wake up, princess. What are you hiding behind those eyes?"

When she didn't stir, he left her to grab some water. Her injuries weren't that worse, she was barely passed out because of shock. But that doesn't work. He liked his prey screaming and kicking while he carved into them. The fear he saw in their eyes while they begged for their lives was such a turn on. Her staying unconscious just won't do. She has to wake up.

He found the steel water jug on the table near the window— the one he filled a long time ago. *Was it last month?* He didn't remember. The only time he came here was when he had to lay low or needed a break from other things. He shook the jug, grunting when it giggled with water.

Sean turned to go to bed, only to find it empty. He looked around the room. The spacious master bedroom came with an in-built closet and a bathroom. She was nowhere in sight. *How did she sneak out of the bed? Was she awake all this time?* He didn't even hear the rustle of clothes.

"You're awake?" he stalked to the bed with a sly grin. His eyes darted to the sides, guessing where could be hiding. Oh, he loved the chase. It was going to be fun.

"I love hide and seek," he whispered as he turned around, confident gaze sweeping the room. "You're sneaky, I like that." He placed the jug on the bedside table.

He peeked under the bed, finding no one. "Where are you?" He put one foot in front of the other, strode to the closet like the predator he was—chest puffed and shoulders squared. He stretched his neck, hearing a satisfying crack when he opened the door with a malicious grin that almost split his face. "Peek-a-boo."

Sean screwed his face when an empty closet stared back at him. "The bathroom then," he said to himself, going to the adjacent wooden door. To his surprise, the door was unlocked. "Peek-a-boo."

The bathroom was empty. His gaze fell on his image on the spherical mirror with rusty edges. He scoffed only to frown when Sean on the mirror did not mimic his movements. Sean lifted a hand, waving at the mirror and tensed when the mirror image stared at him in response. His breath hitched when he noticed the unnatural black eyes with no hints of white.

What the fuck?

Sean laughed. Fuck. *Did Mike add some shit in the booze?* The buzz of alcohol he felt was the usual. It was nothing out of the ordinary and he wasn't a lightheaded drinker. He could hold his booze for longer than anyone else in his gang could.

Was it the new meth he sampled earlier?

He met the mirror image defiantly, making faces and laughed out. Sean ran a hand through his hair and spun on his heel.

"Don't leave me here."

The feminine voice sounded distant yet too close, barely audible. He whipped around, wild gaze searching. His heart almost stopped this time to see an empty mirror.

Sean waved his hands in front of the mirror. Still nothing. Letting out a stream of curses, he clutched his head, closed his eyes and counted from ten to one. When he opened his eyes to look back at the mirror, he saw everything was normal. But the relief did not last long.

"Come, find me."

His eyes snapped to the mirror. An arm shot out of the mirror, clawing at his face. He jumped back from the mirror, a silent scream stuck in his throat. The apparition in the mirror cocked its head to the side with a sinister smile. His heart cartwheeled in his chest. Sean shook his head to shake the image off and even hit his head to clear whatever fuck this illusion was. This cannot happen.

A sigh of relief drifted out of his mouth when the fog cleared in his brain. He backed off from the bathroom and slammed the door shut. Before he could move further, he felt a cold grip grabbing his ankle. He fell face first and twisted his body to come face to face with the ugliest face. The sickening stench was something his mind registered first. Dark eyes peered at him with a growl rumbling out of its chest. Sean screamed pushing at whatever creep it was, scrambling back, his arms and legs flailing blindly. His eyes fell close on impulse and the hand left him.

Fuck.

He was out of his mind.

Crap.

Sean never experienced fear in his life, not as an adult at least. The last time he sensed something close to fear was at the age of ten while he still believed in Boogeyman sneaking on him from under his bed. But his father had beat the fear out of him that day. He never dared to fear again.

As his gaze swept around the room, he sensed the discomfort settling in his bones for some unknown reason. His breathing came out in pants. He wiped off the cold sweat from his forehead using the back of his hand. Once again, he was met with an empty room. *Where did she go?*

Sean staggered to his feet, shaking his head again. *It must be the new shit.* That was it. He concluded. Some drugs resulted in hallucinations. That was fucking insane. A swift glance around the empty room eased his mind. He laughed amused at his reaction and directed his thoughts to the girl. He didn't hear the door opening or closing.

The master bedroom had the least amount of furniture—a queen-sized bed, two one-seater couches, a small coffee table and head side table. Nothing that could hide a woman from his view. He frowned, unlocked the room and walked into the dark corridor. The light from the room spilled into the corridor and he was met with silence. *Where did the fools go now?*

Sean once again looked inside the room, double-checking, she wasn't there. He marched outside, took a left turn at the L-shaped corridor and froze on his spot. A woman stood in front of the open window, looking outside. *What the—*

His heart flipped as he took in her appearance. She looked like a royal, elegant and ethereal, her skin glowing under the moonlight, rich, colorful clothes draped around her curvy frame. His tongue darted out unconsciously licking the seam of his lips when he noticed her thin waist. Clear porcelain skin peeked from under the red material wrapped around her hip. He had no doubt her flawless skin would feel like silk against his hand. And those damn curves... His fists clenched in growing anticipation.

"Fuck me."

The curse slipped out his mouth when he caught her side profile. Never in his life had he encountered such a mesmerizing beauty. Lust clouded his senses. Straight nose, high cheekbones and plump lips had his hormones raging. She glowed like a fucking crystal. And fuck that long neck. Oh, he could lick and suck that neck for days.

What a night!

Sean swallowed, his dick hardening at the sight. The idiot didn't slow down to think how an otherworldly beauty entered the mansion. With his dick taking the front seat, he closed the distance between them.

She turned around just before he put a hand on her shoulder. "Peek-a-boo," her lips barely moved as the ghostly whisper brushed his ears. Her eyes, glinting like silver, morphed into something right out of his nightmare and the predator found himself stumbling on his feet, his heart cartwheeling inside his chest.

"W-who are you?" He jumped back, pressing his back to the wall as his breathing grew heavier.

"Not so strong now, are you?" the woman whispered, her pearly-white teeth glinted in the moonlight.

"What the fuck is wrong with you?" He was frozen to the spot, glaring at the most beautiful woman he had set his eyes on. But there was something definitely wrong about her. She didn't look like someone from around here. The meth must have had a horrible side effect when mixed with alcohol. There was no way this could be real. He hit the side of his head with his hand, trying to clear his thoughts.

"What the fuck is wrong with you?" she mocked in the same ghostly whisper before bursting into laughter. A shrill sound that bounced off the stonewalls and echoed into the corridor. It was a sort of laughter that created a creepy sensation when something crept over one's skin.

"S-stop..." he wheezed. "Stay away from me."

"Or what?" she hissed. Her eyes darkening, face morphing to something sinister. The glow on her face dimmed. The skin grew darker with purplish veins popping all around. Redness seeped into the black of her eyes, almost glowing like embers.

His heart lurched to his throat. "I-I'll kill you."

"Mhm..." The woman laughed again. "I'd like you to try that."

With that she reached out to him, Sean tried to swat her hand but the moment her cold fingers contacted his skin, he sensed a suffocating presence inside him before his world went dark.

Mike stumbled on his feet; his body swayed as he ran aimlessly through the forest. *It's just a nightmare,* he kept chanting.

The girl was nowhere in sight, and he didn't know where he was. His foot tripped on a stone, falling unceremoniously. A sharp object cut into his palm, making him yelp. He heard footsteps approaching and staggered to his feet, wild gaze looking around. His heart almost stopped upon seeing who it was. It was easy to make out the familiar features under the bright moonlight. A relieved sob left his mouth. "Sean!" He ran to his leader. "Thank fuck you're here. There's something seriously wrong with this place, man, or I don't know if I'm drunk. Let's just leave this place." Sean didn't respond. Mike shook him again. "What are you looking at? Come on. Let's go."

"That fast?" Sean tilted his head, speaking in a shrill girlish voice that didn't belong to him. "Don't you wanna scream, *daddy?*"

Mike's eyes widened as he stumbled back. "N-no. S-Sean."

This...this can't be real. He sobbed. *This can't be true. I'm seeing things.*

"You're scaring me, man." Mike chuckled without humor, hands planted on his hips as he tried to make sense of the situation. "I know this is all a shitty prank. You win."

"Did I?" Sean titled his head.

"Sean?"

"Yes, daddy."

It was then Mike noticed Sean's unnatural eyes, black covered his pupils and then his sclera.

"What the fuck, man?"

"Don't you like it, daddy?" Sean's face morphed to that of the woman he was running from.

Mike screamed.

"I love it when you scream."

Johnny was running blindly behind the woman. It didn't take long to figure she was the one they picked from the road. He recognized the t-shirt and golden-brown hair. His chest heaved as his body protested to match her speed.

"Fuck!"

Why the fuck would Sean let the bitch run around like this?

"Stop!"

She wasn't stopping, she kept running. He panted hard. He wasn't one for exercise and his stamina sucked. Johnny couldn't believe their stupid luck when they stumbled on not one but two girls to play with. The same shit luck now had them running out of breath tonight. One bitch was locked inside the room while the other ran like a cheetah into the woods. *How is she so fast? Was she an athlete or something?* Again, how the girl could even run without the help of light was beyond his knowledge. Even with the flashlight, he barely saw anything clearly.

He was deep into the woods when he heard the screams. *Mike?* His feet came to a sudden halt and he pivoted, turning to the direction of the scream.

"Mike!"

He wheezed, his lungs burning and legs slowing down as he reached the area.

"Sean, what the fuck, man?"

Johnny gasped absolutely horrified by the scene in front of him.

Their boss had a naked Mike bent over as he fucked him. Mike's face was bloody as he begged him to stop. The painful cries were falling into dumb ears. It must be his mind playing tricks. Johnny blinked. One. Twice. And then rushed to Sean, pulling him off Mike.

"What the fuck is wrong with you man?" he growled, pulling a staggering Mike behind him. "If you wanted men why didn't you say so? You let your girl runaway and now railing one of our own?"

Sean, however, responded with a punch that knocked the breath out of him. "Scream for your daddy..." The ghostly growl didn't belong to Sean. Johnny's eyes bulged, but it was too late because Sean's fist was the last thing he saw before darkness enveloped him.

Johnny cracked his eyes open, pain exploding the back of his head. He squinted at the bright light, trying to hide his eyes with an arm, only he couldn't move.

They were back in the living room. He lay on his side on the floor, his hands and feet tied. He scanned the room, tugging at the rope that secured his hands behind his back. A burst of cruel laughter caught his attention and he jerked his head in that direction.

A silent scream erupted from his lips as he attempted to scramble away. Sean looked nothing like the man he remembered. He bathed in blood. His skin was glowing eerily. Blood dripped from his arms and pooled on the dirty carpet. The mad look on Sean's face was something he had never seen before. *Were his eyes glowing too?*

Johnny choked on a mixture of sob and scream.

Mike, his once confidante, was now nothing more than a bag of mangled flesh. His stomach churned and he dry heaved, bringing up his knees and rolling to his stomach. He had to get away. Escape this shitty place. His body barely moved an inch. Soft whimpers left his mouth when he realized how helpless his situation was.

A low growl caused Johnny to half his feeble movements. He strained his neck to Sean, whose soulless, glowing eyes now fixated on him. No.

Johnny's eyes widened as Sean climbed to his full height with a sinister smile on his face.

"N-no!"

Sean boomed with laughter. "No? Doesn't that mean you want more?" He cocked his head to the side, then added, "Daddy…"

Johnny whimpered. What happened to him? He thrashed in his binds. "S-Sean."

"Alina…" Sean whispered. "My name is Alina Garrison." He

licked his lips.

Johnny swallowed, flopping unceremoniously on the floor as Sean boomed with laughter. "Forgot me already? Am I that easy to forget?"

Sean cocked his head to the side. Johnny blinked once and when he opened his eyes, he saw the girl standing in his place. That face... He remembered now. One of his best kills. He shook his head multiple times. *Shit, I must be dreaming.*

"This is not possible." He laughed. "You're dead."

"Yes," the woman whispered. "Because you killed me!"

The air was knocked out of his back and pain exploded from his back. He wheezed as the girl approached him with slow, steady steps. "Does it hurt?"

He could only whimper in response. Fear paralyzed him to the spot, her menacing aura holding him a tight grip.

"Don't you love to play?" Alina drawled mockingly. A vengeful smile danced on her lips.

Johnny couldn't believe it was happening. Those were the words he said to her while torturing her to death. His heart pounded in his ears. "Y-You're not real."

She took a step toward him and he flinched.

"Don't come near me."

She laughed, taking a step.

"Stop."

Another step. The cold smile on her face was unwavering.

"N-no, please..."

"No?" Alina closed the remaining distance in a blink of an

eye. Hard hands grabbed his head and tugged his hair painfully. "What does no mean?"

"No."

"Say that again," she taunted.

"No."

"Right. No means no," she snarled, slamming his head on the floor and Johnny saw stars, dark spots clouded his vision. "What did you tell me that day?"

Johnny whimpered. "Please…"

"I asked you a question," she hissed and pulled at his hair that made his neck stretch at an odd angle.

"That no means you wanted more," he sobbed.

"That's right. And that's exactly what I'm going to give you."

"Please…Let me go."

The girl laughed; a ghostly sound bounced off the walls. Then she stopped. "Not enough," she licked her lips. "I need more."

"M-more?"

She nodded and flipped him so he was on his back. His vision blurred and then he saw Sean hovering above him.

Loud screams that didn't belong to him resonated in the room. Soon he realized they belonged to his victims. With every scream, with every word spoken Sean carved a mark on his skin and Johnny realized his mistake when the same pain was inflicted on his body.

But it was too late.

Too late for redemption.

Too late to beg for forgiveness.

Mithravathi

Too late for everything.

6.

Fools.

Joe Martinez smacked his lips. They never saw it coming. None of them did until it was too late. These imbeciles always loved to believe they were in control. All too powerful but it was always too late when they realized they were not.

His Toyota Tacoma smoothly made its way through the dirt road. The hunt was on and a familiar thrill boiled in his blood. He cut the lights off and parked the car in front of the fenced gate. With a hand resting relaxingly on the backrest of his passenger seat, he waited for the command.

Six months ago,

"She has marked you for death," Mr. Singh whispered as he slumped in the chair. "That's…that's…"

"I know that already." Joe was terrified inside. He didn't need a verbal confirmation to know that the entity had marked him. But he didn't believe it was for death. He had figured that earlier when he was inside the bathroom. "Tell me more. Tell me about *her.*" He leaned forward, waiting for Mr. Singh to speak.

The older man opened and closed his mouth multiple times. An uncomfortable silence settled between them and Joe watched the other man intently. After fifteen minutes, Mr. Singh finally picked the courage to utter the next words. "She is an ancient legend that lives right at the heart of Mussoorie." He exhaled weakly and reclined in his chair, head on the backrest, his eyes staring at the ceiling.

"My great grandmother once told me a story about a woman who lived here in the sixteenth century. She had an ethereal beauty that drove men crazy. Women envied her commendable presence. She was the daughter of a high minister, who had a great influence in the king's court."

Joe tilted his head to the side as he listened studiously.

Mr. Singh intertwined his hands over his stomach and glanced at Joe. "Men vied for her attention and it is said that even the king himself wanted her to join his harem, which she refused. It was a bold move from a woman of that era, you know." The older man licked his lips as he straightened slightly, and then ran a hand over his weary face. "My memory is vague, but I remember my grandmother telling me that the king plotted revenge. A day before her wedding, she was abducted and the next day she was found dead in the forest. They…" The man swallowed. "They ruined her and destroyed her beauty."

Joe pursed his lips, his heart racing.

"Soon…the men in the kingdom started to die. Every month on the night of the full moon, she claimed a life, killing them in the same way they killed her. It went on for years before the king performed a ritual to bind her to the ruins."

"Bind her? As in she can't get out."

The older man chuckled. "That's what they believed because she stopped killing."

"But it never stopped," Joe assumed.

Mr. Singh nodded. "She was well respected among the villagers," he said. "They began worshipping her and offered her sacrifices. They believed serving her would protect virgin women."

"What happened?"

"Time has changed. People stopped believing. She became a myth."

"But there are still people who believe," Joe argued.

His gaze subconsciously went to the painting that caught his attention earlier. It was of a woman. Now he looked more clearly, he realized it wasn't just any woman, but the one he met in the woods. He would recognize those features anywhere. No veil covered her face this time. She was beautiful—an ethereal beauty that warranted men to wage wars. What caught his attention were her almond-shaped eyes. Her piercing gaze was intense and even though it was just a painting, Joe could sense her commanding presence as if she was in the room with them.

"What's her name?"

Joe blinked and willed his gaze to Mr. Singh.

As Joe watched, he noticed a strange glint in his eyes. It was also then he noticed the change in the atmosphere. The pristine office did not look pristine anymore. Cobwebs and dust-covered every inch. He flicked his nervous gaze around the room, zooming in on one photo he hadn't noticed before. Mr. Singh smiled in a thick-framed photo, a dried garland hung around it. He had to blink several times when he read the dates under the photo. *Was he reading that right?*

Joe's world froze. Mr. Singh was dead. He has been dead for over ten years now. He whipped his head to the person standing in front of him and watched with horror when Mr. Singh's eyes morphed into something more piercing and intense. Then he replied in a voice that belonged to a woman he met in the forest, *"Mithravathi."*

Joe believed that he was going to die that day. His heart hammered in his chest, the loud buzz of his blood rushing to his brain drowned the other sounds around him. A small smile curved Singh's lips before his form morphed to that of the woman. God, she was beautiful. Now in broad daylight, he saw her clearly. The painting did no justice to her beauty.

Joe's knees shook and he found himself dropping to his knees, his shoulder hunched on impulse. Her lips curved into a smile that brightened the entire room and Joe felt a compulsion to bow. He couldn't comprehend his actions but he bowed at that moment, completely surrendering to her.

"You're not like those men," her voice still rang with authority, but there was a hint of gentleness and borderline amusement.

"I...I have a daughter too, Ma'am." He clenched his fists to hide the trembling. "And Alina was like my daughter. They..." He choked on a sob, remembering the broken body of the girl he once knew. "They killed that little girl and they're still *alive*," he growled the last part like a curse.

"Singh is dead." There was a strange softness to her voice when she spoke his name. She turned and moved around the room or more like glided smoothly so he couldn't see her face. "You promised me something yesterday."

Joe nodded. "I still stand by my promise. I'll do anything."

"Do you pledge your loyalty, Joe?" she asked with a pleasing hum at the base of her throat.

"I do." The words tumbled out of his mouth without his permission. That was it. He sensed when the promise bound the entity to him. It was as if there was another presence in his body. His body shook and he breathed through his mouth.

That day, he learned the mark she left on him wasn't for death. She was merely testing his loyalty. Mithravathi, now a malevolent entity, couldn't leave the ruins upon free will. She had to be summoned. The last time someone summoned her was a decade ago when Mr. Singh was still alive. After his death, the villagers stopped anyone from going to her out of fear.

The entity thrived in fear and fed on souls. Joe understood why she sought him out. She needed souls. The more the merrier. However, unlike the others feared, she only wanted the souls of the men who didn't deserve to walk on this earth. She needed his help to leave the ruins, break the binds that were holding her captive in the place she despised. She needed someone who offered themselves to her willingly.

That was exactly what he did.

Present day...

Joe knew exactly when he received the command. The gates opened automatically and he cranked the engine, driving through the uneven road to reach the mansion that stood tall in the darkness.

He slipped out of the vehicle and then through the open door, immediately regretting his life's decision. Alina stood in the middle of the room, bathed in blood. Three mangled bodies lay at her feet. As much as the sight repulsed him, he also couldn't help the satisfaction that filled him. He didn't have to ask what happened. After all, he was doing this for the past two months, ever since he freed Mithravathi. The world was free of three serial killers who killed for fun.

Alina aka *Mithravathi* flicked her eyes upward and he knew the victim was upstairs. He avoided the blood and gore, fighting nausea as he climbed up. Finding the girl was easy. Without wasting time, he hoisted her into his arms, loaded her in his car and drove off.

The girl looked broken, but she'd survive. Thank the fucking heavens they were on time. She'd wake up tomorrow mostly with no memories of the night. As he drove off into the night, he saw the newspaper resting on his dashboard.

Man arrested for rape-murder of 3-year-old Tennessee girl.

His lips curved into an obnoxious smile.

You'll never lay your finger on another human being again.

Mithravathi will return...

ABOUT THE AUTHORS

Mark Boutros: Mark Boutros is an International Emmy nominated screenwriter and fantasy author. He mostly likes sleeping and saying no to social gatherings.

M.M. Ward: Mama Magie Ward- Farm mom and author who writes as part of my stroke recovery. My stories are a walk between shadow and light. I write stories about and for those who have been through much. There will be triggers for survivors, things I would wish on anyone, but sadly, these are the trials many face in today's world. Some of will overcome, some will succumb, and I encourage all to seek help. Weep, cope, reach out. You are not alone. There is always the choice... Become Better, not bitter.

D.A. Schneider: D.A. Schneider is an author of multiple genres who makes his home in Louisville, Kentucky. He has two sons and started his writing career in 2007 with the self-published novel, Avenging Autumn. After trying for some time to break into the comic book industry with his artwork, D.A. instead decided to focus fully on writing. He signed with KGHH Publishing in 2017 and Poe Boy Publishing in 2020. D.A.'s latest releases are the horror novels The 9 Ghosts of Samen's Bane and the Ghost Hunter Z Trilogy. His work has also appeared in several short story anthologies and online literary magazines.

Phil Hore: Phil likes to point out he was one of the last children born before man walked on the moon. He's worked at Australia's National Dinosaur Museum, the Australian War Memorial, National Film and Sound Archives, the Australian National Botanic Gardens, London's Natural History Museum, the Field Museum in Chicago and The Smithsonian's National Museum of Natural History. Published in newspapers and magazines across the globe, Phil is the paleo-author for the world's longest running dinosaur magazine, The Prehistoric Times. He's also been a comic shop manager, a cinema projectionist, a theatre technician and gutted chickens for a deli. All of these influences seem to make an appearance in his writing, especially the chicken guts bit. His first novel Brotherhood of the Dragon contained another Amun adventure, while 2020 sees the release of his WW1 trench murder mystery, Golgotha.

Brandon Ebinger: Brandon Ebinger is a horror/dark fantasy author who lives in upstate New York with his fiancé and two cats.

He holds a BA in creative writing. He enjoys horror films,Gothic rock and punk music and video games. He is a huge fan of haunted attractions, and spends October as a haunt actor. Brandon has written four horror/dark fantasy novels, Ash, Hollow Hills, The Afflicted and Rose. He has also published a handful of short stories within the genre. He has recently finished his most recent novel Broken Night and is at work on a new one.

Danielle McNeill: Danielle McNeill is an author who writes paranormal/supernatural, which include vampires and werewolves, and ghosts. Her works include The Immortals Saga vampire series and the Bane Werewolf Colony series. She's working on a revenge crime series of short stories and a science fiction series. She's a graduate of Full Sail University with a Bachelor of Fine Arts degree in Creative Writing for Entertainment. She has experience with script writing, comic writing and game writing. When she's not writing, she enjoys reading books specifically paranormal romance novels and watching anime. She loves to listen to classical music, rock music, and kpop.

Catherine Edward: Hailing from India, Catherine is an author and law graduate, specializing in Intellectual Property and

Copyright Infringement. She is passionate about Lycans, Werewolves, Witches and Vampires, and writes sizzling tales of love and betrayal. Her love for books started from a very young age,

when her loving father would gift her books like Russian Tales woven with fantasy. But it was in late 2015 when she found the books of Paranormal Romance author Cynthia Eden, whose books introduced her to the whole new world of paranormals. The more she read the more she got enticed and she penned her first novel in 2016. When she isn't writing, she likes to travel and read. Music and writing goes hand in hand for this night owl. Her family and furbabies are her world. She also loves to chat with her readers and fellow authors. You can find Catherine often chatting on Twitter or on her Facebook page.

WANT TO READ MORE HORROR STORIES ?

CHECK OUT BOOK 1 FROM THE HALLOWEEN SERIES

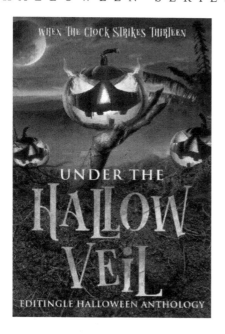

UNDER THE HALLOW VEIL

Halloween Anthology Book One

In the dark of night, they come to life. Whispers through haunted tombs. Cackles beneath a dreaded moon. Malevolent spirits from the twisted mind. Be mindful of whose door you knock on. A reaper may greet you. For those that care of Halloween scare, abandon intent and take the dare.

Made in the USA
Las Vegas, NV
04 February 2022

43056704R00210